STAKED!

By Denise M. Baran-Unland

Illustrated by Christopher Gleason

This book is lovingly dedicated to the reader, whoever you might be.

"Think now and then that there is a man who would give his life, to keep a life you love beside you!"

— Charles Dickens, *A Tale of Two Cities*

FORWARD

Generally speaking, I am not much for fantasy or science fiction.

Sure, I've enjoyed several Ann Rice books – who, after all cannot love Lestat? – and a few Ray Bradbury classics. I am aware of the genius of Isaac Asimov, though, I confess I have not read anything of his.

I have watched the first three of Peter Jackson's magnificent *Lord of the Rings* saga. Still, I have not read any of Tolkien's master works. After seeing the movies, I don't think I ever will, though the entire collection sits right now in my attic library. Just too much…I don't know, "complication" for my brain, already stretched, strained and stressed with reality's many rigors.

Staked! hits many of those fantasy/science fiction notes.

It is about 17-year-old John-Peter Simotes, who is a changeling straight out of Irish folklore. His father was a vampire who was staked by a friendly vampire hunter. His mother doubles as a living bank of her dead husband's vampiric blood. His "uncle" conjures up a world of fairies and sprites in his imagination that is as real as rain (and as dangerous as lightning) for John-Peter. His Tarot card-reading best friend chats with John-Peter via mental telepathy and she practices astral projection. And he dreams of the day when he will rescue the princess trapped in the mirror hanging in his bedroom closet.

Yet I loved it.

Truth be told, I loved both of its predecessors, too.

The first, *Bryony,* told the tale of a 1970s teenager, Melissa Marchellis. Missing her recently-deceased father, Melissa falls head-over-heels in love with the idea of love – or, more precisely, the vampire who embodies it, and offers it to her. That love comes at a steep price, but the girl is more than willing to pay it, as so many teen girls are.

Visage continued Melissa's story, now as a young adult. Melissa heads off to college, her vampire fling having ended in flames. Even there, though, Melissa cannot – or does not want to

– leave her past in the past. So, when she falls for a hot music professor who bears an uncanny resemblance to her dead (undead?) vampire lover, well...

Complicated books, sure. Overflowing with elements that don't usually trip my literary wire, certainly.

Yet I enjoyed them precisely because they aren't really about what they seem to be about.

In all great literature, the truest, most powerful drama comes in the lonely longing for passion; the physical, emotional and spiritual intimacy that comes with new love; the personal validation and romantic affirmation to mature love brings; and the consolation that follows when love fails or abandons us.

Staked! has all of this, and much more.

To be sure, John-Peter Simotes is a strange kid with a bizarre past.

Yet, in all ways meaningful and important, he is a normal 17-year-old boy. Voraciously hungry. Geeky and gawky with his growing body. Bright to the point of arrogance. Sometimes brooding. Often resentful of his step-father who has taken his father's place in his mother's bed, but not in John-Peter's estimation.

And as obtuse about romantic love as the day is long. Even, especially, when it's staring him right in the face. (Interestingly, John-Peter's apple does not fall far from his mother's tree. She is also blind to the flashing neon signs of romance, until... well, you'll just have to read the book.)

Ms. Baran-Unland has done a wonderful thing in this book. She has created a unique "fantasy" world peopled with interesting characters, at turns enchanting, scary and thrilling. At the same time, she has put these "magical" characters on paths cluttered with hurdles that any teenager or parent will recognize, having probably tripped over many of them themselves.

The ability to capture and convey the challenges and rewards of human interaction: pain and joy, celebration and sorrow, heartache and elation. These are the difference, to paraphrase the immortal Truman Capote, between "typing" and "writing."

With apologies to Mr. Capote, I will add that it is no coincidence that "literature" and "love" start with the same letter.

6

"Staked" is a great story. Not because it's about something as fantastical a vampire's need for blood, but rather the human heart's very real need for love.

Tom Hernandez, author of *Chocolate Cows and Purple Cheese, and other tales from the homefront*

TABLE OF CONTENTS

THE PROLOGUE

The shrunken man sat behind the counter smoking his clay pipe.

Business had been slow that day, although he had hoped the dreary, steady drizzle might have influenced people's spirits, enticing them to part with their goods or seek a cheap bargain, the custom on such a day. Calmly, he reached onto the shelf for a wooden match to relight the pipe. Well, no matter. He'd earned enough today for the beer he'd drink while working on this night's project, his finest yet.

He leaned back, puffing contentedly, grinning. How they had jeered at him, back home. Sure, his father had been a cobbler as had his father had been before him, but if Glorna could progress, why not he? He had practiced his new craft, working in solitude and silence until he could approach the steward with his request. Oh, the rejoicing when the steward granted it. No one laughed at him now.

The rusty, dented bell at the top of the door jangled as three men entered the shop. The shopkeeper glanced at the Roman numerals on the large stone wall clock. They certainly were prompt.

The first man, the tall one carrying the large paper sack, shook out his long blond hair. "Be quick. I don't have much time."

Painfully easing himself to a standing position, the shopkeeper hobbled past the men and hung his *Out to Lunch* sign before locking and bolting the door. Then he tottered to the back and flung aside the ragged shamrock green curtain hiding the cellar's entranceway.

"This way, gents," he said.

They followed him down the dank, stone steps to the underground. He gestured to a series of rotting tree stumps where, to his satisfaction, the men seated themselves, even the oldest of the group. The shopkeeper squatted down and dug his heels in the soft earth. It was the moment for which he'd been waiting.

"Your request departs from our established method," he said, relighting his pipe and waiting for their response. He observed the men as they exchanged looks.

"One you promised to fulfill, Eircheard, when you commissioned this project," the oldest of the three said, stroking his white Santa Claus beard, a decided contrast to his blue jeans and red and white striped shirt.

Eircheard drew hard on the pipe and then paused. "John, have you the payment?"

John's eyes gleamed in the dim light.

"Yes," he said. "I have a child."

The shopkeeper leaned forward, his heart leaping into his throat. "It's here?"

The third man adjusted his thick, black-rimmed glasses and nervously smoothed back his slick, dark hair. "The child is not quite ready."

Eircheard puffed again. "How long, Dr. Rothgard?"

"Soon."

Eircheard relit his pipe as he considered. "It's such a special project…a month?"

Dr. Rothgard shrugged. Eircheard appealed to the leader.

"Steward…and the program?"

Smiling, Ed Calkins, the Steward of Tara, nodded, held up a small, plastic leering leprechaun. Its tiny black eyes glinted under a pair of bushy red eyebrows. A thatch of wild red hair slid out from under its tall green hat. In the center of its belly, a series of numbers in the billions spiraled downward. "It's ready to find its first home."

"So," Eircheard said, "an even trade at the time of delivery?"

"Wait." John opened the sack and brought forth a piano leg. "Use this."

"Solid oak?" the shopkeeper said.

"See for yourself."

Eircheard puffed again and examined the piece carefully. It was as John claimed. Although he preferred his own materials, this object surpassed his specifications. The varnished wood would definitely extend its serviceability.

"Significantly?" John asked.

Eircheard started at the question and nearly dropped the leg. It was almost as if that man had read his mind.

"A decade, maybe."

John did not blink. "I need two."

"Impossible."

"Doctor Rothgard!" And John turned eyes of stone on him.

"John," Dr. Rothgard shuffled nervously on his narrow stump. "I'll do my best. It's not been done."

"Don't worry," Ed said with a confident nod. "It's programmed to synthesize it. Just give the leg plenty of water and sunlight."

The steward leaned back and smiled. Clearly, Eircheard thought, this was the best he'd coax from them. Disappointed, he rose to dismiss them.

"If there's nothing else," Eircheard said around his pipe. "I must return to work."

"Wait," John said, sliding a hand into his pant pocket.

He brought forth a knife and sliced a deep gash across the palm of his left hand. Then, with slow deliberation, he rubbed the seeping blood along the oak until the wound clotted.

Turning to the steward, John said, "Be certain it accepts no blood but mine."

He crushed the paper bag, tossed it into a corner, and started up the stairs. Dr. Rothgard followed. Ed Calkins watched them leave until they disappeared behind the curtain. Turning toward Eircheard, Ed smiled and said, "I have a second commission for you."

Eircheard removed the pipe from his mouth. "Oh?"

"I have a box of wood I saved from the oldest oak tree in France," Ed said. "I want you to make something from it."

"And that is?"

"A mirror."

CHAPTER 1: RETURNING HOME

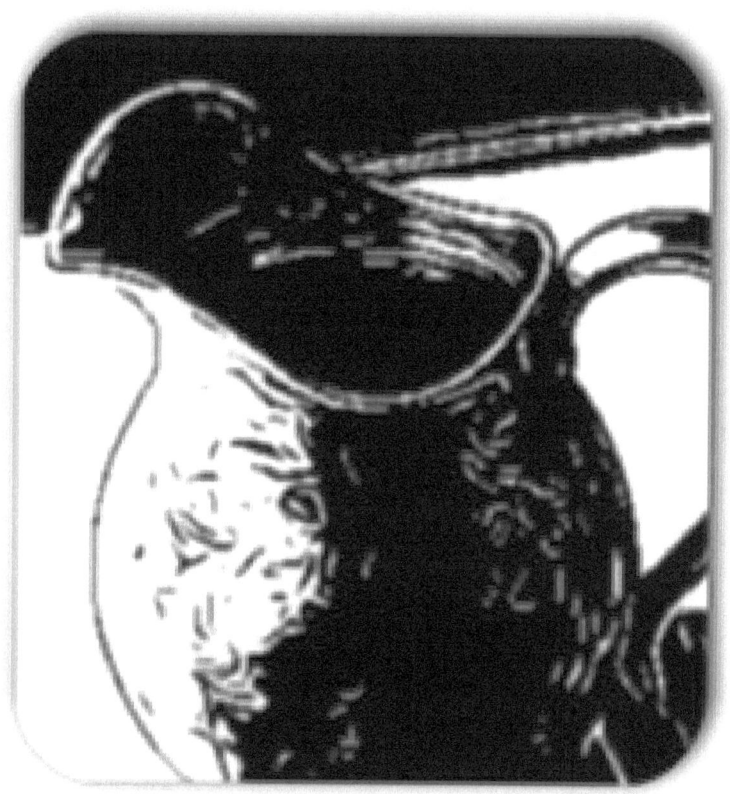

Seventeen-year-old John-Peter Simotes poured the bucket of black water down the drain of the old porcelain sink, careful not to splash it onto the wood floor and create another mess he would have to clean. He was exhausted and hoped his mother was ready to go home. He had begun his day well before midnight, and it was now late afternoon. Uncle Ed would be waiting on his doorstep in a few hours.

His mother, Melissa Wechsler, mop in hand, emerged from the tiny bedroom, pausing to brush the dark hair from her eyes.

"Well," Melissa said as she surveyed the parlor and kitchen one last time. "I guess that just about does it."

"What time is Grandma coming tomorrow?"

"About noon."

"I can't believe they're staying this time." John-Peter slid off the green bandana and shook out a thick, wild mane of long red hair.

"Me neither. But your grandfather has always wanted to come back, and your grandmother saw no reason why she shouldn't make the sacrifice this time, especially now that your Uncle Brian has taken over the cleaning business."

"They'll be bored. I give it a week."

Melissa smiled, but she looked weary. "Your grandmother may be bored, but your grandfather won't be. He's content to spend his days fishing and reading his Bible."

"An exciting prospect, to be sure."

"He'd probably feel the same about writing piano compositions."

John-Peter fell silent and filled his jug for one last drink of water. Further debate was pointless. Last winter's heart attack had changed his grandfather, who had never considered retirement, until his doctor recommended it. The heart attack he survived wasn't called "widow maker" for nothing.

"If you want to add a few years to your life," the cardiologist had told Steve in the hospital the day his grandfather could finally welcome visitors, "you might want to quit work and take it easy for a change."

Darlene, John-Peter's grandmother, had been sitting on the bed beside Steve when the doctor had made his pronouncement, and John-Peter had noticed the pleading, loving look Steve had given Darlene when he squeezed her hand. Nevertheless, John-Peter was surprised when his grandfather announced he was turning the entire cleaning business over to Uncle Brian. Everyone, including Uncle Brian, knew he would inherit it someday, but John-Peter never fathomed "someday" would arrive so soon. Even more surprising was Steve's sudden moral fervor. When John-Peter used to visit his grandparents, Sunday morning was "their" time: his and his grandfather's.

His grandmother liked to sleep late on the weekends, the perfect opportunity for Steve and John-Peter to enjoy a large leisurely breakfast before tackling the yard. His grandfather always booked cleaning jobs on Saturdays, so Sunday was the only time Steve had for catching up on chores at home.

But in June, when John-Peter had spent a week at his grandparent's house in Grover's Park, the routine had changed. Uncle Brian now maintained the lawn, and Sunday morning breakfast didn't happen until after they had attended church services, with Darlene in tow because Steve no longer had his doctor's permission to drive.

Well, once they moved to Munsonville, his grandmother would have to drive all the way into Jenson if his grandfather expected to go to church on Sunday. John-Peter had never seen a minister assume duties at Munsonville Congregational Church, and, on more than one occasion, he'd heard his mother and stepfather discussing whether or not the village board should tear the building down or convert it into a tourist attraction.

John-Peter didn't care one way or another. He considered it ludicrous that a man of the cloth could be frightened away by a ghost story, especially in nineteen ninety-four, yet his mother had insisted that, ever since Reverend Brown had died shortly after they had moved to Munsonville, no minister lasted more than one night at the parsonage. Naturally, his mother did not believe the stories.

"No one ever mentioned that old parsonage was haunted, not one time when I used to live here," Melissa had said. "I think the rumor started as a way to attract visitors to Munsonville after Simons Mansion burned down."

Like that would persuade world travelers to the bromidic village.

John-Peter helped his mother carry the cleaning supplies to her car. "I can't imagine Grandpa and Grandma living in a three-room fishing cottage with nothing more than a water closet for a bathroom and Lake Munson as a front yard."

"Well, your grandfather can. He grew up in it."

"I know he did. I just can't visualize it. He seems made for suburbia."

Steve had sold the fishing cottage to Jack Cooper's father long before the Marchellis' had moved to Munsonville, back when his mother and Uncle Brian were just kids. But Bob Cooper had died years ago, and Jack was tired of playing landlord to tourists. Then again, it seemed as if Jack Cooper had no interest in anything besides drinking and fishing, although, to be fair, he did work hard at Sue's Diner. His mother said Jack was only too happy to resell the cottage back to his grandfather.

As John-Peter closed the trunk, Melissa touched his shoulder. "I know you want everything to stay the same, but think how nice it will be to see your grandparents every day instead of waiting for a school holiday."

"I'd have more fun if Uncle Brian was coming, too." He changed the subject. Talking about his grandfather's transformation made his stomach hurt. "What's for dinner?"

"I'll have Mabel throw some burgers on the grill while you shower. They'll cook quickly, and then you can go straight to bed."

"Mind if I run home?"

"Not at all."

John-Peter tossed his shoes and socks onto his mother's back seat, crossed Main Street—the only paved road in the village, and sprinted toward Bass Street, reveling at the grass prickling his soles, his heels pounding the dry earth, and the late afternoon sun warming his skin. A house-lined hill with hard-packed gravel roads, Munsonville's only neighborhood, lay to the north of Main Street; the fishing cottages were at the south, overlooking Lake Munson. Main Street's downtown area was a single street of plank sidewalks, and weathered brick buildings identified with painted wood signs: *Village Hall, Joe's General Store, Harper's Grocery, Dalton's Dry Good*s, *Walker's Apothecary*, and *Munsonville Public Library*. *Munsonville Inn* had a three-story turret. Munsonville Congregational Church, small, cream-colored, clapboard church with arched windows and an ornate steeple, sat farther back. The three-story, redbrick Munsonville School stood near the end. To the east was the mouth of the dark and mysterious Simons Woods, which extended for many miles before one came to another village, Evansville. Right before the turn of the century, renowned pianist and composer John Simons had fallen in love with seventeen-year-old Bryony Marseilles, daughter of Munsonville's minister, and had built the mansion in the woods as his wedding present to her. John Simons had also covered the house and filled the grounds with pink-flowered bryony, specially bred for his wife. The bryony still covered the property; the old, gray, four-story stone and reputedly haunted building, with its numerous bay windows and a large porch, wrap-around porch, had succumbed to a fire long before John-Peter was born, destroying Munsonville's plans to revitalize industry by restoring the mansion as a tourist attraction. To reach real civilization—the historic town of Jenson, the quaint and touristy Shelby, and the city of Thornton—one traveled west.

John-Peter lived in a three-story, wood-frame house at the top of the hill, a few doors away from where a girlhood friend of his mother's, Julie Drake, had grown up. They didn't see much of her. She and her husband David lived in Washington State where they both practiced psychology. The best part of his house was the view from the backyard. From his perch in the old oak tree, John-Peter could see all of Munsonville: its neighborhoods, Main Street, the lake, the cemetery, and even the ostentatious motor home at the top of Blue Gill Road where his best friend, Karla Dyer, lived.

He hadn't communicated with Karla in a few days; maybe he'd call her tonight. The girl's sympathy might soothe his tangled feelings. Karla had lived in her grandparent's backyard almost her entire life, ever since her own father had died. Worse, Karla had witnessed the gradual deterioration of not one grandparent, as he had, but both her grandparents.

The circumstances surrounding their fathers' deaths should have placed enmity between John-Peter and Karla; instead, they had forged deep friendship bonds between them. No one at school teased him for being close with a girl, not after John-Peter broke the nose of the smart aleck in his kindergarten class who had tried.

He remembered the fuss the day it occurred. The teacher panicked and sent a third-grader for the principal, who had called his mother from her own classroom and into the Munsonville School office.

"John-Peter, what's gotten into you?" his mother had said in a shocked voice. "You know better than to hit people."

"Even when defending the honor of a girl...."

His mother glanced at the principal, who quickly busied herself with some papers on her desk.

"... and her right to be friends with the boy who shields her from harm?"

Neither of them had known what to say to the little boy who had folded his arms across his chest and stared at them with a cool, defiant expression in his brown, green-flecked eyes. With a half-hearted verbal warning about keeping his hands to himself, the principal had sent John-Peter back to his classroom.

He reviewed the bizarre story in his mind as he cut across yards, kicking a rock up the hill. John-Peter's father, a former college music professor, had died of a mysterious, news-breaking illness. Karla's father, Cornell Dyer, self-proclaimed occultist sleuth, medicine man, and vampire slayer, had sneaked into the funeral home and staked the human remains lying in the coffin. Then Cornell had fatally stabbed himself, a fitting end to one who had probably become delusional from inhaling the noxious vapors of one too many magic potions.

The funeral director, who had been working late that night, heard the commotion and stumbled upon the gruesome scene. Neither John-Peter nor Karla had any idea why Cornell Dyer thought Professor John Simotes was a vampire, but the incident apparently had no devastating effect on John-Peter's mother. She soon afterward married the funeral director, which only proved to John-Peter the shallowness of women. I'm never marrying, he thought. A world famous musician can pick and choose a woman, when he decides he wants one.

And he already knew which one he wanted.

John-Peter had never known his father, for he was barely more than a baby when the drama had occurred, but his mother maintained that Professor Simotes resembled the Munsonville Library oil painting of classical pianist John Simons. He guessed if anyone would know, she would. After the death of her "real" father, his mother had lived inside the servant's cottage on the former estate, until the fire destroyed Simons Mansion. John-Peter had studied that painting and carefully compared it to the photograph in the yellowed newspaper clipping that had reported his father's desecration, safely hidden in his closet's false bottom, since, in theory, neither he nor Karla were supposed to know their fathers' story. Both John Simons and John Simotes had long fair hair, but John-Peter didn't consider that characteristic significant, despite their similar names. Lots of men had long hair.

Still, for as far back as John-Peter could recall, his mother had credited Professor Simotes for the musical talent in the son, but John-Peter had scoffed at her fancies. Whatever meager accomplishments a college professor might have possessed had no bearing upon John-Peter's current aptitude or his future potential. Everyone knew genius was inbred, not inherited.

As John-Peter crossed the front yard, he heard his mother's car door slam and caught a glimpse of his stepfather, Kellen Wechsler. A silent house greeted him, but if his parents weren't getting along again, it wouldn't be silent for long. He flew up the stairs two at a time and then grabbed a towel from the hall closet before his stepfather could lay claim to the shower.

He turned the water on full blast and peeled off his clothes while waiting for the spray's temperature to rise. It took a five full minutes for the results of the basement water heater to reach the top floor, another of his stepfather's gripes, along with the home's gravity heat, and a fair one, too, John-Peter mused as he tested the icy stream and then dipped his head under it for a long drink. Kellen owned a chain of funeral homes across the country; they could have lived anywhere. If John-Peter had his way, they'd reside in Paris. But no, his mother wanted to stay in Munsonville, and Kellen, for some unfathomable reason, accommodated her.

John-Peter shut the shower door behind him; the steam engulfed him. He hadn't quite conquered his aversion to water, but now that he was older, a shower offered certain advantages not associated with getting clean. He generously lathered up the soap. The door handled rattled, and he heard Kellen's muffled cursing.

"Almost done!" John-Peter called out.

Soon, he was stepping onto the shag rug and hastily rubbing an oversized towel across his body, not looking at his bony legs, the only part of him he truly disliked, as they were remarkably thinner than the rest of his skinny frame. Because of them, John-Peter never wore shorts, even during the summer. Wet hair tied away from his face and leprechaun moved from his dirty jeans pocket to his shorts pocket, John-Peter tossed his towel in the direction of the laundry room hamper and scampered toward the stairs.

Kellen looked up disapprovingly from the newspaper as John-Peter bounded into the tiny dining room, still barefoot, and plopped down beside him. The entire house, although large, was a maze of small rooms. Antique buffets and china cabinets lined the dining room; an old heavy table that accommodated fourteen ruled the center. To sit, one carefully pulled his chair away from the table, barely, if he didn't wish to scrape the furniture behind it. His stepfather reached into his pocket, removed a ten-dollar bill, and flipped it near the edge of John-Peter's plate. Even the tableware proved a source of contention between stepfather and stepson, for Kellen preferred bone china above others, while John-Peter refused to partake of a meal off a dish that contained animal fragments, necessitating a set of dishes especially for him.

"Get a haircut while you're in Grover's Park. You look like a fairy."

As a toddler, John-Peter had considered Kellen, with his black clothes, black hair, black mustache, and black goatee, the personification of death himself. John-Peter could understand why a funeral director, especially one that marketed himself as an ex-vampire, might wear black at work, but even at home or during social engagements, Kellen never wore any other color; his lapel always boasted a red rose. John-Peter had briefly wondered if his handsome stepfather might appear more attractive if he wore other colors and eventually concluded that Kellen, a married man, didn't want to seem too attractive, despite the fact he slept separately from John-Peter's mother.

Without saying a word, John-Peter slid the bill across the table to Kellen, who snorted and stuffed the money into Melissa's back pocket as she eased into her chair. Mabel Brown, Reverend Brown's widow who'd cooked and cleaned for the household as far as back John-Peter could remember, set a platter in front of Kellen and a pitcher of ice water before John-Peter.

"Maybe you can talk sense into that boy," Kellen said as he removed four hamburgers.

"It's not an issue as far as I'm concerned," Melissa said. "Besides, it's a waste of time to cut it. You know how fast it grows."

John-Peter poured ketchup over his garlic bun, Mabel's specialty, and then carefully layered leaf lettuce, tomato, onion, and cucumber onto it. "Sorry about the shower. I didn't know you were home."

Kellen sighed. "Never mind, I'll take one after dinner. I only earn the money. By the way, I brought your shoes and socks inside the house again."

"Sorry. I forgot."

He passed the plate of food to John-Peter, who reached for a burger. John-Peter didn't have to ask which ones contained only isolated soy protein. The nauseating smell of beef gave it away; his only satisfaction was in knowing Kellen reacted the same way about Mabel's garlic buns. She had to make plain ones especially for Kellen. Too late, he averted his eyes away from Kellen's plate. He saw the blood from the rare hamburgers drip onto it. He wished it had dripped right into Kellen's black goatee. Cows didn't bother anyone. They only contentedly grazed on grassy fields. Did that deserve death by dinner?

Mabel returned with a pitcher of water and a vitamin for John-Peter and the potato salad, which she placed near Kellen and then brought in the tossed salad. Kellen plopped two large spoonfuls of potato salad onto his plate and then slid the bowl to John-Peter. He, in turn, passed it to Melissa and waited for the inevitable comments.

"Look, kid, it won't kill you."

"I don't eat eggs."

Kellen grabbed the bowl and stirred the spoon throughout it, spilling the potato salad down the sides of the bowl. "I don't see a single egg in here."

"They're in the mayonnaise."

"Maybe a life of poverty would teach you not to be so picky."

John-Peter took a bite of his sandwich. Why did parents always resort to the, "When I was your age?" routine. So Kellen had once lived a hard life. Big deal. That was ages ago. Time to get over it.

He did not, however, say that to Kellen.

Kellen looked at Melissa. "I'm flying into New Jersey tomorrow morning and will probably be gone all week. Think John-Peter could go into Thornton when I'm gone? I'll leave him a chore list."

Melissa scooped potato salad onto her plate. "He won't be here next week, remember? He's helping my parents pack."

"So he can help your parents, and he can help the aging paper boy, but he can't help me."

Melissa said nothing. John-Peter knew his mother disliked the irreverent nature of the Happy Hunting Grounds funeral home, but John-Peter didn't mind working there when his schedule permitted it. He hoped his cooperative nature might persuade Kellen to buy him a car for his seventeenth birthday, something like a vintage convertible.

John-Peter did not say that to Kellen, either.

"I'll help upon my return," John-Peter said. "The cottage contains only four small rooms so there won't be much unpacking, and I'll have another week until school starts."

Kellen grunted. "Always on someone else's terms."

"I mean it sincerely." He turned to Melissa. "Shall I take a plate to Grandma before I go to bed?"

"No, I'll feed her when I'm done. Just say good night to her. She always looks forward to it."

Carol Simotes, white hair perfectly groomed despite wearing an oversized, floral house dress, stared blankly at the television set in her first floor bedroom. Kellen would have preferred this master bedroom with the full bath for himself, but Grandma could no longer negotiate the stairs and this made it easier for Melissa to care for her, even if Grandma did wear diapers.

John-Peter kissed the bare, pink spot at the top of Carol's head. "I'm off to bed," he said in a loud voice.

She turned at its sound and scrunched her face in thought. Her chin uncontrollably quivered. "Papers?"

"Yep. Uncle Ed will be here before midnight."

"School?"

"Not for two weeks yet, Grandma. Have a good night."

He slipped from the room and shut the door before Carol could continue the conversation. With his stomach full of food, the drowsiness he had fought back the last hour was gaining on him, and he still wanted to call Karla before he went to sleep.

After refilling his water jug, John-Peter took the stairs more slowly than he had an hour ago, pausing outside his bedroom, listening hard. He quietly pushed open its door, tiptoed into his room, and noiselessly adjusted the latch. Then he peered into the closet door that stood ajar.

Nothing.

With a backward glance, John-Peter strolled across the room and closed the gently fluttering curtains before pulling down the shades. This was against Uncle Ed's explicit wishes. He felt sunlight was healthy for a growing boy, but John-Peter slept better in the dark. The good thing about living near a lake in a northern state, however, was that summers, on the whole, were relatively mild. The entire wall facing the woods was filled with windows, but that was not the main reason why John-Peter had selected this location for his bedroom. By removing the screen from the middle window, John-Peter could easily grasp the farthest branch of his oak tree and swing himself up into the tree's branches, his private library on long, summer days, he'd read *The Odyssey* in Greek last week, and his favorite nesting location on sleepless nights.

He kicked off his shoes before settling onto his four-poster bed, oak and from the seventeenth century, but that was all. Why remove his clothes? He'd only have to dress again in a few hours, not worth losing precious extra minutes of sleep. No need for a wake-up call tonight. Uncle Ed always yelled at him from outside. He pulled the leprechaun from his pocket, slid it under his pillow, stretched his toes, and called Karla.

Karla, however, had just sat down to dinner, but she was willing to accommodate him. "If you really need me," she added.

He did not need any stupid girl. He just felt like talking, that's all.

"Nothing important. Maybe tomorrow."

"Okay. Good night, John-Peter."

CHAPTER 2: THE LEATHER-BOUND DIARY

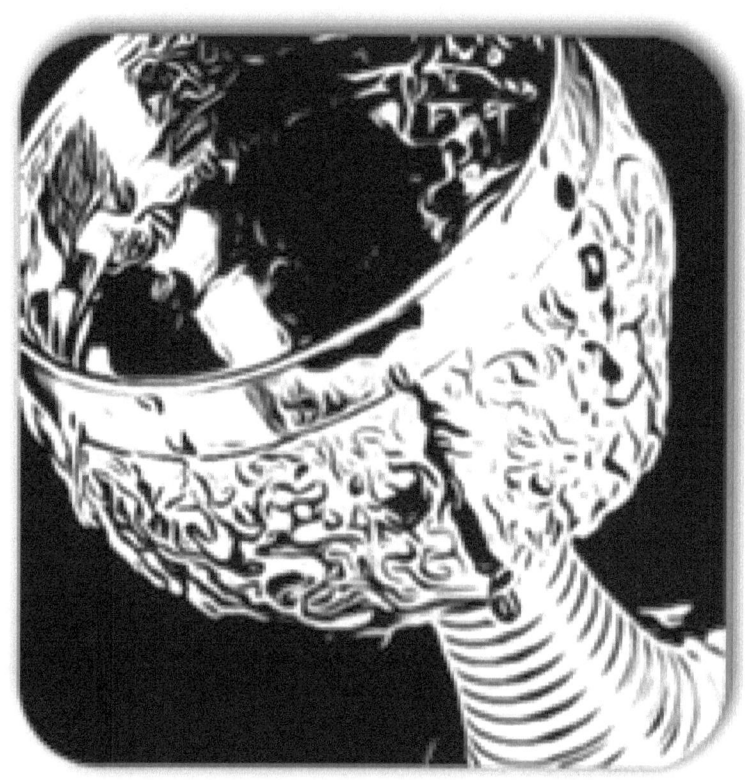

John-Peter had just sat down in the sunny kitchen with a hummus sandwich and the vitamin he had forgotten to swallow that morning when his grandmother returned for another cup of coffee.

"I'm glad you're taking a break," said Darlene, petite and pretty, whose corn-silk hair was just beginning to hint at gray. "When you're done, join me in the attic."

"Ten-four."

"I saved the rest of the fruit salad for you." Darlene brought another glass of water with the bowl.

"Much appreciated, ma'am."

John-Peter bit into his sandwich, then tasted the oranges and pineapples. Too bad she hadn't added some strips of purple onion and a sprinkling of black pepper as his grandfather might have done, back when he was allowed to cook. The drone of the living room television in the Barnes' living room meant his grandfather had again fallen asleep while listening to the solicitations of yet another evangelist. How would his grandmother have packed up the entire house without John-Peter's help?

"As many times as I've moved, you'd think this would get easier," his grandmother had grumbled on Tuesday as she taped shut another box.

With a large, black marker, Darlene wrote "garage sale" on top. Boxes marked thus were for Aunt Cindy. John-Peter hoped the items netted a fair amount of money, so Grandma could provide a stipend in gratitude for his help. He wasn't counting on it, though. Now that his grandfather wasn't working, they needed the extra money, at least until their tri-level sold. He peeked in the living room on his way upstairs. Sure enough, Steve's head, and his silver-blond hair had flopped over the back of the recliner. John-Peter hurried to the attic. It disturbed him to see his once busy grandfather so still.

For the next several hours, John-Peter trudged up and down the ladder, lugging boxes and stacking them on the second floor landing. The August sun radiated through the roof and sucked up the dusty air. Only his grandfather was enjoying the central air conditioner this afternoon. Finally, her face streaked with sweat and dust, his grandmother emerged from the attic. Dismayed, she stood, hands on her hips, and examined the mess. John-Peter looked, too.

"You're taking all this to Munsonville?"

Darlene laughed. "Not if I want someplace to sleep. I'm only taking the boxes with Grandma Marchellis' things inside them. Uncle Brian is saving the rest for the garage sale. I couldn't see sticking him and Cindy with all this work."

"Grandma Marchellis?"

"My first husband's mother. I've haven't opened those boxes since I packed them up after her death, but I can't seem to part with them." She glanced at her wristwatch. "Three-thirty, already? Heavens! Brian will be here by five. I'm going to shower and start dinner."

She hugged John-Peter who squirmed only on the inside because he didn't want to hurt her feelings.

"Thanks for all your help today," Darlene said. "I don't know what I would have done without it. We make a good team."

"Like Bonnie and Clyde?"

Darlene raised her eyebrows and then continued as if she hadn't heard him. "Can you bring down the last few boxes and then raise the ladder?"

"Milady, your wish is my command."

One by one, John-Peter transported the remaining five boxes down to their siblings. As he lifted the final box, the bottom literally fell out, scattering its contents onto the attic floor.

Squatting, John-Peter stacked the items, mostly photograph albums. One leather-bound book, smaller than its mates, caught his attention. He opened it and studied its spidery script, mostly prosaic news of daily life: the weather, a pointless argument with parents, the woes of babysitting. John-Peter was closing the diary when two words caught his attention.

John Simons.

He quickly flew back through the pages, but could not relocate the name. He jumped as a pot clanged, a sure signal his grandfather had beaten his grandmother to the kitchen.

Leaping over the stack of boxes, John-Peter flew to the spacious guest room where he always stayed when he visited his grandparents, the same room once belonging to his mother. He didn't mind its stark whiteness or tan shag carpeting. What difference did it make when he was asleep?

He softly closed, and then locked, the door. John-Peter knelt before the bed and dragged out his suitcase, stuffing the diary beneath his jeans. He had just snapped the valise closed when he heard a knock on his door.

"John-Peter? Are you in there?"

"On my way out, Grandma."

"Would you believe your grandfather started dinner?"

John-Peter enthusiastically followed the heavenly scent of garlic and onion. Steve stood by the stove. Sunlight still shone through the large windows that covered two sides of the kitchen. Darlene, for all her exasperation, was nowhere in sight.

"What are you making, Grandpa?"

"Rice pilaf. Brian's throwing steaks on the grill when he gets here."

John-Peter opened his mouth to object, but Steve interrupted him. "Look in the refrigerator, young man. I'm becoming quite the vegetarian chef."

Sitting in a shallow glass dish on the second shelf were three, thick slices of firm tofu, swimming in a brown soy sauce marinade. John-Peter smiled with satisfaction as he shut the door. "Will Uncle Brian grill these, too?"

"You bet. Want to chop vegetables for the salad?"

"Which ones?"

"Whatever suits your fancy."

John-Peter stuffed his hands inside his pockets and whistled Mozart's *Sonata Facile* as he strolled to the garden he and his grandfather planted back in the spring, the last big project they had accomplished together. He wandered among the plants and decided on two large cucumbers, four beefy tomatoes, and a handful of green onions and radishes. The boy returned to the house just as a teal minivan pulled into the long concrete driveway. John-Peter checked his green wristwatch, a Christmas present from Uncle Ed during the Queen of Christmas coronation. Four-thirty. Uncle Brian was early.

Aunt Cindy stepped from of the van and opened the sliding door. Three slender, little girls with the mother's tight blonde curls scampered out. His aunt reached inside and removed a large watermelon.

"Deanna! Shut this door."

The tallest girl, who had just turned nine last month, dragged her feet back to the van.

"Why me?" Deanna whined. "Just because I'm the oldest."

She slammed it for good measure.

John-Peter grinned at her. "Now you can open the back door for me."

Deanna stuck her tongue at him. "You're not my boss."

"No, but I am." Brian lightly cracked her rear, but he grinned at John-Peter. "Mom's had you working like a slave all week?"

"Slaves have it easy," John-Peter said with a smug look at Deanna as he re-entered the kitchen. Deanna let the metal screen door slam and then stomped into the kitchen. Brian pointed to the living room. "Time out. Ten minutes."

Deanna opened her mouth to retort and then closed it when she noticed her father's stern look. Her seven-year-old sister stood on tiptoes to watch John-Peter scrub dirt off the vegetables.

"Can I help you, John-Peter?"

"Sure, Ellie."

Ellie clapped with delight. "Oh, boy!"

"Wash your hands first," Cindy said, cutting a slice of the watermelon and setting it on a platter.

The five year old had wrapped one hand around her mother's bare, tanned leg as she sucked the thumb of her other hand and watched the kitchen action with large, blue eyes.

John-Peter popped the thumb from her mouth on his way to the kitchen table. "Cut it out, Fawn. You're too old."

Fawn whimpered and wrapped two arms around her mother. By the time John-Peter had set the colander and the knife on the kitchen table, Fawn's thumb was back inside her mouth.

Deanna returned to the kitchen. "My ten minutes are up."

Brian was rubbing spices into the steaks, but he glanced up at the clock. "So they are. Now find Grandma and tell her we're here."

"Bring the cutting board first," John-Peter said.

With a sidelong glance at her father, Deanna objected, "I don't know where it is."

"Second drawer on the right," Brian said.

Ellie ran to the kitchen table, waving her hands for John-Peter's approval. "I'm ready to help!"

Deanna pouted, but she did bring the plastic cutting board. "Can I help, too?"

John-Peter cut a tomato in half. "Ellie asked first. Besides, you're the pony express."

"Grandma's probably in her room, writing."

"Deanna!" Brian called out.

She dashed away. John-Peter waited for Ellie to add the uniformly cubed tomatoes to the salad. Then he sliced the cucumbers while Ellie watched him.

"John-Peter, I can say my twelves."

"Bet you can't."

"Can, too."

Ellie began to recite and she had just reached twelve times twelve when Deanna's voice excitedly rang out, "I helped Grandma with her story!"

A mournful howl erupted from Ellie. "You messed me up!"

Darlene entered the kitchen, smiling. "Deanna double-checked every date."

"See?" John-Peter chopped the last cucumber. "The advantage of years. Your sisters can't read that well."

"Can, too!" Ellie's voice rose with indignation.

"Me, too!" Fawn echoed from across the room.

"Tiny, baby words," Deanna mumbled, with a sidelong glance at her father.

Thirty minutes later, John-Peter was sitting at the old wood picnic table and staring at the food on his plate while Steve said grace. John-Peter tuned out the pious words. He'd heard them nearly every meal this past week. Instead, he admired the nice grill marks on the tofu from his grandfather's new gas grill, Uncle Brian's present to him last Father's Day.

The boy ignored the dinner conversation and mentally reworked a section of his new composition. At his left, his three cousins were holding court at the small picnic table, his old one that he and his grandfather had repainted pink last summer. Each of the girls wore matching, turquoise shorts and ponytails tied with turquoise yarn. Tiny golden hoops dangled from their ears. They didn't spill any ketchup from their hot dog buns onto their bright, white shirts nor on the lace trimming the collars and short sleeves.

"What's that?" Ellie pointed to John-Peter's plate.

Deanna licked a drop of ketchup from the end of her bun. "Tofu. John-Peter doesn't eat animals."

John-Peter flashed a wicked grin. "I prefer them for pets, not dinner."

"Daddy won't let us have any pets," Deanna said in her saddest tone. "Not even a tiny little kitten."

"He's mean," Ellie said.

"Mean, mean," Fawn echoed.

"More rice, John-Peter?" Darlene said, passing the dish to him.

"Thanks, Grandma."

"Brian?"

"Sure!"

Brian spooned a generous serving of rice onto his place and ate a forkful before he spoke. "Steve, since you're reading the Bible, maybe you can answer a question for me. Remember that new guy I hired last week, Bob Watson?"

"About your age, right?"

"Yeah. Well, his uncle, who lives on the east coast, died last night. He was in an automobile accident and needed a blood transfusion. His family refused it saying his religion didn't allow it. Have you ever heard of such a thing?"

Steve cut into his steak. "They're probably referring to the scripture passage where Moses tells the Israelites to pour out the blood and eat only the flesh. The verse says something like, 'The blood is the life.'"

"What's the connection with blood transfusions?"

"Well, some denominations believe a blood transfusion is identical to consuming blood."

"Even to save someone's life?"

"Even then."

Brian look disgusted as he shook his head. "That's plain wrong. A stupid belief cost a man his life."

Ellie tugged John-Peter's shirt. "Fawn kicked me."

"Who wants an ice cream cone?" Darlene set a tub of chocolate ice cream on the picnic table and opened a box of cones.

"Oh, me!" Deanna flew to throw her paper plate into the garbage can.

"One scoop or two?"

"Two!"

Deanna proudly brandished her prize in front of Ellie's face and took an exaggerated lick. "You can't have one because you left a mess at your place."

"I did not!" Ellie hurried back to the picnic table. "I'm getting rid of it now!"

Darlene set a small, single scoop in a dish before Steve. Deanna snuggled near him and licked the edges of her cone. "Will you play badminton with me?"

"Steve," Darlene said as she handed the eager Ellie a cone of her own. "Remember what the doctor said."

"Now, now. How tiring can one little girl be?"

Brian and Cindy exchanged looks. John-Peter suppressed a yawn. "Mind if I shower and go to bed?"

Steve looked surprised. "So early?"

"My body operates on newspaper time."

"Go right ahead," Darlene said. "I need you rested for the morning."

John-Peter wasn't nearly as tired as he claimed to be, but he did wish to linger in the shower and then browse through the diary before sleepiness did hit him. Dusk had fallen by the time John-Peter finally made it to bed and slid the leprechaun underneath his pillow. Yawning, he turned the pages more carefully this time, but he still found no reference to John Simons. His traitorous eyes fought against the faint hum of the central air conditioning and drooped before he scanned a fourth of the entries. Reluctantly, the boy tucked the diary underneath the pillow, next to the leprechaun. Half-awake, half-asleep, John-Peter dreamed vague dreams about chasing his cousins in the yard with a beach ball when he heard the familiar click. The back yard vanished; an old-fashioned parlor replaced it. Even in the dim light, John-Peter noticed the shabby brown furniture, worn beige carpet, bookshelves covering two walls with oil paintings covering the remaining two. The hearth fire blazed high. Sweat glistened on the faces of the men, some standing and some sitting, but all smoking cigars or pipes and drinking brandy or wine. All eyes gazed fixedly upon the Amish-looking man sitting in the corner and reading aloud from a large book. John-Peter noted its gilt letters: Holy Bible.

"Then thou shalt kill of thy herd and of thy flock, which the Lord hath given thee, as I have commanded thee, and thou shalt eat in thy gates whatsoever thy soul lusteth," the Amish man read.

A slight movement caught John-Peter's eye. Slowly, one of the men turned to face John-Peter. It must have been John Simons, for he resembled the library painting.

"The unclean and the clean shall eat of them alike," the Amish man's voice droned. "Only be sure that thou eat not the blood. For the blood is the life."

John Simons stretched his hand toward John-Peter, as if offering the dark crimson liquid in his half-full goblet.

"For the blood," John Simons echoed, "is the life."

CHAPTER 3: PARADISE IN THE OLD OAK TREE

John-Peter took one last bite before dropping the core. "Ow!"

He yawned and turned a page.

"John-Peter, you dropped that apple on my head!"

"Sorry, Karla."

"You'd better pick them up before Kellen gets home."

John-Peter stretched his toes and then curled them tighter around the branch.

"How long are you going to stay up there? I've been calling you all morning."

"Telepathy's on the fritz."

"Oh! You are so annoying!"

The boy reached into the knapsack hanging on the branch next to him and grabbed another apple. As he bit into it, he glanced down at the ground. Good. Karla was gone. He knew she had called, and he had ignored her on purpose. With only one week left before school began and having to work the graveyard shift with Uncle Ed, John-Peter intended to enjoy his final, free moments alone, nestling in the oak tree, his favorite reading spot ever since he and Karla were young enough to enjoy the fairy tales his mother had read to them. While Karla sighed over *Rapunzel, Sleeping Beauty*, and *Cinderella*, John-Peter imagined himself commanding a fine white horse and rescuing the princesses. In gratitude, they'd worship at his feet even as they met his every need because they, as well as his entire kingdom, relied on his superior wisdom, strength and judgment.

So real were these tales to John-Peter that he was not at all astonished when he encountered a real princess. He had arrived barefoot at the dinner table, and Kellen had sent him back upstairs for his shoes. Not bothering to flick on the light switch—the dark had never bothered him, even at three years old—John-Peter had swung open the closet door and caught a quick glimpse of the little girl with the golden hair standing inside his mirror.

His own reflection quickly replaced the fantastic one, but not before John-Peter noticed the melancholy in the toddler's rich chocolate eyes. Who had imprisoned the princess? Certainly not his jovial Uncle Ed, who had hung the mirror soon after John-Peter and his parents had moved into the Munsonville house, shortly after his father's death, when John-Peter was only two years old. Uncle Ed, known as the Steward of Tara due to his love of all things Irish, had purchased the mirror from his favorite pawn shop in Jenson as a housewarming present.

When John-Peter was very small, Uncle Ed told him the shop was enchanted, which explained why the merchandise appeared different each time they visited it. Of course, John-Peter now understood the consistent turnover in pawn shop items, especially one so close to Jenson College. Undoubtedly, the main beneficiaries of the transactions between the shop's owner and the students were Berkley's restaurant and Crossroads Tap.

Nevertheless, the pair never left without an interesting "find" of some kind. After the initial trips, John-Peter stopped showing Kellen what Uncle Ed had bought for him, thus saving the tedium of listening to his stepfather's disparaging remarks about bringing home other people's garbage, since, to John-Peter, these trinkets were treasures. Of course, the boy had told Uncle Ed about the princess, but his uncle had merely laughed and said he wasn't surprised because anything could happen with a mirror when it possessed supernatural powers.

As the years passed, the princess in the mirror grew with John-Peter, transforming from a wispy-haired, sorrowful toddler into a dejected-looking young woman. What did not change was John-Peter's resolve to one day rescue the princess from her solitary confinement within the glass and sail away in a magical craft to the land John-Peter was destined to rule. Even now, at seventeen, John-Peter did not consider his fantasy a childish one, not with an authentic princess living inside the mirror in his bedroom closet.

When John-Peter and Karla outgrew story time, John-Peter claimed the tree for his own and continued his love affair with the printed word several feet in the air. An ideal summer day meant shoes and socks kicked to the ground, a book on his lap, and a knapsack filled with apples, a heavenly combination and one that saved him from chastisement, since Uncle Ed always seemed to know when John-Peter spent too much time in the shade. John-Peter only wished he wasn't so dang prone to splinters, a nuisance that increased in frequency and intensity with each passing year. His mother often spent an hour or two removing thorns from his limbs, which generally invited the scorn of his stepfather.

"Let him suffer a bit. This happens every time the boy climbs a tree. You'd think he'd develop some sense by now."

"I don't mind," Melissa would say as she removed another sliver from John-Peter's palm. "It saves a trip to Dr. Rothgard's office."

Kellen never argued with her logic.

By the time his classmates had graduated to chapter books, John-Peter had completed the entire works of Dickens, Dumas, and Tolstoy. He doted on C.S. Lewis and Tolkien and read Shakespeare's plays before he was ten. It amused him to see the panic in Mrs. Clements' old eyes when he entered the Munsonville Library, knowing full well he probably had a request she could not readily fill.

Today, however, it wasn't literature that interested him, but the diary. The packing and unpacking of Grandpa and Grandma Barnes from Grover's Park to Munsonville had left precious little time for any serious reading. The reference to John Simons still intrigued him, and that was the second reason he hustled Karla away. He wanted to discover the reason behind it on his own and without help, a significant challenge when one's best friend is psychic. Since he still hadn't relocated the entry, John-Peter decided to start at the beginning, at the one account not dated.

Although the aide has already closed the shades, from my position in bed I can peer through the narrow space between the shade and glass to watch the softly falling snow, the only white in the dark, evening sky.

The doctor has come and gone and, unless I have a relapse, is unlikely to return this weekend. But it is not my outcome, which most concerns me. It is what will happen to my family once I am gone. For that reason, I am documenting this strange tale.

Frank, please do not be shocked by what you are about to read. I have no fear of Divine Retribution for I have confessed my sins and been forgiven. I have tried to lead a godly life, and I believe I have been as good a wife and mother as was possible under the circumstances.

First of all, you should know that the Lenkes, your grandparents, were not my parents. They were an older, devout couple who had always longed for children of their own. When I became orphaned, I was left in the care of the local pastor's housekeeper. It was she who paired me with the Lenkes.

Up until I was eight years old, my life was quite uneventful, although I had spent part of my days inside the great walls of Simons Mansion. My father, John Simons' former valet, had already died; I have no recollection of him. My mother was Simons Mansion's senior housekeeper. She and I lived inside the servant's cottage, some distance away from the main house. The remaining servants either commuted from the village or lived in attic quarters. I was the only child on the estate, but my days were happy. John's wife, Bryony, was only eighteen years old when they married, and, in my company at least, was as much of a child as I, although I was but six. John spent most of his day at the piano, filling the mansion with his music.

Bryony, when she had no social obligations, loved to frolic with me. During mild weather, we rolled hoops across the spacious lawn, played hopscotch, bounced a ball on the back walkways, or sat cross-legged inside the gazebo playing jacks. Occasionally, Bryony could induce Alfred Jackson, the night coachman, to row us across Lake Munson to explore the other side of Simons Woods. We'd make a day of it because Mama would always pack a picnic lunch. During inclement weather, Bryony and I played dominos or checkers in the morning room.

When John—Mr. John as my mother had instructed me to call him—was away from home, Bryony might spend part of a day in the servant's quarters playing dolls with me. I had two, both presents from Mr. John. One had a paper mache head with a cloth body, and the other was a real wax doll from Europe. Of all the games we played, Bryony liked our doll games the best. She longed for a real baby of her own, but no stork had yet brought one to her.

On other occasions, I'd lie on Bryony's bed and watch her maid dress her while I sighed in delight at all of Bryony's pretty things, especially her cherry-wood music box. It was painted in pale green bryony vines and pink bryony flowers, the very same plant that grew all over Mr. John's estate, the bryony vines that he had ordered specially bred for her.

John-Peter stopped in mid-chew. The music box's description matched the one sitting on his mother's dresser. He was not allowed to touch it nor recreate its ridiculously simple music, which baffled him, since the object was most precious to his mother. Once, many years ago, when she had not responded to his knocking, John-Peter had caught her curled up on her bed, eyes closed, and cradling the box close to her heart. He had quickly slipped away, confused by her fascination, since even his casual interest elicited her wrath. Now, he contemplated her reaction with new awareness. The diary had fallen from a box of Grandma Marchellis' photograph albums. Quite possibly this diary, as well as the music box, had once belonged to Grandma Marchellis, too. That might explain his mother's irrational possessiveness of the item. He dropped a core and reached for another apple.

That music box, when opened, chimed a very special song, also called "Bryony," which Mr. John had composed for Bryony as his wedding present to her. "Bryony," had become John Simons' signature piece, the one which concluded his concerts, and the very last one he played at home before closing the piano lid for the night. The song also became part of my bedtime ritual. If I was good that day, my mother would let me spend a few minutes in Bryony's room where I could actually sit and hold that glorious music box and listen to its magical notes. The bliss ended when Bryony finally became pregnant.

At first, the reality that she would actually have a baby filled Bryony with indescribable, overflowing joy. With excited whispers, Bryony shared the news with me. My mother would have been furious with Bryony had she known. It was not considered proper that I, a mere child, should know such things about our master and mistress.

But a strained atmosphere on the estate soon replaced a happy one, especially inside the mansion itself. Mr. John, often away on business, now rarely left the house, yet few people saw him. Bryony moped; the servants moped; and even Mr. Matthews, Mr. John's house steward, who could always be counted upon for a ready smile and a hearty laugh even as he slipped a few peppermint bits inside my pocket or tweaked my hair, shut himself up in his study and only occasionally made an appearance. I missed Bryony and the fun we'd had together.

One morning before dawn, my mother pulled me from my warm bed, bundled me into shawls, and hurried me up to the main house. After a solitary breakfast in the mansion's kitchen, I hid under the staircase so I could observe the excitement. The walls fairly shook with Mr. John's voice roaring for Mr. Matthews. Soon afterward, Mr. Matthews gathered the servants around him, dispensed quite large sums of money and informed them that, because Mr. John was so pleased with their work, he was giving them an extended holiday. I thought that was mighty nice of Mr. John.

Only my mother remained, but she was busy upstairs. Lunchtime came and went. Just when I decided no one cared if a little girl went hungry, Mr. Matthews himself appeared downstairs, announced he was famished, and invited me to share a little repast with him. I nodded, uncertain what to say. In the space of a few, short hours, my entire world had gone topsy-turvy. Servants never ate with the household elite and, certainly, the house steward would never venture into the kitchen.

But Mr. Matthews trotted down the cellar steps as naturally as if he had executed those same motions hundreds of times. I meekly followed, for the sight of him rummaging throughout the ice box for food was a hilarious sight. Yet if Mr. Matthews found that funny, he did not show it. He told me to be a good girl and fetch him a tray, and I did, upon which he piled all sorts of interesting things: cold chicken slices, an entire lobster, a loaf of bread from yesterday's baking, a jar of pickles, and several apples. These he carried up the stairs with great care. As he laid our sumptuous feast on the dining room table, I hung back. My mother had promised me a whipping if I ever entered that room.

Nevertheless, Mr. Matthews drew up a chair beside him and patted the cushion. Still, I hesitated. I couldn't disobey my mother, but neither must I insult the house steward. Mr. Matthews apparently noticed my distress, because he told me the rules had changed for today, and only today, because we were celebrating the very first baby of John and Bryony Simons. His voice caught a little as he delivered that speech, and his gaiety seemed rather contrived. Nevertheless, we had a pleasant lunch, he and I, and as Mr. Matthews told such funny stories, I barely noticed the shouting on the mansion's second floor.

Just as we'd gathered up the remnants of our little banquet, my mother stormed into the room. I nearly dropped my tray, anticipating a spanking. All color drained from the house steward's face, and I briefly wondered if he was in trouble, too. My mother's words tumbled from her mouth faster than I could comprehend them. Mr. John had changed his mind, she said. He wanted Mr. Matthews to immediately fetch Dr. Gothart.

Without a word, Mr. Matthews dashed out the mansion's back door, and I soon observed one of the small, open carriages whiz past the front window as if the devil himself chased it. I hadn't known Mr. Matthews could handle horses and drive a carriage with such admirable skill.

It seemed only minutes had passed before he returned with the doctor. I had only a brief glimpse of their troubled faces before Mr. Matthews hustled Dr. Gothart up the stairs to Bryony's room. Neither one returned.

For a while I sat on the bottom step, faced hunched into my hands, waiting. But no one came for me, and I felt forlorn that no one remembered me. The lunch and waning daylight made me drowsy, and I finally sought refuge and a nap behind a sofa in the parlor, where, hopefully, no one would discover my trespassing, since I dared not return to the cottage without my mother.

I woke to unearthly screaming, but the house was black and silent, so I knew the shrieks had been a dream. For a long time I huddled behind the sofa. Moonlight streamed through the front windows. Why, with all the servants gone, had not my mother closed the curtains or lit the lamps? Then I remembered. Bryony had her baby! Why, everyone knew a new mother and her baby needed their rest. That must be why the house was so dark and quiet. Surely, my mother must be upstairs helping her. She would be worried about what had happened to me.

These were my thoughts as I gripped the handrail leading me to the second floor and, ultimately, to Bryony's bedroom. No light seeped from under the door. I knocked. No one answered, so I turned the handle, and the door creaked open. As my eyes adjusted to the dark, I saw the curtains drawn around the bed. Was the baby in there with Bryony or in the nursery? I couldn't resist a peek. Boldly, I peeped around the curtains and beheld only a lumpy quilt. Puzzled, I pulled back the bedclothes and gazed into the unseeing eyes of Bryony and her baby. My head whirled; my stomach heaved, and I ran about the room screaming until my fingers closed around the only item in the room that was still real: Bryony's music box.

How long I crouched in the corner of Bryony's bedroom crying and repeatedly listening to her song, I do not know. But at some point, Mr. John rushed into the room wearing the most appalling expression. He stopped short at the sight of me and collapsed onto the floor, breathing hard and looking most untidy. His hair hung damp and disheveled; his torn shirt was stained red; and even in the room's dim light, I saw the ghastly pallor of his face. I shivered at the calculating look in his eyes and wailed, "I want Mama!"

"You're a big girl now," Mr. John coldly replied.

"Oh, Mr. John, I'm so scared!"

Mr. John reached into his pocket, removed his handkerchief, and dried my eyes.

"You must be brave. You will soon have a new home."

"No!" I clutched the music box closer to my chest.

He pressed my fingers over the lid and lifted my chin to look at him. "It's magic."

"Magic?" I stupidly repeated, momentarily jolted from my fright.

"I am going away."

"No! No! No!" I flailed my legs with each syllable.

Mr. John raised the lid, and my taut muscles obeyed the enchanting notes and slowly, slowly, loosened their grip.

"If you need me," Mr. John rose, looked beyond me, and nodded. I turned around and saw Mr. Matthews standing in the doorway. A cold hand gripped mine and pulled me to my feet. It was Mr. John.

"If you need me," he repeated, "play it."

How events transpired from there, I don't quite recall. In a rapid, jumbled form, Mr. Matthews wrapped me in my shawls, sat me into one of the covered carriages, and drove me to the parsonage where he bade its housekeeper with my care. That was the end; I never again laid eyes on the house steward.

With a face full of sympathy at my plight, the housekeeper shed my wraps, sat me at the table inside the warm kitchen, and spooned up some very delicious vegetable soup. My eyes soon drooped, and I think I might have dropped my head into the dinner if the housekeeper had not noticed and bundled me off to bed.

The next morning I woke with the birds, thinking, at first, that I was in the servant's cottage and that last night had only been a horrible imagining. But the nightmare for me had only begun. I wanted my mother, and my mother never came.

The housekeeper mistook my listless behavior for docility, which fared me well with my new parents, Jozsef and Sophia Lenke. Within days, I had moved to Detroit where Jozsef worked as a bookkeeper in a large hardware store below the Lenkes' rented apartment. I was apprehensive about my new life—well, who would not be?—so far away from home and everyone I had ever loved. I bore it as bravely as I could, but on the third night. I broke.

Lying in the dark, I wailed into my pillows, hating my fate and wishing the past could be reversed. Gradually, as my torrents subsided. I unburied my face, rested my cheek on my drenched pillow, and gazed at the nearby music box. Would Mr. John really appear as he promised he would?

Squealing tires jolted John-Peter to reality. Kellen was home. The boy downed the last of his water, slid down the tree, and hastily collected the apple cores.

CHAPTER 4: MIDNIGHT APPRENTICE

John-Peter wearily pulled the pallet jack down the row of hastily assembled plywood work tables in the large warehouse, neatly dodging the zombie-like carrier pushing a shopping cart of newspapers toward an exit to load into vehicles. Despite the service doors opening into the night, the air hung heavy and lifeless with the overwhelming heat and humidity the building effectively trapped by day. It had been a long, laborious week, not one filled with the reading and relaxation.

At the dinner table Monday night, Kellen had unveiled a list of chores for John-Peter to complete that week at the Happy Hunting Grounds funeral home because Kellen's secretary was on vacation. None of the tasks were difficult, only time consuming. John-Peter had spent the last three days filing and running brochure orders to and from the local printer, as well as tearing apart and cleaning the display cases before refilling them with souvenirs and then carefully dusting the enormous picture of Agnes Scofield, the first client of Happy Hunting Grounds. Kellen had once told John-Peter that Agnes, a ninety-three year old resident of Jenson Nursing home, had given Kellen the permission of feasting on her blood in exchange for being forever immortalized as "the first."

Tomorrow, John-Peter would return to Thornton with his mother for a physical—two physicals to be exact—before beginning school on Monday. Then John-Peter could only help Uncle Ed on weekends and school holidays. Between running newspapers with Uncle Ed by night and helping Kellen by day, John-Peter had not read anymore of Grandma Marchellis' diary. Any free time he had acquired, whether at home or riding in the car, was spent in sleep.

"Hey, John-Peter!" a large, burly man called from across the aisle. "I didn't get my *Thornton Times*!"

"Count?"

The man stretched his tight and faded blue T-shirt over his hefty belly, trying to cover the last inch of skin and failing. "Thirteen."

John-Peter handed them to the man who belched in reply. He couldn't blame the carrier, or any of the other drivers, for being grouchy tonight. Their boss, Joe Reece, had tucked a policy change into their paycheck envelopes stipulating that only a certain number and colors of bags would be distributed. If carriers required more than that amount, the cost would be deducted from the next week's pay.

That move prompted Uncle Ed to express his displeasure with a limerick:

> *There once was a cheap boss named Reece*
> *Whose supplies to carriers decreased*
> *When the carriers cried, "Foul!"*
> *Reece spat as he howled,*
> *"I'll make you share one sleeve apiece!"*

"Someday," Ed said, leaning close to John-Peter and dropping his voice, "people will refer to cheap acts as 'doing a Reece.'"

No negative situation existed where Uncle Ed could not compose an appropriate limerick.

"The limerick is the most superior kind of poem," Uncle Ed had often him. "Not only can people pronounce it, they can remember it and it flows freely from the tongue. This sort of poetry works in two ways. The words I say create fear in others, fear of how they will be remembered. This fear then promotes a willingness in your enemy to compromise, to confront you in more friendly terms, or maybe to ally with you."

But if Joe Reece, or anyone else for that matter, cowered in terror before Ed Calkins, he never showed it. Even the carriers themselves rarely expressed the respect and appreciation John-Peter felt was due Ed for his hard work.

Ed printed and sorted route books, oversaw the unloading and distribution of entire truckloads of products, including bag shipments and fifteen different publications totaling over ten thousand newspapers. In addition, Ed fielded complaints, dispensed bags, retrieved and carried garbage to the dumpsters, and swept the warehouse. This was in addition to his regular, carrier responsibilities. Ed delivered newspapers to the outlying and remote areas no driver wanted to touch, including Munsonville.

On school days, if John-Peter rose early, he'd grab a jug of water and sprint barefoot down to Main Street under the early morning sun, just in time to catch Ed Calkins filling the newspaper boxes outside Sue's Diner. If Ed had a few minutes to spare, which he always seemed to have, he'd share an Irish joke, adjust John-Peter's leprechaun, and point to John-Peter's watch.

"Bet you can't say 'Irish wristwatch' ten times."

And John-Peter could, every time.

"John-Peter, if you want to make an Irishman laugh on a Monday, tell him a joke on a Friday."

"John-Peter, while at the wake of his atheist friend, the Irishman said, 'Poor lad. All dressed up with no place to go.'"

"John-Peter, do you know it takes four Irishmen to change a light bulb? One removes it from the socket and the other three remark, 'What a grand, old light bulb it was!'"

If Ed ran late, he'd acknowledge John-Peter's existence with a jovial nod before he dropped the bundles at the machine, fully expecting John-Peter to fill them.

John-Peter, of course, always did. He understood newspaper deadlines. He had grown up with them. His father, Professor Simotes, not Kellen, had delivered a country route under Uncle Ed's authority. John-Peter not only accompanied John on the route, he helped prepare the papers for delivery and consulted the route book when his father had a question about the location of an obscure address, a delivery instruction or code, or which combination of publications a particular customer might receive.

The problem? John-Peter did not remember any of it.

He had been too young, a tender twenty months of age when the professor had died. His memories of the newspaper business centered around Uncle Ed, who was not really his uncle, but a man who had been a good friend, as well as the boss, of John Simotes.

Ed seriously undertook his news agency responsibilities, even referring to himself as a "ruthless dictator" who expected compliance within his ranks, although he rarely obtained it. The carriers snatched extra newspapers from the pallets, invented excuses for customer complaints, and stole inserts, hooks, and bags from each other's stations. Never did one week pass without a carrier calling Ed with a crisis of why he could not deliver his route that night, and could Ed please do it?

And of course Ed did, while hard at work composing a penalty limerick, which that said carrier would hear upon walking in the warehouse door the following night. However, Ed did not limit his control tactics to mere verse. No new carrier slipped through the ranks without at least one request to sign Ed Calkins' petition. Ed's birthday fell between Abraham Lincoln's birthday and Valentine's Day, a fact significant enough, Ed felt, to warrant a three-day national holiday.

"The time will come when everyone around the world will eagerly anticipate the Ed Calkins Day parade," Ed always said, beaming, as he pressed both paper and pen into the hesitant carrier's hands.

In the meantime, Ed himself offered the joys and excitement of his parade to the elite crowd fortunate enough to deliver newspapers in the middle of the night from the Jenson warehouse.

For as long as John-Peter could remember, he celebrated each February thirteen watching a carrier pull Uncle Ed through the building on the pallet jack, one John-Peter had decorated with green streamers and balloons for the occasion, while an exuberant Ed waved to his constituents with one hand and tossed bite-sized, wrapped pieces of candies from the other one toward the work stations.

So although John-Peter had no time to read the diary this past week, he could and he did spend much time reflecting upon what he had read as he busied himself with his required duties.

Had Grandma Marchellis really lived part of her life inside Simons Mansion or was the entry simply the ramblings of a demented mind? Surely if she'd had a connection to the musician, his mother, grandparents, or even Kellen would have mentioned it. Besides, who knew if her son Frank even had read it? Grandma Marchellis chronicled the tale in her personal diary. Maybe she went completely senile before she shared it with Frank.

"John-Peter! Where's my *Detroit Daily News*?"

"In transport."

"Late again?"

"Afraid so, Dave."

John-Peter dragged the jack back to the dock. He had nothing left to disperse until the final truck arrived for the night. He closed his fingers around the leprechaun before heading toward Uncle Ed's work station.

With lightning speed, Ed bagged the *Jenson Reporters* for a carrier who took his year old daughter to the emergency room last night. Eyes down at his work, Ed said to John-Peter, "Stuff all the papers for Munsonville, and bundle my papers for Sue's Diner."

John-Peter refilled his jug from the water fountain and then went in search of an empty grocery cart. He found one overturned near Joe's office, in front of the rusted, dented metal shelves holding back issues of the previous week's publications. The cart worked better than he had guessed. Its handle only slightly wiggled and three of the wheels actually rolled.

He stacked the newspapers from Ed's work area into the cart and dragged the load to the strapping machine. Three other carriers stood in line to belt their store drops. One short, round woman fidgeted with growing impatience.

"Hurry it up, Kurt. You're not the only dang carrier in this building."

But Kurt ignored her and continued strapping bundles with a steady pace. Soon the metered beep-beep of a truck's back-up alarm broke into the carriers' low, rumbling chatter.

"'Bout time," groused a tall, thin man as he scratched under his scraggly, bronze beard. "Gotta go to work this mornin'. Boss said if I'm late again he'll can me."

John-Peter wondered if John Simons ever paid that promised visit to Grandma Marchellis. If he did, John-Peter doubted the musician entered through the front door. He believed the story of the magic music box. He might even have seen it.

Ed tugged a pallet jack full of *Detroit Daily News* bundles past John-Peter as the boy strapped the last bundle.

"John-Peter! Get that cart back to the station and help me get these *Detroits* passed."

"Affirmed, sir."

Carriers swarmed the dock and Ed's pallet, opening bundles and grabbing stacks of papers, heedless of Ed's loud orders to wait their turns. Joe Reece charged five dollars for every newspaper a driver delivered late. John-Peter plopped onto a work table, fished inside his other pocket for an apple, and wished the princess had given it to him. He took a bite and leaned his weary body against the table's back. As punishment for disregarding his stern commands, Uncle Ed would be tormenting offenders tomorrow morning with a fresh supply of limericks.

"John-Peter!"

The boy woke with a start. The apple core lay on the floor. The warehouse was devoid of carriers. Uncle Ed must have already loaded his car because he looked ready to leave.

The first rays of dawn were breaking through the dark the sky as the pair entered the parking lot. No chance of a nap this morning before he and his mother would leave for Thornton.

"What time is your appointment?"

"Eleven-thirty."

"Hmm." Ed frowned and looked at his own green wristwatch. "I'll hit the country roads later. Let's deliver Jenson, and then I'll take you back to Munsonville. You'll never survive the day without a nap."

"Much obliged, Steward, much obliged."

With a light heart and a steady supply of apples in his left hand, John-Peter threw newspapers into the driveways of Jenson's neighborhoods and fumbled for whatever publication Uncle Ed needed with his right. He was glad to skip the country roads. The joggers who inhabited them at three o'clock in the morning made him uneasy. Once, Ed nearly collided with a man who rode his bike straight at Ed's car. Other carriers might have signaled their anger with a finger or colorful language. Instead, Ed soothed his jangled nerves with a limerick.

> *O cyclist who rides in the night*
> *Making sure you're hidden from sight*
> *One day you will find*
> *A driver's who blind*
> *Who'll flatten you without any fight.*

"John-Peter, did I ever tell you about the four great treasures of the Tuatha de Danann?"

Ed had just reached the part about the endless food supply of the Cauldron of Dagda when he threw two newspapers out the window into the driveway of the house before the stop sign.

"Wait, Uncle Ed," John-Peter said, reaching above the visor for the route book. "The *Jenson Reporter* is a vacation stop."

"What about the *Thornton Times*?"

"Active, your honor."

John-Peter ran across the road to pick up the extra newspaper. Although the sun was now fully up, the absence of traffic made delivering papers almost a joy. After tossing the renegade paper back into the smudged, cracked laundry basket that held its clones, John-Peter, gradually perking up under the brightening sun, grabbed a handful of *Munsonville Weeklies*.

"Can't understand why that newspaper is still in business," Ed complained. "How much news can that village report in a week?"

"The Daltons bought a parakeet."

"Three more blocks and then we can do the stores. Keep up with me because I want to stop at Eircheard's Emporium before we go back to Munsonville."

"Anything in particular you're seeking?"

"Another tin whistle."

Ed Calkins saved the pawn shop's bundle for last, after first pulling off the road to adjust John-Peter's leprechaun, a pocket-sized creature with a leering face, tiny black eyes glinting below a pair of bushy red eyebrows, and a thatch of wild red hair sliding out from under its tall green hat. In the center of its belly, a series of numbers in the billions spiraled downward. The lull in the action always caused John-Peter to nod off, but he always reawakened feeling as refreshed as if he'd slept the night. By waiting until daybreak to deliver the Eircheard's Emporium, Ed could be certain that Eircheard himself would have unlocked the front door, prepared the tea, and, if the wizened shopkeeper was feeling particularly ambitious that day, prepared a loaf of warm, Irish soda bread, using vinegar instead of buttermilk and a vegan spread from Brummings in Shelby to top it, out of respect for John-Peter.

But no whiff of freshly baked bread greeted John-Peter's nose that morning, only the pungent scent of the tobacco that emitted from Eircheard's clay pipe. When John-Peter was a small boy, the sight of this leprechaun-like old man intimidated him and became the source of a recurring nightmare. Since early childhood, John-Peter had often dreamed of the shopkeeper, sitting on a tree trunk and carving a misshapen piece of wood with a long-handled knife. A series of incantations followed the store owner's act of jamming the wood into the ground. While Eircheard chuckled in glee, John-Peter's leering face emerged from the top of the wooden post.

But the Eircheard's fearsomeness now only existed in John-Peter's dreams. Inside the pawn shop, he was simply an old man making a dime from those wanting a quick buck and parting with their possessions to obtain it. The one-room, wood shop was not large, but Eircheard had filled it to bursting with all manner of furniture, knickknacks, clocks, lamps, signs, clothing, wall hangings, books, record albums, toys, dishes, household furnishings, and so forth, all stacked haphazardly and without category consideration.

"No tin whistles today," Eircheard said, leaning back in his desk chair, puffing on his pipe, and gesturing to a side table. "But some fellow brought in a whole stack of records. All bagpipe music."

Uncle Ed made a dour face and recited:

A pygmy did sit in his chair
Luring the innocent into his lair
He said, "Why not you stay
And buy something today?
If it's garbage I really don't care."

Eircheard grinned around his pipe and watched Ed weave through the card tables, laden with assorted figurines, plaques, and jewelry, to flip through the albums.

John-Peter poured a cup of tea, popped his vitamin, and polished off the remnants of yesterday's bread while Eircheard puffed and watched some more. The boy wished he had topped off his jug before leaving the distribution center. His parched throat screamed for water.

"Saved the last from yesterday. Had a feeling you gents would stop this morning."

"Thankee, Mr. E."

Eircheard smiled through the black gaps between his broken teeth. "Anytime."

Ed looked up from the stack of records.

"Want to drive Kellen nuts?"

"I'll pass, Uncle Ed."

Kellen's disparaging remarks about classical piano music were the bane of John-Peter's life. No need to blare bagpipes, too.

Ed selected three albums and brought them to the counter. Eircheard rose painfully to his feet to ring up Ed's purchases.

"That will be five dollars even."

"You drive a hard bargain."

"Got to keep a roof over my head, same as you."

Ed picked up the records and turned to John-Peter, who spread margarine on this third chunk of bread. Three-fourths of the loaf had disappeared into the boy's growling stomach. "Let's drop Munsonville, and get you home."

"Think Reece will be mad the country route is late?"

"Not mad enough to find someone else to take it out."

The combination of the sun's glare off the windshield and the warm snack sent waves of sleepiness through John-Peter's numb brain. Twice he nodded into slumber against the window glass before he and Ed reached Munsonville.

Ed parked his car in front of Sue's Diner and reached for the newspaper bundle. "You rest. I'll fill the machines." In less than five minutes, Ed was turning onto Bass Street over John-Peter's objections.

Only the muffled sounds of his grandmothers' voices from Carol's bedroom greeted John-Peter as he entered the house. It was past seven o'clock, very unlike his mother not to be awake by now. Kellen would already have departed for Thornton. They would meet him later for lunch.

"Mother!" John-Peter called.

He wandered into the kitchen, the only modern part of the entire house. Munsonville's oldest homes once all had basement kitchens, but Kellen said he'd be damned if he'd go without modern conveniences just to placate Melissa's sentimental attachment to charms of the past. Melissa had posted a note on the black refrigerator: *Setting up my classroom. Be ready to go at nine. Hope you had a good night with Uncle Ed. Mabel prepared a wok full of vegetable stir-fry. Don't forget your vitamins. Love, Mother.*

After reheating the stir-fry in the microwave, all the while drinking straight from the faucet, and tucking a carton of soy milk under each arm, John-Peter settled into the black leather recliner of the small television room and picked up the remote. He wished Kellen would buy a big screen for the house as Kellen had for the funeral home, but Kellen refused to waste his money for shoddy Munsonville reception and viewing selections. John-Peter actually enjoyed some of the Jenson College documentaries the students produced, but Kellen would not budge. So as he ate, the boy randomly surfed the stations until the face of his smiling stepfather appeared on the screen.

"Hello, this is Kellen Wechsler, former vampire and founder of the Happy Hunting Grounds funeral home with a special offer for you."

John-Peter crushed the first carton and opened the second.

"For the next two weeks, I will add a Happy Hunting Grounds bereavement selection or support group to any of our regular or deluxe funeral packages at no cost. This is your opportunity for Grandma to have that vampire slaying she always wanted, to express appreciation to your deceased first grade teacher, or to meet with other mythological figures as they, too negotiate their place in today's society."

John-Peter set the empty bowl and fork on the coffee table and proceeded to finish the soy milk.

"Plan your next funeral at Happy Hunting Grounds, where the dead bury *your* dead."

Scanning through the stations, John-Peter stopped at a pre-recording of Jenson Junior High School's participation at a band competition. He popped back the chair, and the music transported him to Simons Woods. Propped against an oak tree in the middle of a grove, John-Peter dozed as the band's tones faded into high-pitched pipes that filled him with its thin light notes. A multitude of fairies danced about his head, the very same fairies his mother's friend Laura had once painted on the bedroom walls inside the house at Jenson. The music weighed against his eyelids and jabbed his face, neck, shoulders and trunk before making its way over his limbs.

"John-Peter!" his mother called.

The music stopped. The boy bolted upright, heart thudding and sweat pouring. He swiped the hair away from his face and scraped his forehead down to his cheek, recoiling from the unexpected sting. Slowly, the boy brought down his palm and saw a thick carpet of splinters.

CHAPTER 5: SCHOOL PHYSICAL

"Here you are!" his mother cried with exasperation. "I've been calling all over the house for you."

"Sorry," John-Peter said, trying to steady his shaky voice. "Dozed off."

"Are you ready to go?"

"Straight away, fair lady."

"Hold on."

Melissa sat on the couch next to John-Peter, picked up one of his hands, and turned it over, examining it. She repeated the same maneuver with his left and then sighed.

"When will you learn to be more careful with trees?"

John-Peter did not reply.

"Well, it's a good thing we're seeing Dr. Rothgard today."

"I can now die a happy man."

Melissa patted his shoulder and smiled. "Come on. Let's go. I refilled your water jug."

John-Peter pushed the leprechaun deeper into his pocket and plodded to his mother's car. The brief nap had revived him just to the point of crankiness. Although the sun felt good, he couldn't wait for the running around to be done so he could really sleep. Uncle Ed would return before midnight.

They were past Jenson and halfway to Shelby before Melissa spoke. "How was work last night?"

"Fine."

"Were the trucks on time?"

"No."

"So you got in late?"

"Yep."

Her voice softened. "I'm sorry. You must be really dragging."

John-Peter did not answer. His mother did not attempt further conversation until they approached the outskirts of Thornton.

"What time is Karla's birthday party tomorrow?"

"Inconsequential."

"Why?"

"I'm not attending."

"You're not?" Melissa sounded surprised. "But she's your best friend."

"Why perpetuate the bourgeois lifestyle?"

His mother looked sharply at him. "Did it ever occur to you that Karla might like to see you there?"

"With the size of her family? She'll never miss me."

Melissa chuckled. "Don't be so certain. You don't exactly fade into the background."

The faint, green hue tingeing the boy's skin since babyhood was a source of both irritation and personal amusement to him. John-Peter's pediatrician never located the source of the unusual skin color although he had run a battery of tests on him.

58

Because John-Peter otherwise enjoyed perfect health, his doctor concluded green skin was a harmless aberration. Too bad John-Peter couldn't say the same about the doctor's perpetual shamrock jokes.

Melissa slowed the car as she approached the parking lot of Thornton Medical Center. "Shall I drop you off by the door? You're five minutes late."

"I can walk." He shot his mother a provocative grin. "However, ma'am, if you are too tired, I can park…"

"Not without a permit."

"Oh ye blind follower of regulations and traditions."

"Cheer up. Driver's Ed starts this fall."

Quite possibly the most annoying aspect of living in Munsonville was the lack of driving opportunities for its youth. Many people in the village still did not own a vehicle, preferring carpooling with one who did whenever a trip into Jenson or beyond was needed. This meant driver's education was offered only to students in their final year of high school, just in case they might attend school or accept employment outside Munsonville.

Inside Dr. Morgan's office, John-Peter yielded to the customary weight check, temperature-taking, and blood pressure readings that were part of every visit to this doctor. The very tall and slightly overweight Dr. Morgan bent low as he peeked inside the boy's ears and down his throat before poking and prodding various parts of his body with soft, poofy hands, all the while asking, "Does this hurt?"

"No, no, no, and no," John-Peter said.

"Ophthalmic migraines?"

"Intermittently."

"Are you still a vegetarian?"

"Only if you don't count rats."

Dr. Morgan's dark bushy eyebrows formed a wide "V" as he smiled and sat John-Peter upright. "I know a joke you might like. Why did the elephant wear his green gym shoes?"

"The red ones were dirty."

"Well, John-Peter, I guess you have gotten older."

"So have your jokes."

Dr. Morgan's hand paused over the school physical form, but he did not comment. The only sounds in the quiet room were the ticking of the clock and the scratching of Dr. Morgan's ballpoint pen.

After what seemed to be a long time, Dr. Morgan rose and returned the school form to Melissa. "I think this will do it," he said.

Then Dr. Morgan turned to John-Peter and extended his hand. "Once again, you're perfectly healthy. I don't expect to see you until next year at this same time."

John-Peter shook the doctor's hand. "Thank you, sir."

Melissa did not speak until Dr. Morgan left the room. "'Thank you, sir?'" she said. "Emily Post would be proud."

"I am not devoid of manners. He took my well-deserved snub like a man."

As Melissa predicted, Kellen had reserved a back table, away from the windows, inside Chuck's Wagon, a family-style, steak and burger house down the road from the Happy Hunting Grounds. Kellen, in black, each rose petal fresh and in place, was pouring cream into his coffee but stood when he saw Melissa and John-Peter.

"How'd the exam go?" he asked, kissing Melissa's cheek and lingering long enough to take a deep breath.

Melissa didn't seem to notice, just as John-Peter tried ignoring the mounted taxidermy specimens and the stench of sizzling cattle from restaurant's kitchen.

"Fine," Melissa said, seating herself on Kellen's right. "John-Peter passed with flying colors."

"So to speak," Kellen said, sitting and then sliding his chair closer to her. "You're still taking him to Dr. Rothgard's this afternoon?"

"Of course."

"You're wasting your time."

"It doesn't cost us anything. And it's my time to waste."

With a grunt, Kellen picked up his menu and studied it. John-Peter regarded him with a mixture of revulsion and placating amusement, even as he stretched back in his chair to allow a sunbeam to fall across his face. Did all men sniff their wives?

The waitress stopped at the table with the coffee pot and refilled Kellen's mug before hovering over Melissa's cup.

"Tea, please," Melissa said. She turned to Kellen. "Do you have a busy afternoon?"

"The Fosters will be in this afternoon to plan Don's funeral, and another family wants to make arrangements for after-care. The Seattle branch called me this morning with a problem they can't resolve. I'm flying there tonight."

The waitress returned with a tray of hot water, tea bags, and sliced lemon, which she set beside Melissa. "I'll be back shortly to take your order."

John-Peter opened his menu and tuned out the rest of his parents' conversation. If Karla ever resorted to drab topics for the mere sake of talking, he'd drop her as a friend.

"Ready?" The waitress had returned.

His parents ordered the cheese steak sandwiches, the restaurant's specialty. Another purgatorial meal awaited him.

"And for you?" The waitress poised her pen over her notepad and smiled encouragingly at John-Peter.

"Three bowls of vegetarian lentil soup, spinach salad, fruit plate, a loaf of plain French bread, and two pitchers of water."

The waitress raised her eyebrows as she documented his order but said nothing. As Melissa and Kellen talked, John-Peter surveyed the dining room's other customers. Two young mothers sat at a corner table with three preschoolers. The chatting women appeared completely oblivious of their offspring's antics. The children crumbled crackers onto the tablecloth, sipped prepackaged creamer, and painted each other's noses with pats of butter. Adjacent to them, two police officers ate a hurried lunch while conversing in low tones. On John-Peter's left, six elderly gentlemen sipped coffee and talked with animation, occasionally laughing heartily at their inside jokes.

A bowl appeared before John-Peter. The waitress had returned with their food as wailing screams ascended from the corner table. One of the preschoolers had tumbled from his booster seat.

"Have you heard anything more from the Chandlers?" Melissa said to Kellen as she handed John-Peter his vitamins.

"Only that they are still looking, but they are definitely interested in the area."

As John-Peter ate, he mentally worked on the new piece he was composing. Now that Kellen would be out of town, maybe John-Peter would have time to perfect it. Of course, that all depended on how long Kellen would stay away and whether or not any trucks would be late tonight. He fervently hoped not. The combination of settling his grandparents into their new home, delivering newspapers with Ed Calkins, and helping Kellen at the funeral home had left John-Peter no time for music, reading, or finishing Grandma Marchellis' diary.

The waitress slid the invoice next to Kellen. He looked at it, grunted, and reached for his wallet. He tossed a handful of bills onto the table and twisted his arm to peer at his gold watch.

"Charge it." Kellen rose and handed Melissa the tab. "I'm late."

Kellen leaned over Melissa's head as if to kiss the top of it, but instead slid his nose down to her neck. This time, Melissa waved him away. John-Peter impaled a cantaloupe chunk and wished Kellen would save his morbid antics for home.

Before heading toward the nursing home, Melissa stopped at Taylor's for John-Peter's school supplies and replacements for the clothes he'd outgrown, but this last was the easiest part of the day, since all he required was jeans and plain T-shirts: green, brown, red, orange, or yellow.

"Well," Melissa said as they waited to checkout. "When Ann calls to complain, I won't be able to relate."

"Lauren is the little fashion princess, is she not?"

Melissa grinned as the cashier moved the items down the belt. "Trenton's demands are not far off either, from what I hear."

"Trenton's style suits the future neurosurgeon. Lauren copies the pseudo-trendy."

His mother leaned down to sign the credit card receipt. "I think your father wishes you were trendy, too."

"He should talk. Basic black is obsolete."

John-Peter carried the packages to Melissa's car and deposited them inside the trunk. His eyelids felt heavy, but his mother would not go home until they had visited Dr. Rothgard, splinters or no splinters. Up until five years ago, a trip to Dr. Rothgard meant a visit to a respectable Shelby office. Today, Dr. Rothgard operated an underground practice from within the walls of Golden Years Retirement & Nursing Home, an upscale senior facility that featured chef-run kitchens, limousine services, high ceilings, granite countertops, solid gold bathroom fixtures, fireplaces, swimming pools, tennis courts, and a movie theater.

It had been that or prison.

Seven years ago, the medical director at Jenson Memorial Hospital had produced convincing evidence that Dr. Rothgard had been stealing patient blood samples and experimenting with them at his home. During the investigation, authorities discovered freezers full of blood on Dr. Rothgard's property. The judge ruled Dr. Rothgard mentally unfit, dissolved his practice, and ordered twenty-four hour supervision. Because of state budget cuts, no other suitable facility could offer mental health services to elderly patients. Thanks to John-Peter's connection with the newspapers, he and Karla carefully followed the story as each step unfolded.

Because Dr. Rothgard was considered a psychiatric patient, he enjoyed none of the home's finer amenities and lived in a stark bedroom in a separate wing reserved for residents with behavior issues.

Nevertheless, Dr. Rothgard continued servicing several of his favorite patients, courtesy of his former nurse Dottie Sherman, now manager of The Golden Years Retirement & Nursing Home. Because Dottie ensured Dr. Rothgard's access to any needed supplies, Dr. Rothgard could continue as John-Peter's primary, albeit unofficial, healthcare provider.

Dr. Rothgard was dozing in bed, but woke with a snort and a hiccup when Melissa shut the door. He blinked several times, replaced the glasses that lay cockeyed across his face, shielded his eyes, and barked in a gruff voice, "Pull those shades!"

John-Peter obeyed immediately, anticipating Uncle Ed's reprimand the next time the paper boy adjusted the leprechaun. Melissa approached the bed and gazed down the old, gray-haired man.

"How are you feeling today?" she said.

"As well as any sane person jailed in this damnable place," Dr. Rothgard said, sitting up straight and rearranging his pillows for leverage. "You're looking well, for someone living with a man claiming to be an ex-vampire. Sit down, and tell me what's new with the boy."

Melissa pulled a chair close to Dr. Rothgard's bed. "John-Peter starts school on Monday. We saw Dr. Morgan today."

"How did that go?"

"Fine. It always does."

"Nothing out of the ordinary?"

"No, nothing at all."

"Well, you've been lucky. Any concerns?"

"Just one," Melissa said, fixing her eyes on John-Peter's face. "Karla invited John-Peter to her birthday party, and he refuses to attend."

Dr. Rothgard glanced up at John-Peter, who, hands shoved into pockets, leaned against the wall near the windows, hoping to catch a warming by osmosis. "A mite too old for 'Pin the Tail on the Donkey,' hey?"

John-Peter peeked around the shades to hide his grin, and Dr. Rothgard did not stop him. Dr. Rothgard often sided with him, which always infuriated his mother.

"It's just a family party at her grandmother's house," Melissa said. "I understand his basic, antisocial nature, but he carries it too far."

Dr. Rothgard opened a drawer and pulled out a pipe. It had a large bowl with a gold lid, gold trim, and gold mouth piece. The rest was a polished dark wood, briarwood, the finest pipe wood since it improved with age, or, at least, that's what Dr. Rothgard always claimed. Dr. Rothgard shuffled to the window, opened it a crack, and then sat in a chair to light the pipe.

"Do you need more vitamins for the boy?"

"Yes, we're almost out."

"Go see Dottie. She'll process them."

After Melissa left the room, John-Peter feigned indifference as he prepared himself for the inevitable extractions.

"Get my bag, John-Peter."

John-Peter slid under the bed, opened the trap door, and removed Dr. Rothgard's black, medical bag, which he promptly brought to the doctor.

"Bring up a chair, and give me your hand."

The boy did and extended his right hand toward Dr. Rothgard. John-Peter flinched at the removal of one splinter after another while Dr. Rothgard contentedly smoked his pipe.

"Slide down that oak tree pretty fast again, eh?"

John-Peter said nothing.

"My boy, why be at odds with the world?"

John-Peter scowled at Dr. Rothgard's remark and winced as the old man removed another splinter. "Perhaps the world should conform to me. What makes its ways so correct?"

"No one said you have to agree with it. Let's see that other paw."

John-Peter held out his left hand and prepared for invasion.

"You should, however, learn how to co-exist in it." Dr. Rothgard paused and looked hard at John-Peter. "A man needs to face himself in the mirror."

"And if he can't?"

"Then you must right the wrong." Dr. Rothgard yanked out the last splinter. "How's your appetite? Pretty good?"

"Customarily ravenous."

"No meat?"

"Animal cadavers, you mean?"

Dr. Rothgard handed John-Peter the tweezers. "Still seeing spots before your eyes?"

"Sometimes. Dr. Morgan said they are ophthalmic migraines."

"But what do you think?"

The door opened and closed. Melissa had returned. John-Peter doused the tweezers in alcohol before returning the bag to its secret home.

"Ready?" Melissa asked as John-Peter stood.

"Melissa," Dr. Rothgard said thoughtfully, around a cloud of fragrant smoke, despite the open window. "Have you had that talk with the boy?"

John-Peter inwardly squirmed. He didn't need his mother, "talking" to him. Isn't that why kids watched television? Dr. Rothgard merely watched Melissa, but she now found her shoes interesting, too.

"I'll think about it," she hedged, opening the door.

As John-Peter started to leave, Dr. Rothgard said, "Consider my words, lad."

"I will."

The sun remained bright despite the lateness of the afternoon; its hot rays beat through the car's front glass. John-Peter closed one hand around the leprechaun and leaned back to receive the sun's full brunt. That should make up for any solar deficiencies, the boy thought as he drifted into sleep. A click, and the heat grew hotter until it blazed high in the hearth. Again, the men smoked and drank, but their faces dripped from the fire's intensity. All eyes gazed upon the Amish man sitting in the corner as he read aloud from the book he held before his face. Even before John-Peter saw its gilt letters, he knew it read *Holy Bible.*

"Then thou shalt kill of thy herd and of thy flock, which the Lord hath given thee, as I have commanded thee, and thou shalt eat in thy gates whatsoever thy soul lusteth," the Amish man read. "The unclean and the clean shall eat of them alike," the Amish man's voice droned. "Only be sure that thou eat not the blood: for the blood is the life."

John Simons rose, turned, and stretched out his hand toward John-Peter, the hand that held the goblet half-full of dark crimson liquid.

"For the blood," John Simons said, "is the life."

In fear, John-Peter edged away from the scene and *Smack!* He had hit his head on the passenger window as his mother turned up Bass Street.

"Are you okay?" Melissa said with obvious concern on her face.

John-Peter rubbed his wet temple and tried to think. "Right as rain." He was as sweaty as the men in the dream. Rain would feel good. No, it wouldn't, he quickly corrected himself. Rain would mean double-bagging on his last night.

"I wish it would rain," Melissa said. "Everything's turning brown."

Darlene was walking from Carol's room as Melissa and John-Peter stepped through the back door.

"I fed and bathed her," Darlene said as John-Peter poured himself a pitcher of water. "I couldn't get her in and out of the tub by myself, but I managed a sponge bath just fine. Hopefully, you won't even have to change her until the morning."

"I really appreciate your help," Melissa gave her mother a grateful hug. "School begins Monday, and I don't have anyone else to stay with her. I can't stand the thought of putting her into Jenson Nursing Home."

Darlene smiled in response. "Steve's been sitting at Sue's Diner all day catching up with old friends, so this gave me something constructive to do."

"Aren't you still writing, Grandma?"

"A little here and there. Nothing too much anymore. I'm spending more time on the other side of the printed word. However, unlike you, John-Peter, everything I'm reading is in English. Well, I need to get going. Enjoy your dinner, you two."

Because Kellen would not be home expecting a large meal, they sat in the kitchen and ate baked beans and vegetarian hot dogs. After taking his vitamin, John-Peter grabbed a jug of water and decided to skip a shower. What was the point when he would be working in a stuffy warehouse in only a few hours? He would clean up in the morning.

John-Peter did, however, crack open the closet door and peek inside. Long red hair framed the familiar face staring back. He crouched down, pressed on the board, and grabbed the diary. He had hoped to catch up with his reading, but he was fast asleep soon after sliding the leprechaun underneath his pillow. He never even opened the cover.

CHAPTER 6: OUTCAST

"Hey, John-Peter!"

John-Peter grabbed his geometry book and slammed a door. Karla leaned against the locker beside his, clutching a stack of books and grinning.

"Well, it's back to status quo education."

That was easy for Karla to say. She lived with a mother who supported her talents. Only after he shut the locker and spun the combination did he face her.

"John-Peter, are you staring at my...?"

"Nice locket."

"What?"

"Are you deaf? I said, 'Nice locket.' Is it new?"

Karla's face turned as pink as her sweater as her hand reached instinctively for the gold chain around her neck. "Grandmother gave it to me for my birthday."

"Oh, yeah, sorry about your party. I had to watch Grandma Simotes for my parents."

"Not a problem." Karla pried open the heart-shaped pendant. "See? She added a picture of her and my grandfather, to keep them close always."

"Nifty."

John-Peter turned on his heel and sauntered down the hall's scuffed wood floors to geometry class. Could he help it that Karla looked better in plain clothes than Lauren and her snooty friends did in plaid miniskirts and knee high boots? Stupid girls!

His encounter with Karla only compounded his irritation. He had begun the day in a terrible mood. First, he had overslept, the result of one too many nights on the route. Then he snapped a shoelace in his haste only to discover Mabel had forgotten to buy soy milk, so he had to settle for a jar of peanut butter on a batch of her garlic buns. All that meant he also missed walking to school with Karla and listening to her rattle about standardized, government-funded indoctrination. Karla detested being late.

All morning, he drifted from class to class, ignoring his juvenile, male peers who drooled over Lauren and company. Knowing Karla was likewise bored consoled him. John-Peter couldn't wait to compare notes with her over lunch. But when he reached the lunchroom, the large open area in the middle of the first floor and furnished with folding wood tables and chairs, Karla announced other plans.

"Do you mind, John-Peter? Megan wants to talk to me about something."

He waved her away from him. "Fait accompli."

It was, after all, only Karla. He scanned the room until he spied the figure of a slight, chestnut haired boy sitting at a back table near a sunny window and reading a thick textbook through his equally thick tortoise shell glasses. Every now and then, the boy took a bite from his sandwich, but his eyes did not leave the pages. John-Peter set his tray opposite Trenton Cooper, read the book's title, *The History of Modern Neurosurgery*, and then topped all four of his plain hamburger buns with the black bean burgers the lunchroom mothers kept for him.

Trenton peered at John-Peter from over the book. "Did you know certain types of hydrocephalus occur only in older adults? Differential diagnoses are Alzheimer's or Parkinson's diseases."

"Grandma Simotes?" John-Peter opened his first thermos of almond milk and quickly drained half.

"Maybe." Trenton buried his face between the book's pages. "The signs are all there: difficulty walking, memory problems, and no bladder control."

"Treatment?"

"A shunt to drain excess fluid."

John-Peter popped the vitamins in his mouth, drank half the jug of water, and then reached for his second sandwich. "Forget it. Kellen would oppose the procedure."

Trenton raised his eyes. "Mom had the same reaction when I proposed a lobotomy for my father, which, by the way, would give me great pleasure to perform."

Since childhood, Trenton had stood apart from the rest of his family, although he fished with his father Jack, bussed tables at Sue's Diner under his mother Ann's watchful eye, stocked shelves at Dalton's Dry Goods, and pretended he acquired valuable knowledge at Munsonville School.

That's where any resemblance to the Cooper family ended.

As a young boy, Trenton had tormented his sister Lauren with the neurosurgical procedures he practiced on her dolls. He shaved their nylon locks with Jack's personal razor prior to slicing open their plastic heads with carving knives, smuggled from the kitchen of Sue's Diner, to remove "malignant" tumors. He slashed wrists with boning knives for carpal tunnel surgery, wrapped coat hanger braces around broken necks, and built custom hospital beds from odd scraps of lumber leftover from clandestine trips into Simons Woods to care for victims of spinal surgery gone bad. Trenton filled any remaining time in his day reading books about neurology and neurosurgery from the interlibrary loan system and disclosed their data to anyone who approached him. That happened but rarely, as most people changed direction when they saw Trenton Cooper with a book between his hands. John-Peter was not one of them. He understood Trenton's fascination with the perfect regulation of the human body's nervous system. It was as orderly as a flawless piano composition.

He rolled an apple across the table, an ordinary, non-magical apple, and Trenton accepted it without looking up. Trenton once told him a budding neurosurgeon required up to twelve years of education before he could legally practice, and he hoped to shorten that time by acquiring some of that information now. Therefore, John-Peter had no desire to hinder his friend's progress. So what if Jack Cooper could decapitate and fillet a walleye? Through informal experiments, his son had learned how the fish's nervous system coordinated swimming and balance. Besides, Jack had nearly peed himself when Trenton, assisting his father, manipulated the correct nerves and then threw his voice to make one walleye corpse talk.

The bell rang. Trenton did not move. John-Peter picked up his tray and headed to the garbage can. Courtney Rogers, the mayor's daughter, sidled up to him. Courtney was Lauren's best friend, which meant she only talked to John-Peter when Lauren was not around.

Courtney adjusted the brown, plush headband holding her blonde hair away from face and brightly smiled. "Geometry's already confusing me."

"You'll catch on," John-Peter said, although he doubted his words even as he uttered them. Girls like Courtney were perpetually confused.

"I'm scheduled all week. Maybe if you work for your father one night you could stop and help me with my homework. The desk gets pretty quiet after seven o'clock or so."

"Forbidden."

"Kellen wouldn't have to know."

Trenton sped past John-Peter with his tray. "Biology, man!"

With a hopeful smile, Courtney linked her arms through John-Peter's right one. "I'll walk with you."

"Where I go, you cannot follow."

John-Peter shook off her claws and stalked away to the men's room, a long, narrow, high ceilinged repository with three metal stalls of peeling blue-green paint and one long, multiple-paned window, propped open with a short stick. He stared in the mirror over the sink at the tangled mass of trailing red hair and decided a ten-minute delay was sufficient for the first day.

At the sight of John-Peter standing in his doorway, the short, stocky, and graying Mr. Peter Miller, one of Karla's uncles, stopped lecturing in mid-sentence about the principle characteristics of organisms.

"I'm sorry, Simotes, but you need an office pass to enter this classroom."

"Give the leprechaun a break. Maybe he had guard duty at the end of the rainbow."

A titter ran through the class. John-Peter sought out at the comedian, a boy with jelled, flipped up blond hair and a blue Dion Monsieur polo shirt, leaning back in his chair and calmly smirking.

"Anyone who finds that funny can join Chandler in detention today." Mr. Miller turned toward John-Peter. "Simotes?"

"Leaving, sir."

"Chandler, out. I'll see you after school."

When John-Peter reached the office, he overheard the boy speak in apologetic tones to Mrs. Joyce.

"It was completely my fault, and I promise to cooperate fully with my punishment." The boy looked at his Gucci shoes and heaved his best, heartbreaking sigh. "I know it's no excuse, but I felt so lost without knowing anyone here. I guess I was just looking for attention."

Mrs. Joyce, squinting at him through the "one size fits all" reading glasses she bought from Walker's Apothecary, smiled encouragingly. "I'm sure a nice boy like you will have no trouble making plenty of friends. Have a seat until Mrs. Princeton returns."

"Thank you, ma'am," the boy said.

He eyed John-Peter on his way to the chair in the corner of the room. John-Peter sidled up to the desk.

"I need a late pass."

"Because?"

"Personal reasons."

Without looking up. Mrs. Joyce reached for the form, scribbled a few lines, and passed it to John-Peter. "In the future, leave yourself enough time at lunch. You're not in second grade anymore."

"Comprendez."

Last period was no improvement. Although his mother offered a varied assortment of literature for her English class, they were all selections John-Peter had read in the third grade. *The Canterbury Tales*? What was she thinking? John-Peter glanced across the room at Trenton who merely appeared to give Melissa his full attention. In reality, Trenton was miles away in some teaching hospital's operating room, extracting a glioblastoma.

Two weeks ago when Melissa had finalized her lesson plans for the fall semester, John-Peter had begged her to assign something challenging for him and dispense the regular material to the subordinate students, a suggestion she disregarded based on a flimsy excuse.

"You know, John-Peter, maybe if you eliminated your superiority complex, you'd make more friends."

"I won't coddle serfs."

"Education is not limited to books, you know."

"You'd rather I fretted about my social status?"

"I'd rather you got off your high horse. There's more than one kind of ignorance."

"And I'll acquire it if I associate with imbeciles."

Melissa had given up, and so had John-Peter. His mother's desire to awaken a passionate love of prose within her students was high and intense. So why did she wish to squelch his zeal? Never would he understand parents, teachers, and especially parents who were teachers. John-Peter said so to Karla as they left the school and walked down Main Street. With no students living on the outskirts of the village, the school had long ago discontinued its bus service.

Karla felt the same way he did.

"Every year, I ask Mom to homeschool me, and every year I get the same answer," Karla said. "She says this is good experience for me. I think it's a huge timewaster, considering the amount of 'other' work she assigns me."

"Karla, oh, Karla!"

They both turned at the sound of Amy Miller's voice, one of Karla's many cousins, who was jumping up and down and waving her hand to attract Karla's attention, as if her Fran Drescher voice hadn't done the job. Karla threw John-Peter an apologetic look.

"She needs to talk about something."

"No problem. I'll call tonight."

The rest of the week passed in a similar manner. Kellen flew home Friday morning from Washington State and joined John-Peter, who had again beaten his stepfather to the shower, and Melissa at the dinner table Friday night.

"The Chandlers' boy, Curtis, started school this week," Melissa said as she passed the pot roast to Kellen. "They're staying in Jenson, but they've talked to the village about buying property on the old Simons Estate."

Kellen reached for the gravy boat. "Unless they're planning on resurrecting Simons Mansion to attract tourists, the village will refuse them."

John-Peter swallowed his vitamins and then devoured at his gluten roast. Mabel threw him a sympathetic glance as she brought him a fresh water pitcher. So his lordship's parents wanted to live in Simons Woods? Good. Maybe the curse would get them.

Melissa sighed. "They're certainly flaunting quite a bit of money. They might make an offer the village will find hard to refuse."

"Let them flaunt. There's other money in this village."

When he finished his meal, John-Peter rinsed his plate before setting it on the counter. Mabel beamed at him and said, "You get your fine manners from your mother."

"You're not our maid, despite what Kellen thinks."

"I've got your grandmother's dinner ready. Shall I feed her?"

John-Peter picked up the rolled napkin of silverware and reached for the plate. "I've got it tonight, Mabel, thanks."

Carol dozed in the armchair, her hand intermittently twitching. She started when John-Peter set the plate on the television tray and dragged it closer to her chair.

"Hungry, Grandma?"

John-Peter fetched a bib from the top of her dresser and tied it around Carol's neck. Mabel had shredded the beef into the gravy and ladled it over the mashed potatoes. He scooped up a spoonful, and Carol obediently opened her mouth. Thunderous applause erupted from the studio audience.

"What did she win, Grandma?"

"Car…and….Hawaii."

"Did you and Grandpa ever go to Hawaii?"

"No…fire..."

Carol's eyes drooped as she finished the last bite, but she managed to swallow it before she fell completely asleep. John-Peter carried the plate to the kitchen, noted with satisfaction that Mabel was using the last of the hot water on the dishes, and trotted to the stairs. When he reached the top, he paused, held his breath, and gently eased open his door. He reached the closet in three large steps and swiftly opened it. The princess stared back. He willed her to stay; his eyes watered from the effort. But when he blinked, she disappeared. John-Peter flicked on the switch and rummaged in his dresser for a pair of flannels. He glanced at his clock as he shut the door. It was Friday night; no need to set the alarm clock.

Before climbing into bed, John-Peter slid the diary from its hiding place under the closet floorboards. After tucking the leprechaun underneath his pillow, he opened the diary to the marked page.

I propped up my head on my elbow and reached out to raise the wooden lid. The music box's tinkle sounded as loud as gongs in the quiet room. I held my breath and waited but saw no sign from Mr. John or even the Lenkes. Bile rose in my throat at this thwarting of my last hope.

At what time I fell asleep I do not know, but when I woke, moonlight filled the room, displaying quite clearly the figure of John Simons standing beside my bed. I blinked in disbelief, but within that brief moment of closing my eyes, Mr. John had disappeared. Had I dreamed it?

Perhaps I did, because I lay awake for a long time, hoping for another glimpse of that familiar person from my past. But he did not reappear, not that night. I had to know if he was real. So on the following night, I once again fell asleep to the enchanting notes of "Bryony" and once again, an indeterminate period of time later, I woke to see the same figure of Mr. John staring at me as I slept. I jerked upright in bed, but the vision had vanished.

Our little cat and mouse game continued for some weeks until one night I felt the sensation of something cold brushing against my cheek. Mr. John sat next to me on my bed. I tightly squeezed my eyes, but when I reopened them, Mr. John was still there, as he was only moments ago. He fixed his lifeless eyes on me; the corners of his mouth drooped. My own sadness lessened as I recalled his loss, even greater than my own, and my heart gravitated toward him. I lay a gentle hand on his; the iciness of that member surprised me.

I commented on how cold he felt, and he nodded gravely and said even his very blood chilled him. I swept aside my blankets and invited him to warm himself under them, hoping he would not leave so soon. He slid next to me, and I observed the dustiness of his ragged clothes and the mustiness that clung to them. I am not certain how long Mr. John lay beside me, but he did not appear to grow any warmer.

Feeling deeply concerned for him now, I inquired if he was ill, and he said no, but if I would only share a bit of my warm blood with him, it might dispel the frigid temperatures of his own. I laughed and said such a feat was impossible to do, but John reassured me of his skill in discharging it, if only I could be so generous in allowing him to take it. Partly from willingness to help him and partly from intense curiosity as to how he might obtain this fluid, I gave him permission to help himself.

Slipping an Arctic hand beneath the collar of my nightgown to hold it away from my neck, Mr. John's other hand fumbled with the tiny buttons to release their hold. I wondered what Mrs. Lenke would say if she happened upon us.

Mr. John slid further into my bed positioning his face quite near my neck. A shudder ran down my spine from the frostiness of his fetid breath, and I might have recoiled from it, but a sudden, sharp pain lanced my throat. I opened my mouth to cry out, but Mr. John's hand crashed over it as he tore into my flesh. My eyes smarted with tears at this betrayal of my trust. Then it happened. As he drank, Mr. John's lips warmed.

My body relaxed as I realized the pain was only part of the process of sharing with him my nice warm blood. I waited for the temperature in his fingers to also rise, but Mr. John pulled away before that occurred. I begged him to take more and warm his entire body, but he buttoned my nightgown, patted my shoulder, and said he felt quite comfortable now, that I needed the rest of my blood, and how proud Bryony would be of me for helping him. I felt quite grown up.

After that night, my life settled into a predictable routine, which I found bearable because of the somnolent visits from John Simons, my secret friend who banished the poignant loneliness from my life.

John-Peter turned a page and yawned hard, but his eyes closed anyway. What a disappointment the diary turned out to be. Either Grandma Marchellis was deranged, or she had one twisted imagination. He yawned, slipped the diary beneath his pillow next to his leprechaun, shut off the light, stretched his toes, and immediately began dreaming of the princess. Because she had refused to marry the dwarf, that shrunken man imprisoned her in a mirror at Eircheard's Emporium, intending to retrieve the glass at a later date.

But Ed Calkins discovered this enchanted mirror and hid it inside John-Peter's closet. When the dwarf discovered the ruthless dictator's plot against him, he began digging through the top of the house to capture the princess from John-Peter's bedroom. Paralyzed under the dwarf's wicked spell, a helpless John-Peter lay immobile in his bed, listening to the scuffling in the ceiling. He must rescue the princess, but how?

The scrabbling moved closer to the princess's asylum, and the princess cried out, "John-Peter, help me!"

The boy struggled to respond, but his voice produced no sound; his limbs refused to move.

"John-Peter!"

Her voice had deepened to masculine tones. The scratching stopped.

"John-Peter, wake up!"

The boy opened his eyes, dazed. How long had Ed Calkins been shouting outside his bedroom window?

CHAPTER 7: MUSICAL CHAIRS

"We have a mouse in the attic," Kellen announced the next morning as he pinned a fresh rose to his lapel. "John-Peter, after breakfast, run down to Daltons and buy traps. I'm flying in a few hours."

John-Peter swallowed his vitamins and then slumped over his large bowl of granola, trying to decide if the effort of bringing his spoon to his mouth was worth it. Stupid late trucks.

"Leaving?" Melissa said as she squeezed lemon into her tea. "You just got back."

"I have to be in Houston tonight for the grand opening of Blakely's HHG funeral home and to guide them through their first week of business. John-Peter, did you hear me about the mouse traps?"

"Yes, sir."

"God, I loathe mice."

John-Peter wouldn't forget Kellen's order. He just had no intention of obeying. While he could not prevent his stepfather's eventual murder of an innocent rodent, John-Peter refused to abet it.

Despite crushing fatigue from a long night in the warehouse, the boy rejoiced at Kellen's impending departure. His stepfather's absence brought the double pleasure of practicing his piano as much as he liked without constant ridicule along, with the temporary suppression of Kellen's musical monarchy.

The stepfather's and stepson's mutual fondness for the arrangement of notes and chords might have bonded them had not their tastes been poles apart, creating a relentless verbal sparring that eradicated the household harmony whenever the pair simultaneously inhabited it.

John-Peter's preferences were decidedly Baroque, classical, and romantic, although he would not dismiss piano arrangements of art songs, as long as he alone played them. Electronic music sufficed only when live was unavailable to him, which, unhappily for John-Peter, was most of the time.

School and work consumed most of his schedule, but when both were complete, John-Peter inclined toward one of three leisure pursuits: reading, composing, or piano playing, all of which became near impossibilities when Kellen was home.

Kellen favored rock music; the harder and louder it blared, the better he liked it. Although Kellen refused to install a large screen television inside the house, he could, and he did establish a whole-house stereo system for blasting his favorite compact discs. Headphones provided limited relief for everyone except Carol, whose partial deafness ensured she heard only her television game shows. Melissa retreated to the library when she corrected papers, and sometimes John-Peter joined her, with either homework or a good book in tow.

But the library offered no refuge when John-Peter required sleep, a necessity that often conflicted with the household routine. The library also failed as a conservatory, the acerbic nickname John-Peter bestowed to the small bedroom at the far end of the second floor where Kellen allowed him to store and practice his small upright piano. The instrument was hardly the concert grand for which John-Peter lusted, or, at the very least, the piano that had once belonged to his father.

Often, when Kellen heard John-Peter playing, he berated his stepson for his "effeminate passion for dead, white, European, highbrow pansies." In return, John-Peter pronounced Kellen a "disciple of fads and all that is tasteless, toneless, and repulsive," a broad-spectrum insult that included Kellen's "miserable sham of respectable funeral homes."

Such remarks usually led to the suspension of John-Peter's library privileges and generous allowance until Kellen was shorthanded at work, in which case he forgave and forgot until the next oral bloodbath began.

Kellen's regular, household absences represented many happy hours of playing previously mastered material for pleasure's sake. It also meant tackling new and difficult pieces without interruption and the freedom to compose piano arrangements of the pipe melodies playing inside John-Peter's mind. His mother had suggested he unconsciously combined the influences of Ed Calkins' Irish background with the classical piano ones of his father, but, if that was true, why didn't Kellen's revolting music selections also dominate his mind?

Melissa had no further explanation for it, and Ed Calkins had no sympathy for John-Peter's plight, other than to produce a limerick denouncing the roguish funeral director.

Hail, Kellen! Friend of the dead.
Their demise keeps Wechsler well-fed.
His wares he does sell
For a grim show and tell.
If only fine print they had read.

A glum John-Peter reached behind the seat for a *Jenson Reporter*. "That's easy for you to say. You listen to Irish fiddle recordings whenever you wish."

"Well, Kellen is gone for the week, and you can spend your time as you see fit. Throw that last paper, John-Peter, and put your shoes back on. We'll stop at Eircheard's Emporium after I adjust the leprechaun. The old magician procured an Irish tankard collection from an estate and promised me first looks."

The scent of newly baked Irish soda bread met John-Peter at the pawn shop's front door. He nodded his thanks to the pipe-smoking shopkeeper seated behind the desk.

"Butter's safe today, I presume?" the hungry boy said as he sliced a thick piece, moved his chair closer to the sunny window, and reached for a gallon of water to wash down his vitamins.

"Butter's always safe," Eircheard said around his pipe.

"Where are the tankards?" Ed asked, holding up a long sterling chain and fingering the Celtic knot hanging from it.

"Back room. I'll get 'em."

Gripping the desk, Eircheard stood and then shuffled behind the dividing curtain. He reemerged a few minutes later, carrying a large box and saying, "Got the goods, Eddie, give me a hand, will ya?"

Ed removed the box from the little man and set it on an empty and wobbly card table next to the desk. He opened the flaps, peered inside, and asked, "About a dozen?"

"Aye, all pewter."

Ed held up a tankard and examined its etching. "They all have Gaelic symbols?"

"Except for two."

He replaced the tankard and brought forth a second to examine it. "A pookah?" Ed turned to face the shopkeeper.

Eircheard nodded and relit his pipe, but said nothing as he watched John-Peter stuff the last of the loaf in his mouth.

"How much, Eircheard?"

"The lot of 'em?"

Ed nodded and resealed the box's flaps.

"Hundred bucks."

The supervisor's face fell. "I don't have it. Can it wait until Friday?"

"Up to you. Tankards might not be here by then."

John-Peter removed his wallet and tossed a credit card on the desk, ignoring the incredulous, gaping looks from the Steward of Tara.

"Easy there, Uncle Ed. Kellen gave it to me for emergencies."

"I don't think this is Kellen's idea of an emergency."

"He never specified. You'll get paid before he gets his statement."

To express his gratitude, Ed Calkins entertained John-Peter all the way to Munsonville by twice singing *The Irish National Anthem* followed by *When Irish Eyes are Smiling* three times. He had just begun *Sweet Molly Malone* when John-Peter broke into the song.

"Hey, Uncle Ed, do you mind filling the boxes? I'd like to see my grandparents before I go home."

Ed's chuckle was weak and weary. "I'd be very ungrateful if I did."

He parked in front of Sue's Diner, where John-Peter leaped from the car, cut over to Lake Munson, and dashed across the grass to the cottage's open side door. Steve sat reading at the table, but he looked up when John-Peter rapped on the glass.

"Well, this is a surprise. Come in!"

John-Peter pushed open the door, stepped inside the tiny kitchen, and immediately recoiled from the lingering scent of frying bacon. He glanced at the white porcelain stove, but no cast iron frying pan squealed on the sins of his grandfather.

"I thought you're not supposed to eat fatty food."

Steve's face looked sheepish. "I figured an occasional slice or two can't do much harm." He pulled a chair away from the table. "Have a seat, and tell me about school."

"Got any soy milk?"

"A brand-new carton is waiting for you in the refrigerator. Glasses are in the cupboard, to the right of the sink."

"I don't need a glass."

John-Peter drank half the carton and brought the remainder to the small drop-leaf table in the center of the cramped room. Its original owner had constructed the walls, cabinets, cupboards, and floor boards from knotty pine harvested from Simons Woods. Steve had returned to his book.

"What are you reading, Grandpa?"

Steve flipped to the cover. The gilt letters on the black exterior read, *Holy Bible*. With a shock, the boy realized it was the same Bible he had seen in his John Simons dreams.

His grandfather noticed and said, "Do you like it? I picked it up yesterday at the village garage sale."

"It looks old."

Steve smiled. "That it does. I like to think that I'm just one of dozens who's gained plenty of spiritual wisdom from its pages."

John-Peter drained the carton. "You don't really believe everything in it, do you?"

A solemn look passed over his grandfather's face. "Well, now, I don't know. I haven't read all of it yet, but I gain fresh insight each day. Look."

Steve thumbed through the sheets until he came to the section he wanted.

"Here you go. 'Greater love hath no man than this, that a man lay down his life for his friends.' John 15:13. Now," Steve said, laying the book on the table, "I wouldn't say I've never heard that one before, but I thought about that verse in a new way today."

John-Peter reached for a napkin from the basket in the middle of the table and asked politely, "How so, Grandpa?"

"I always aimed to live my life looking to the needs of others and trying to meet them. Now that I'm nearing the end of it, I hope I was successful."

John-Peter winced. He hated when his grandfather talked as if death was imminent. So the boy quickly changed the subject.

"I'm experiencing that verse today, Grandpa."

Steve appeared puzzled. "I don't understand."

"At the pawn shop in Jenson, Uncle Ed wanted to buy something, but he didn't have the money so I charged it. If Kellen finds out, he'll kill me."

Steve chuckled and lightly punched John-Peter's shoulder. "I don't think you could have laid your life down any more than that."

Darlene walked into the kitchen, adjusting the back of her earring as she did. "John-Peter, why aren't you in bed?" she said, bending to kiss his cheek.

"Leaving now, Grandma. I just stopped to say, 'Hi.'"

"Tell your mom I can sit with Carol this afternoon if she wants to escape for a few hours."

"Will do."

Steve walked John-Peter to the door. "Join us for church tomorrow?"

John-Peter avoided his grandfather's beseeching gaze. "I'd really like to, Grandpa, but with working all night..."

"If you can find time to run newspapers, surely you..."

"Steve, let the boy alone." Darlene interjected. "When you were his age..."

"I know." Steve looked tired, but he smiled at John-Peter anyway. "Still, if I could do it all over again..."

"I'll try, sometime, Grandpa, okay?"

The fishing cottage suddenly felt oppressive, and John-Peter couldn't escape it fast enough. Once outside under the sun, exhaustion hit, despite the warmth. His leaden legs struggled to climb Bass Street. Once home, the boy dragged his resisting body up the stairs and fell asleep on the bed before he ever kicked off his shoes.

John-Peter woke to waning light. He groped for his clock and held it up. Two o'clock! Now he'd never get to bed at a decent time tonight. Thunder grumbled in the distance with restrained anger. Good. Storms this afternoon meant clear skies later and no double bagging. He scurried to the conservatory and entertained himself for hours, free of intrusion from the master of the house, until a knock severed his muse.

The boy abruptly stopped. "Who is it?"

"Your mother. Why aren't you in bed?"

"My stupid fault. I slept too long this afternoon."

Melissa opened the door. She was wearing her purple robe and matching slippers.

"Why don't you grab a bite to eat, shower, and try to relax? The storm is supposed to last all night."

"Sure."

"Don't forget your vitamins."

Might as well. His trespassing mother had broken his musical spell, the beginning of a series of events that only compounded his irritation. The vegetable curry caused indigestion; the shower brought only limited relief; and the princess remained hidden. Furthermore, as John-Peter restlessly tossed in bed, the rain pattered on the roof with unrelenting intensity. When agitation hit near-screaming level, John-Peter kicked off the sheets, flicked on the light, and padded across the room to the still-empty closet. Maybe, John-Peter thought as he settled back beneath the sheets, another chapter from Grandma Marchellis' unstable mind might bore him into slumber.

After that night, my life settled into a predictable routine, which I found bearable because of the somnolent visits from John Simons, my secret friend who banished the poignant loneliness from my life.

Unfortunately, grief and the dirty city air had weakened my health. At least that's what Dr. Mroviak said. He encouraged periodic trips back to Munsonville, where Mr. Lenke owned a fishing cottage, so I could breathe pure air and run free in the warm sunshine.

It sounded like a sensible plan, except that it didn't help. Whether I dwelled in Detroit or rested in Munsonville, my skin had attained a sickly pastiness, and my limbs moved only with languor. I was never well enough to attend school; a tender-hearted local teacher provided me with lessons in the evening and on weekends.

When I finally did realize John Simons was a vampire, I was almost fourteen. Nor did I discover this fact with my own mind. Dr. Gothart told me.

Because he kept his office in Munsonville, whenever the Lenkes and I vacationed there, he paid daily visits to me to assess my health. One evening at bedtime, he ordered Mrs. Lenke from the bedroom due to the delicate nature of the next exam.

To my surprise, the meek woman stood her ground, but Dr. Gothart assured her he would not compromise the bounds of decency, but he required privacy to produce an accurate result. He would need only several minutes.

My insides quaked as Mrs. Lenke closed the door. What would Dr. Gothart do to me that could not be accomplished with her in the room?

The answer was nothing.

Removing his stethoscope from his bag, Dr. Gothart listened to my heart and my lungs while I observed him as he conducted the exam. I liked the way he looked. His auburn hair was neatly combed and his gold spectacles made him appear wise and scholarly.

He sighed, removed the instrument from his ears, and regarded me with a grave expression.

"I forbid any further helping of John Simons unless I manage it,'" he said to me. "He will kill you if blood-letting continues in this haphazard fashion."

My jaw almost hit my blanket. How did Dr. Gothart know about the secret ritual I shared with Mr. John? But. Dr. Gothart seemed nonplussed by my reaction.

"It's my experience in treating vampires that a slow, steady acquiring of the host's blood will eventually cause a remission in the symptoms that are characteristic to the undead. But unless such treatment is supervised, both parties are risking permanent harm."

I struggled to speak as I digested his words. Mr. John was a vampire? A flurry of questions formed in my mind. How? When? Why?

Acting casual, as if I already knew this information, I asked him, "Why did you never tell me of this risk?"

Dr. Gothart rose and replaced the stethoscope into his bag. "Until very recently, I only suspected the source of John's therapy. I am not here to dissuade you, only to notify you of my next action should you disobey me."

"You'll tell the Lenkes?"

"You've weakened your heart with this foolishness. Again, you will now help John according to my orders."

I huddled in my bed, too stunned to argue with him, while he outlined Mr. John's method of treatment. Mr. John could only visit me once a week, and he must only consume five minutes worth of blood. If he transgressed Dr. Gothart's instructions, I was to immediately send word to Dr. Gothart. After the doctor left, I lay in bed, watching the shadows of dusk lengthen and fade into night as I pondered this new information. Mr. John was seeking more than comfort. Somehow, he had died, and he now sought a new life, a life that only could be made possible with my blood.

Up until this point, Mr. John controlled the timing and the amount, but, with Dr. Gothart's knowledge and advocacy, I decided the time had come for me to assert a few, additional demands of my own.

Because now I could."

Karla called at that moment. John-Peter closed a door and the diary to talk with her. He still was not yet ready to share Grandma Marchellis' information with her. He leaned over the bed for his water jug and took a long draught.

"I saw the light in your room," Karla said. "I can't believe you're not sleeping."

"Napped too long."

"Will you get up in time for Ed?"

"Hope so." John-Peter yawned loudly, also hoping his body, and Karla, would get the idea. "Give me a wakeup call?"

"Sure. What time?"

"Eleven-fifteen."

"Not a problem. Sweet dreams, John-Peter."

"Bonne nuit."

He groped for his leprechaun under the pillow, stretched his toes, and then lay wide-awake in the dark, listening to the rain fall and trying not to contemplate the inevitable double-bagging of the large Sunday newspapers. To soothe his overactive mind, John-Peter fixed his eyes on the closet door, imagining the princess had left the mirror and was now rushing toward a fragrant grove, the edges of which he glimpsed beyond her golden hair. With an apple, she beckoned him to follow, and, enthralled, he rose from the bed and danced the Fairy Reel with her while Ed Calkins fiddled.

Suddenly, Karla appeared. "Wake up, John-Peter," she said.

"No!" John-Peter guided the princess away. "Go away, Karla! I've changed my mind."

She sprang close to his ear. *"Wake up!"*

John-Peter bolted upright. The grove was gone; the music was gone, and, disheartening of all, the princess was gone. Only Karla's voice remained.

"Are you okay, John-Peter?"

He squinted at the luminous numbers on his clock. Eleven twenty-five. If he didn't want Uncle Ed shouting outside his window again, he'd better hurry.

"It's cool, thanks, Karla."

Although he probably would never say it aloud, much less admit it to himself, John-Peter felt profoundly grateful for the lone sanctuary in his life where he could freely express his true nature without any restraining boundaries.

And that was within his intimate friendship with Karla Dyer.

CHAPTER 8: THE LEGACY OF CORNELL DYER

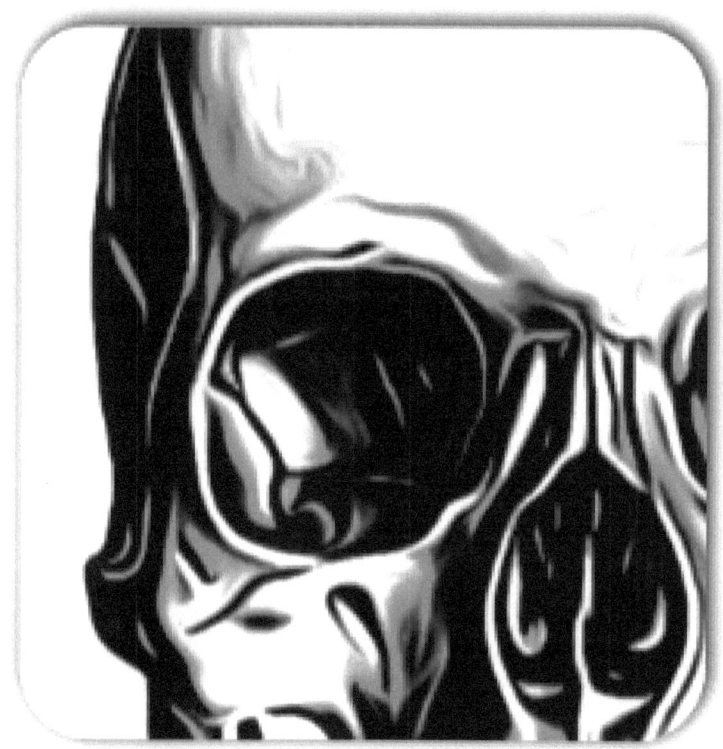

John-Peter could not remember when Karla taught him telepathy. She had always claimed their ability to communicate so uniquely was instantaneous, and he had no reason to doubt her, especially since Karla remembered everything that happened in her life since the beginning of her conception.

Still, Karla rarely dwelled upon that knowledge. She maintained that life in the womb was repetitive and mundane; furthermore, much of daily life was not worth recalling. Nevertheless, Karla's superior memory had one advantage, and, of this, John-Peter was most jealous. Karla could remember her father.

No one else could assert possession of such abilities without inviting ridicule and disbelief. But Karla was not like everyone else. Although not even her mother, Katie Dyer, had ever realized the full extent of Cornell Dyer's extrasensory abilities, a clue to their vastness resided inside his daughter.

John-Peter had never met another being with Karla's supernatural proficiency; even Kellen paled when compared to her. To cultivate Karla's inherent paranormal talents, Katie augmented Karla's academic studies with a unique home program. Katie herself designed the curriculum from Cornell's records, research, and documentations. Katie's stance was that Karla had a single reason for living: to reestablish and advance Cornell Dyer's psychic balm for mankind's woes.

Because he believed his destiny was to save the world from nefarious spiritual forces, Professor Dyer dwelled in a large motor home, always ready to travel to the next adventure. To alert the living, the dead, and the demonic of his approach, Cornell had covered the white exterior of his motor home with amateurish paintings of astrologic symbols, hexagrams, and magic wands. A sign painted across one side read: *The Thaumaturgical World of Professor Cornell Dyer: Amulets, Fortune-Telling (with and without cards), Ghost-Hunting, Horoscopes, Numerology, Palm-Reading, Potions, Séances, Spells, and Vampire-Slaying.* While staying in Munsonville, the professor had parked his motor home on the property of Karla's grandparents. After his death, Katie and Karla remained at the site of Cornell's final home, the most fitting place, Katie believed, to prepare his daughter to resume his benevolent mission.

"It's like going to school twice," Karla often complained while walking home. "But Mom is against homeschooling me exclusively. She thinks I should mix with regular people."

"To solicit future clients?"

"To understand them, dodo."

"Same thing."

Most of the time, Karla unquestioningly accepted her lot. Her metaphysical skills were second nature to her; their maturation was inevitable. No one but John-Peter ever knew the occasional distress those abilities caused her and, even then, they were both in junior high before he ever actually witnessed it.

He had strolled through the motor home's side door as he did nearly every afternoon and found Karla slumped at the dinette table, head buried under her arms, sobbing inconsolably. The boy had scooted past her to the refrigerator for Katie's soy milk before dropping into a chair, still gulping, and wondering what had happened. Karla was not a crybaby. "You're rather gloomy today." John-Peter eyed her as he downed the carton.

Karla raised a tear-stained face. "Oh, John-Peter, I can't stand it. Amy invited me to go to the movies with her on Saturday, and I can't go because of this horrid crystal ball lesson."

"Who cares about a sappy movie?"

She narrowed her eyes. "You're not getting it. Why can't I be normal for just one afternoon?"

"Normal like Amy? Come on, Karla, she's a goon."

"It's so tiresome to be special."

"You should embrace your greatness."

"You don't have to sit through math class without sharing the memory of Mr. Andrews' morning quickies."

"A perspective infinitely more thrilling, to be sure, than his wife's."

"I knew you wouldn't understand!"

John-Peter catapulted the carton at Karla where it bounced into her lap. She slammed it on the table and glared at him.

"You have a gift," he gently said, ignoring her outburst.

"Sometimes, I don't want it."

"That's the trouble with your gifts. They have no exchange receipt."

"I said, 'Sometimes.'"

"Well, clear your mind. You won't master the lesson when you cloud your mental faculties with a trivial emotion."

"Spoken like a real boy. Emotion, for your information, weirdo, is not trivial."

"I never said it was. But self-pity won't get you to the movies."

John-Peter reached under the black and aquamarine dinette table where Karla had flung Cornell's *Concise Crystallomancy* and set the large binder near Karla. She hesitated, heaved a large sigh, and then obediently located the lesson. She then pushed the textbook back to John-Peter, and slid the quartz ball closer to her. He read the instructions for predicting future job prospects while Karla sulkily recorded her visions.

"Got a secret," John-Peter said, turning a page, closing that door, and peering sideways at Karla from under his lashes to gauge her reaction.

"Go on," Karla said, continuing to write and not looking up.

"Kellen's opening a San Francisco branch next month. No one knows yet, not even my mother."

Karla scrawled the information in her notebook. On Saturday morning, when Katie called Kellen to verify the information, a jubilant Karla transmitted the victory to John-Peter. She was allowed to go to the movies.

Had they not combined their resources to prevent it, Karla's extra-curricular obligations might have left her very little free time to spend with John-Peter, something neither one would tolerate. In study hall, they halved their homework time by mentally swapping answers so that, after school, John-Peter could hang about the Dyers' motor home where Karla practiced her metaphysical lessons on him. Their ingenuity was not without risk.

Years ago, Melissa and Katie agreed that neither John-Peter nor Karla could "play" at each other's house unless a parent was on the premises, a rule based on history so ancient that John-Peter and Karla found it laughably absurd since the offending incident had occurred when they were both under age three. The trio—Katie, Karla, and John-Peter, had been sitting on the couch watching some banal, pseudo-educational program about the wonders of the human body when Katie left the room to answer the telephone.

During the half hour she chatted to one of Cornell's former clients, John-Peter and Karla embarked upon their variation of "doctor," which Katie rudely interrupted with shrieks of protest when she returned to the living room.

"Is she ill?" John-Peter mentally asked as he rolled off the couch. He had never seen anyone's mouth actually froth.

Karla sat up and vehemently shook her black curls. "Mad," she communicated back. "Real mad."

"Don't you ever, ever do that again!"

Katie yanked Karla's ruffled shirt over the little girl's head. John-Peter said nothing as he dressed. He could not understand why Katie made such a fuss. Her lips pursed into a tight, thin line as she tied Karla's shoes.

John-Peter perched on the arm of the couch and swung his legs. "I tied my own shoes," he said, hoping to appease her.

Katie glared at John-Peter. "Next time you watch television here, keep your clothes on."

"So much for, 'Learn, explore, discover.'"

When Melissa later arrived to take John-Peter home, Katie related the incident to her in hushed, strained tones while John-Peter and Karla gazed at each other in astonishment over the block castle they were building on the carpet.

Karla wordlessly spoke, "Next time, we'll be more careful."

Which meant that, although the pair never stopped examining one another's body cavities and other interesting areas, "doctor" ceased to rank as their number one amusement. Much more intriguing to John-Peter was his silent investigation into Karla's mind, a virtually unlimited and untapped realm of possibilities and surprises, infinitely more fascinating.

Sometimes John-Peter felt jealous of Karla's advanced telepathic prowess. Unless she consciously blocked the continual flow of information, she read everyone's minds with ease, whether she desired it or not. John-Peter's telepathy was limited only to Karla and what she chose to broadcast to him. However, experimentation had fine-tuned their skills until they had developed a unique method of relaying information over distances, as well as the ability to shut off, either partially or completely, each other's near perpetual, cerebral presence, simply by closing one or more mental doors.

Because mothers would be mothers, John-Peter and Karla did not waste time with futile explanations about their activities. It was, as Karla had said, simpler to be discreet.

Getting past Katie was easy because she worked at Klever Cuts in Jenson until seven o'clock each weekday night and most Saturdays. As long as Karla produced physical evidence of compliance to her father's program—research papers begun, experiments logged, and predictions made, Katie never suspected John-Peter's invasion of her home.

Melissa posed the greater challenge, the downside to having a mother who kept a parallel school schedule. Fortunately for John-Peter, numerous distractions—Carol Simotes' care and homework to correct—usually kept Melissa busy until dinner time.

Just in case, he never left home without his decoy in place. After setting the timer on the portable compact disc player to render three hour's worth of classical piano music, John-Peter, shoes in hand, tiptoed back to his bedroom. Rarely did Melissa disturb him while he practiced, and he silently thanked his father for setting this important precedent.

After checking first on the status of the princess, who almost always was absent, John-Peter opened the bedroom window, slid down the oak tree, and bounded away to Karla's house for an afternoon of adventure. They compared and interpreted their dreams, studied the etymology and uses of herbs, and fine-tuned their ESP skills. When Karla learned the basics of astrology, John-Peter's natal chart was the first one she calculated.

"Your moon is in Leo, and that makes you very charming," Karla said.

John-Peter grinned as he twirled Karla's compass between his fingers. "Surprised?"

"Your sun is Capricorn," Karla continued, ignoring him, "So you are devoted to the ones you love, but it is also near Mercury, which means you get off sharing your opinions with everyone."

"Why be selfish and hoard premium knowledge?"

Karla grinned back at him. "Your sun also opposes Jupiter."

"Meaning what?"

"Meaning you nurture gigantic dreams and goals and plan to leave your mark on the world."

"Like playing to a full house at Carnegie Hall?"

Karla grimaced as she documented her results. "Doesn't sound like much of an aspiration to me."

"That's because you're not a great artist."

"I wish I was a great alchemist. But Mom won't let me play with potions until next year."

"Are supplies easy to obtain?"

"Sure, if I had Internet."

"Mademoiselle, prepare a shopping list."

While completing her numerology assignments, Karla added the digits of John-Peter's name and discovered that four represented both his destiny number and his dream number.

"Duh," Karla said. "That means you have an organized mission you intend to fulfill."

"Oh, what a surprise."

"But too many fours make you rigid and pessimistic."

"Only when fools interfere with my plans."

Nevertheless, it was John-Peter's palm reading that confused Karla.

"The lines on your left and right hands are identical," she said, holding John-Peter's hands in her smaller, softer ones as she compared one to the other. "That's downright impossible. Daddy says your left hand tells what is inbred and the right hand is the one that records how you live. The only thing I can figure out is that you're already living your destiny."

"Stuff and nonsense. I was created for glorious purposes."

"Such as?"

John-Peter hesitated. He had always closed a door whenever he indulged his "knight in shining armor" fantasies, nor had he shared with Karla the vision of the princess who dwelled inside his closet, the princess he planned to one day rescue from her prison. And he kept that door closed now.

Karla shot him a triumphant look because John-Peter couldn't answer her. He said nothing as she dropped his hands to consult Cornell's binder on hand divination.

"I'm stumped, John-Peter."

He found his voice at last. "Better discern it before your mother comes home."

Karla sighed and picked up John-Peter's left hand. "Well, first of all, you have an earth hand."

"A what?"

"An earth hand. See? You have a square-shaped palm and only a few deep lines. That means you are serious, responsible, and stubborn. Your short fingers tell me you view reality only from your own perspective."

"The correct perspective."

Karla ignored him. "Your life line is very small with no breaks. This means you are rarely sick…"

"I've never been sick," John-Peter interrupted.

"…but you will die young."

"Better a short, fulfilled life than a long, mediocre existence."

"Your head line is longer and clearer than your heart line, so you're the kind of person who makes rational decisions. Being right is more important to you than being in love."

John-Peter contemplated the princess, and his heart skipped a beat. Karla looked up and frowned.

"And your mounts are way over-developed," she said, releasing his hand to jot her findings, "which means you over-react in just about every area of your life. Pretty accurate, huh?"

"I yield to your superior knowledge and wisdom…hey! Those aren't my results you're writing."

"Of course not. This is stuff I made up. You're not supposed to be here, remember?"

Most interesting to John-Peter was Karla's systematic decoding of his inner self with a deck of cards.

"This is you," Karla said. She laid the card in the center of the table. John-Peter read the caption: King of Wands.

"How so?"

"That's the card for any male under forty with red hair."

John-Peter gazed at the flowering stick the man held. "Is that oak?"

"How should I know?"

"You're the diviner."

Karla laid the High Priestess card over the King of Wands. "This is what covers you," she said. "There is a secret in your past that will affect your future."

She placed across the High Priestess a card depicting two dogs barking at a moon. "Hidden enemies and deception cross you."

A seated man holding an upright sword and a pair of scales went above John-Peter's identity card.

"This is 'Justice,'" Karla said. "This is what crowns you."

Below the center cards, Karla set an upside down Ace of Wands. John-Peter reversed it, but Karla returned it to its original position.

"The card has two meanings," she said, "depending how it lands. This one shows something that happened in your past."

"Which is?"

"A fall or disgrace of some kind."

Her answer puzzled him. Such an event had never occurred in his life as far as he knew, and Karla's precise memory confirmed it.

"Unless it happened before I was born," Karla said thoughtfully.

"You'd know it anyway."

"Maybe I'm not reading it right. I'm just a beginner."

"Lay another card."

Karla set the Four of Wands on the right hand side of the center card. "This is the influence moving away from you."

John-Peter contemplated the dancing people between the four, flowering wands. A house stood in the card's background. "And that is?"

"Peace and harmony."

"Figures."

"Well, the card on the left represents what's moving into your life."

It was a knight riding on a horse. In one hand, he upheld a wand.

"A journey?"

Karla beamed. "Good job!"

Maybe that Paris vacation *would* become reality. "What's with all the wands?"

"I don't know, John-Peter. You cut the deck."

She laid a card on King of Wands' right, a horseman wearing a laurel crown. "This is the Six of Wands. This shows you waiting and hoping for something."

An image of the princess flashed through John-Peter's mind, and he squelched it before Karla saw it. She set the eighth card above the seventh one: a hanged man. John-Peter looked at Karla.

"Good news, I hope?"

"It says your life is currently hanging in suspension."

"The lot of a frustrated musician."

"Cheer up, John-Peter. I think you'll like this one better."

Karla laid another card. This one showed a naked man and woman, The Lovers, which made Karla laugh out loud. "Okay, John-Peter, who's the girl of your dreams?"

Had she read his mind after all? "Lauren Cooper, who else," the boy carefully said as he closed all doors.

"You're so funny I forgot to laugh. Now this last card will tell us what your future holds."

Karla started to turn the final card and then abruptly set it back on top of the deck.

"Game over," she said and rapidly began picking up cards.

"Hey, what about the last one?"

She shook her head. "I need more practice. I'm not doing it right."

"So what? We've never expected perfection. Come on, Karla, let me see the card."

John-Peter extended his hand. Karla wavered and then placed the card, face down, on the boy's palm. Wondering, John-Peter turned over the card. It was a skeleton riding a horse. The card was labeled, *Death.*

Karla Dyer subsequently abandoned her practice of the Tarot, and John-Peter stopped pestering her to renew it. They had other ways to occupy their time, and Katie had other lessons for her daughter to learn. Instead, they concentrated on séances, but all they ever conjured up were common souls, voices of the past who had lived ordinary lives and had nothing prophetic to share. Moreover, many of these specters arrived with their own requests. A nineteenth century homesteader wanted the thief that stole his life savings from behind the barn wall. A frontier schoolteacher demanded to know who started the house fire that killed her. A stillborn girl wailed for her mother.

"Maybe we did something wrong," Karla said, flipping through Cornell's notes.

"Perhaps we should call upon a specific shade."

"Like who?"

"Why not one of our fathers? Wouldn't you want to know exactly what happened that night at Kellen's funeral home?"

Karla sighed and closed the notebook. "Mom would kill me if she found out. She said Daddy strictly forbade it. He must have known she'd want him to come back."

"She wouldn't have to know."

"Do you think Daddy wouldn't tell her if we resurrected him?"

"Good point. So now what?"

She chewed her pencil eraser and thought for several minutes. "We could explore the parsonage."

"You mean breaking and entering?"

"Only entering. Get on the couch."

With a knowing wink, John-Peter grabbed his gallon of water and sauntered to the living room where he blissfully stretched out on the faded psychedelic patterns of green, blue, and purple that held many blissful memories of other entertainments. Karla sat on the edge next to him and loosely curled her fingers around his hand.

"Okay, John-Peter, close your eyes."

"When do we take off our clothes?"

"We don't, unless you want to walk through the parsonage naked."

"Point taken. Why waste exquisite beauty on the deceased?"

With her free hand, Karla jabbed John-Peter's ribs to get his attention. "Now imagine your spirit is growing lighter than your body."

"Why?"

"John-Peter, just do it!"

"All right, all right."

"Now picture it sliding out your body, just like a snake sheds its skin."

"Do I get it back?"

"Your spirit's not totally leaving. See? It's still attached to your body with a silver cord."

"Long enough to reach the parsonage?"

"As long as you make it."

As John-Peter visualized himself walking down Blue Gill Road, he could feel his spool of silver unravel with each floating step. For several minutes, John-Peter only sensed the steady rise and fall of Karla's chest as she breathed.

He cracked open one eye. "How am I doing?"

"Shut your eyes, or you'll break the spell. Are you there yet?"

"Approaching the bottom of the hill."

"Let me know when you get inside."

"I don't have a key."

Karla giggled. "Just walk through the door. You're disembodied, remember?"

"Is this safe?"

"I hope so."

Neither one mentioned John-Peter's *Death* card.

John-Peter slid through the front door. "Should I look on the first floor or go upstairs?"

"Go upstairs. That's where most of the sightings have been."

"I can't see."

Karla heaved an impatient sigh. "Then pretend you have a flashlight."

A huge flood light popped into his right hand. John-Peter swung the powerful beam around the main floor as he ascended the stairs. "Won't the light scare away the ghost?"

"It's not a real light."

John-Peter illuminated each bedroom as he peered inside it. "Karla, unless you count a bunch of old furniture covered in dusty sheets as ghosts…."

The crunch of gravel interrupted his statement. The silver cord attached to his waist dragged him down the stairs. Before he reached the parsonage's front door, John-Peter caught a jolting glimpse of the parlor. He knew that room, the very one where he had dreamed of John Simons offering him a glass of blood.

John-Peter bounced out of the house and back up Blue Gill Road. He felt a lurch and thump as his soul reentered his body.

Karla pried his cold, shaking fingers off her hand. "Sorry about rewinding it so fast, but Mom's home early! Grab your shoes, and get out of here!"

John-Peter leaped to his feet and ran to the passenger door of the motor home as the side one opened. He heard Karla loudly say, "Mom, how come Mr. Klever...." before he quietly shut the door behind him.

Only once did Karla allow John-Peter a glimpse of Cornell Dyer's favorite crystal ball. By peering between the cracks of one of Cornell Dyer's locked cabinets, John-Peter glimpsed its pale, green glow.

"Crackerjack!" he whispered in awe.

"I know. It's even got a solid gold stand. I can't wait to use it. But Mom says I first have to be more accurate with my crystal ball readings."

"What if the batteries run down by then?"

"Oh, you're funny."

On school holidays, when Ed Calkins returned John-Peter home well before daylight and well before any parents had stirred, he and Karla would mount bikes and head for Simons Woods to study vibrations.

Karla had learned from her mother that Cornell was stationed in Munsonville to study spiritual energy, which he deduced pulsated clearly, strongly, and regularly near the former Simons Estate, especially the former site of Simons Mansion. Yet, as many times as they had roamed the property, neither John-Peter nor Karla had ever sensed any supernatural activity there. Because the summer had been an unusually busy one for John-Peter—a combination of his grandparents' move, numerous employee summer vacations at the funeral home, and multiple down newspaper routes—the pair had postponed further examination of the place.

So when Karla called John-Peter during Friday's geometry class and asked if he would bike with her to Simons

Woods on Labor Day, his affirmative response was swift and enthusiastic.

"Let's leave extra early. I'm not helping Uncle Ed that day."

"You're not? Why?"

"Early family picnic with the grandparents. Mother doesn't want me cranky and tired."

"Two o'clock?"

"Works for me."

That night, as John-Peter drifted into unconsciousness and high up into an oak tree, where he stretched across a sturdy branch, curled his toes around a leafy limb, turned his face to the sky, and sent the clear notes of a tin whistle straight to the moon, Karla's voice broke into his hypnagogic imagery: "Hey, John-Peter, do you need a wake-up call?"

The boy recalled the last time, when Karla had entered his princess dream. He couldn't risk it happening again.

"No." He dropped the door and sank into sleep.

The pillow muffled his alarm clock so well, it had rung a full five minutes before John-Peter heard it. His hand fumbled under the pillow to silence its annoying beeping and then groped along the headboard for the leprechaun.

After first gulping down a jug of water and loading a backpack with a second gallon and sack full of peanut butter sandwiches and apples, the boy pedaled as fast as he could to the Dyer's motor home, but not fast enough. Karla sat on her bike waiting for him, a reproachful look on her face.

"I knew you'd oversleep," she said in a haughty tone.

John-Peter yawned to show her comments merely bored him. "Coming?"

Karla waited until she cleared her driveway before clicking on her headlight. In silence, except for the crunching of packed gravel under their wide tires, they coasted down to Main Street and then turned left toward Simons Woods, their bicycle lights providing the sole illumination. Dawn was still several hours away. Neither one spoke until they had pedaled far past the estate and deep within the woods.

"I really hope we learn something today," Karla said, her voice cutting through the eerie stillness.

"Me, too. Mother claims Father passed his talent to me, but I disagree. I think, perhaps, there is something in those tremors your father sensed. Munsonville does seem to attract genius, first John Simons and now me."

"You're delusional. John Simons was already great when he came here."

"My point. He didn't have to come here. He could have gone somewhere else."

"But he did go somewhere else. Lots of somewhere elses. Remember? He toured all over the world."

"But he chose Munsonville as his home. Doesn't that say something to you?"

"John-Peter, how can you be so dense? John Simons chose to stay here because he was in love."

"But what was the initial attraction? Consider the possibility a supernatural energy might have lured him here."

"As it did my father?"

"Perhaps Cornell Dyer was not the first to perceive it. I wonder if there is a connection between his research and my father's mutilation."

"I wish I could figure out why Daddy staked him. I can't see Professor Simotes being a vampire. Everyone always talks about him with tons of respect."

"Maybe he only pretended to be a vampire."

"Like Kellen?"

John-Peter looked over at Karla and grinned. "Kellen's reformed, remember?"

She sighed in mock exasperation. "It seems everyone these days wants to be a mythical creature."

"Sickening isn't? Bet it drives the real legends underground."

"The opposite seems to be true for Kellen. He's attracting them left and right."

"Ah, yes, nothing like a wanton, ex-pranic vampire."

"There's nothing 'ex' about him. Instead of feasting on people's blood or energy, Kellen drains their wallets."

"'The Pecuniary Vampire: A Case Study,' by the illustrious Karla Dyer."

"I'd love to know what Daddy had to say about vampire subtypes. But I'm not allowed to read any of his parasite research until I'm eighteen."

"Let me know when you do. I want your take on this dream I'm having. It appears to contain vampire elements."

"Shoot."

With painstaking detail, John-Peter verbally reproduced his John Simons dream, including the troubling detail of the parsonage parlor, which he swore he never saw until last week when he metaphysically entered it with Karla's guidance.

"Cross my heart." John-Peter started to add "and hope to die," but remembered the Tarot cards and changed his mind. So he spat three times on the ground to prove his sincerity and nearly collided into Karla's bike.

Karla dismissed his concerns. "Lots of Munsonville houses look alike. It's probably a coincidence, that's all."

"But why offer me his blood? Everyone knows I can't stand meat."

Karla considered that statement. "What if you're not dreaming about John Simons? Didn't you say that your father supposedly looked like him? Maybe you're taking the vampire story about your father and dressing it up in John Simons' clothes?"

"So the dream is merely a conglomeration of unrelated impressions?" John-Peter did not mention Grandma Marchellis' stance that John Simons was a vampire, but Karla's theory made sense.

The ground trembled; the boy's bike lurched; and he braked to a squealing stop.

"Karla!"

"What is it?"

"The ground moved!"

Karla skidded to a stop, jumped off her bike, and let it fall. "What did the motion feel like?"

John-Peter shoved his hands inside his pockets, his left closing around the leprechaun, and thought. Karla paced several yards in both directions on the grassy patch beside the path. She paused every few paces to stomp her feet and listen.

"Did it feel like a shake?" Karla said, head cocked, and face tense with concentration.

"No, it rumbled."

Karla glanced up at him. "Then the energy here is not good."

"Evil?"

"I don't know."

"Sad? Angry?"

"I told you. I don't know. Anyway, it's getting light. Let's go to the park before we have to go back."

Thoughts of the mysterious vibration preoccupied them both until they reached the drive leading to the old estate. As they turned onto the road, Karla said, "Mind if I take a peek at that dream?"

"No. Why?"

"I want to take some notes about the room. The next time we go back into the parsonage, we can compare them."

Her suggestion excited him. "So we are going back?"

"Of course. We didn't even come close to finding that ghost. Race you to the swings!"

With a burst of speed, Karla reached the top of the hill and dashed toward the playground and picnic area, the former site of Simons Mansion. John-Peter slipped off his shoes and flew after her. As the swing set came into view, he saw Karla had flopped tummy first over a swing and was dragging her fingers through the dirt as she swayed back and forth. John-Peter selected a thin sturdy piece of grass and straddled the swing next to Karla's, winding the chain round and round as he stretched out the blade.

"John-Peter, I've been thinking. Maybe we should call up someone in particular."

He blew lightly into the grass, and it responded with a satisfying high-pitched whine. "The subject?"

"John Simons."

"Elucidate, mademoiselle." He tossed the blade and reached inside his backpack for a sandwich.

"Maybe he can give us information about the negative vibrations in his woods. Maybe something bad happened here.

Maybe that is why he is offering you blood. Maybe he wants you to know."

"That's a lot of maybes."

Karla dragged the tips of her shoes through the dust. The swing stopped. "So you don't want to do it?"

"Au contraire."

She abruptly stood up, sat on the swing, and vigorously pumped her legs. The swing soared in the air. "I'm coming back here later to get some mandrake root. Then maybe we'll be successful."

"Whoa, missy!"

John-Peter unwound his swing and quickly reached her height. "You don't need mandrake root for a séance."

Karla looked uncomfortable. "I know."

"You're not trying to bring him fully back, are you?"

"Got a problem with that?"

"Just a tiny one. Mandrake root does not grow in Munsonville."

"No, but bryony does. The two are interchangeable."

"They are not."

"Since when do you know more than Harriet Sturnam's classic, 'The Primer of Magical Herbs?'"

"Mandrake will scream when you rip it from the ground. Bryony produces no sound."

"I never said they were identical. I said they were interchangeable. You know, for spells and things."

"I thought you didn't know anything about casting spells."

"I said I didn't know anything about mixing potions. There's a difference."

"I think your plan will fail."

"And I think you're just jealous because you don't know as much as I do."

"Well, be careful. Bryony is poisonous, and I can't accompany you when you gather it."

"Thanks for the vote of confidence."

Sulky and sullen, Karla remained silent during the trip back. She didn't talk to John-Peter again that day until he settled into bed for the night.

"I got the bryony, Mr. Smarty Pants. Tomorrow, we bring John Simons back from the dead."

"Okay."

"How was your family picnic?"

"Okay."

"You're not very talkative."

"Keep your door up. I'll wake you if I have that dream again."

The next day's dark experiment failed, which left Karla shaking her head and re-reading Cornell's instructions on raising the dead.

"I just don't get it. We did everything right."

"I told you bryony is no substitute for mandrake root."

"Well, you don't have to get all superior about it. Lots of people use bryony."

John-Peter tugged her sleeve as he stood. "Let's go."

"Where?" she said, slamming shut the book and rising from her chair, wondering, but ready.

"Library. I'll prove it to you."

He moved amongst the green painted shelves, and these stood as a strange contrast to the library's dark wood floors, gleaming paneling, and cinnamon-scented air. The library boasted only ten of these shelves, except for three waist-high bookcases near the circulation desk that held children's stories, an eternal source of frustration for John-Peter as he had read all of those volumes before his fourth birthday. Within twenty minutes, John-Peter and Karla sat at a back table, huddled over several volumes of open books.

"I told you so," Karla whispered, pointing to an entry about white bryony.

It said how European practitioners of magical arts often substituted the less expensive and more widely available bryony for the rarer mandrake, especially in the formation of love potions. Karla wore an annoying, victorious expression. Well, that would soon vanish.

"You didn't read far enough," John-Peter said, directing her attention to the next paragraph. Karla pursed her lips as her eyes skimmed the text.

"I don't get it," she said, shaking her head. "It said black bryony isn't true bryony. The stuff that grows on Simons Estate is pink bryony, not black."

"Pink bryony is not authentic bryony. It's something John Simons cross-bred especially for his estate."

Karla looked suspicious. "How do you know that?"

"My mother told me. She wrote a paper on it once."

"You could've told me that yesterday."

"You wouldn't listen."

Karla closed and stacked the books. "I'm taking these home to write a research paper on real and fake bryony and their different properties. Betcha that's something my mother never even considered for a topic. Maybe it'll buy me some temporary freedom and privileges."

"Go slowly, or you'll get your own motor home for Christmas."

Mrs. Clements a gray-haired woman in a brown-striped skirt, beige blouse, and glasses hanging on a chain, quickly checked out Karla's books.

"Here you go, Karla," Mrs. Clements said, sliding the reference books across the counter.

"Thanks!" She turned to John-Peter. "Okay Professor Simotes the Second, let's go. I want to start this report before Mom comes home."

They turned toward the door when they heard a woman's voice say, "Excuse me, young man."

John-Peter and Karla stopped. An older woman, each gleaming white hair resting perfectly in place, gold discs clipped to her ears, and green-tweed suit hugging her slim waist, laid three romance paperback books on the counter and pleasantly smiled.

Mrs. Clements began stamping the due date cards.

"I'm sorry for eavesdropping," the elegant woman said, "but did the girl just say your last name is 'Simotes?'"

"Yes, ma'am."

"I used to know a Simotes family from a long time ago, when I lived in Bradford Heights."

John-Peter exchanged glances with Karla. "Where, ma'am?"

"It's in Ohio, dear. Their names were Marvin and Carol. Perhaps you're related to them?"

"They're my grandparents."

The woman's face softened. "Oh, sweetie, never mind. We must be talking about different people. The Marvin and Carol Simotes I knew couldn't have any children."

CHAPTER 9: NATURE OF THE BEAST

During study hall Wednesday afternoon, Karla called John-Peter and asked if he felt like exploring the parsonage after school.

"Can't," John-Peter leafed through his biology textbook to the chapter review questions. "Stoking fires today for the Prince of Darkness."

"Oh."

He sensed her disappointment but did not further elaborate.

"Can you go tomorrow?"

He flipped back to find the definition for "exocytosis."

"John-Peter?"

He jotted the answer into his notebook. "Consult your crystal ball, and get back with me."

Bang! Karla had slammed a door. Good. She was gone.

He could waste no more time with her. Arthur would be waiting outside when the final bell rang. With Grace leaving early for a dentist appointment, he anticipated a busy evening, one that did not include homework. Later, as he flew through a literature test, John-Peter hoped his mother might dismiss him early. Karla huddled over her work. John-Peter didn't care. Who needed help with literature?

His mother dashed his hopes for early release. After collecting their papers, she spent the remaining five minutes launching into a discourse *Tale of Two Cities*, the novel they would read that semester. When he finally reached his locker, Karla, wearing a hurt look, had to lean against the side of it anyway.

"John-Peter, what's your problem?"

"Move. In a hurry."

As he closed the locker door with a clang, John-Peter felt Karla's fingers in his back pocket. He sped down the hall toward the front door. A black HHG stretch limousine sat waiting in front of the ancient red-brick school building, blocking Main Street. Arthur stepped from the car to open the door. As he slid into the vehicle, John-Peter looked around him, hoping Curtis Chandler had caught a glimpse and pissed his pants.

"Refrigerator's full," Arthur said.

"Good man!"

Arthur shut the door behind him.

John-Peter dug a compact disc from his book bag. A touch of a button and Chopin's "Fantasie Impromptu" filled the air, putting him in better humor than he'd felt all day. Humming under his breath, he opened the refrigerator and removed the chilled antipasto salad Kellen had ordered from Brummings, complete with chef-created garlic and caper-laced marinade for the tofu, the best part of spending an evening at the funeral home. The vegan deli also sold exotic juices, which Kellen stocked in his cars for John-Peter and clients alike. He moved a few bottles aside and found papaya, hidden in the back behind the iced chamomile tea. Now he could relax and study for tomorrow's Old World History quiz. It was a two hour ride to Thornton.

But after he swallowed his vitamins and as he shoved the first forkful of artichokes and red peppers into his mouth, yesterday's strange conversation at the library flooded his mind and unsettled him. Why did that strange woman say his grandparents had no children? John-Peter's first impulse when he raced through the back door was to approach his mother and simply ask her. But the stench that hit him when he passed through the kitchen told him Grandma Simotes had experienced another rather unpleasant bowel accident. He could hear his mother and Grandma Barnes talking to each other as they bathed her.

He tossed the salad container into the garbage, drank up all the bottles of papaya juice, and opened his textbook. John-Peter had never flunked a quiz in his life, and he did not intend to begin now. Sumerian civilization so absorbed the boy that he never checked the clock until Arthur pulled into the employee parking lot. Grace had to leave soon, and the drive-through line was full. He'd have to change quickly.

The second the limousine stopped at the building's rear entrance, John-Peter leaped from the back seat, not waiting for royal treatment. Kellen would be mad, but he didn't care. Kellen would survive.

He glanced at the first room on his left. Excellent. It was empty. John-Peter quickly peeled off his clothes, tossed them onto the floor, and then, with equal speed, slid into his black HHG uniform, remembering to tie back his hair before placing the cap on his head. He hoped Kellen noticed how extra neat he looked today. Might be worth a bonus. Before stuffing his school clothes into his book bag, John-Peter removed the leprechaun and pushed it to the bottom of his uniform pocket. On the way out the door, John-Peter lightly kicked the book bag in the direction of the sunken marble bathtub.

The boy hastened down the hall to the opposite end of the funeral home, passing the row of conference rooms where Kellen and an elderly couple sat conversing in one of them, the table full of scattered brochures.

"Now, if you should rise as one of the undead," Kellen said, "would you like to try the predator's lifestyle, or do you prefer one of our vampire slaying packages?"

John-Peter flew past the main display cases and bounded into the first station, causing Grace, a short, stocky woman with a deeply lined, but cheerful, face, to look away from the window and place an index finger to her lips. He tiptoed to the log book to check the day's orders. Grace returned her attention to her customer.

"Good afternoon, and welcome to Happy Hunting Grounds," Grace said. "May I take your order?"

A man's deep voice boomed over the loudspeaker. "I'd like a number four."

"What color, sir?"

"Do you have lime green?"

"We do, but it's a special order. What day would like to schedule the wake?"

"Next Thursday, if possible."

Grace scanned the chart by the window. "We can't order lime green that soon. You'll either have to postpone the funeral or choose another color."

"Man! Lime green was my aunt's favorite."

"We do have a florescent green that's reasonably close to the lime."

"Wait a minute. Let me ask my wife."

John-Peter heard the droning of background voices as he opened the gallon of water Kellen kept in the station especially for him.

The man said, "Okay, the fluorescent will do. Does that coffin come in an extra-large? My aunt weighed over 400 pounds."

"Yes, for an additional $600."

"That's fine. Oh, hey, I almost forgot. I have a coupon for a tombstone."

"Redeem it with the cashier, please. Your total is $12,552.76. Pull up to the second window."

Grace closed the glass. "You're dad told me to remind you about the bereavement sale."

"I just read the flyer."

She removed her cap and fluffed her matted gray hair. "I sure do appreciate you helping out tonight, John-Peter. This tooth is killing me. It kept me up all night." One of the blood-red "H's" in "HHG" had peeled away from her shirt, but Grace hadn't noticed.

"Grace, you shameless transgressor of child labor laws."

Grace smiled weakly as she grabbed her purse. "Don't grow old John-Peter. Everything falls apart."

A car horn sounded through the speaker. John-Peter, every letter properly in place on *his* cap and shirt pocket, hurried to Grace's spot and slid the glass aside. "Good afternoon, and welcome to Happy Hunting Grounds. May I take your order?"

"Yeah, I want a number three in sky blue."

John-Peter typed the order into the computer. "Shall I tell you about today's bereavement sale?"

"Sure. What do I get?"

"Three séances, two card readings, and a T-shirt."

"How much?"

"$550."

Static crackled through the speaker as the man considered.

"Nah, I'm pretty sure we don't want to see her again."

"Okay. Your total is..."

"But I'd like a T-shirt."

"Full price without the bereavement package."

"That's fine. What's my total?"

"Ten thousand even. Pull up to window two. Let the cashier know your shirt size."

Crackling and more static as the next customer approached the menu.

"Good afternoon, and welcome to Happy Hunting Grounds. May I take your order?"

"I'm still looking," the woman's high-pitched voice answered.

A few seconds passed.

"Oh dear, I can't make up my mind. I know my brother would like the steel guitar option—he really loved last year's vacation in Hawaii—but he was so religious, I'm afraid he might also think it was irreverent."

"Would you like to make a personal appointment with Mr. Wechsler? He could accurately assess what makes your brother happy."

"Oh, that's right! Mr. Wechsler was once dead, wasn't he? Maybe I *should* talk to someone who can ask my brother. I'd sure hate to be wrong."

"Ellen can make that appointment for you. Pull up to window three."

A rusted pick-up truck took the place of the woman's compact car.

"Good afternoon, and welcome to Happy Hunting Grounds. May I take your order?"

"I'd like a number one in mahogany, please."

"What color lining?"

"I like the red checks."

"I see we have that in stock. Standard size box?"

"Yes. I also have this brochure that says I can protect my wife's wishes with an HHG insurance policy. Is there an extra charge for this?"

"No, sir. That insurance policy is complimentary to all of Mr. Wechsler's customers."

"What about poltergeists?"

"Happy Hunting Grounds offers a full range of options. When you pay for your order, you will receive an information packet. Just indicate your preferences and mail it back to us. No postage is necessary."

"Cool!"

"Will there be anything else?"

"When do I decide about the refreshment room?"

"When you book the actual funeral. Just tell the cashier you'd like a menu. That will be $15,437.36. Pull up to the second window."

"Shit! I forgot my credit card."

"No problem. We accept cash."

For the next two hours, John-Peter negotiated the steady stream of cars passing through the Happy Hunting Grounds parking lot. At seven o'clock, he shut and locked the glass and then rose and stretched hard. He wondered what time Kellen would be ready to leave.

John-Peter walked out of the cubicle, past the main entrance, and down the hall to the offices. The entire area was dark. He turned on his heel and retraced his steps past the drive-through area and toward the meeting rooms. A glimmer of light shone from the last room. Of course. Wednesday night was Kellen's support group. He paused, hoping his stepfather would notice him through the slightly ajar door.

"…welcome you here tonight," Kellen said. "We're proud you've chosen to take that first step, and I hope that here, at HHG, you find all the support and encouragement you need to live a reasonably human lifestyle, free of the pain and stigma of the past."

Another man piped up. "It took me eight years to come out of the closet."

The quavering voice of another man responded. "Well, actually I crawled out from under the bed. Scared the crap out of little Tommy Wright."

John-Peter loudly cleared his throat. Kellen looked up and handed the woman on his left a card.

"Diane will now lead everyone in 'The Reformed Monster's Creed.' I shall return in a moment."

The tiny, shriveled woman who looked long dead accepted the card with a proud smile.

"Now, everyone, repeat after me," she said in a croaky voice. "I, a hideous freak of nature…'"

Kellen shut the door behind him. "I'm stuck here another two hours with this blasted group. Arthur can take you home now, or you can wait and leave with me. Your choice."

"Got any food?"

"Vegan pizza in the freezer."

"Can I have two?"

"You can eat the whole damn case if you want." Kellen turned toward the room.

"Can I watch television?"

Kellen stopped and looked back. "Restock the display area first."

"Will do."

"And stay out of my office. The last time you fiddled on my computer, you deleted several major files, and it cost me thousands of dollars to retrieve them."

"Acknowledged."

Kellen tossed John-Peter the keys and returned to the meeting. As a boy, John-Peter wondered how Kellen's rose never wilted or lost scent by the end of the day. Eventually, John, Peter concluded that a funeral director able to raise the dead would have no problem preserving a plant.

John-Peter shed his uniform in exchange for his jeans and green shirt and then strutted toward to the kitchen, noting that all five viewing areas were closed, which meant they were full. Good. Should mean a juicy allowance this week.

John-Peter found the pizzas in the kitchen freezer, removed three, and popped one into the microwave. He cooked the second one while he devoured the first, remembering his vitamins without maternal promptings. He glanced at the clock as he unwrapped the third pizza and drained another gallon of water. He'd better hurry.

He sped to the reception area and slid to a halt before the first case. Three of the pamphlet sections were low, so John-Peter walked behind the counter for the extras, thumbed through the stack, and pulled the three he needed: *Missing that Special Loved One? How to Create Your Dream Funeral*, and *Waking the Dead*.

Within thirty minutes, he had refilled the cases with the funeral home's signature pens, mugs, toy hearses, and T-shirts that read, "I'm an HHG Ghoul." He still had eighty minutes.

Jubilant, John-Peter relocked the cases, pushed the keys into his pocket, and slid off his shoes and socks. Swinging the tied laces from his fingers, John-Peter first dashed back to the kitchen for another gallon of water and then to Kellen's office. No need for the light switch. The glow of Kellen's rain forest screen saver provided plenty of light. He dug into his back pocket for the paper Karla had tucked there and placed it between his lips as he dropped his shoes and settled cross-legged into Kellen's leather desk chair. He swiftly typed Kellen's password and signed online.

Searching under the heading "magical herbs" John-Peter found several suppliers for whole mandrake. He glanced at the rest of Karla's order, wormwood, hyssop, and camphor powder—and then scanned the headings until he found an occult store that carried all four. He clicked onto the link, tapped the mouse several more times, and proceeded to check out. He' memorized Kellen's credit card number long ago. Overnight delivery? Worth it. It'd be stupid to have the order show up on Saturday when Katie was home.

Before John-Peter signed off, he checked to see if his stepfather had added any new women to his vast collection. Naked image after naked image filled the screen, women of all shapes, sizes and endowments. They had only one commonality: their various shades of red hair: fiery, carrot, auburn, strawberry blonde, titian and copper. Kellen had only added seven new women, and none seemed particularly spectacular. Yawning, John-Peter logged out and glanced at the large, wall clock. A skeleton ruled the center; its spindly arms marked the minutes and hours, its numerals constructed from bone shapes. Sixty minutes to go. He unlocked the door to the adjoining den, and his feet sank into plush crimson carpet. After grabbing the television remote, John-Peter propped a black, satin sofa pillow for head support and stretched full length on the overstuffed couch, his body melting into the soft black cushions. He heard a click, a series of colored lights leaped up before his eyes, and he shook his head. They obediently dispersed. Yawning again, John-Peter surfed through new movie releases, music videos, nature shows, stand-up comedy routines, talk shows, and reruns on home repair.

A rough hand shook his shoulder. "John-Peter!"

The sudden alertness was an electric shock. A second, harder shake followed the first one.

"John-Peter! Wake up! We're going home."

The boy bolted upright. "What time is it?"

"Ten o'clock." Kellen was holding up John-Peter's book bag. "Somehow, this found its way into my private quarters again."

"Strange."

"Where are your shoes?"

"Don't remember."

"Well, find them, and get out to the car. Arthur's had it running for ten minutes."

"Yes, sir."

He waited for Kellen to leave and then retrieved his shoes from under his stepfather's desk. Inside the limousine, Kellen sat against the back seat and shuffled through a stack of paperwork. The reading lights were off, but, then, Kellen never needed them. The open briefcase lay on the floor near his feet. He did not look up as the boy took a seat across from him.

"Sorry I'm late," John-Peter said, not sorry at all.

His stepfather only grunted.

"How did the support meeting go?"

"Fine, as usual."

"Sales were consistent all night."

"I see that."

John-Peter looked out the window. Downtown Thornton at night was so different from Munsonville's Main Street. After the evening news passed, the only lights in the village were the celestial ones. In Thornton, the sleek ebony sky served only as a backdrop to the bright white street lamps that lit the road clear as day. As the limousine neared the country roads between Thornton and Shelby, the streetlights grew sparse and then vanished all together.

"I had quite the compliment on you this evening," Kellen said. One hand held his forehead as he read the sheet of paper before him. From the headlights of a passing car, John-Peter saw the pale features of Kellen's waxy skin.

"Interesting."

"It came from the woman who wanted the Aloha band for her brother. She called me this evening and scheduled a counseling appointment. She said it was your kind and professional attitude that inspired her to make it."

"Jest a li'l ol' county boy a'doin' his job."

"And you did it well."

Praise did not often flow from Kellen's lips. He must be ill.

"Do you need me tomorrow?"

"We'll see. I talked to Grace after the meeting. The dentist gave her an antibiotic and something for pain, so she should be good for work tomorrow."

120

The car's jostling made him drowsy, but John-Peter fought against the urge to sleep. He didn't need Kellen to wake him again, as if he was a baby. Instead, he thought about the parsonage. He hoped Karla could get him inside tomorrow.

The dark night swirled before John-Peter's weary eyes. It twisted and turned until he heard the click and clearly saw the familiar figures sitting the parsonage's parlor. The fire roared high in the hearth. Great beads of sweat trickled down the faces of the men who lounged in chairs, sipping wine and brandy and smoking fragrant cigars and pipes. All eyes were riveted onto the Amish man sitting in the corner of that room as he read aloud. The gilt letters of "Holy Bible" were stamped on the book's front cover.

"Then thou shalt kill of thy herd and of thy flock, which the Lord hath given thee, as I have commanded thee," the man droned, "and thou shalt eat in thy gates whatsoever thy soul lusteth."

Apprehension rose inside John-Peter. "Karla!"

"The unclean and the clean shall eat of them alike. Only be sure that thou eat not the blood."

John Simons turned, stretched his hand toward John-Peter, and offered him the dark crimson liquid in his half-full goblet.

"For the blood," John Simons said, "is the life."

A hand slapped John-Peter's knee with a loud crack.

"Wake up, boy," Kellen said. "We're home."

John-Peter blinked against the brilliant porch light. He fumbled on the floor for his book bag and quickly found it, but his shoes eluded him.

"Here." Kellen tossed them into John-Peter's lap. "They rolled under the seat."

The door opened, and John-Peter stumbled from the car.

"Good night, John-Peter," Arthur said.

His mother sat in her favorite chair, her legs curled around her as she read. She closed the book when she noticed John-Peter. "How was work, dear?"

John-Peter sagged against the door frame. "A customer complimented me to Kellen."

Melissa smiled. "My son, the people-pleaser."

"Yeah, go figure."

John-Peter heard the back door close again, so he quickly kissed his mother's cheek and proceeded to the stairs. He brushed his teeth, threw his clothes and his dirty uniform in the direction of the hamper, and trudged to his bedroom. Ignoring the light switch, John-Peter opened the closet door and studied his reflection. The mirror rippled slightly. He held his breath and waited.

Nothing happened.

Suppressing a sigh, John-Peter shut the door and shuffled to bed, hoping his body would take the hint from the slow motion of his legs. Still wide awake, John-Peter slid his leprechaun under his pillow, set his alarm, and turned off the light.

He paused again and listened.

Nothing.

He climbed into bed and stared at the ceiling, pondering the mysterious vibrations inside Simons Woods, Karla's desire to call up the spirit of John Simons, and the woman at the library. Reflection turned to irritation. Some friend Karla turned out to be. She promised to examine John-Peter's recurring dream and then didn't even show up when he needed her.

John-Peter kicked away the blankets and turned on the light. He sat motionless for a moment, debating, and then slid his feet to the floor and marched back to the closet for the diary. Maybe he should've told Karla about it, since she was so determined to revive John Simons. He replaced the board and climbed back into bed.

John, for I had decided our relationship no longer required the formality of a title, did not visit me that night or the next, but I was not worried. Dr. Gothart seemed encouraged by the little progress John had made, so I knew sooner or later John would return to me. And when he did, I would be ready for him.

He came to me the first night back in Detroit. I had fallen asleep to the sweet notes of "Bryony" and awakened to find John Simons poised over my chest and unbuttoning the top of my nightgown. I moved his hand away from me and quickly said, "I want you to kiss me first."

A glimmer of surprise passed over his face, but John's voice was steady.

"Not in the bargain," he said.

I turned my face away from him. "Then you can't have any of my blood."

"Suit yourself."

John rose to leave, and I panicked.

"Wait! Where are you going?"

"To locate other blood sources."

"You might not find any that work as well as mine."

"Don't flatter yourself."

I had to make him stay. He wanted my blood; I was certain of it. "Please don't leave me. I'm scared."

John hesitated. He obviously liked that. I doubted his resolve.

"You're afraid?"

"Oh, yes!"

"Pray, tell."

"What if no one ever kisses me?"

"Unlikely."

"I could die first. What we're doing is dangerous. Dr. Gothart said so."

"I trust Dr. Gothart's instructions."

"You could pretend I'm Bryony."

Now that was a bold move, but I swear I detected a hint of longing in his flat, blue eyes. I continued rallying my cause. "Maybe if you remembered kissing, you might enjoy one."

John said nothing. I mustered my most beseeching expression.

"Just one kiss. Please."

He scowled, but he leaned toward me just the same. "This won't be repeated."

"I just want to know what one is like."

John closed his eyes and inched toward my face where, with cold, parted lips, he briefly tasted my warmer ones. He backed slightly away and, without saying a word, headed for my neck. This time, I offered no resistance. I only said, "Next time, maybe you should take some blood first so your lips won't be so cold."

"There won't be a next time." And his fangs lanced my skin.

He was wrong.

Over the next few years, we—John, Dr. Gothart and I—observed a slow, steady progress in John's re-humanization. Each time we overcame a hurdle, I raised the bar of my conditions for cooperation. We progressed from lips barely touching into long-drawn-out passionate kissing, and more. That left me feeling weaker than any lack of blood ever had.

During those moments, I wondered if John really pretended I was Bryony, or if he was merely sharpening his skills for the day when his vampire nature vanished forever. I really didn't care. I had fallen in love.

"Melissa!" Kellen's voice roared from the main floor. "Come look at this credit card bill, and see what your son considers an emergency!"

John-Peter heard the inaudible tones of his mother followed by the louder, and fortunately equally inaudible tones, of his stepfather. He ditched the diary underneath his pillow, switched off the light, and flung the covers over his head.

By the time his mother knocked on his bedroom door, John-Peter's gentle breathing could have fooled even Karla.

CHAPTER 10: TEACHER'S PET

"Let's go, boy! School!"

The boy squinted against blinding sunlight as he groped for his alarm clock. The pounding continued.

"John-Peter!"

"I'm up," John-Peter mumbled and rubbed his aching head, an act immediately rewarded by rows of colored lights.

"I want you dressed and at the table in ten minutes!"

Kellen thumped on the door one last time, and then his footsteps grew faint. John-Peter threw the blankets over his head. The colors faded; he remembered the history quiz. He had to get up, the boy thought as he groped under his pillow for the leprechaun. He could not risk flunking it.

Fifteen minutes later, John-Peter was swallowing his vitamin and scooping granola into a mixing bowl. He had not eaten anything since the pizzas last night, and he was ravenous. Kellen, the black of his clothes highlighting the pallor in his face and the blood red of his rose, stood by the stove, eating a plateful of partially cooked calves' brains and gulping a final cup of coffee.

"I've already talked to Grace this morning. She's feeling much better today, so you're off the hook."

John-Peter nodded against the knifing pain in his temples and poured a carton of soy milk over his cereal.

Kellen glanced at his watch. "I don't have time to get into it with you this morning, but you and I have a few things to discuss when I get home tonight."

"An authentic father-son talk? Oh heart, be still."

"Don't get smart. I'm not happy with the credit card bill."

A car horn blared, and Kellen pushed the plate away.

"Melissa, Edgar's here!" Kellen called as he picked up his briefcase and tossed John-Peter a harsh parting glance. "Tonight."

Kellen opened the back door, and Darlene walked in. With a curt nod and a polite "Ma'am," Kellen was gone. Darlene dropped a light kiss on the top of John-Peter's head, but even that soft caress felt like the downswing of a sledgehammer.

"You look beat," his grandmother said, stroking his hair. "What time did you get in last night?"

John-Peter remained silent, too irritable for her sunny demeanor, so his grandmother tried another approach.

"Where's your mother?" Darlene asked.

"Feeding Grandma Simotes."

Darlene squeezed his shoulder as she passed him. "I'll take over. She'll be late for work."

John-Peter was rinsing his bowl when Melissa dashed into the kitchen and pressed the "start" button on the microwave.

"I've heated that tea three times and haven't drunk it yet," she grumbled, more to herself than to anyone.

"Haven't you eaten?" John-Peter set the bowl on the counter. Mabel would take care of the dishes later. The well hadn't sufficient pressure to support an automatic dishwasher.

"Not yet."

Karla's voice broke into the confusion. "John-Peter, why aren't you ready?"

Like he felt like talking after the way she abandoned him last night.

Karla persisted in her knocking and calling out, "John-Peter, are you there?" So he dropped a door.

The microwave "dinged," and Melissa removed the mug of tea. She started to leave the room with it, but John-Peter blocked the doorway. Melissa stopped so fast the tea sloshed dangerously close to the edge.

"Scoot out of the way. I almost spilled it on you."

"Eat a bowl of cereal."

"I don't have time. You'd better move, John-Peter."

"No."

Melissa glared at him. "Lose the disrespect. You're in enough hot water."

John-Peter held firm, and his mother relenting, said, "Get my briefcase from upstairs. I'll have a piece of toast."

"And a glass of milk," John-Peter said, turning to leave.

Darlene roughly pushed past him. "Melissa, there's something wrong with Carol."

Melissa set down the tea and fled from the room. John-Peter put two slices of bread into the toaster and poured his mother a tall glass of milk. A loud thud from the other room froze his heart.

"John-Peter!" Melissa called out.

He hurried to the room. Melissa was easing Carol into her chair. Both women were splattered in the oatmeal Carol had recently consumed. Darlene sat hunched on the floor, clasping her foot.

"My ankle," she groaned. "I think I sprained it."

"Here, Grandma, sit down," John-Peter helped up Darlene and eased her onto Carol's bed. "I'll get ice."

The boy dashed to the kitchen for an ice pack from the freezer and ran back into the room as his mother emerged from the bathroom, wrapped in a towel.

"Mom, I'm going upstairs to change," she said, "and then I'll clean up Carol. John-Peter, stop at the office and tell Mrs. Joyce I won't be teaching today."

Carol made a face and clutched her head. "Hurt," she moaned. Her face contorted; she retched again; and John-Peter flew into the bathroom for more towels.

He arrived at school as the first bell rang and reached his classroom with his water jug just as Mrs. Miller, one of Karla's aunts and Amy's mother, distributed the history quizzes. She gave John-Peter a stern look as he entered the room. Curtis Chandler monitored the exchange, delight plainly showing on his face.

"I have a pass," John-Peter said serenely, holding out his pink slip.

Mrs. Miller accepted the note. Fortunately for John-Peter, everything on the history quiz pertained to Sumer, the very last subject John-Peter had studied. Confident of the correct answers, John-Peter flew through the material, pausing only to organize his thoughts for the lone essay question:

"Hey, John-Peter," Karla called. "What's number five?"

He dropped another door. With a flourish, the boy signed his name and raised his hand. Mrs. Miller nodded for him to approach her desk. Despite the closed doors, he still felt Karla's impatience.

Mrs. Miller smiled at him as she accepted the completed assignment. "Well, you're done in record time," she said in a low voice.

"Yes, ma'am." Take that, Karla.

She scribbled on a yellow notepad, tore off a sheet, and held it out toward John-Peter. "Here's tonight's assignment. You may begin it now, if you like."

Karla made peace with him at the doors of the lunchroom.

"I'm sorry I got mad at you yesterday. I just really wanted to go back inside the parsonage. Next you time have that dream, I'll show up. I promise."

"C'est la vie."

"Do you have to go to Thornton today?"

"No."

Amy appeared in the doorway. "Karla, we can't plan anything else without you."

"Be right there." Karla turned to John-Peter. "Today, okay?"

Karla linked her arm through Amy's and walked into the lunchroom. John-Peter watched them go, their heads close together as they giggled at some private joke. He headed for Trenton's table and tossed him an apple. Immediately, John-Peter thought of the princess, and he reached inside his left pocket for his vitamin bottle.

"Hey, John-Peter," Trenton said, deftly catching the apple without looking up, "did you know acoustic neuromas grow on the eighth cranial nerve in the inner ear?"

"I do now."

"You've got to be careful removing them, too, or you can damage the seventh cranial nerve, maybe even cause hearing loss. Boy, I wish I had that now."

"An acoustic neuroma?"

"No, hearing loss. I'm tired of listening to Lauren's obsession with Curtis Chandler. She hangs on the phone all night yakking about him."

"So decapitate the sycophant."

Trenton lowered the book. "You okay? You sound tired."

"I'm rethinking my allowance. Faust had it easy."

"I know what you mean. I bussed tables until eight last night."

After school, the boy trudged barefoot up Bass Street under a very pleasant afternoon sun, wondering if he had the energy to spend the rest of the afternoon at Karla's and considering using his fatigue to punish her for refusing to help him last night. He smelled the fried potatoes before he actually opened the back door. Mabel had already begun cooking dinner.

"You're early today, Mabel," John-Peter said as he closed the door behind him and set his water jug on the counter.

"I've been helping your ma all day. Your Grandma Barnes sprained her ankle, but she insisted on walking home so you mother wouldn't leave Carol."

"She didn't!"

"No, but she tried. Your ma called Jack Cooper to give her a ride. I made some banana bread for you. Would you like one or two loaves now?"

"Two, please. Where's Mother?"

"She's upstairs taking a break. Carol fell asleep about half an hour ago. I've been washing laundry all day."

With a loaf in each hand, John-Peter ascended the stairs to Melissa's bedroom. Through the partly open door, John-Peter heard his mother talking on the telephone. Without looking away from her desk, she motioned for him to enter. He sat on the bed and waited for her to finish the phone call.

"No, I'm sure they won't be expecting it. I really appreciate you taking my place today."

Melissa listened while the person on the other end talked.

"That's the plan right now. She's doing better and even kept some broth down this afternoon."

Melissa paused again and then nodded. "Well, John-Peter is home now. Thank you once again. 'Bye."

She replaced the receiver into the base. "And how was literature class today with Miss Elbert?"

John-Peter popped the last of the banana bread into his mouth. "I can't believe you assigned 'Tale of Two Cities' for this semester. Are you trying to drive me from your class?"

"You can read great literature more than once."

He sniffed. "Mother, you insult my intelligence."

"I'm glad you think so. You should have no problem passing tomorrow's quiz on the first three chapters."

Melissa picked up the receiver and dialed. Watching her, John-Peter made up his mind. He sprinted downstairs for his water jug, back up again to the conservatory to arrange the compact discs, and then away to his bedroom. He opened a window, leaped into the tree, slithered down, and then pranced away to the motor home.

Karla was sitting at the table practicing candle gazing. John-Peter scooted past her for the soy milk. By the time he'd claimed a chair, the glassy look had left Karla's eyes, and she was chronicling her impressions.

"See anything, missy?"

"A long, dark tunnel. So are we going or what?"

"Pining for you to make it so."

Karla shut her notebook, and John-Peter, soy milk in one hand and water jug in the other, followed her to the couch.

"Okay, John-Peter, same as last time. Close your eyes, and imagine your spirit is growing lighter until it floats right out of your body."

"Done."

"See the silver cord?"

"Verified."

"Then hurry up, and get over to the parsonage."

"Mademoiselle is feeling domineering today."

"Just do it, John-Peter. Let me know when you're in."

John-Peter once again passed through the parsonage front door, summoning up a large flashlight as he entered the dark house. He still saw nothing except outlines of covered furniture.

"Why aren't you going to the second floor?"

"Have patience, my pretty."

A blast of cold air rushed through John-Peter, and his flashlight went out. He switched it on and off, but nothing happened.

"Hey, Karla, the flashlight stopped working."

"So make up another one. Figures you'd get one with old batteries."

"No, it's something else."

Karla's fingers tightened around his hand. "Like what?"

"Like, I don't know. I felt something…"

Tinkling from the parlor interrupted his thoughts. He knew that melody.

"Felt what, John-Peter?"

Sudden light deluged the room. The flashlight had turned back on. The music was gone.

"John-Peter!"

"Reel me back, Karla."

The cord hummed as it wound back inside him. A jerk, a jolt, and John-Peter re-entered his body. He opened his eyes and gazed into the incredulous ones of Karla Dyer.

"I met the ghost," John-Peter said.

Karla's eyes widened. "Oh, gosh, John-Peter! Stay right there. Don't move."

She ran into the kitchen for her notebook and returned just as lightening flashed across the room.

"Now tell me what happened."

"I just told you."

"Details! I want details!"

"A gust of something that felt like cold air passed through me. That's when the flashlight stopped working."

"Then what happened?"

"I heard music."

Karla scribbled furiously. "Music? What kind of music?"

John-Peter paused and dropped a door. He did not want to tell Karla, not yet. "I don't know. Just music."

"Then what happened?"

"I came back."

Karla's face glowed with joy. "This is great, John-Peter, just great. I can't wait for tomorrow."

"I can't tomorrow. It's Friday, remember?"

Her face fell. "That darn route! Now we'll have to wait until Monday. What about Simons Woods? Can we go there if you get back early from papers?"

"'Early' is the key word."

A clap of deafening thunder caused them both to jump.

"John-Peter, you'd better get home before the storm breaks, or you're going to have an awfully hard time explaining your wet clothes."

"Parting is such sweet sorrow."

John-Peter got caught in the downpour anyway. He was just slipping through his bedroom window when he saw Kellen's car turning up the street. Half an hour later, John-Peter was still rinsing the shampoo from his hair when he heard Kellen's bellowing. "How long does it take one skinny kid to get clean?"

John-Peter nearly laughed out loud. Kellen really didn't want an answer to that question.

"Five more minutes," he shouted over the water's spray.

"Forget it. I'll wait until after dinner."

Ten minutes passed until John-Peter emerged from his sauna. He paused at the laundry room door just long enough to toss his dirty clothes near the hamper. He was almost to the stairs when he heard his parents' voices coming from downstairs. He stepped from view to listen.

"Face facts, Melissa. You're over your head."

"You're overreacting."

"She's deteriorating beyond your ability to handle her."

"Oh come on, Kellen. It's the stomach flu."

"And tomorrow it will be something else. You feed her, bathe her, diaper her, and shuttle her back and forth to the doctor. You also teach fulltime—ridiculous considering the amount of money that flows through here—and you're raising a teenage boy. I think a nursing home will be kinder on everybody, including Carol."

"I'm not institutionalizing John's mother. If you're so worried, why not hire a private nurse?"

"Is that what you want?"

"It's better than a nursing home!"

"Have it your way. I'll call tomorrow, right after I schedule an exterminator. That damn mouse kept me awake all night. I'd certainly like to know where that boy set those traps. I went into the attic and didn't find a single one. By the way, where is John-Peter? Dinner is getting cold."

John-Peter bounded down the stairs on cue, ate a fast dinner, and then politely excused himself to devote the remainder of the evening to his studies. It had nearly worked, too, until John-Peter reached the door.

"Not so fast," Kellen said. "We've got a little something to discuss." He reached inside his shirt pocket and withdrew a folded piece of paper. "I want you to explain these charges. What do you know about a cash advance on July twenty-seventh for five hundred dollars?"

"Karla went to Thornton's festival and needed the money."

"Five hundred dollars!"

"She took three friends."

"Do you realize the amount of interest charged to a cash advance?"

"And here I thought you paid the entire balance each month."

"Watch your mouth. Then I have not one, not two, but ten separate one hundred dollar charges in August for Berklys. Can you explain that one?"

"I ordered some food."

"Ordered some food! You already eat me out of house and funeral home!"

John-Peter met his stepfather's eyes and shrugged. "I had a taste for Mrs. Berkly's vegetarian lasagna."

"Jenson's thirty minutes away!"

"They charge more for delivering long distance."

"And what in the hell is an Eircheard's Emporium?"

"A pawn shop."

"A pawn shop!"

"Yes, in Jenson."

Red with fury, Kellen screamed, "You spent one hundred of my dollars at a Jenson pawn shop?"

"Not exactly. Ed needed to borrow the money, or he'd lose a good deal on a dozen pewter tankards. He's paying me back on Sunday."

"Your allowance is suspended until further notice."

John-Peter didn't care. He still had Kellen's credit card.

Kellen shoved the statement back inside his pocket. "You're dismissed!"

More gagging came from Carol's bedroom. John-Peter headed for his room before his mother asked for his help. He could refill his jug from the bathroom sink. In his room, he opened the closet door, noted just his reflection, and retrieved Grandma Marchellis' diary from its hidey hole. He leaned against the closet wall, opened the diary to his marked spot, and began to read.

A certain Peter Marchellis now owned and operated a butcher shop next door to the Panchuk's grocery store and deli where, since I was eleven years old, had a regular sitting job with the Panchuk's little boy Alexis. The job had been an excellent means for me to contribute to the Lenkes' income without taxing my health—which had improved considerably under Dr. Gothart's care—but it now had become the perfect opportunity to sneak passing looks at the handsome, young entrepreneur on my way to and from work.

I shan't bore you with the details of our relationship since they bear no relation to this story, except to say that the succulent kisses of a bashful, living man in love erased from me any desire to accept similar kisses from a dead one.

Suffice it to say that John voiced strident objections to the announcement of our engagement. "You belong to me, Anna."

"Only my blood does, and you can still have that until you're human again."

Dr. Gothart defended my position and ordered John to discretion. My love for Peter blossomed despite the clandestine, nocturnal rapport I maintained with John. I was eager for him to become whole again and find the same happiness I now had.

During our initial year of marriage, Peter expanded his successful business by opening a second store on the other side of town even as we anticipated the birth of our first child. About midway through the gestation, the old symptoms of my childhood illness returned, completely stumping Dr. Mroviak, who suggested I spend a couple of weeks breathing the pure Munsonville air.

My condition further weakened during my stay at the fishing village, and my darling husband yielded to my pleas of summoning Dr. Gothart, who was optimistic about my return to vibrant health, if we but followed one condition.

"No visitors except your husband and doctor," Dr. Gothart said, gesturing with his pipe as he spoke. "It's much too taxing for you."

Peter nodded in understanding. Dr. Gothart resumed his smoking. Despite my distress, I couldn't help admiring his pipe, with its large bowl of polished dark wood, a gold lid, gold trim, and gold mouth piece.

"No one?" I asked the aging doctor, anxiously meeting his eyes.

"No one," Dr. Gothart repeated, with heavy emphasis on his words. "Your husband and I will make certain of it."

I did not see John again my entire pregnancy. The very day Dr. Gothart loosened my restraints, John paid a middle of the night call to me. He tugged at my nightgown with such force he popped the buttons.

"Stop," I whispered, restraining his arm with my hand. "You'll wake my...."

John clamped his teeth onto my neck, ripping its flesh as he swallowed a huge, mouthful of blood. I screamed in agony and fright. Peter sat up, fumbling for a candle.

The baby, you Frank, began to cry in the cradle. I leaned over the bed to lift you and comfort you at my breasts. John was gone. Peter blamed the wound in my neck to vermin and laid bait and traps.

John-Peter paused to listen, and he heard the knock again. "Who is it?"

"Your mother. I want to talk with you."

"Can it wait? I'm getting ready for bed."

"Be in my room in five minutes."

"Over and out."

John-Peter replaced the diary under the floorboard, changed into his pajamas, and then scampered down the hall. He'd waited far too long for this conversation.

Melissa sat at her desk correcting papers by the tiny lamp. It was the only light in the entire room except for the pink candle she burned near the vase of the fresh purple roses she always insisted Kellen buy for her.

"Yes, Mother?"

Melissa threw down her pen and swerved around. "Grow up already!"

"Beg pardon?"

"You heard me. Your antics may have been cute and forgivable when you were small, but they are not funny now."

"On my honor as a gentleman, I am not trying to be funny."

"Then, what?"

John-Peter leaned over her dresser, stretched out his arms across her lace runner, and buried his head in them. "You would not understand."

"Try me."

The boy raised his head and pried open her antique music box with his thumb. Why had he heard this chiming melody inside the parsonage?

"I met a woman this week," John-Peter softly said.

"Oh?"

Had he detected a note of surprise in his mother voice?

"A very classy, older woman, she was." John-Peter traced the painted green bryony vines on the side of the box. "Claimed she used to live in Bradford Heights."

Silence.

"Are you acquainted with the town, Mother?"

"You're well aware that I am. Your father's parents used to live there."

John-Peter slammed the lid and whirled to face Melissa. "That's a lie! The woman said Marvin and Carol Simotes never had any children. Explain *that*, Mother!"

"John-Peter," Melissa calmly answered, "did you ask her when she knew them?"

"You're evading the question."

"No, I'm not. Your father is adopted."

"You expect me to believe that Marvin and Carol Simotes adopted a son and never told anyone?"

Melissa chuckled and retrieved her pen. "Well, actually, I think your father adopted them."

"And why did you withhold this from me?"

"Because it wasn't important, that's why. Look at how you're overreacting. If this bothered you so much, why did you stew about it so long?"

"I loathe family secrets. They nauseate me to the very core of my being."

Melissa bent over her homework. "John-Peter, you're a little dramatic."

"Am I?"

He glided across the room and paused behind her, peering over her shoulder. Melissa paused, pen in mid-air, and frowned. "Do you mind?"

The boy swiftly grabbed a handful of hair and yanked her head to one side. His right index finger touched the lobe of her ear and traced a line down her neck all the way to her shoulder.

"Is this how Kellen looks at you?" John-Peter whispered. "You must know I've watched the way he sniffs your neck, wishing he was a real vampire, burning with lust for that first bite."

Melissa slapped his hand off and jerked away from him. "You touch me like that again, and I'll have you committed so fast you won't know what hit you."

"Empty threats."

"John-Peter, you're pushing your luck."

"Melissa!" Kellen's voice rang out. "Get down here! Hurry!"

Melissa again tossed the pen and sped from the room with John-Peter following. Kellen was halfway up the stairs.

"I've called an ambulance for Carol. I think she's had a stroke."

CHAPTER 11: A NEW FRIEND

As the date approached for Carol Simotes' release from Jenson Memorial Hospital, Kellen gave Melissa two choices: Golden Years Retirement & Nursing Home in Thornton where Dr. Rothgard lived or Jenson Nursing Home. Melissa cajoled and cried, but Kellen refused to budge.

"Thornton is too far away, and Jenson is so dreary," Melissa wailed.

Kellen didn't care. "Personally, I'd choose Golden Years; it's classier," he said. "But that's up to you. Either way, she's not coming back here."

"How can you be so heartless? Just because she's John's mother!"

"Melissa, you know better than that!"

John-Peter released his hold on *Tale of Two Cities* and the paperback landed on the grass next to his shoes. Having to re-read the book was bad enough without his mother and Kellen disturbing his concentration.

"I won't do it! And you can't make me!"

"If you won't, I will! But don't come crying to me, Melissa, when you don't get the facility of choice!"

"I hate you!"

"No big revelation there!"

The boy slipped another core into his bag, grabbed the last apple, and wondered what was up with Karla. She'd been quiet all weekend, but quite possibly Karla was studying up on mandrake carving, since they planned to do that on Monday. Maybe John Simons could explain the vibrations inside Simons Woods.

"John-Peter!" Mabel's voice rang out. "Dinner!"

He quickly polished off the apple, retrieved his bag, water jug, and book, and then sprinted into the house just in time to see Kellen pause at the dining room entrance to glare at him.

"Hurry up! The food's getting cold!"

"Yes, sir."

"And put your damn shoes on!"

The silent, oppressive atmosphere at the dinner table nearly spoiled John-Peter's enjoyment of the tofu quiche Mabel had prepared for him. Kellen scowled as he ate and said nothing. Melissa picked at her steak and whimpered.

The second John-Peter placed the last bite to his lips and emptied the water pitcher, Kellen's fist slammed down hard. The boy startled and the tofu chunk rolled under the table.

"Do you know starving children in the Tristan de Cunha would die for the food you waste in this house?" John-Peter said calmly as he let his fork fall to his plate.

"Shut your mouth!" Kellen rose from the table. "Gotta call Don Cates. I want that mouse gone by Monday." He left the room in a hurry.

That settled it. Tonight would have to be the night. John-Peter summoned Karla for a wakeup call, just to be sure.

But Karla didn't answer any of his calls. Even if she was still at Megan's house, Karla never let social activities interfere in their communications. What was up with that? No matter. He'd probably catch her before he fell asleep.

Returning to his room after a long hot shower and a full water jug, John-Peter checked the mirror and then removed Grandma Marchellis' diary from under the floor. Why was the princess hiding? Climbing into bed, John-Peter messaged Karla again, but she did not respond, a true annoyance, since that meant he'd have to rely on his alarm clock, which he slid underneath his pillow before opening the diary.

One night when Peter worked late, we met: John, Dr. Gothart and me. The blood treatments had stopped working. Dr. Gothart stressed to John the urgency of abandoning me and quickly locating another compatible host.

"If you do not soon find someone whose blood marries with your chemistry, you may regress into full-blown vampirism," Dr. Gothart said. "Should that occur, we will have to begin anew. But I must warn you, John, each time you repeat the process, you lessen your chances for permanent success."

I did not like the sly expression crossing John's face as he said, "The best match would be one closest to Anna's chemistry, correct?"

"Yes. A girl would be ideal, if that were possible."

"But it is possible," John said, turning to me with an ardent smile.

The horror of John's insinuation washed over me. He wanted me to conceive another child, and, if it was a girl, to offer her as the next host.

"You can't make me have a baby!" I cried.

"Can't I?"

Dr. Gothart removed his pipe. "I wouldn't force the girl's hand, John. Remember, she safeguards your secret."

This empowered me, so I decided to test this muscle, previously unknown to me. "Threaten me, and I'll expose you to the world."

"Expose me," John said, "and I kill Frank."

His words stunned me into silence. I looked at Dr. Gothart for help. My hero merely puffed on his pipe and watched the exchange, not with sympathy, but with high amusement. Dr. Gothart had no regard for me or even for John. This exchange of blood wasn't benevolent scientific discovery. It was sport.

I turned savage eyes on John, but kept my voice low, so as not to waken Peter. "You've destroyed my marriage."

"I don't care."

Rage boiled inside me long after John and Dr. Gothart left my house. I would not, could not, conceive and deliver up a child to John. Nor, would I risk a granddaughter to that same fate. Peter Marchellis' progeny must end here; I would do everything in my power to achieve it. To that end, Dr. Gothart did help me. Speaking privately to my husband, Dr. Gothart bluntly stated that another baby would kill me. Peter, crushed, complied by keeping a safe distance.

You, Frank, grew healthy and strong, until you reached adolescence. Deliberately, I raised you in a flurry of self-doubt, praying you might never seek marriage and perpetuate my former master's crimes. Instead, I placed a camera into your hand and encouraged you to see the world through the eye of its lens. As you mastered its skill, my confidence grew. I just might triumph over John Simons' evil plan for this family.

Following a high fever, you went into diabetic shock, and as you recovered, I impressed upon you the devastation your illness could bring a family, through your inability to work and through the passing down of this disease to your children.

I joined your father's church and raised you there. In due time, the pastor retired, and Alexis Panchuk, the little boy I once babysat, now fully grown, was ordained and given command of the church. As our faith grew, Peter's dissipated until it disappeared all together. He had taken a chance with opening his heart. I knew he would never do it again. Peter instead, poured his passions into his business, and it thrived under his hands. He made more money than we could ever spend in a lifetime. Anyway, what good was money without love?

During these years, I never encountered John, and I grew hopeful that I had seen the last of him. Then, one night, he appeared in my solitary room. He did not touch me or seize any of my blood. He came with an ultimatum.

Buy Simons Mansion. Or else.

John's condition had deteriorated. His persistent quest for the right host had destroyed any remaining appearance of life; he was truly hideous to behold. The time had come to falsify his death. Only in hiding could he pursue his goal. It was up to me to ensure his safety while he pursued it.

A click, and John-Peter was standing inside the parsonage parlor, its fire blazing high and fierce. Sweat ran unheeded down the men's faces and onto their clothes as they hypnotically fixed their eyes upon the Amish man sitting in the corner as he read aloud from the Bible.

"Karla!"

"The unclean and the clean shall eat of them alike," the Amish man's voice droned. "Only be sure that thou eat not the blood."

Slowly, slowly, slowly John Simons turned toward John-Peter, his outstretched hand once again offering the half-full goblet of crimson fluid.

"For the blood," John Simons said, "is the life."

A muffled jangling jolted the boy awake, and he fumbled for the alarm clock. Its silence only intensified the buzzing in his head from lack of sleep. He closed the crumpled diary. Ed Calkins would soon arrive. If John-Peter was going to save that mouse from senseless death, he'd better do it quickly.

After emptying a shoebox and plucking an apple core from his knapsack, John-Peter sprinted down the hall on bare toes. The faint television sounds from the first floor master bedroom suggested Kellen might still be awake, but the silence from his mother's bedroom didn't necessarily mean she had gone to bed, since it was only eleven o'clock. The attic door gave a slight creak as he opened it, but that was all. No parent stirred; no parent called out. John-Peter noiselessly sped up the stairs.

Once in the attic, he rolled the core across the floor and crouched, box opened, waiting for Kellen's potential victim to approach. Several minutes passed with no mouse. John-Peter remained motionless. More time elapsed, and still the mouse had not appeared. What if Ed Calkins...

A scuffle, a scratching, and WHAM! The mouse was his.

Back inside his bedroom, John-Peter taped the box shut and punched several air holes in the top. He had just buried the box inside his closet when he heard a car door slam. He snatched his shoes and sprang for the tree.

No trucks were late that night; even the route itself was uneventful. A quiet house awaited John-Peter upon his return Sunday morning. His mother and Kellen were settling Carol Simotes into her new bedroom at Jenson Nursing Home.

John-Peter spent the day napping, reading *Tale of Two Cities* up in the oak tree, and feeding Bertrand, for that was his name for the mouse, a concoction of oats and millet seed. He did not call Karla, and he hoped she was miserable wondering why he avoided her. Maybe he'd even pass on Monday's mandrake carving, unless she pleaded hard enough. A little begging would be good for Karla.

While heading for his locker Monday morning, John-Peter discovered the source of her weekend distraction, and he nearly threw up. With her cheeks flushed pink, and her face lit up like the Northern lights, Karla leaned against the wall where the lockers divided and animatedly chatted to Curtis Chandler. He stood before her, resting one hand on the wall above her head, listening intently and smiling.

Looking neither to the left nor to the right, John-Peter sauntered past the pair, knowing just mere seconds would pass before Karla would scamper after him. When he reached his locker, he gave a sidelong glance down the hall. Neither Karla nor Curtis had budged. He grabbed his books and slammed the locker door. With a warm smile, Curtis lightly touched Karla's shoulder and headed for the office. Karla trotted down the hall toward John-Peter.

"Hey, John-Peter, we're still carving the mandrake this afternoon, right?"

"Are we?"

She blinked at his coldness and drew back, puzzled. "That's what we agreed to do. You're not working for Kellen today, are you?"

"Nope."

"Then what?"

"Seems to me you've found a new toy."

He turned toward the library. The hurt look on Karla's face provided small satisfaction, even though it served her right. She needed a shock to snap her back into reality.

The morning was unending. Imagining Karla and Curtis stealing saccharine glances with each other disturbed his concentration. Once, John-Peter tapped the side of his head to clear the images, and a series of lights flashed before his eyes. Dr. Morgan had called them ophthalmologic migraines. Harmless. Ignore them, and they'd soon fade.

He planned to shun Karla in the lunchroom, too, but she'd beaten him to it. She and Curtis had retreated to a corner table where they sat side by side, heads close, doing more talking than eating. He dragged leaden feet to the kitchen for his lunch sack and fresh water jug. Strange that he didn't feel hungry.

"Melissa, how much do I charge for one slice of pizza?"

His heart stopped, and he felt cold. Turning toward the sound of the voice, John-Peter saw the strange woman from the library, the one claiming to know his grandparents.

"Pizza's a dollar," Melissa replied from her table.

Munsonville School did not have a teacher's lounge. Teachers ate in the room where the students' parents did the serving. John-Peter did an about-face, took three steps, and bent close to Melissa's ear.

"Mother," he said in a low voice. "Who is that female?"

"That's Evelyn Chandler, Curtis' grandmother," Melissa said, moving her head away and looking up at him. "Why do you ask?"

"She works here?"

"Why all the questions? I thought you didn't like Curtis."

That took the boy aback. John-Peter had never discussed Curtis with his mother. "I never said it."

"You didn't have to say it. It's obvious every time you're in my classroom."

For once, John-Peter had no comeback. He found his lunch and turned heavy feet toward Trenton Cooper, who sat at the opposite end of the lunchroom nibbling a hamburger and reading, *Neurosurgery of the Nineteenth Century*. Without breaking concentration, Trenton reached for the salt shaker and heavily sprinkled his French fries with one hand and caught the apple John-Peter rolled to him with the other one.

"John-Peter, I can hear the weeping now. I'm going to have a bad night."

"You broke your forceps?"

"No, Curtis Chandler broke Lauren's heart. Haven't you noticed him hanging all over Karla?"

John-Peter didn't answer. Trenton turned a page and asked, "Taking Courtney to the homecoming dance?"

"I'd rather be drawn and quartered."

Trenton looked at John-Peter as if he'd lost a lobe or two. "Well, heck, I'll take your leftovers. Courtney's hot!"

As if on cue, Courtney sidled up to their table, supposedly on the way to the garbage can with her tray. "I can't believe our dippy little school is finally having a homecoming dance."

Instead of making his big move, Trenton buried his face deeper into his book, the tips of his ears glowing bright red. On the inside, John-Peter was broadly grinning. Trenton only reached Courtney's shoulder.

"The dance is but a small portion of the event," John-Peter said. "Homecoming is really more a reunion for the alumni."

"Oh, John-Peter! Everyone is going."

"Even Trenton."

"Is he? That's nice," Courtney murmured, still looking at John-Peter.

Just then, the bell rang. Courtney didn't move. "Are you working for Kellen this week?"

John-Peter rose. "He hasn't compiled the schedule."

He moved briskly toward the garbage can, Courtney trailing behind him.

"Well, if you do, you're always welcome to stop in."

"Good to know."

The boy tossed the paper bag in the can, grabbed the jug, and sauntered out the door. Exactly three hours later, John-Peter strolled through the Dyer's motor home where Karla was sitting at the dinette table studying advanced palmistry from her father's notes, diagrams of hands scattered everywhere.

"Where's the mandrake?" John-Peter said, reaching for two cartons of soy milk.

"Hidden." Karla's head moved back and forth as she compared her findings with Cornell's instructions.

"Well, stash the sacred tomes and retrieve it. I haven't got all day."

Karla looked up, astonished at John-Peter's brusque remark, but the boy suddenly found Cornell's footnotes extremely interesting. Without a word, Karla piled her school material and carried it from the room. She soon returned with the mandrake root and a white-handled knife.

"This was Daddy's." Karla handed the knife to John-Peter. "He always used this when he carved mandrakes."

John-Peter turned the knife several times and noted the angles of glinting light.

"It looks rather old," he said. "Your mother allows you to cut with it?"

Karla looked uncomfortable as she snatched the knife back. "I never said she lets me use it. Anyhow, when did you get all righteous?"

"Settle down, my spirited filly. I bow to your superior shrewdness."

"Fine. Let's start cutting."

She made the first crude marks and then held up the root for John-Peter's approval. Although the notches were precise, something didn't appear right about them.

"The image eludes me."

"I'm not done yet, John-Peter."

Her face creased, and her lips pursed as Karla whittled away. As the likeness took shape, John-Peter realized what Karla had done wrong.

"That's not John Simons."

"Close enough."

"Not when it resembles Curtis Chandler. Are we performing necromancy or a love spell?"

Karla's eyes narrowed as she viciously jabbed the mandrake root. "And what's that supposed to mean?"

"You're obviously obsessed with the one-dimensional pretty boy."

She slammed down the knife. "How dare you say such a thing to me?"

"How dare I? Because you've gone to extreme lengths to hide this twisted relationship. And now you've ruined the mandrake. Poor deluded Karla."

Karla's face flushed with anger. "Who are you to talk? With what you've kept from me!"

The next breath caught in his throat, but the boy managed to choke out, "Elaborate, please." When did Karla find out about the princess?

"You hid Grandma Marchellis' diary from me! I thought we were best friends and partners!"

"Historical inaccuracies are not generally admitted as evidence," he said, his voice shaking with tremendous relief. His secret was still safe.

"Stop talking in circles!"

"I'm talking fiction. Don't be so stupid, Karla."

"Don't call me stupid!"

"And don't upbraid me for a judgment call. Must every private amusement be subject to your prying mind?"

"John-Peter, I'm warning you...."

"Because I can provide quite a show."

Karla jumped up, eyes blazing. "You're disgusting! Go home!"

"Halfway there, darling."

John-Peter left so quickly, he forgot his water jug. He did not call her all week, nor did Karla make any effort to connect with him, allowing the boy to double his piano time. He polished three previous works, composed a new piece, and trained Bertrand to scale of wall of blocks. Despite these accomplishments, John-Peter slept terribly and even debated the merits of spending one of those insomniac nights exploring Simons Woods. In the end, he decided against it, and that further irritated him. If he encountered any vibrations, he couldn't decipher them without Karla's help.

Everything went wrong at the distribution center that night. Three trucks arrived late, the strapping machine broke, and the manager's toilet spewed its contents into the office, obstructing access to the computer to print route lists. Furthermore, Joe Reece had shorted the checks again, and five carriers walked away from their routes because of it. Ed barked at anyone who approached him. John-Peter unloaded truck after truck, so Ed, growing paler by the minute, could distribute newspapers as rapidly as possible. In between arrivals, John-Peter bagged abandoned routes, refilled his water jug, and ate up all the apples in his knapsack.

"Who's taking them out, Uncle Ed?" John-Peter said as he tossed another paper into the overflowing cart.

"I'm doing one; Joe's passing one; and three carriers offered to split the rest."

"Which one's yours?"

"Evansville. I'm running it after I take you home. Can't you find a working cart?"

"There are no more carts."

Ed leaned against the work station and breathed hard. "Throw the papers on my table. I'm going out for a bite. Let me know when the Munsonville Weeklies get here."

John-Peter clicked his heels together and saluted. Ed smiled weakly and wobbled toward the service door.

The last truck pulled into the dock an hour later. John-Peter had finished rolling; Ed had not yet returned. John-Peter reluctantly grabbed the pallet. He did not relish the idea of single-handedly unloading and distributing the last of the newspapers.

The first two bundles disappeared as quickly as the boy dropped them. Another impatient carrier snatched a bundle from the second pair, unstrapped it, and grabbed a handful of papers, scattering the remaining contents over the floor.

Ed's voice rang out. "Any carrier seen on the dock area gets their papers last!"

John-Peter threw two more bundles onto the pallet and breathed a sigh, thankful Ed was back. The respite had rejuvenated the old Steward, while John-Peter's mood grew dark and brooding.

"Need a nap?" Ed Calkins said, backing up when John-Peter missed his third driveway in a row.

"No," the boy said, flinging out the newspaper.

Ed didn't speak again until he turned down the road that led to the unincorporated area between Shelby and Jenson. "Then what?"

John-Peter had not intended to tell Ed about Karla and Curtis, but it somehow spilled out... Ed clucked his tongue in sympathy, and said, "I didn't know you liked Karla."

"We're friends, nothing more."

Ed chuckled softly. "Sounds to me like you're jealous."

"Of what? A plastic excuse of the male species?"

Ed threw a paper and slapped John-Peter's arm with an excited, "Hey! I've got it!"

Curtis, the new golden toy
With the girls he loved to be coy
When he asked Karla out
She said with shout,
"I prefer a red-headed newsboy."

Feeling blacker than ever, John-Peter finished off the apple, then reached over the seat for a Munsonville Weekly, and said no more. Ed apparently didn't mind John-Peter's brooding as long as the boy kept on task. The Irishman filled the gap with stories of the fairies who foretold death, from the headless Dullahan who rode a black carriage to the wailing banshee.

"There a lots of theories about the banshee." Ed pulled to the side of the road and stuffed a Thornton Times into a tube. "Hand me a Detroit, John-Peter."

The boy reached up onto the dashboard and gave Ed the newspaper. Ed drove back onto the road and threw the newspaper into the next driveway.

"Now, some people say the banshee is a shriveled old woman, and others swear she is a beautiful maiden," Ed said. "A few stories claim she is the ghost of a person who died a violent death. But whether the banshee is friendly or unfriendly, this much is known. She only appears to certain families; she is always a woman; and she always heralds death."

The sun was high in the sky when they finally made it to Jenson.

"I can smell the Irish soda bread now," Ed said, patting his stomach and sighing with pleasure. "Let's pull over a minute, and I'll adjust that leprechaun."

John-Peter didn't argue. The brief nap in the sun would feel good. He handed over the leprechaun and sank into blessed sleep.

"You're late," Eircheard said from behind the counter as Ed and John-Peter entered the pawn shop. He reached for a match. "There's only half a loaf left."

"Go ahead, John-Peter," Ed said, handing a Jenson Reporter to Eircheard. "I can catch a bite in Munsonville."

John-Peter sliced the bread in half, spread each side, and then dragged the chair closer to the window. Ed picked up a multi-colored suit jacket and held it over his chest.

"What do you think, John-Peter?"

"Too small."

"Ha! Just you wait and see."

After struggling to pull the jacket over his potbelly, Ed struggled back out of it and tossed it on the card table, adding, "Not my style." He turned his attention to a stack of Irish novels. "How much?"

"A buck a piece," Eircheard said, between puffs.

"The thrift store down the street sells paperbacks for a quarter."

Eircheard smiled around the pipe. "Then take your business there."

The boy's eyes traveled over the suit coat. Its red, orange, and yellow checks, crisscrossed with heavy brown lines, reminded him of autumn leaves at Simons Woods. He slid his arms into the sleeves and easily buttoned it.

"That'll be ten dollars," Eircheard said as he rang up Ed's books.

Ed looked at John-Peter. "You're not thinking of buying that, are you?"

The boy did not answer as he joined the Steward by the cash register. Without any hesitation at all, John-Peter pulled his wallet from his back pocket, removed Kellen's credit card, and tossed it on the counter.

CHAPTER 12: LAST CHOICE

At school Monday, Karla was leaning against his locker, waiting for him.

"I threw away the mandrake root," she said, avoiding his eyes.

"Move."

Karla meekly stepped aside, and John-Peter flung open the door. "Good. You ruined it."

"Can you get me another? I'll let you carve it."

"I can't do Curtis Chandler justice."

Karla blushed and bowed her head. "I didn't mean for it come out that way. It's just that...."

Her voice trailed off. John-Peter slammed the door and spun the dial, but as he turned to leave, Karla caught his sleeve.

"John-Peter, have you ever been in love?"

His mouth went dry. He dropped a door and asked in a low voice, "Why do you ask?"

"Because I think I'm in love with Curtis Chandler."

The boy flinched as if she had punched him, but he only said, "Shouldn't you be telling this to Curtis?"

"I wanted to know what you thought. We used to tell each other everything."

Karla's voice broke, and John-Peter glanced at the crowd of students filling the hall. He hated Mondays.

"Sure, I'll get you another mandrake, but I can't order it until Wednesday night."

She flung her arms around his neck. "Oh, thank you, John-Peter! I swear I won't touch it."

As he pried off her fingers, the first bell rang.

"We're going to be late for class," the boy said.

"So are we still friends?"

John-Peter's throat tightened. "Of course we're still friends."

Relief flooded Karla's face. "Oh, good! For awhile, I thought you were mad because I liked Curtis. Are you coming over this afternoon? We could explore the parsonage again."

He hesitated. Karla had a lesson to learn. "No. I have a composition to polish."

"Oh, well," Karla said, disappointment creeping into her voice. Her eyes traveled down John-Peter, and her face brightened. "Where'd you get such an awesome jacket?"

"Eircheard's Emporium."

"The place you go with your Uncle Ed?"

"The very same."

"I've never been inside it. My mother says it looks seedy."

"Your mother lives in an old motor home."

This time, Karla did the flinching, so she quickly changed the subject. "So what do you think I should do?"

"About what?"

"About Curtis Chandler. Do you think he likes me, too?"

"You're the mind reader."

She shook her head. "I can't read his mind. My feelings for him get in the way."

The second bell rang. John-Peter looked away from Karla. The hall was deserted.

"Good job, Karla. Now we need late passes."

"I'll tell Mrs. Joyce it was my fault."

"I don't think Mrs. Joyce cares."

At lunch, John-Peter steered away from the hand-holding love birds and headed for the kitchen to claim his sandwiches and a fresh water jug. His mother was eating a bowl of soup and reading.

"The soup is vegan," Melissa said. "No meat, not even the broth. Evelyn Chandler made it."

He closed the refrigerator door. "I'll pass."

Melissa looked up at him in surprise. "Is everything all right?"

He didn't answer, so she returned to her mystery novel. "I'm staying late at school today."

"Detaining a wayward student?"

"No, I'm in charge of the decorating committee for the homecoming dance. I've got a planning meeting."

"Great. My mother is leading a school campaign for the color selection of streamers and balloons. Shall I have Mabel hold dinner for you?"

"Actually, I'm thinking of bringing a sleeping bag and camping out in my classroom. The dance is less than two weeks away, and I've got lots to do," Chuckling, Melissa turned a page. "Come on, John-Peter, why don't you join us? Even Karla is helping."

"I have my music to consider."

Melissa looked straight at him. "You mean the CDs you play when you sneak to Karla's after school?"

He stood in stunned silence.

She winked. "I was young once, too, you know. Don't worry. Your secret is safe with me."

That remark further irritated him. John-Peter stomped from the kitchen and headed for the back wall, but today Trenton, his book laying closed before him, had Courtney to keep him company. Courtney gave Trenton polite smiles as he enthusiastically talked, but her eyes scanned the room. In the far corner, Curtis had unwrapped Karla's straw and was now wedging it into her milk carton. John-Peter's stomach spun like a top, and he returned to the kitchen.

"Back so soon?" Melissa said, opening a package of crackers. John-Peter caught a glimpse of the book's title: *The Portrait of a Lady*. Typical English teacher pick. His mother only read literature or novels by her former high school English professor, Harold Masters.

"No seats."

Tuesday didn't fare much better than Monday. Karla spent so much time with Curtis that even Amy and Megan—from John-Peter's view at his lunch table—looked annoyed.

"I see you made a new friend," John-Peter said to Trenton. He stirred chopped raw onions into his vegan chili, leftover from the previous night's dinner, and reached into his left pocket for his bottle of vitamins.

Trenton set down *Minimally Invasive Spinal Surgery: Pros and Cons* and grinned. "Score!"

"Score what?"

"Score Courtney. I'm taking her to homecoming."

"My deepest sympathies."

The beaming smile vanished. "You could congratulate me. Do you know how much nerve it took to ask her out?"

"You'll need nerves of steel to last an entire night with her."

By Wednesday, John-Peter was almost glad to see Arthur waiting outside. The entire world had gone mad around him, and he felt thankful for furnace duty. He downed several bottles of papaya juice, opened his marinated tofu salad, and leaned against the leather seats. The respite was short-lived. John-Peter bumped into Kellen at the funeral home's back door.

At the sight of John-Peter's jacket, Kellen's mouth dropped and then twisted into a sneer. "Don't tell me you're wearing that thing in public."

"I won't tell you."

Kellen yanked John-Peter by the collar and moved him into the direction of his bathroom. "Hurry up, and get your uniform on before someone sees you dressed in that ridiculous coat."

John-Peter almost laughed out loud, but he dutifully shut the bathroom door. Kellen had built an empire that catered to the aberrations of nature, and John-Peter's clothes embarrassed him?

For the next four hours, John-Peter parroted, "Welcome to Happy Hunting Grounds. May I take your order?" so many times he almost forgot about Karla and Curtis. After he convinced a solid third of the customers to add Kellen's new ghost-hunting option to their packages, Kellen ordered a triple serving of vegetable kabobs from Brummings and gave John-Peer access to his private rooms.

"So I may go online?"

"Yes, if you stay away from my private work files."

"Like I care about dead people."

"Don't knock it. They keep a roof over your head and parsnips in your belly."

Kellen had no sooner closed the door to his monster support group than John-Peter grabbed his bag of food and fresh water jug off the display case and headed for his stepfather's office. Immediately, the boy opened Kellen's store of red-headed women. How many pictures had Kellen added in the last couple of weeks? Twenty? Thirty? Some of the girls didn't look old enough for high school. He clicked *zoom* for a closer view of the last girl. Was Kellen insane?

Feeling uneasy about this discovery, John-Peter quickly shut the file and signed online. Four advertisements for homecoming dresses popped onto the screen. Annoyed now, John-Peter clicked them away. He ordered the mandrake, with standard shipping this time, and logged off. With drooping eyes, John-Peter shoveled the last bite into his mouth, grabbed his water jug, and headed for the television and a nap.

On Thursday, John-Peter told Karla he was available to explore the parsonage, but Karla had a decorating committee meeting and declined his offer. The following day, Karla boarded a bus into Jenson to meet Katie after work. They were going shopping for a homecoming dress. John-Peter crashed early on Friday and distanced himself from Ed's prying questions all weekend, preferring to mentally rework a composition, which he planned to practice Sunday afternoon.

However, even that pleasure was denied him. Kellen was home packing for a business trip to New Mexico. His music blared so loudly, the walls shook. John-Peter stayed at the library until closing time and then amused himself by building a maze for Bertrand on his bedroom floor. The mouse quickly negotiated any plotting deviances as long as John-Peter dotted the way with cooked brown rice. When Bertrand tired of the game, John-Peter turned his attention to Grandma Marchellis' diary.

I can only guess what thoughts ran through your father's mind when I approached him after all these years. Wary at first, he soon made love to me with an ardency I had missed. So when Simons Mansion went to auction the following month, your father purchased it for me. I rejoiced for I believed my obligation to John had ended.

But your father had other ideas.

Peter researched the history behind Simons Mansion, became fascinated with John and Bryony Simons' story, and concluded that the mansion's restoration would benefit the village. There was little I could say to the contrary. Peter had the money to do what he pleased with it, and I could propose no convincing argument to dissuade him from his plans. After all, why else would I want him to buy a dilapidated, old building and not fix it up?

John entered my dreams, warning me to keep Peter from intruding into his sanctuary. But the more I attempted to sway Peter away from his illusory notions, the more tenacious those notions became in his mind.

One sad morning, I woke to find Peter lying dead beside me, his features frozen in terror. I can only speculate what horror he beheld in those final moments of life.

The first stroke I suffered caused me to realize the extent of John's power and the finiteness of my days. I prevailed upon you to assume legal ownership of Simons Mansion, impressing upon you the necessity of keeping the house and never relinquishing to the village or any other soul all the days of your life.

Even before the ink dried on the papers, I congratulated myself. John would have to find some other family to haunt. We were safe. A week later, you called to announce the good news. You had met a woman, fallen in love, and eloped. You were now a married man.

I prayed you might never have children. I feared for Peter Marchellis' posterity. I longed for someone to save us from the curse of John Simons.

Frank, you may shrug off my tale as the ranting of a feeble old woman. But I caution you to think twice about doing so. Shelter your daughter!

The last few pages were blank. If he had been Frank, he would have skipped the nursing home and chosen a mental institution. The old lady was bats.

An excited Karla met John-Peter at his locker the next morning. In honor of homecoming week, Katie had canceled all of Karla's extracurricular studies. That, in combination with a three-day school week, meant Karla had plenty of time to enjoy the festive activities and prepare for Saturday night's dance.

"Too bad you're not going, John-Peter," Karla said. "You should see my dress. It's lavender with..."

"Listen to yourself. You sound like Lauren Cooper."

Karla giggled. "Lauren Cooper is hopping mad. She got invited to the dance more than anyone else—a couple of guys from Jenson High even called her—but she turned them all down, because she was convinced Curtis was going to change his mind about taking me and ask her instead."

John-Peter gasped and clutched his chest. "I still have a chance?"

"Are you serious?"

"Lauren Cooper? Get real!"

He had to get away. Now. What had happened to Karla? She used to be so normal.

For the next three days, John-Peter buried himself in homework, dreading the upcoming weekend and thankful his newspaper job would shield him from much of the hype...until

Melissa, full of parental authority, called Ed and told him John-Peter wasn't available for work this weekend because of homecoming activities. Too late, John-Peter tried wrenching the phone from her hands. The serene smile on her face was maddening.

"Mother, I'll thank you not to interfere in my career!"

She glanced briefly at Mabel, who quickly bent her head over the vegetables she was chopping for dinner.

"For your information, young man, you're seventeen and living under my roof. This weekend, your spacious freedom is curtailed. You *will* attend the carnival on Thursday night, and you *will* attend my reunion picnic at Simons Woods on Friday afternoon."

"So why can't I work Saturday night?" He felt control slipping away from him, and he did not like it.

Melissa smiled and patted his cheek. "Since you're such a night owl, I volunteered you for the dance's clean-up committee. That leaves you Sunday to rest up before you return to school on Monday."

"And just who's heading this clean-up committee?"

"The Chandlers. You'll report to them."

"Will no one storm the Bastille and free me?"

"That will be I. On Sunday."

The only good part about Thursday night was that Steve planned to attend the carnival with Darlene. She wouldn't allow him to ride any rides or play any games, but he could sit at the tables, eat the native food, and visit with people, something his grandfather was more than happy to do.

"Are you sure this is what Grandma had in mind?" John-Peter said as he brought Steve his third hot dog.

Steve peered inside the wrapper. "What's on it?"

"Everything, Grandpa, just as you asked."

"Even the hot peppers?"

"Even the hot peppers."

Steve handed John-Peter a five-dollar bill. "Can you bring me another order of onion rings, my partner in crime?"

"Anything else?"

"A giant chocolate chip cookie. Come back if you need more money."

John-Peter grinned as he moved away from the picnic tables near Lake Munson and wove through the crowds. Steve was taking full advantage of his furlough. Darlene was manning the information booth for the next couple of hours, and Melissa was helping Ann bus tables at Sue's Diner for those people who wanted a full, home-cooked dinner instead of bratwurst or nachos. His grandfather had no one to spy on him.

Rollicking music from the merry-go-round and flashing lights from the Ferris wheel beckoned the brave to the half dozen rides blocking the entrance to Simons Woods, leaving access via bike trail only. Beyond them, food and game booths formed two lines all the way to Munsonville School. Vendors manned their wares in front of every store along Main Street. Just before the food booths stood the art tables, hawking everything from Celtic pottery to landscape oil paintings. The boy paused at the table displaying on-the-spot caricatures and asked, "How much?"

Its gaunt, greasy, and gray-haired artist slouched in a canvas folding chair chewing a dirty finger.

"Ten bucks," the artist replied.

"Can it be someone in the crowd?"

"Nope, gotta be you."

"A hundred dollars to draw him." John-Peter pointed to Curtis, standing at the bank of Lake Munson and feeding Karla little bites of pale blue cotton candy.

The artist spat a large nail on the ground. "You're on."

"Excellent."

The boy headed to Dalton's Dry Goods, the location of Munsonville's only ATM machine. Within minutes, John-Peter returned with the money. With a "How's that?" the artist held up a large sheet of paper for John-Peter's approval. The man had delightfully widened and elongated Curtis' large eyes, even teeth, and sappy smile. John-Peter rolled up the paper, tucked it under his arm, and turned to leave when the artist asked him, "Aren't you the Simotes kid?"

The question took him aback.

"What of it?" the boy asked evenly, but he disliked the gleam in the old man's eyes.

"I knew your father."

"Doubtful," John-Peter said.

"Your real father," the artist added.

"My real father was a well-respected college music professor."

He started to walk away, but the artist leaped from behind the table, grabbed the boy's arm, and hissed, "Well-respected men don't buy other men's babies."

John-Peter's heart stopped and then quickly restarted with a hard thump.

"Do yourself a favor, kid. Ask your mother about Derek Granger. And don't let her put you off with one of her fairy tales. You deserve to know the truth."

The boy flung off the arm and quickened his pace to the food court, but the artist's words had badly shaken him. As he stood in line for the onion rings, with the chilly night air seeping past his jacket and into his bones, the boy recounted the truth about himself as if reciting facts in Mrs. Miller's history class. He was John-Peter Simotes, son of music professor and amateur pianist John Simotes, who died from a baffling illness. His mother, an English teacher, claimed John-Peter received his musical abilities from his father, but now...

"Can I help you?" the chubby woman behind the booth said.

"Large order of onion rings."

"Two-fifty."

John-Peter laid the bill on her sweaty, outstretched palm and waited for the harried woman to ring up the sale.

"One, two, and fifty." The woman placed tacky bills onto John-Peter's hand and set the onion rings on the counter. "Have a good night."

"Thanks," the boy said absently and walked toward the cookie booth. His mother had brushed away Evelyn Chandler's assertions that Marvin and Carol Simotes never had children by explaining how the Simotes had welcomed his father into their family long after they had broken contact with the Chandlers. Was it true?

"One giant chocolate chip cookie, please."

"Two dollars."

John-Peter accepted the cookie. The throngs pressing against him seemed surreal. Did any of them doubt their identity?

Once, his background had seemed perfectly logical. His best friend's father had driven a stake through Professor Simotes' heart before committing suicide inside his stepfather's funeral home. The vampire slayer's daughter was psychic. His stepfather claimed to be an ex-vampire, collected nude photographs of red-headed women, and sold séances along with his coffins. Now, nothing made sense.

Well-respected men don't buy other men's babies.

His grandfather's table came into view. Steve was no longer alone. A woman sat opposite him, her back toward John-Peter.

"Here's your food, Grandpa." John-Peter placed the items between Steve and the woman. "And your change."

Steve handed the quarters back to John-Peter. "Keep it, and buy something for yourself."

John-Peter slipped the money next to his leprechaun. Nothing at the carnival cost fifty cents. Maybe he could bargain with Eircheard.

"Onion ring?" Steve held the package toward John-Peter.

"No thanks, Grandpa," John-Peter said, retrieving his water jug. "I'll see you later."

"John-Peter, have you met Evelyn Chandler? I believe she's the grandmother of one of your classmates."

Curtis' grandmother turned around and faced John-Peter. "We finally have a real introduction. It's a pleasure to meet you, John-Peter."

Stunned, John-Peter reluctantly shook her outstretched hand. "Likewise, ma'am."

Steve chuckled. "I used to date Evelyn in high school until a certain Horace Chandler came into town and swept her off her feet."

Evelyn softly tapped his wrist. "Now, Steve, tell the boy the truth. You had already jilted me when I met Horace. Actually, John-Peter, I had asked your grandfather to marry me, but he declined to take care of his parents, who were elderly and in poor health."

"Well, maybe that's how the story went," Steve said with a grin he tried to smother and failed. "Time fogs the old brain. Anyway, my decision provided you with a life of ease."

She closed her manicured hand over Steve's. "There's more than one way to be rich, Steve."

Obligations fulfilled, John-Peter slipped through the hordes filling Main Street and toward home. Amy and Megan were shooting mechanical ducks. At a table beyond them, Courtney was applying face paint to one of the first grade girls. Lauren and some boy stood behind a Victorian cut-out. Silly to waste ten bucks for a stupid picture. Trenton leaned against the general store, reading a book by flashlight. A bit of pink on the boy's cheek caught John-Peter's eye.

"You didn't!"

Trenton started rubbing away the rainbow. "I forgot it was there. Courtney was only practicing."

"Wouldn't a red heart be more appropriate?"

"I thought so. But I had to wipe off the heart—and the frog, to make room for the rainbow."

The rollicking music gradually faded and the hum of the crowds turned to murmurs. Shoes in hand, John-Peter trudged up Bass Street. Strange to enter an empty house. He still could not get used to Grandma Simotes' absence. Kellen's use of her room seemed almost sacrilegious, but what was his stepfather supposed to do? Build a shrine for her?

He opened his bedroom door a tiny crack, slipped through the narrow space, and peered into the closet door, but only his reflection stared back at him. Another blow. He groped along the top shelf for his weapons and then tacked the caricature on the back of his bedroom door.

The first dart nailed Curtis' left nostril. The second dart split his lip, the third landed beside it, the fourth missed altogether and landed on the floor, but the fifth lodged into Curtis' right eye. John-Peter threw the fourth dart again for good measure and pierced Curtis' other eye.

"Vous etes un homme tres elegant," John-Peter said. Then he readied himself for bed.

On Friday morning, John-Peter ate bowlful after bowlful of granola as Melissa gathered picnic items. She had given Mabel a paid holiday for the rest of the week since Kellen wasn't due home until Sunday night.

"So, Mother, when do the grand festivities commence?"

"Noon." Melissa opened a cabinet door, and, hands on her hips, surveyed its contents.

Sitting behind a school desk would have been a more productive way to spend the day, even a sunny autumn one.

"Will the Coopers be there?" John-Peter reached across the table for a napkin.

"They're supposed to be. Don't we have any ketchup?"

"Kellen finished the last bottle. Besides, who cares?"

Melissa looked inside the refrigerator. "I care. I'm supposed to get all the miscellaneous food items, and I really don't want to fight the carnival crowds to get inside the general store."

"Then call the Coopers. I'll bet Sue's Diner has plenty of ketchup. It's not like you're expecting a crowd. How many kids did you have in your class? Five? Six?"

"Seven." Melissa reached for the phone. "Maybe I will call Ann. I just hate to ask. She and Jack are bringing all the meat."

"Ahem!"

"Don't worry. Katie's bringing a box of soy burgers. Did you take your vitamins?"

They divided the spoils between two backpacks, with John-Peter carrying most of the water. Together they coasted down the hill, but once on flat land, John-Peter shot past Melissa, enjoying his only taste of freedom in this tortuous weekend. As he neared the mouth of the woods, he slowed and waited for his mother to pull alongside him.

"Boy, am I out of shape!" Melissa said, huffing. "I guess I should do this more often. The problem is finding the time. There never seems to be enough of it."

A toddler crossed the path. John-Peter braked hard, and Melissa skidded to one side.

"Kyle!" The large, pregnant woman threw one last piece of bread into the lake then wobbled after her child. She did not look at John-Peter or Melissa.

"Maybe we should have walked," John-Peter said as they waited for an elderly couple to pass. Behind them, a father pulled a wagon full of children while the mother led a large collie.

"It's just for one weekend. The business is good for Munsonville."

"What if the picnic grove is taken?"

"It won't be. Dan and Joey camped there last night."

"At substandard accommodations?"

She glided back onto the road. "They're radio personalities, John-Peter, not celebrities."

John-Peter followed her. "Not to hear Lauren and her cackling elite talk. They tune into them every day until classes start. Amy plastered her locker with their pictures."

They reached the hill that led to the park. Melissa jumped off her bike and began to push it, so John-Peter did the same.

"Lightweight."

She grinned. "Believe it or not, I used to pedal this every day."

They walked in silence until they reached the top of the hill where Melissa stopped to remount her bike. A shadow passed over her face as her eyes swept across the former estate. A knot tightened in his stomach at the wistful expression and longing in her eyes. To cover it, John-Peter leaned over her bike, jiggled his mother's handlebars, and said, "I have an exposition of sleep come upon me."

Melissa startled, blinked away the reverie, and then stared hard at John-Peter. "What did you say?"

She was angry at him? That made no sense.

"I said, 'I have an exposition of...'"

"I heard you. Why are you quoting 'A Midsummer's Night Dream?'"

A simple literature quote upset his English teacher mother? "A feeble attempt to be amusing, nothing more."

Melissa pedaled away. When he reached her, she gave him a sheepish look.

"I'm sorry for overreacting. I guess I'm just a little nervous about today. I haven't seen Julie in years."

"Is she bringing David?" John-Peter only knew the couple from Christmas cards.

"Yes, they flew into Detroit last night."

They glided past the swings full of squealing children toward the orchard where two of John Simons' apple trees still grew. Beyond that was the picnic grove, where a dilapidated gazebo once stood, if his mother's memory was correct. Manning the grill in a cloud of thick smoke were the all-too-familiar profiles of the Detroit radio disc jockeys Dan Turner and Joey Brown, otherwise known as Danny T. and Joey B. Ann stood before an open cooler and handed a package to Lauren, who carried it to Joey. Jack was lugging a second cooler into the pavilion.

Katie looked up from the red checked cloth she was spreading across a wood picnic table, smiled, and waved. John-Peter parked his bike near a tree trunk, stepped around Trenton and his book, and set the backpack near the tables. Katie had brought an entire cooler of water jugs. Good.

"How shall I help?" John-Peter asked.

"You can set out the salads and desserts on this table over here." Katie gestured to the back wall. "Leave the lids on them until the meat is done. Hey, Dan, how long before we eat?"

"Ten, maybe fifteen minutes." Dan flipped a hamburger and squashed it hard.

Melissa began unloading the contents of her backpack. "Where's Karla?"

Katie unfolded another tablecloth. "She's in the woods with Curtis looking for sticks for the marshmallow roast."

Curtis?

"Oh my God, it's been so long!"

He turned to see Dan embracing a slender woman with short dark hair who fit into jeans and T-shirt as nicely as Karla. A second man, his blond hair streaked with gray, stood near them cleaning his glasses. Joey, still holding the tongs, waited expectantly for his hug.

Katie smoothed the creases from the last tablecloth, pushed back her limp hair as she watched them, and said, "I swear, Melissa, she hasn't changed at all."

"Is that Julie?" John-Peter asked in surprise.

"Melissa!"

Within seconds, Julie was wrapping his mother, and then him, in a tight embrace. Washington cologne, John-Peter decided, had a distinct edge over Michigan varieties.

"Would you believe the first flight was cancelled? It turned out to be some stupid mechanical problem. David wanted to drive here and make a proper vacation of it, so I kept hearing 'I told you so' during the entire trip. But what did he want me to do, cancel an entire week's worth of clients? Flying is quicker."

A movement in the trees caught John-Peter's attention. Karla and Curtis had emerged from the woods, clasping hands and carrying long branches. Karla's face lit up when she saw him.

"Hey, John-Peter!"

Karla dropped her branches next to the backpacks and hurried to greet him. John-Peter busied himself with the careful arranging of potato salad, fruit salad, and brownies, and Karla waited for him to notice her. Without looking up, the boy merely asked, "Do you mind?"

"John-Peter, what's wrong?" Karla asked, almost anxiously. "I thought we were cool."

"We're cool. You're impolite."

"What are you talking about?"

He gestured at a picnic table where Curtis sat across from a chattering Lauren and looking uncomfortable. "You've abandoned your beau."

"We don't own each other. We're just...."

"Please, Karla." John-Peter held up a hand. "Spare the gory details."

"I don't get you. You're acting almost as if you're jealous."

"Jealous? Of that moth?"

"Yes, jealous!"

"I'm disillusioned by your blindness. Our friendly mandrake has more testosterone than he does."

"Food's done!" Dan called.

Karla shot John-Peter one final withering look and joined Curtis. During lunch, laughter bubbled around John-Peter, but he could not rise to the lighthearted mood. His only consolation was that Julie chose to sit next to him. Silently, he ate one soy burger after another and almost forgot to take his vitamins.

Dan popped a baby carrot into his mouth. "Hey, what's invisible and smells like carrots?"

Joey slapped him on his back. "Rabbit farts."

Lauren giggled into her hamburger, but her eyes swept over the table to where Curtis and Karla, sitting at a separate table, talked quietly together. Jack smothered a grin and absently passed Ann the mustard. Ann wasn't smiling.

"Honestly, you're acting like a bunch of idiots," Ann's blue eyes behind her tortoise shell glasses looked stern; the occasional gray streak in her hair intensified their severity. "Can't you grow up?"

Dan piled more slaw on his plate. "Hey, Joey, other than radio, what's the three most efficient means for broadcasting news?"

"Telegraph, telephone, and tell a woman."

Jack snickered, glanced up at Ann, and abruptly stopped. Trenton, bent over a book, was oblivious to everything except the printed words and his food. What a stupid picnic. John-Peter rose from the table, scooped up several of Katie's vegan brownies, and meandered into the woods.

Well-respected men don't buy other men's babies.

Aimlessly, the boy walked around, kicking a twig out of the way here and brushing a clump of grass there, hoping to trigger a vibration. He was just heading back when the ground briefly buzzed beneath his feet and then stopped.

"What are you doing?"

With a start, he turned to face Karla. "I felt them."

Karla's eyes grew very large, and she gripped his arm. "The vibrations?"

"The very same."

"John-Peter, we've got to study these!"

"Then pare back your social schedule."

Karla looked more annoyed than disappointed when she said, "I can't this weekend. You know that."

"I know. Don't call us; we'll call you."

He spun around and sauntered back to the group.

On Saturday morning, Melissa invaded John-Peter's sanctuary by actually climbing up the tree and thrusting her face between the leaves, rudely close to his face. In her hand, she clutched an envelope.

"Katie just called me. Apparently, Curtis is sick and can't take Karla to the dance tonight."

John-Peter stretched his toes and turned a page. "Sucks to be Karla."

Melissa wrenched away the book and threw it on the ground.

"No, it sucks to be John-Peter," she said. "You're taking her to that dance."

John-Peter stared into the distance. "Mother, go correct some papers. If she truly wished to save face, Karla herself would have asked me to take her."

"Karla knows better than to ask you to do anything ordinary people do."

"A sensible girl, Karla."

Melissa waved the envelope before John-Peter's face. "Do you know what this is? It's Kellen's new credit card bill. Watch it mysteriously disappear after—and only after—you take Karla to that dance."

"You drive a hard bargain, Mother."

"So let's go." Melissa began climbing down the tree.

"Go where? The dance isn't until tonight."

She paused to smile up at him. "We're going to buy you a suit and get you a haircut."

John-Peter leaned his head against the bark and groaned. "I can feel the screws tightening."

"And then we'll have Dr. Rothgard remove your splinters. You wouldn't want to snag Karla's dress."

"Of course not. I wouldn't be able to rest at night."

Melissa's mood switched to sunny for the ride to Thornton. She flipped through several pop radio stations and sang along with whatever tune caught her fancy. John-Peter looked out the window, counted telephone poles, and tried not to think. At Klever Cuts, the barber on duty took one look at John-Peter, standing defiantly and clutching his water jug, and blanched.

Melissa remained nonplussed. "My son needs a haircut."

The man ran a hand through his balding head as he scrutinized John-Peter. "How short?"

Before Melissa could answer, John-Peter said, "I'd like a Mohawk."

The barber glanced at Melissa.

"Take off a foot and half," Melissa said. She leaned close to John-Peter. "Cut the crap."

"A special occasion warrants a special haircut." But he submitted to the shears.

The razing of John-Peter's head was nothing compared to shopping for a suit as Melissa insisted he complement Karla's lavender gown. In the end, she selected a gray suit, gray and black-striped tie, and a lavender shirt. Then she searched for gray socks and black shoes to match.

"It's homecoming, Mother, not Halloween," John-Peter said as Melissa paid for the costume.

She smiled. "I'll let you pick out the corsage."

"Flowers? For Karla?"

Melissa slid her credit card back into her wallet. "Oh, by the way, Kellen called this morning. He's sending Arthur to the house tonight."

"Kellen is a fool. Why waste good money for Arthur to drive all the way from Thornton just to transport us one block."

"It makes the event more special."

"That, dearest mother, is a matter of highly speculative opinion."

Even Dr. Rothgard had no sympathy for John-Peter. "I'm very proud of you, my boy, for stepping up to help a friend." He pulled the last splinter from John-Peter's right hand and then picked up the left one.

John-Peter peered at his mother, sitting in a nearby chair and monitoring every word. "My boundless generosity will one day be the death of me." The tweezers slipped and stabbed John-Peter's hand, but the boy only grimaced.

Another jab as Dr. Rothgard said, "It's conquering these little life challenges that strengthen you for the bigger battles yet to come."

"Alas, 'tis my only comfort."

That evening, John-Peter was buttoning his suit coat when he heard his mother knock and call, "May I come in?"

"Entré, sil vous plait."

She undid his tie and added a perfect knot; she adjusted his collar. John-Peter scowled at her efforts, but his mother appeared not to notice. Melissa held him away from her for a closer look. Her countenance softened.

"You look very sweet."

Her eyes misted, and John-Peter looked away. Stupid dance.

"Your father cut an impressive figure in white tails. I loved dancing with him. I…"

She stopped short and hung her head before speaking again. "You have more of your father inside you than you'll ever know."

Well-respected men don't buy other men's babies.

"Anyway, Arthur is here. I'll meet you at Katie's. Don't forget Karla's corsage."

"You're going to the Dyers?"

Melissa smiled. "You know. For pictures."

"Yeah, this is one for the memory books."

Karla opened the door for him, her face flushed pink with excitement. John-Peter held out the corsage.

"My mother said to give this to you," he said.

She accepted it with a smile then, impulsively, kissed his cheek. "Oh, thanks, John-Peter. Come inside a few minutes. Our moms want to take a bunch of pictures before they go set up refreshments."

The sooner he relinquished himself to fate, the sooner the persecution would end. He smiled broadly for picture after picture, only too happy to sprawl across the back seat of the limousine, water jug nearby, for a brief respite before round two of torments began.

"So Golden Boy misled you about his true intentions for this evening?"

Karla shifted her gaze to the window. "John-Peter, I don't want to talk about. I'm really upset at Curtis, and I just want to have a good time tonight."

"So it's true? He isn't sick?"

"Look, I said I don't want to talk about it. If you can't respect that, I'm going home."

Yes! Salvation…at hand. Then John-Peter remembered the credit card bill.

"My lips are sealed, fair maiden."

Arthur stopped in front of Munsonville School. Karla's eyes grew big. "Wow! Look at all the people."

The entire building was lit from top to bottom. Students and adults jammed the lunchroom, which was lavishly and colorfully decorated. Every man and boy wore a suit; the girls and women swished their pastel gowns. Lauren Cooper was nowhere in sight. Yeah, he'd have looked out of place in a green T-shirt and blue jeans.

Microphone feedback cut through the chatter. Karla giggled and held her ears.

"Helloooooooo, Munsonville!" Dan called out. "You've heard us on the radio, but we're yours for the next four hours. So get ready to mix it up with Danny T. and his sidekick Joey B. Bust out those dancing shoes and, start scraping up the gym floor!"

Amy grabbed Karla's hand and dragged her out to dance. Good. Time for Karla to be charitable. Amy did not have a date. Even Trenton gave his best attempt at dancing, although he jerked his limbs as if Courtney, despite forcing a cheerful smile, was sticking them with hot pokers.

"Boy, oh boy, oh boy, oh boy." Trenton quickly gulped a glass of punch. "Is this a great dance, or what?"

"Thrilling. Where's Cinderella?"

"Bathroom again. I wish she'd hurry. I don't want to miss any of the slow songs."

"You're sister really had no escort?"

"Nope. She was holding out for Curtis Chandler, which was stupid. Even if he'd asked her, she would have sat home, with him being sick and all."

Dan's voice broke through the din. "For all you lovebirds out there who need an excuse to put your heads closer together, here's a tune by..."

From across the dance floor, Karla's eyes sought those of John-Peter. Right then, he found an interesting mark on the floor to contemplate. He knew what she wanted. He just didn't want to give it to her.

"It's conquering these little life challenges that strengthen you for the bigger battles yet to come."

"Alas, 'tis my only comfort."

He was a number four. His sun opposed Jupiter. He was destined to accomplish great things. Hadn't Karla said so?

"Your short fingers tell me you view reality only from your own perspective," Karla had once said.
"The correct perspective."

John-Peter winced at the memory of words that, tonight, only sounded shallow in his ears, and he did not know why that mattered to him. He looked up. Karla was still gazing at him, expectation clearly written on her face.

Well...what the heck.

The boy took a deep breath and headed straight to Karla. He reached her as the music began playing, but as she held her hands out to him, he stopped, paused, and swallowed hard.

He couldn't touch her.

They were best friends. They shook hands over deals, held hands during séances, and high-fived over victories. They lay on the grass in the middle of woods during the pre-dawn hours and shared their dreams. *Learn, explore, discover.* He was as comfortable with her body as he was with his own.

But not tonight, not with her dressed in lavender except for her bare shoulders and with the muted gym lights streaking gold through her black curls. This was not the Karla he always lost to arm wrestling.

"It's okay if you can't dance," Karla said, misinterpreting his discomfort. "I'm not very good either."

Pride rose inside him, and he squared his shoulders for the challenge.

"I can dance," he said and accepted her outstretched hands.

He could, too, and his easy ability surprised him as he expertly and flawlessly moved her around the dance floor. The music enveloped them; the other couples melted away. Suddenly, and without warning, Karla pulled back her hands and wrapped them around his neck. His mouth felt dry as he lowered his hands to her waist. They were barely moving now. Where had he learned to dance?

Karla's eyes never left his face. She did not smile. Was she feeling it, too, this strange magic that was happening to them? The gym walls disappeared as they became one with the music, and Karla was so very close.

John-Peter felt a tap on his shoulder. Quickly, he whirled Karla away, but Curtis had the audacity to follow. Again, John-Peter changed directions, and again that leech fastened himself to Karla's heels.

Karla abruptly pulled back. "John-Peter, knock it off, all right?"

"Isn't Curtis' date a hot water bottle?"

Curtis grabbed Karla's hand. "Karla, I am really, really sorry about tonight. Please, forgive me. Please, let me make it up to you."

The happiness on Karla's face was more than John-Peter could bear. His last act before leaving the gym was tossing his tie into the trash can. Maybe the janitor could use it. He hoped Karla and Curtis enjoyed their short limo ride.

He dragged his bare heels up Bass Street feeling more alone than he ever had in his life, and he silently berated himself for allowing the contrived atmosphere to affect him, and with Karla of all people. She'd probably lost all respect for him. He certainly had none left for himself.

Entering a dark and silent house was becoming the norm. For a fleeting moment, he considered heating up some leftovers, but the thought of food sent his stomach churning. Or maybe Curtis' memory was nauseating him. Ascending a steep mountain required less effort than climbing the staircase to the second floor. He couldn't wait to lose the straightjacket and get to bed. He needed sleep: long, deep, black, and dreamless sleep.

He snapped on the light, flung open the closet door to kick his shoes inside, and stopped, stunned, at the sad brown eyes of the princess staring back from inside her mirror prison. Instead of vanishing, as she usually did, she stood motionless and watched John-Peter watch her.

This couldn't be happening.

John-Peter closed his eyes and shook his head, but when he looked again, the princess was still standing there, solemn, unblinking. In wondering awe, the boy edged close to the mirror.

174

Slowly, he raised his right hand, and the girl raised her left one. With light and easy movements, John-Peter made circular motions in the air. The princess did the same.

Gently, he pressed his hand against the glass. The princess rested hers against his. John-Peter only felt the cold, sleek surface, and the princess hadn't offered him an apple, but for tonight, that was enough.

CHAPTER 13: THE MAD SCIENTIST

WHAP!

The dart hit Curtis between the eyes.

How long since his school physical with Dr. Rothgard? One month? Two?

"I think it's time you had a certain talk with the boy," Dr. Rothgard had told Melissa. John-Peter laughed bitterly and threw another dart.

Well-respected men don't buy other men's babies.

John-Peter's bedroom door opened.

"WHAP!

The dart bounced off the wall dangerously close to his mother's face.

"You almost hit me with that!"

John-Peter threw another dart.

Melissa marched across the room, yanked the remaining dart from John-Peter's hand, and slammed it onto his nightstand. He responded by crossing his arms over his chest and leveling his most ferocious glare at her. Undaunted, Melissa sat on the edge of his bed and rudely stroked his hair for a long time before speaking.

"John-Peter, I'm sorry about last night."

The icy stare remained.

"If I had known Curtis would pull a stunt like that, I would never have insisted you take Karla to that dance."

Silence and an unwavering gaze.

"Honest."

Bile burned the boy's throat as John-Peter choked out, "'Honest,' Mother? What do you know about honesty? You couldn't utter the truth if your soul depended upon it."

Melissa blinked, dropped her hand, and drew back in surprise. "What are you talking about?"

"I'm talking about commodities."

"I'm not following you."

"Am I adopted?"

She hesitated and then answered, "Yes."

"Was this what Dr. Rothgard wanted you to tell me?"

His mother again paused and looked down at the bed.

"Yes," she said in a low voice.

John-Peter bolted upright, eyes blazing. "Why did you hide this knowledge from me?"

"Will you lose the paranoia already? This isn't some conspiracy against you. I didn't tell you because there was no reason to tell you. Your father and I always considered you our son, plain and simple. We never wanted you to question it."

"Adoptive parents don't buy their children."

"What?" His mother jumped to her feet. "John-Peter, I don't know what's gotten into you, but until you speak like a rational human being, this conversation is finished." She turned to leave.

"Wait."

Melissa whirled around, her face full of fury and hurt.

"Please stay and talk to me."

Reluctantly, Melissa sat back down, but her face was tense and guarded.

"An artist spoke to me Friday night at the carnival."

"The one who drew that monstrosity?" Melissa jerked her head toward Curtis' picture.

"The very same. He said Father purchased me from a Derek Granger."

Melissa's eyes filled with tears, and she no longer looked mad. She lightly touched John-Peter's cheek with the back of her hand.

"Honey, I'm so sorry. I don't know who this artist is, but he shouldn't have said those things."

"So it's not true?"

"Of course it's not true. Your father and I adopted you in the conventional, legal way any couple adopts a baby."

"Why would he say it?"

"I don't know. Maybe he knew Derek."

"My real father?"

His mother sighed. "Do you really want to hear all this?"

John-Peter didn't like the strained expression on her face. A look like that could only mean trouble.

"Derek Granger was your biological father. His girlfriend took private piano lessons from your adoptive father. One night she quit the lessons because she was pregnant and couldn't afford them."

"So?"

"So she didn't want the baby either and asked your father if we would be interested in adopting you. We most certainly were interested because we couldn't have any children of our own. The only money that transpired between us and them was for the doctor, the lawyer, and the hospital bills."

There is a secret in your past, Karla had said, and a disgrace of some kind.

"John-Peter, would you like to see the receipts?"

"I want to meet them."

"You can't."

178

"And why not?"

Melissa turned away, and John-Peter knew she was crying.

"They're dead," she whispered.

John-Peter flinched at this news; he closed his eyes to absorb it.

Peace and harmony are moving away from you. Your life is hanging in suspension.

"Your mother, Debbie, died on the operating table when Dr. Rothgard delivered you." Melissa's voice quavered. "Derek committed suicide the following year. I never wanted you to know. I wanted to spare you this pain."

He reopened his eyes, hoping his mother could see his loathing for her. His identity was shadows; his entire life was a lie, and it was all because of her.

"So that excuses your deception? Mrs. Wechsler, next time you suggest I need professional help, please look in the mirror." John-Peter rolled onto his side, and splashes of light obstructed his view.

Melissa grabbed his shirt and yanked him onto his back. The spots vanished.

"You watch what you call me!" She was crying hard now. "You're John Simotes' son, and I'm the only mother you'll ever have. You'd better not forget it!"

She fled from the room, slamming the door behind her, just as he hurled the last dart. John-Peter lay there, brooding. Sleep, when it came, brought menacing shades and sinister images. He drowned in anguish and let it engulf him.

Karla's voice pierced the gloom. "John-Peter, I know you're in there."

He dropped the door and swam to the bottom of his despair, but her voice bubbled through the murky gray... Karla persisted.

"I'm sorry about last night," she said. "It was all a mistake."

A sleazy artist slouched in a canvas folding chair. With quick, light, scratchy strokes, he sketched the feathery outline of John-Peter's head. Karla pushed in and tugged the boy's ear.

"John-Peter, you listen to me. Lauren Cooper coaxed Curtis into coming home with her after the picnic. One thing led to another and...well...she threatened to tell the whole school what happened if he took me to the dance."

"That's twice your invertebrate boyfriend thought with the wrong head. Lauren can't tell without incriminating herself."

Eircheard leaned over the artist's shoulder and puffed on his clay pipe as the latter man added a log under John-Peter's head. Wispy smoke curled over the drawing and hid the emerging image. The scratching grew insistent, even after the artist laid down his pencil. John-Peter opened his eyes. Bertrand continued his obnoxious scratching. The boy glanced at the clock. Two-thirty. Bertrand wasn't the only one hungry.

After feeding the near-hysterical Bertrand, John-Peter eased open the bedroom door and noted the muffled sounds of the radio coming from Melissa's room. Good. His mother was the last person he wanted to see. He sneaked down to the main floor on bare feet so light they scarcely touched the stairs and returned shortly, bearing a platter of peanut butter sandwiches, a fresh water jug, and a left pocket full of vitamins. He ate while stretched full length out on the floor and teasing Bertrand with occasional bits. The mouse didn't care he was adopted. He probably never gave a backward glance to the field mouse that bore him. So why should John-Peter care that the professor and Melissa adopted him?

"Bertrand knows I adopted him," John-Peter said aloud as he tossed a fragment of sandwich across the floor. The eager mouse scampered after it. "I, on the other hand, am suffering greatly from their hoax."

Bertrand snagged the chunk with fully extended claws and greedily devoured it as exhaustion dragged John-Peter into the leafy top of a tall oak tree. Below, Ed Calkins sat and played a tin whistle. A cool breeze flitted across the boy's cheeks. A full golden moon cast its beams through the leaves. He stretched his toes and savored the blood still lingering in his mouth.

Click.

The beams grew leaner and larger until its sharp rays grazed the parsonage ceiling and thickly covered it with soot. The Victorian men, their suits heavy and soaked with dripping sweat, noticed only the Amish man sitting in the corner and reading aloud from the Bible.

"Then thou shalt kill of thy herd and of thy flock, which the Lord hath given thee, as I have commanded thee, and thou shalt eat in thy gates whatsoever thy soul lusteth," the Amish man read.

No surprise that John Simons was there, his back facing John-Peter.

"The unclean and the clean shall eat of them alike. Only be sure that thou eat not the blood."

John Simons turned malicious eyes toward John-Peter and again offered him the goblet of crimson.

"For the blood," John Simons said, "is the life."

A scream pierced the air. Cornell Dyer, face contorted with rage; his eyes madly glinting, hammered a stake deep into John Simotes' heart, splitting the chest in two. The professor's eyes wildly darted above a mouth stuffed with garlic. The stake disappeared into black hole; Cornell pulverized John's bones to powder. The pummeling grew louder and louder until John-Peter woke, wet hair fused to his face, body drenched with sweat, and blood pulsating through his ear with deafening thumping. Electric guitars rattled the glass in the bedroom windows. John-Peter smirked through the pain in his head as he pulled clean clothes from his dresser. Time to have some fun.

So elated was he, the boy nearly skipped from the bedroom to the stereo controls and silenced the so-called music. From downstairs, Kellen roared, "Turn that back on, you little scamp!"

John-Peter took three steps down and leaned over the banister. "Oh, Kellen! Guess what came in the mail the other day?"

Kellen's bedroom door banged against the wall as he sped into view. "Give me that credit card bill right now!"

Melissa rushed out of her room. Panic filled her face "John-Peter, what are you're doing?"

"Gosh, Kellen, I wish I could, but Mother intercepted it." John-Peter turned and leered at Melissa. "Isn't that right, Mother?"

Kellen's face burned purple with rage. "Melissa! Bring me that bill!"

John-Peter erupted into giggles the second he shut the bathroom door. The steaming shower felt good against his clammy body. He would have sold his soul to witness the ensuing conversation between his mother and Kellen. And he bet his mother would think twice before lying to him ever again.

That night, John-Peter was Sydney Carton from *Tale of Two Cities* and Curtis was Charles Darnay, rightly imprisoned for treason. Karla, as Lucy Manette, begged John-Peter to die in his place. John-Peter laughed at her.

The next morning as John-Peter was getting dressed, Karla, on cue, broke into his mind and said, "The mandrake arrived over the weekend."

"Have fun." John-Peter stuffed the leprechaun into his pocket.

"Can you come over today and help me carve it?"

John-Peter dropped a door. No mercy until she paid the price. As he predicted, whatever happened between Curtis and Lauren stayed between Curtis and Lauren. John-Peter doubted Lauren had anything over Curtis except the fact he went to her house. That alone would be enough to humiliate anyone. John-Peter almost sympathized with Curtis.

Indian Summer came and went; chilly November winds blew off Lake Munson, replacing the village's crisp autumn days with a foreshadowing of a brutal winter. Because John-Peter no longer spent his afternoons at Karla's house, he had the time to perfect three original piano compositions and teach Bertrand to chase a tiny rubber ball. Each night now, the princess waited for him inside his closet. Her eyes spoke of poignant loneliness and profound misery that John-Peter longed to relieve. He wished he could read her mind as he had once read Karla's, but he could only stand with fingertips pressed against the glass and return the stare, which he exulted in doing as long as she remained. Sometimes the princess stayed only for a few minutes; other times, her presence lingered for hours. Whether minutes or hours, she always faded from view far sooner than John-Peter wished.

Karla had stopped trying to contact him, which would have suited John-Peter just fine if he hadn't missed her so much.

Even Trenton wasn't much company these days. After the dance, Courtney had decided they should remain "just friends." Trenton was still moping behind his books and refusing to talk to anyone, especially John-Peter, for Courtney wouldn't leave John-Peter's side. She pestered him about the correct way to measure angles. She begged him to drill her history questions. She manipulated the seating to ensure they were lab partners.

Even Ed was no longer much fun. He shared only the legends John-Peter already knew and threw a fit whenever the boy rested his bare feet on the dashboard. On more than one occasion, Ed punished John-Peter for missed throws by refusing to take him to the pawn shop for Irish soda bread.

Kellen increased John-Peter's hours to work off a bill Kellen could well afford to pay. Day after day, John-Peter dusted the endless pieces of expensive furniture; vacuumed numerous rooms, stocked cases of *Dirges and Other Funeral Music,* and sold untold quantities of Kellen's new *Mourners for Hire* program.

"I'm worried about you," Melissa said one night, entering John-Peter's bedroom when he was nearly asleep, sitting very close, and flitting a soft hand across his forehead.

"Well, don't be." He covered his head with a pillow and turned toward the windows just as a series of colored lights appeared before his eyes.

Melissa sat there for a long time, and John-Peter stayed awake an even longer time. He refused to allow the luxury of slumber until he was confident she would not return to pester him. He could no longer trust her. Gradually the lights faded and so did his commitment to full alertness.

But the oak tree stretched high into the sky and through the clouds until its boughs grazed the moon. Here, John-Peter played the pipe music Ed Calkins had taught him. The captivating melodies enchanted the stars; they twinkled to its beat. Far below the tree, past the earth's crust and into the lower region of the underworld, the princess cried out in pain and fright. The boy immediately ceased playing and slid down miles of tree to save her, heedless of the bark lacerating his body. Just before reaching the bottom, John-Peter sat upright, shaking against the heated stinging in his limbs. He was still sitting cross-legged on the bathroom stool removing splinters when his mother, blinking against the morning light, stumbled into the bathroom.

"John-Peter, what happened?"

He wearily, but methodically, removed another splinter. She squatted beside him for a closer look. "How long have you been doing this?"

"All night."

"I'm calling the school. We're going to Thornton this morning."

It took four hours for Dr. Rothgard to remove every last splinter. Neither one spoke until only a few remained, and even then, it was Dr. Rothgard that broke the grim silence by saying, "Cat got your tongue?"

"Nope."

"Then spare a few details of your life."

"Nothing to tell."

"That so?"

John-Peter said nothing, only grimaced against a particularly vicious jab.

"How was homecoming?"

"Fine."

The doctor glanced at Melissa who had just returned to the room and then back at John-Peter. "How's Karla these days?"

"Fine." Why couldn't the silly old fool shut up?

"Your mother tells me you have a pet mouse. Bertrand?"

Aghast at yet another assault on his privacy John-Peter blurted out, "Mother, you spy!"

The doctor set down his tweezers and looked at John-Peter long and hard. "All right, let's talk."

But John-Peter was still glowering at Melissa, who shifted uncomfortably and frowned.

"He's upset because I never told him about the adoptions," Melissa said, averting her eyes.

Dr. Rothgard's annoyance turned to incredulity. "The what?"

"The adoptions," Melissa hastily replied, still looking down. "John-Peter knows how the Simotes family adopted his father and how John and I, in turn, adopted him."

What little color the doctor had drained from his face. "You didn't tell him!" Dr. Rothgard grabbed John-Peter's arm and gave it a rough shake. "Listen to me, boy. You're not human."

"Oh my God!" Melissa leaped from her chair and flew to the door.

"Your father was a vampire."

The door banged against the wall as Melissa cried out, *"Help! Now!"*

"Beware Kellen!"

Men in white jackets rushed into the room and restrained Dr. Rothgard. Melissa pulled John-Peter toward the door, but he dug his heels into the floor. A hypodermic needle sunk into Dr. Rothgard's arm.

"Guard your mouse," Dr. Rothgard mumbled as he closed his eyes.

CHAPTER 14: TIME OUT

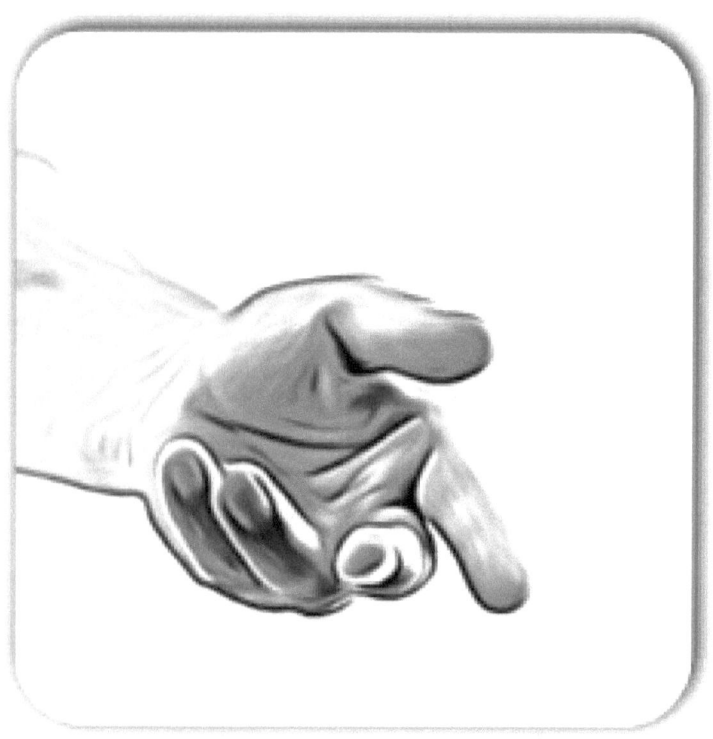

Neither John-Peter nor Melissa spoke until they neared the two-lane highway between Jenson and Munsonville.

You're not human.

"I'm sorry about today," Melissa said. "He's apparently more out there than I had realized."

Your father was a vampire.

"Forget it," John-Peter said, pondering the trees in full autumn bloom zipping past his window. Was Dr. Rothgard referring to the posthumous staking of his father or his stepfather's claims for being an ex-vampire. If only Karla hadn't gone off the deep end...

"It's not that important."

Beware Kellen.

"Well, it's important to me," Melissa said. "I..."

A ringing from the inside of his mother's purse interrupted the rest. "John-Peter, answer that, please."

He reached his hand inside her purse for the phone and flipped it open. "Hello?"

"Where's your mother?"

"Driving."

A pause. "Well, tell her I'm flying to New York tonight, but I still plan to make Thanksgiving dinner."

"Understood."

"Don't forget."

"I won't."

"Yeah, like you remembered to buy the mouse traps."

The line went dead. John-Peter shut the phone and dropped it back into the bag. "Kellen said..."

Guard your mouse.

"I heard." Melissa pressed her lips together and tightened her grip on the steering wheel.

Maybe his mother was right, although why would he trust a liar? Besides, why would Dr. Rothgard express concern for a field mouse?

You're not human.

Mabel was covering a frying pan as John-Peter walked through the back door.

"Just a quick, easy dinner," she said. "I can't see leaving food in the refrigerator when no one will be home to eat it."

He peeked under the lid. Mabel hadn't made tofu burgers in months. His mother would eat them, but Kellen would not. "Uh, Mabel..."

"Kellen already called. I know he's not coming home, so I didn't even bother making anything for him." Mabel turned on the water to rinse the mixing bowl. "How many franchises does he own now? Twenty? Thirty?"

The back door opened, and a blast of crisp air blew in.

"Brrr," Melissa said, rubbing her hands together. "I hope it's warmer in Grover's Park. Oh, by the way, catch!" She dug into her coat pocket and tossed a large bottle at John-Peter.

"Good," John-Peter said. "I took the last vitamin this morning."

He waited until after dinner to pack his suitcase, tucking the vitamin bottle between his T-shirts and contemplating last night's telephone conversation between his mother and Uncle Ed. The Steward had sounded miffed when Melissa informed him John-Peter would not be available for papers this weekend.

"Melissa, he needs to be on that route this weekend."

"This isn't his decision, Ed."

"It's extremely important for the boy to spend time with me on a regular basis."

"Ed, ever since John died, my son has spent each weekend, every holiday, and all summer with you. I don't think the two of you have gone seven consecutive days without seeing each other."

Your father was a vampire.

"Melissa, you don't understand..."

"Ed, he's going to Grover's Park."

At the "click," John-Peter quickly hung up the extension in his stepfather's bedroom, the one to his mother's private line she didn't know Kellen had. Ed should be thankful he didn't have to pay John-Peter for a four-day weekend. He'd have more money in his pocket for Atlantic City.

John-Peter woke before the alarm sounded, stretching forth one hand to deactivate the ringer and groping for the leprechaun with the other. He leaned over for the water jug and heard the muffled sound of his mother's voice followed by that of his grandfather. John-Peter wavered as drowsiness enveloped him then kicked back the covers. Better get up now before someone else made him do it.

Twenty minutes later, John-Peter was carrying his suitcase past Melissa's bedroom. The door was slightly ajar. Darlene was leaning against the dresser, drinking from a steaming mug while Melissa snapped close the suitcase on the bed. He felt Karla knock at a door.

"John-Peter, are you awake yet?"

"No." He trotted down the stairs.

"Do you still want me to watch Bertrand?"

Guard your mouse.

188

He set the suitcase and water jug by the staircase and ran back upstairs to his bedroom.

"Fine! Act all snooty. I won't keep your..."

Stupid Karla! "An hour, I guess."

John-Peter hadn't really expected to see the princess in the daylight, with or without an apple, but hoped he might just the same. Sunday night was more than half a week away.

Bertrand squeaked fretfully inside his box. Now that his secret was out, John-Peter saw no reason why he couldn't feed the mouse in the kitchen. He tucked the shoebox under his arm, reached for the feed, and once again sailed past his mother's room and down the stairs.

Steve sat at the kitchen table drinking decaffeinated coffee and reading a newspaper. He looked up when John-Peter entered the kitchen.

"Well, all ready for a little road trip?"

"Almost. Want to see my mouse?"

"Mouse?" Steve frowned as he set down his cup.

"Bertrand. I caught him in the attic. See?" John-Peter pulled off the lid and set Bertrand's home on the table.

Steve peered into the box and then raised his eyes. "Does your mother know you have him?"

Bertrand climbed up to the edge, and Steve slapped the cover on it. The mouse let loose a series of high-pitched squeaks.

"You hurt his paws!"

Steve roughly pushed the box to the center of the table. "Has he had any vaccinations?

"His insurance won't cover them."

"See here, young man..."

"He's never bitten me, Grandpa." John Peter lifted the lid and added a scoop of the oat and millet mixture.

"That's not the point. Mice carry all kinds of diseases. I can't believe your mother isn't concerned about it."

"Isn't concerned about what?" Melissa said as she walked into the kitchen with Darlene and her coffee mug following behind her.

"Do you think it's wise to allow your son to keep a field mouse for a pet?"

Melissa filled a mug with water and set it inside the microwave. "Let's just say the mouse is a recent discovery and leave it at that. Mom, do you want another cup of coffee?"

Darlene kissed the top of Steve's head. "Sure. John-Peter, can you carry the suitcases out to my car?"

"Ten-four."

"Melissa, he really should have some kind of shots."

"He will, Steve," Melissa said. "When we get..."

John-Peter slammed the screen door behind him. What difference did it make to Steve anyway if Bertrand had his shots or not? He sounded as paranoid as Kellen.

Beware Kellen.

John-Peter quickly loaded the car and returned to the kitchen. Two bags sat on the counter, one filled with peanut butter sandwiches and the other with apples.

"Well," Darlene said as she rinsed her cup and set it on the drying rack. "I think we're ready to leave."

"We have to stop by Karla's house." John-Peter seized Bertrand's box and his food and strutted to the car.

Karla was waiting outside the motor home when his grandmother pulled into the Millers' driveway. John-Peter had just cleared the doorway when Karla, right behind him, lifted the lid to peek at the mouse. "Aw, John-Peter, he's adorable."

"Mice are not adorable. Think Bubonic plague."

"They're still cute. What does he like to eat?"

The boy handed her Bertrand's feed bag.

Still cradling the box, Karla sat on the couch and removed the lid. Two paws, then a set of whiskers appeared at the edge. She stroked the mouse's nose with one finger. His grandmother's car horn sounded, but John-Peter didn't move.

"He doesn't have his shots," John-Peter said.

"I don't care. You wouldn't hurt me, would you, Bertrand?"

John-Peter shoved his hands into his pockets. His fingers closed around the leprechaun and held it fast. He had to know.

"I hope you and your mother have a nice Thanksgiving at your grandparents' house. Are all your cousins coming?"

"Mom said I didn't have to go this year, so I could have dinner with Curtis and his family. John-Peter, do you think Bertrand likes turkey?"

Another blare from the horn, this one longer and louder.

"What?" The boy felt his heart race.

"Turkey. You know, the stuff most people eat on Thanksgiving."

"How should I know if Bertrand likes turkey?"

Karla put the lid back onto the box. "Well, I wouldn't want Bertrand smelling all that yummy food and not get any."

"You're taking my mouse to the Chandlers?"

"Did you think I'd leave him here where my mother might find him? Oh, hi, Mrs. Wechsler."

"Karla, I hate to be rude," Melissa said, but she was glaring at John-Peter, "but my son really needs to cut this short."

John-Peter instantly pictured Bertrand scampering across the Chandlers lace tablecloth or hanging from an antique chandelier. "He loves turkey. Gotta go."

Steve was already dozing in the back seat, but his eyes fluttered open when John-Peter clicked his seat belt.

"That's a mighty bright suit coat," Steve said. "Where'd you buy it?"

"Pawn shop in Jenson."

"Oh," Steve said, his voice drifting away. A light snore escaped his lips.

John-Peter unwrapped his first sandwich. Main Street faded into the back roads that led to the highway. His mother had already begun correcting papers.

You're not human. Your father was a vampire.

He shook his head to clear his thoughts and immediately rewarded with rows of bright lights. He waited; they vanished; and then he fished inside his backpack for *Tale of Two Cities,* not to read but to study. Melissa had scheduled a quiz for Monday. He drank half a gallon of water and immersed himself into the story of the French Revolution and Sydney Carton's sacrificial offering of himself to save the woman he loved.

Steve stirred in his sleep and slid further into the seat. John-Peter unwrapped his last sandwich and finished the gallon. For a brief, weak moment, he wished Karla was still tapping into his mind, but she had apparently shut out all his thoughts. Maybe he should let her read Grandma Marchellis' diary. Karla could use the distraction.

"Anyone need to stop?" Darlene called over her shoulder as John-Peter finally put away the book.

Steve stirred and stretched slightly. John-Peter strained to see the clock on the dash. Three more hours and they would be in Grover's Park.

"That's probably a good idea, Mom," Melissa said without enthusiasm.

"May I have a dollar?" John-Peter asked.

Melissa did not look back at him. "For what?"

"Water."

John-Peter took his time inside the gas station, deliberating over the different brands and prices and enjoying the respite from the cramped car. A wall had grown up between him and the people he once considered family and that suffocated him more than the vehicle's tight space.

Everyone was waiting for him in the car when he finally returned, and John-Peter wondered who would chastise him first. His mother and grandmother had switched positions during his absence. Darlene merely gazed out the window. Melissa turned the ignition key. Steve leaned his head back on the seat and watched him with a queer expression on his face as the boy fastened his seat belt and uncapped the bottle.

"John-Peter, about Bertrand..."

"No."

Steve began again. "The Old Testament says mice are unclean animals."

"Grandpa, don't start."

"There was a practical reason for it. Mice and rats carry many germs that are harmful to humans."

Melissa piped up. "Steve, I already told you I'd have Dr. Samuelson check him out next week."

John-Peter turned accusing eyes at his grandfather and waited for his reaction. But Steve was looking at Melissa and hadn't noticed it. "Melissa, I'm talking to John-Peter, not you."

"Just stop badgering him, okay?"

"I'm trying to make a point. God made those rules so humans could live long in the land He would give them. John-Peter, the mouse doesn't have to bite you to hurt you."

"I know about hantaviruses, Grandpa. 'I heard every living creature in heaven and on earth and under the earth and in the sea, and all therein, saying, 'To him who sits upon the throne and to the Lamb be blessing and honor and glory and power for ever and ever! Amen!'"

Steve's mouth dropped.

"That's Revelation 5:15, Grandpa. It says 'every living creature.' Maybe God likes mice. Maybe Moses got it wrong. Do you think God shut the door on the ark when the mice got close? Don't be so narrow-minded; I read, too."

John-Peter dug his heels into his seat, hunched his knees to his chin, and stared out the window. He wished Steve never had a heart attack. He didn't like how preachy his grandfather had become.

It was mid-afternoon when Melissa pulled into Brian's driveway. She and Darlene both looked exhausted.

"You two go ahead," Steve said. "I want to talk with John-Peter a minute."

John-Peter watched his mother and grandmother exchange looks, but neither one commented. They simply left the car. Steve watched them go and then turned to John-Peter.

"I forgive you," Steve said.

"Great, Grandpa. Can we go inside now?"

"Not yet. I want to clarify something. I'm new at being a Christian. Perhaps I come off a little strong at times, but that's only because I'm excited about living my life with God in it, even if I am late in getting there."

John-Peter's face grew hot. This was not the conversation he had expected. "Grandpa, you don't have to explain yourself."

"You're right, but I don't want you thinking I'm cramming my beliefs down your throat."

"Grandpa..."

"You have to find your own way to God."

"Grandpa..."

"But I want you to know that He exists, that He loves you—more than your family or friends ever could—and that He died to heal your broken humanity and to repair the damage sin did to you."

"Grandpa..."

"God's laws are there to help us, not frustrate us. If we're frustrated, maybe we're not doing things the way God wants us to do them."

"I got it, Grandpa. Now can we go insi..?"

"You know, John-Peter, if I had become a Christian when I was well, I'm not so certain you would have noticed it. It's not really my faith you resent. It's my illness. We can't have the same kinds of fun anymore. I can't clean with you. I can't do yard work with you. I can't throw a football with you. Heck, I can't even drive myself around the block. You're not the only one who misses those times. I miss them, too. Brian especially misses them. I can't help it."

"Grandpa."

"But I hope and pray our relationship is still important to you. I know it is to me." Steve held out his hands and examined his fingernails. "Now, that the things I can't do are on the table, let's talk about how I do try to bless my family."

"Grandpa."

Steve looked John-Peter in the eye. "I pray."

John-Peter shifted his weight and gazed around the car. He studied the numbers on the clock, the radio knobs, and the passenger-side visor that hung halfway down. Had anyone ever found the missing glove box key?

"I pray for your salvation. I pray you will grow in wisdom and understanding. I pray for your protection from all evil influences. I pray for your future and that God will be in it."

The boy said nothing. He did not know what to say.

"Did you know that I admire you, John-Peter? The Bible says—yes, I'm quoting the Bible again—that you should not be conformed to this world, that you should be transformed by the renewing of your mind. I admire you because you do not conform to the world. You do what you think is right for you, and I respect you for that."

"Grandpa."

"And you are always renewing your mind. You're the smartest person I know and that's a fact."

"Grandpa."

"I hope you can put aside anything negative between us and enjoy the next few days. It's wonderful we can come together and be a family and give thanks to God for His blessings to us. Who knows if we'll have this same opportunity next year?"

"Can we go inside now?"

Like any of what Steve said could matter. He wasn't his real grandfather.

"Sure." Steve opened the door and eased his legs to the ground.

Fawn jumped up and down behind the screen door when she saw Steve and John-Peter walk up the front steps. "They're here! They're here! They're here!"

A hand shoved her aside. Ellie pushed open the screen door. Fawn ran wailing up the staircase for Cindy. Ellie smiled brightly and threw her arms around Steve's waist with an enthusiastic, "Hi, Grandpa!"

"Hello to you, too," Steve said and patted her head.

Deanna sidled up to John-Peter and tugged his hand up and down. "I've got a surprise."

"Hold on, Deanna. I've got to bring the suitcases."

"I'll help you. I'm really strong."

"If you wish."

Deanna skipped after John-Peter. "You're going to be really proud of me."

"That so?" John-Peter set two suitcases on the driveway and reached inside the trunk for the ones belonging to his grandparents.

Deanna dragged Melissa's suitcase toward the front door. "What does she have in this thing?"

"Homework." He picked up his suitcase and then took his mother's. Deanna sped ahead and opened the door. "Hurry up, John-Peter!"

"One more trip."

Aunt Cindy was walking downstairs holding Fawn's hand when John-Peter returned with the remaining suitcases. "John-Peter, would you carry them upstairs? Both guest rooms are on the left. You don't mind staying in the family room, do you? The couch pulls out."

"I'm easy."

Deanna was at his heels all the way to the second floor. "Don't forget, John-Peter."

"I won't."

John-Peter set his grandparents' suitcases in the first guest room. Deanna leaped on the bed. "Do you like the bedspread? I picked it out."

"Sure, if you're into wildflowers."

"I am. Look how pretty the cornflowers are."

After John-Peter brought his mother's suitcase to her room, Deanna flew past him to the main floor. "Can I show you now?"

"I'm all yours."

He followed her lead to the rear of the house. At the far wall of the family room sat a small, upright piano.

"Some guy died, and we got his piano and a whole bunch of sheet music," Deanna said excitedly. "I'm taking lessons. Want to hear me play?"

"Deny me no longer."

With exaggerated poise, Deanna assumed her position at the piano and raised the lid. She dangled her fingers above the keys, thinking, then launched into a version of three blind mice that required only single notes and one, well-practiced chord.

She played without blemish until the very last note, which she hastily corrected. She bit her lip and looked up at John-Peter who answered with an encouraging smile and a question: "Can you play another?"

"Yes! I know five more songs."

"Can you play them alphabetically?"

Aunt Cindy walked into the room. "John-Peter, will you cut some apples for me?"

Deanna dropped the piano lid with a bang and slid off the bench. "I want to help!"

They spent the next hour seated around the kitchen table. John-Peter peeled and cored, while Deanna carefully sliced. Ellie then dunked the wedges into a bowl of lemon juice and coated them with the spicy sugar-flour mixture. Fawn carefully layered the pieces into the pie crust and occasionally licked her fingers.

Deanna caught her and groaned. "You're gross! Go wash your hands."

Fawn began to cry, and John-Peter pinched her arm. Aghast, the little girl immediately stopped wailing.

"Hurry up, and wash your hands. We'll wait for you."

He tossed the core into the garbage can, polished an apple on his green T-shirt, and devoured its flesh in three bites. Ellie watched him, with interest.

"How come you like apples so much, John-Peter?"

He reached for another. "Hoping for a magic one."

Deanna lifted her chin in disdain and shook her head. "There's no such thing as magic, and you know it."

Fawn ran back into the room, waving her dripping hands. John-Peter handed her a napkin, tossed the cores into the garbage, and began working on another apple.

"Surely you've heard what happened to Connla the Fair. Ellie, watch your nose."

Ellie moved her face away from the apple. "What 'fair?'"

"'Fair' means he had a light complexion and was very handsome. He was the son of Conn, the Hundred-Fighter."

"He's making it up," Deanna said.

Ellie stuck her tongue out at Deanna. "Well, I want to hear John-Peter's story."

John-Peter handed Deanna the peeled apple.

"One day, when Connla the Fair was sitting with his father on the Hill of Uisneach."

"A pretend place," Deanna scooped the slices into her hands and set them before Ellie.

"Tell that to the ancient Druids. They considered it to be the very center of Ireland, the ancient seat of the Kings of Meath."

"What's a doo-rid?" Ellie said.

"A very wise man."

"I still think you're making it up," Deanna said.

"There is a huge limestone there that resembles a cat watching a mouse. Someday, I'll show you the picture."

Fawn looked at John-Peter with large, round eyes. "Tell the story, John-Peter."

John-Peter watched as Fawn laid the slices onto the pie crust. She began to pop her fingers into her mouth, looked at Deanna, and grabbed a napkin instead.

"While Connla the Fair was sitting with his father and his father's druid, a beautiful woman appeared and said, "I belong to a race of people called the Sidhe…'"

"What's shee?"

"Fairies, Ellie."

"Oh." She stuck her face close to the paring knife.

"Ellie!"

"Sorry." She edged away.

"The woman said to Connla, 'We dwell in a land of peace where death does not exist. Connla, if you follow me, you will always remain young and fair.'"

Ellie scooted closer to John-Peter as he cored another apple, and he nudged her away with his elbow.

"Now Conn could not hear the woman's voice, but the druid did. He noticed how she bewitched Connla so he uttered magical words, yes, Deanna, real magical words, against the power of her voice. She vanished, but not before tossing an apple to Connla."

"Where'd she get the apple?" Fawn asked.

"Be quiet, Fawn," Deanna said, curiosity overtaking her superiority, as she sliced the apple.

John-Peter set down his knife, smiled, and continued.

"For the next month, Connla refused all nourishment except the woman's apple, yet the apple never diminished in size or in its ability to satisfy him. At the end of the month, the woman returned in a crystal boat and once again extended her invitation for him. Although Connla loved his people, he loved the enchanting woman more.

"Did he go with her?" An apple slice slipped from Ellie's hand and splashed lemon juice onto the table.

"He did," John-Peter said and bit into the last apple. "No one ever saw him again."

"Well, these apples didn't come from a beautiful woman," Deanna said, eyeing Fawn as she set the final slices onto the crust. "They came from the grocery store."

"They did so come from a beautiful woman!" Ellie said, wiping away the lemon juice with the sleeve of her pale blue sweater. "Mom bought them, and she's beautiful. Right, Mom?"

Aunt Cindy set the rolling pin on the counter and brought a piece of dough to the table. She laid it over the bottom crust and pinched the edges together. "That's a lovely story, John-Peter. Did you learn that one from your Uncle Ed, too?"

"Mais, oui."

"I want another story," Fawn said.

Brian walked through the back door carrying a stack of boxes. "John-Peter, give me a hand with these pizzas. The top one is yours."

"Why does John-Peter get something special?" Ellie said, pouting.

Deanna carried a pie to the stove. "Because he doesn't like regular food. He won't even eat turkey tomorrow."

John-Peter squeezed Ellie's shoulder. "That leaves more for you, honey."

After dinner, Steve consulted the newspaper for a nearby church that offered a Thanksgiving Day service and asked Darlene to drive him. Cindy insisted she needed both Melissa and Darlene's help in the kitchen and suggested Brian do the driving and take all three girls with him. Of course, Brian assumed John-Peter would rather go with him and Steve than cook with the women. In reality, John-Peter hoped for a couple hours on the piano, but after locking eyes with his mother, realized he hadn't a voice in the decision.

For a day that celebrated the joys of feasting on animals, a surprising amount of people crowded Living Water Worship Center. A woman wearing a bulky fur coat and heavy make-up scooted closer to the elderly man on her left in a futile attempt to make room for them.

"Go ahead," Brian whispered to Steve. "I'll take Ellie and Fawn and look for another seat."

Deanna resisted John-Peter's nudges to get into the pew first, but since he refused to cozy up to the giant raccoon, he grabbed Deanna's arm, pushed her into the seat, and quickly slid beside her. Steve squeezed next to him and blocked further movement.

"That was a dirty trick," Deanna mumbled.

John-Peter grinned open-mouthed at her and then said, "Shh. The music is starting."

An off-key guitar band opened the service. John-Peter gazed about the bare white walls and tried to ignore the grating twangs. Steve closed his eyes, smiled, and tapped his foot. Deanna squirmed restlessly and jabbed her elbow into his ribs.

"Sit still," John-Peter hissed.

"Make me," she hissed right back.

At the song's completion, everyone clapped, and the guitarists immediately began another. Deanna yawned loudly, and John-Peter slid his finger in her mouth. She slapped his hand and whispered angrily, "You messed it up."

"Cut it out, Deanna."

"You're not my boss." She yawned again, this time wider and louder.

Finally, the pastor assumed the podium. For the next forty-five minutes, the man recounted every food-related story in the Bible, beginning with The Garden of Eden and continuing through Peter's vision of the unclean animals. Deanna's eyes drooped. John-Peter stifled his own yawn and accidentally bit his tongue.

"But all the food in the world will never satisfy our hunger for God, who made everything that sustains us." The pastor raised his hands. "Let us all stand and sing our thanks to God."

The nauseating smell of dead fowl assaulted John-Peter's stomach the moment Ellie opened the front door. Even the garlic from the mashed potatoes couldn't mask it. Cindy walked from the kitchen and noticed his discomfort.

"Whew, it's hot in here." She wiped the back of her hand across her forehead. "Brian, can you open the window by the sink? It's stuck."

"Cindy," Darlene called out. "I can't tell if that lentil loaf is done."

Brian kissed Cindy on the cheek and started up the stairs.

"How was church?" Aunt Cindy asked.

"Packed. But the girls behaved themselves."

After they had all gathered around the table and Steve had begun the blessing, the front door blew open.

"Sorry I'm late," a red-faced Kellen said as Cindy rushed from the table to take his coat. "My flight was delayed."

Brian said, "Ellie, let Uncle Kellen sit by Aunt Melissa."

"I wondered what happened." Melissa looked up as Kellen assumed the vacated seat and unfolded his napkin.

"Arthur was supposed to call," Kellen said, huffing between words.

"He did call when you were taking a shower," Darlene passed the platter of turkey to Kellen. "I forgot to mention it."

John-Peter carefully observed Kellen's pouring of gravy over everything on his plate. Kellen stopped in mid-stream and stared back. "Is there a problem?"

"Your face is bloated and blotchy."

Kellen puffed the air from his cheeks as he set down the gravy boat. His hands were ruddy and swollen; the veins were engorged "It's a little warm in here, that's all."

Brian opened another window. Kellen picked up his fork. Steve cleared his throat. Melissa nudged Kellen. He raised blood-shot eyes as red as his lapel rose, noticed Steve's folded hands, and laid the fork against the plate.

Steve bowed his head. "Heavenly Father, we give you thanks and praise for bringing us here today to celebrate your bountiful goodness."

John-Peter studied the lentil loaf Aunt Cindy had sliced. A little dry, but not bad for a first attempt.

"And we thank you for providing us with family, people we can love and who love us. We ask you to continue blessing us in the coming year so we can once again join together to give thanks. Amen." Steve reached for the cranberry sauce. "How's that? The food didn't even have time to get cold."

The phone rang.

"You sit," Brian said to Cindy. "I'll get it."

"There's pineapple in the sweet potatoes, Grandpa," Deanna said.

"Well, it's a good thing I like pineapple."

"I helped make them yesterday, before you guys got here."

"Then I'll have to take an extra helping."

John-Peter gestured his fork at Ellie's plate. "You haven't touched your Brussels sprouts."

"Brussels sprouts are pukey."

Brian reappeared, looking grim. "Melissa, it's for you."

"We'll wait to go around the table," Darlene said.

John-Peter had hoped this year they might skip the "I'm thankful for..." ritual his grandmother always insisted they perform. Be thankful for what? His best friend was in love with a marionette; he was related to no one in his deceitful family; and his doctor just told him he wasn't even human.

"More turkey, Kellen?" Brian said.

Melissa sat back down, biting her lip to keep from crying.

"It's Carol," she said, picking up her napkin and placing it on her lap. "They're not sure what happened. The aid who brought her dinner tray found her unconscious so they called an ambulance."

"Thanks, Brian," Kellen said, taking three large slices and then checking his watch. "Do you want to fly back with me tonight, Melissa?"

She shuddered and rested her head in her hands. "I don't know what to do."

Darlene interrupted. "I'll be fine driving alone. I'll have Steve and John-Peter to keep me company."

"Grandpa," Ellie said. "We have two kinds of pie tonight: pumpkin and apple."

"Make up your mind, Melissa," Kellen said. "I haven't got all night."

"Maybe I should go," Melissa said. "I'll go call the hospital and tell them I'll be there tonight."

Steve pushed away his plate and patted Ellie's hand. "Your grandmother won't let me eat two pieces."

"You probably shouldn't have one," Darlene said.

"John-Peter helped us make the apple ones."

The girls grew whiny after Melissa and Kellen left. Cindy asked Brian if he could ready his daughters for bed while she and Darlene cleaned up the kitchen. Fawn clung to John-Peter's waist and cried, "I want John-Peter!"

Cindy transferred the leftover turkey to a plastic container while Darlene began rinsing the plates and stacking them in the dishwasher.

"Fawn," Aunt Cindy said, "John-Peter is not going to..."

"I don't mind," the boy quickly said.

Fawn dug her fingers into his waist. "Hurray!"

Cindy turned around, looking doubtful. "Are you sure? They can be a handful at bedtime."

"We'll be good," Ellie said.

"For a story," Deanna added with a smirk.

"If you guys are in bed in fifteen minutes, I shall tell about the king with the silver hand."

The girls raced each other up the stairs with John-Peter close behind them. Deanna reached the bathroom first and slammed the door, narrowly missing Ellie's fingers. Ellie beat on the door with her firsts, and Fawn joined her.

"No fair! Open up!"

Fawn's lips puckered as she tried not to cry. "I need to brush my teeth."

John-Peter grabbed Fawn's hand, pulled her into the bedroom, and briefly noted the lavender painted walls. "Where are your pajamas? You can beat Deanna getting dressed."

"I can get them, John-Peter." Ellie pulled out the bottom dresser drawer and stood on it to reach the top one. She tossed a white nightgown on the floor. Fawn sat on the floor and cried, "I want the pink one!"

"I'm done!" Deanna announced as she rushed into the room. "John-Peter, you get out while I'm getting dressed."

"Ellie, get Fawn the pink nightgown. Come on, Fawn, let's brush your teeth."

Fawn scrambled to her feet and skipped into the bathroom.

"She can brush her own teeth if you put the toothpaste on for her," Ellie said, kicking off her buckled shoes.

Deanna pushed John-Peter toward the door. "Out!"

Ten minutes later, John-Peter was sitting on the double bed Ellie and Fawn shared and leaning against the wall with all three girls snuggling next to and looking up at him; the soft light from the ballerina night light illuminating their scrubbed and excited faces. He recounted how Nuada the King had lost his right hand in the battle, which forced the Tuatha De Dananns to choose a new leader.

"Why, John-Peter?" Ellie asked.

"Because no king could rule with a physical blemish or infirmity."

The new king, Bres, was handsome and forceful, but lacked Nuada's charismatic personality. He grew meaner and meaner until the people begged Nuada to rule them once again.

"Now the doctor for the Tuatha De Dananns had kept Nuada's hand in a jar with a special solution to preserve it," John-Peter said. "With a combination of the old hand and silver, with surgery and with magic, the doctor fashioned a new hand for Nuada. Now the people could throw off the tyranny of Bres and crown Nuada as their rightful king. And thus he became known as 'Nuada of the Silver Hand.'"

His left arm was numb where Fawn had fallen asleep against it. Ellie moved so John-Peter could lay Fawn's head against the pillow. She snuggled next to her sister, and he covered the two of them with the blanket. Deanna moved to her bed.

"Tuck me in, too, John-Peter," Deanna whispered.

Ellie grabbed John-Peter's face between her two hands and brought him down for a kiss. "Someday, a princess will bring you a magic apple," she said, her voice fading away into sleep.

John-Peter's heart caught in his throat.

"You mean 'fairy.'" Deanna corrected.

John-Peter tucked the bedclothes around Deanna. She sighed happily and dove deeper into her pillow. He straightened and turned to leave the room.

"John-Peter?"

"Hmm?"

"Can fairy tales come true?"

"Why?"

"Because I want...."

Deanna's voice caught; she said no more. John-Peter thought of the princes in his bedroom and understood. The light from a passing car shone through the windows. He saw the ruffled curtains, the Teddy-bear lamp on Ellie's dresser, and the row of dolls inhabiting the window seat. For a fleeting moment, John-Peter envied Brian and all that was his: a pretty wife who loved him, children who adored him, a comfortable home, and a job he relished. He couldn't wait until the princess was truly his.

"Yes," John-Peter said as he opened the door. "They come true."

At breakfast the next morning, Brian decided to take John-Peter with him to clean an office building. Another opportunity at the piano, gone. Brian noticed the boy's downcast face.

"If we get out of here in the next half hour," Brian promised, "we can be done by noon."

Deanna nudged Ellie. "Good. We can practice for our concert."

"What concert?" Cindy said as she poured a bowl of cereal for Fawn.

"The one tonight after dinner," Ellie said. "John-Peter, you're playing too, right?"

"John-Peter doesn't need to rehearse," Deanna said, stirring the pumpkin-shaped bits in her milk. "He's naturally good."

Brian stood up. "I'm going to check the van to make sure I've got everything. I'll meet you outside."

"I'll help you," Steve said, rising.

John-Peter moved back his chair. "I left something upstairs. Be right back."

"I want to play music, too," Fawn whined around a mouthful of cereal.

"Yuck!" Ellie shouted. "Close your mouth when you chew!"

With everyone occupied, John-Peter decided to take a chance. He dashed to the second floor and into the guest room his mother had abandoned.

"Golden Years Retirement & Nursing Home," the voice on the other end of the receiver said.

"Dr. Rothgard's room, please."

"Password?"

"I'm sorry?"

The voice grew impatient. "What is his password?"

"I never needed a password to speak with him."

"Well, it looks like you need one now."

Only the fear of being discovered prevented John-Peter from slamming down the phone. A password! How sneaky could his mother get?

He sulked during the entire trip across town with Brian and answered in monosyllables whenever his uncle spoke to him while they cleaned. Brian lost patience with him by the third bathroom.

"Okay, what gives?"

John-Peter dragged the cart to the row of sinks, and, still scowling, began swabbing them.

"Hey, I'm talking to you." Brian flushed a urinal and moved to the next one. "You've had a chip on your shoulder all morning."

"You're dismissed."

Brian threw the swab on the floor, seized John-Peter's shirt, and pushed his nephew up against the wall. "That does it. Now you tell me what your problem is or I'll..."

John-Peter's eyes were slits. "Or what?"

"Quit acting like you're better than everyone else in your family!"

John-Peter shoved his uncle away. "Keep your unrelated body parts off mine!"

"We're the best family you're ever going to have, and don't you forget it!"

"Forgotten."

John-Peter retrieved his swab and returned to work.

"John-Peter," Brian said, and the concern in his voice now sounded genuine. "What happened?"

The boy said nothing as he moved to the next sink.

"Is this about finding out you're adopted?"

Silence.

"You're preaching to the choir."

John-Peter pointed his dripping swab at Brian. "*You* grew up with your father."

"And you call that a blessing, getting to watch my dad die, piece by painful piece?"

John-Peter tossed the swab into the cart and reached for the glass cleaner.

"Do you know what it's like having a father who is always sick, unable to see or walk, just sitting at home in that dang wheelchair? On the other side of our rec room in our basement, past the washer and drier, was his home dialysis unit where Mom hooked him up three times a week, in between raising us and working her butt off. Then one morning I woke up, and I didn't have a dad anymore."

John-Peter unrolled more paper towel.

"I supposed you think Steve had a lot of gall trying to take the place of my dad. After all, what could some backwoods, single guy offer me? Not much, right? And yet, he cooked so Mom didn't have to do it and helped me with my homework so Mom didn't have to do it. When she moved back to Grover's Park, he left his world behind him and moved with us. He started a business to support the entire family and trained me to work alongside him. Occasionally, he played a board game with us, or we watched TV. That's it. So if taking the girls and spending an hour in church with him makes him happy, so what?"

John-Peter sprayed another mirror. "You didn't even like my so-called father. Admit it."

"You're right. I didn't like him. But I can't fault him as a father. He loved you, John-Peter, and that's the truth. You were his world. Anyone with half a brain could see it. And now you have Kellen who hustles his ass off to give you a good life. That's more than most fellows get in two lifetimes."

John-Peter tossed the glass cleaner back into the cart. "You don't like Kellen either."

"I don't dislike him. For some reason I can't understand, my sister is attracted to strange men, and I guess that's her prerogative. But Kellen is a hard worker. I don't think I've ever not seen him work. The difference is that Kellen likes fancy gimmicks, and I prefer to simply do a good job and treat people like I want to be treated."

More silence.

"Like Steve does," Brian added.

"Whatever."

Brian picked up his swab. "Look, I'll finish the stools if you'll empty that bucket of water that's in the hall. Then let's call it a day, okay?" Suddenly drained of all energy, John-Peter dragged the oversized bucket to the utility closet. As he lifted it, the boy screamed and dropped it. The water flowed down the hall and into the bathroom.

"John-Peter!"

Brian raced and skidded on water to where John-Peter leaned against the sink, clutching his right arm.

"What happened?"

"Don't...know."

"Let me see."

Brian's face turned grey when he saw the angry swelling in John-Peter's arm.

"Holy smoke you hurt it good! I'm getting ice."

After hastily mopping up the water, Brian headed for the emergency room, where he and John-Peter spent the bulk of the afternoon. Once back at the house, his grandmother insisted on settling him on the sofa bed and keeping his water jug full. Aunt Cindy surprised him with another lentil loaf. Even the little girls were subdued.

"You don't have to play tonight," Ellie said between mouthfuls of her dinner, which she insisted on eating right next to John-Peter "so he wouldn't be lonely."

"Fair lady's kindness is appreciated." The pain in his arm made his stomach hurt, despite the prescription from the hospital.

Deanna brought John-Peter the last slice of apple pie. "But you still want to hear us play, right?"

"Right."

Deanna's piano-playing dominated the brief, after-dinner concert. For every two nursery rhymes she played, Ellie hummed made-up songs on her kazoo while Fawn clanged away on her xylophone. But everyone politely clapped anyway.

"Maybe you can play for us tomorrow night, John-Peter," Ellie said. "If your hand feels better."

"But make them fun songs," Deanna added. "Not that classical stuff."

John-Peter smiled despite the throbbing inside his arm. "That 'classical stuff' is the product of genius minds."

208

Fawn looked anxious. "But I like 'Pop Goes the Weasel!'"

The next day, Cindy ran errands with the girls; Steve watched a television evangelist with Brian; and John-Peter settled into the sofa bed with several volumes of Brian's encyclopedia collection and the last three apples in the house beside him. They returned at lunchtime, and the girls' happily chattered about their morning.

"Grandpa, my boots are prettier than Fawn's. They have white fur."

"Daddy, feel how soft my mittens are."

"My new snowsuit is pink!"

The little girls burst into the family room.

"John-Peter, can we show you…" Ellie began.

His grandmother rushed in and ushered them from the room. "John-Peter's busy resting right now."

"But…" Fawn said.

"Out. Now."

Deanna poked her head around the corner. "John-Peter, is your hand well enough to play tonight?"

Darlene scooted her back out. "I doubt it."

"Yes!" John-Peter rebelliously called from the couch.

During that second after-dinner concert, Deanna glued herself to John-Peter while he, left-handed, played unfamiliar ragtime music, to which she appreciably bounced.

"John-Peter can play anything." Deanna's face shone with unusual pride at her cousin's accomplishments. The phone rang, and Brian left to answer it. Fawn ran from the room.

Ellie clapped her hands. "You're not done yet, are you?"

"I think he's had enough for one night," Darlene said.

"Oh, please, just one more!"

Brian returned and bent over Cindy. "That was old Mrs. Ostrem from next door. Her toilet's stopped up. I'll be back soon."

Steve slowly and stiffly rose. "I'll go with you."

Ellie's mouth turned down at the corners. "You'll miss the concert!"

Steve patted her head. "You can tell us all about it when we come back."

Fawn bumped into Brian and Steve as she ran back into the room and handed her prize to John-Peter.

"Can you play this?" Fawn breathlessly asked.

The boy took the tin whistle from her and turned it over in his hand. "Whose is it?"

"It's Fawn's," Cindy said, settling into the recliner with a cup of clove-scented tea. "She bought it at rummage sale."

"I can blow it," As proof, Fawn snatched it back and gave a long, loud blast. Deanna and Ellie covered their ears. Even Cindy winced.

"That's not music," Deanna said.

"That's only because Fawn has not yet learned to play it." The boy held out his left hand. "May I?"

Fawn set the whistle on his hand. John-Peter wavered, and, then, with both hands, began playing, hesitatingly at first, and growing more confident with each note he blew. The music floated around his head and lifted him far into the oak tree where he rested among the branches and played. The simple tune enveloped him; contentment flowed freely. He leaned farther into the leaves, curled his toes around the branch for support, and sent the music up. The moon bade goodnight; the stars blew good-bye kisses; and the first pink rays of the sun became his next audience, but still John-Peter blew each enthralling note. The sun bowed its appreciation; the birds suspended their flight to listen. The trees surrounding him dipped and swayed with the rhythm.

"John-Peter," a choked voice said.

The boy abruptly stopped playing. Deanna brushed her hand across her eyes and laid her wet palm across the injured arm. She was crying, but so was everyone else in the room.

"I believe in your magic," she whispered.

CHAPTER 15: MOUSE IN THE HOUSE

They were almost to Munsonville when Karla called.

"Hey, John-Peter, may I keep Bertrand one more night?"

"I don't care," the boy said, looking sideways at his grandfather. "Any particular reason?"

Steve had fallen asleep soon after they had left Illinois and hadn't stirred once, not even when they stopped. His grandmother had switched between pop radio stations and talk radio all the way home.

"Just lonesome. I broke up with Curtis this weekend."

He should have rejoiced at the news, but he didn't and wasn't sure why.

"Tribulation in paradise?"

"He got really mad about Bertrand."

"Curtis doesn't like mice?"

"He doesn't like you, so he didn't like me mouse-sitting. He told me I had to choose: our friendship or him."

"You can't have a best friend and a boyfriend?"

"He didn't see it that way."

"What a drip."

"Anyhow, thanks for letting me keep Bertrand. I'll see you in school tomorrow."

She dropped a door before he could answer. Well, she'd soon find out. He wished he could sleep like his grandfather, but his throbbing arm had other plans.

Darlene's soft voice broke through his thoughts. "John-Peter, would you please wake up your grandfather for me?"

John-Peter nudged Steve's shoulder. "Hey, Grandpa."

Steve grunted in his sleep, and his chin bumped his chest. John-Peter shook his arm back and forth. "Come on, Grandpa, wake up. We're almost home."

His eyes fluttered for a few seconds and closed again. John-Peter pushed hard on his shoulder. "Grandpa! We're home."

Steve snorted and weakly opened his eyes. He looked confused and then gave John-Peter a weak smile. "Sorry I wasn't much company." He now seemed coherent. "How's that arm of yours?"

"Fine."

Pain followed John-Peter right into his dreams where he ruled as Nuada until he enemies severed his right hand in battle. The ache in his stump traveled up his arm, but at least his hand was safe, preserved in a jar of blood next to Dr. Rothgard's bed at the Golden Years Retirement & Nursing Home.

The new king, Kellen, was handsome and forceful, but lacked John-Peter's charismatic personality. He grew meaner and meaner until the people begged for John-Peter to rule them once again.

"What shall I do?" John-Peter said as Dr. Rothgard picked splinters from his left hand.

"Stop sliding down oak trees."

John-Peter scowled and said nothing. He didn't know the password.

"My boy, why be at odds with your king?"

"Ow!"

"Give me your right hand."

"I don't have my right hand, you dimwitted quack!"

Dr. Rothgard set down the tweezers. "If a man can't face himself in the mirror, he must right the wrong."

"Replace my hand!"

The boy woke covered in sweat. Melissa sat next to him, holding a glass of water. He pulled the quilt over his head. "The pills aren't working."

Melissa retracted the quilt. "It might be worse if you stop taking them."

John-Peter started to object, let it go, and then sat up to accept the pain medicine. He didn't have the stamina to argue with her.

"How did you hurt arm?" Melissa asked, handing him the water.

John-Peter swallowed and then answered, "Don't know. Curiosity satisfied?"

"John-Peter, it's called concern."

"Then ask Uncle Brian. He's got all the answers."

She smoothed the damp hair off his face, and then bent down and kissed his forehead. "You've had a lot happen to you over the past few days. You wouldn't be human if you weren't upset."

You're not human.

He relaxed at the softness of his mother's genuinely caring touch and felt the rage he'd harbored against her slipping away. "Thanks for being a nice mom."

She stroked his cheek. "Try to get some rest, okay? Shout out if you need me."

"Bonnuit."

One look at John-Peter's right arm the next afternoon, and Dr. Morgan forgot all green jokes. The boy winced and grimaced during the examination, but he did not cry out. Torture was becoming routine.

"How did you hurt it?" Dr. Morgan said.

"I lifted a bucket of water."

"That's it?"

"Are you calling me a liar?"

The forcefulness of John-Peter's remark took Dr. Morgan aback.

"Of course not. It doesn't take much to cause some damage. My father used to lift heavy cartons all day long, but he wound up with a herniated disc after bending over to pick up a pencil." Dr. Morgan pulled a pad of paper and a pen from his shirt pocket and began to scribble.

"Here," he said, giving Melissa the prescription. "Discontinue the other medication, and use this for the pain. The swelling should go down in a few days. And as for you." he turned toward John-Peter, "I think you should stay out of trees for the rest of the week."

"Avec plasir." The doctor was out of his mind if he thought John-Peter felt like climbing anything.

"And speaking of trees..." Dr. Morgan grinned. "What's big, green, and fuzzy and would probably kill you if it fell out of a tree?"

John-Peter looked at his shoes. The man was a total idiot.

Dr. Morgan snickered. "A pool table! Get it?"

The next stop was Dr. Samuelson's, who kept a small office in the back of Walker's Apothecary. The space was a jumble of filing cabinets and cages, for the veterinarian's office doubled as the village's humane society.

Dr. Samuelson, navel-length white beard on a round and ruddy face and tufts of white hair sticking up on a round pink scalp, pronounced Bertrand "in perfect health," as John-Peter knew he would.

"What about vaccines," Melissa asked.

"No vaccines," Dr. Samuelson said as he returned Bertrand to John-Peter and walked to the sink to wash his hands.

John-Peter couldn't help giving his mother a triumphant smirk. Melissa, looking uncertain, said, "But don't rats and mice carry disease?"

Dr. Samuelson looked up as he grabbed two sheets of paper towel. "They can, hantavirus and salmonellosis, to name two." He glanced back at John-Peter with a solemn face but his eyes danced when he winked. "I'm assuming you're old enough to understand the importance of washing your hands?"

"Assumption correct." John-Peter lay Bertrand back into his box and headed for the sink.

Kellen called on the way home from Dr. Samuelson's office. He had returned from his business trip and would be home for supper. Too bad. That meant yet another dinner amidst the smell of roasted animal flesh.

Mabel had just set vegan rice pilaf on the dining room table when someone knocked on the front door. Melissa started to rise from her seat, but Mabel flapped her hands for her to sit down.

"You eat. I can get the door."

John-Peter was spooning raw chopped onions onto his black bean casserole when he heard Mabel say, "I can give it to him. They're just starting dinner."

"Thanks!" Karla said.

Bertrand!

John-Peter rushed to the door, almost bumping into Mabel as he snatched the box from Karla. "It's cool, Mabel, I can handle this one."

John-Peter waited until Mabel left the room before he lifted the lid. Bertrand was nosing a trench through the shredded paper. Karla reached inside the box, stroked his fur with the back of her hand, and said, "I buried some sunflower seeds in there for him. I thought maybe he might like to hunt for his food."

"Cool."

"How come you weren't in school today? I even tried calling you. Is something wrong?"

"Doctor's appointment."

"Are you all right?"

Katie's car horn honked.

"Gosh, she's impatient," Karla said. "Think you might be well enough to carve the mandrake tomorrow?"

"Perhaps."

The horn sounded again in three sharp bursts. Karla heaved a large sigh and pushed open the screen door. She wavered and then turned around to wink at John-Peter. "By the way, you were right. Bertrand *does* like turkey."

By the next morning, the softball in John-Peter's right arm had significantly decreased. He called Karla in geometry class and confirmed one mandrake carving for later that afternoon.

"Great!" Karla messaged back, sounding like her old self.

Karla was sitting at the kitchen table reading from one of Cornell's binders when John-Peter closed the back door of the motor home. As he eased between her and the counter on the way to the refrigerator, he paused to look over her shoulder.

"What are you reading?"

"All about vibrations."

He set both the jug of water and carton of soy milk on the table. "What about vibrations?"

"Dad says they're like ghosts."

"Another earth-shattering testimony from the great, late Cornell Dyer."

"Well, duh. He found thousands of vibrations all over Simons Woods, and none were positive, not a single one."

"Your dad's claiming the woods are full of ghosts? Even if you counted everyone who died in Munsonville since the beginning of time you couldn't fill those woods with their ghosts."

"That's the part that stumped my dad. That's why he stayed here so long, so he could study them." She sighed and closed the binder. "I wish we had gotten back out there before it got too cold. Now we can't investigate until spring."

"Well, if you hadn't symbolically eloped with..."

"Knock it off, okay? I'm in no mood."

John-Peter drank the carton in one gulp and then said, "So where's the mandrake?"

"Hidden. I'll get it."

While Karla was gone, John-Peter flipped through the binder, shaking his head at Cornell's illegible shorthand. Although Karla had long ago learned his codes, if Cornell had intended his work to be a legacy for future generations, he really should have first practiced his penmanship.

Karla returned with the mandrake and the ritual knife.

"You can do it all," she said. "I'll just watch."

He held up his hand, and Karla's eyes grew large. "What'd you do to your arm?"

"War injury. The mandrake's all yours."

"But I screwed up the last one."

John-Peter pushed the items away. "You, at least, make the first cuts." He watched, jealous, of the quick, precise way Karla could form an image. "So how was Thanksgiving at the Chandlers?"

"It was okay."

"You actually brought Bertrand to the table?"

Karla stopped in mid-cut. "Are you nuts? Everything is so elegant there. I folded some turkey into my napkin and smuggled it to Curtis' room."

"You were in his bedroom?" John-Peter felt sick at the thought. Karla had never seen the inside of his bedroom.

"Well, where else did you expect me to hide a mouse? The oven?"

In silence, they together carved a decent John Simons likeness into that plant, amazing them both. Karla eyed the results of their work.

"I don't know, John-Peter. Maybe I should give it to Miss Elbert for a Christmas present. Might get me extra credit for art class."

"I shudder to think what she'd do with it."

"You're sick. Are you coming back tomorrow to resurrect the real John Simons?"

"Wouldn't miss it."

The battered cuckoo clock in the living room chirped six times, and he heard a car door slam. He hadn't even seen Katie pull into the driveway. Karla ran outside to distract her mother so he could slip away. He returned promptly after school the next day.

"Your mother needs to buy more soy milk." John-Peter drained the last drops from the less than half full carton.

"You need to quit drinking it so fast. Mom's getting suspicious." Karla crawled on her knees as she unrolled a ball of twine into a large circle. "We have to conduct the spell inside the string to keep us safe from demons, if they show up."

"I sense them trembling now."

Karla looked at him from her perch on the floor. "Do you want to help or not? Daddy gave very specific directions for practicing necromancy with a mandrake. If you're not going to take this seriously..."

John-Peter's gaze fell onto the compact disc sitting on the coffee table. "Where'd you get this?"

"The library. I figured if I played it, John Simons would be more likely to hang out."

He set the water jug on the table and picked up *The Best-Loved Compositions of John Simons.* Why hadn't his mother bought him a copy? He could learn most of the pieces in an afternoon. That ought to put Munsonville on the map, birthing two world-famous, classical pianists. He turned to the back to read the song list and stifled a gasp.

There, next to the short history of John Simons' signature tune, *Bryony,* was his mother's music box.

Karla stood and stretched. "You ready?"

Feeling dazed and unsteady on his feet, John-Peter sank into the couch, still holding the compact disc. "Karla, look at this."

"What?" She sat beside him and patted her locket into place.

"It's a picture of a music box John Simons supposedly made for Bryony." His heart beat fast against his will. "My mother owns it."

"You're kidding!" She gave the picture a long look. "Are you sure it's the same one? I mean, weren't there supposed to be replicas..."

"It's the same one, Karla."

"Are you sure? How would your mother get it?"

"I think she got it from Grandma Marchellis. You really should read her diary. She claims to have grown up in Simons Mansion as the daughter of one of the maids."

"Wow! That's really exciting. I'll bet the village would love to own that diary."

John-Peter opened the compact disc and played the last track. It matched the melody of his mother's music box, the same melody he heard when...

"John-Peter?"

He took a deep breath and then faced Karla. "Grandma Marchellis said John Simons was a vampire who regularly partook of her blood."

Karla's eyes grew big, and her face turned white.

"Oh, John-Peter," she breathed. "Do you think it's true?"

"I originally dismissed it as fiction produced by a maniacal mind, but now..."

"Can I read it?"

"Sure."

"Would you get it now?" She began to rewind the twine.

"I thought we were resurrecting John Simons."

"Can't today. Dad says never bring back vampires; it's too dangerous. You might think Grandma Marchellis was crazy, but we're not taking any chances until I read that diary. John-Peter, are you listening to me?"

"Just thinking. You know, I heard a music box the last time we visited the parsonage. I'd like to go back in there."

"Okay. But get the diary first."

Half an hour later, the diary had a new hiding place in Karla's bedroom, and John-Peter was lying on the couch in the motor home while Karla guided him into the parsonage.

"Do you see anything?"

"No."

"Hear anything?"

"No again."

"Well, keep looking."

"I'm going to the parlor."

"Why there?" Karla leaned over him to grab the pen and paper she had balanced on the back of the couch, and her locket hit him in the eye. She was close enough to touch. He wouldn't, but just the same...

"Because it might be the one in my dream. And that's where I heard Bryony's music box."

"How do you know it's hers?"

"It's the same song on the CD."

John-Peter shone his flashlight around the parlor, but saw nothing except the sheet-draped furniture, nothing at all resembling the scene in his dream. He waited for the cold blast of air he felt the last time or the faint tinkling of the music box, but nothing happened.

"Reel me in, Karla. It's a futile trip."

Nevertheless, Karla felt it was worth a few notes. "If I read them all at once, maybe I'll find clues I didn't notice."

"Good point."

She closed the notebook and chewed on the pen cap. "Do you think the ghost is Bryony?"

"Why would she haunt the parsonage? Doesn't local myth state she was happiest at Simons Mansion?"

"But Simons Mansion burned. Maybe she's lost. Her old home would be familiar to her."

"What about John Simons?"

"I'll make up my mind about him after I read the diary."

"We've wasted another mandrake." And another credit card statement.

Karla grinned. "Maybe I'll give it to Miss Elbert after all." The smile faded. "Hey, Mom said your grandma had another stroke. Is it true?"

"On Thanksgiving. She's supposed to go back to the nursing home tomorrow. The doctors can do nothing more for her."

Her face softened. "I'm really sorry, John-Peter."

"Yeah, me, too."

John-Peter had not realized how much he had missed the mouse until that night. Lying on the floor and leaning on one elbow, he coaxed it to leap into the air for tiny bites of toast. Bertrand ate half a slice before he lost interest in food and decided to explore the blocks John-Peter had snaked from his closet to nightstand. The boy observed him for a while, but when Bertrand became enthralled with a particular corner and refused to be moved, John-Peter grew bored. He fished out the leprechaun from his pocket and held it before his eyes. He studied its tiny black eyes, bushy red eyebrows, wild red hair, tall green hat, and downward spiraling numbers in the center of its belly. He wondered why it had stopped bringing him the good luck Uncle Ed had promised it would, why it needed periodic adjustments, and what might happen when the digits reached zero.

A row of blocks fell, and a gleeful Bertrand scuttled past before John-Peter could stop him. He set the leprechaun on the floor and inched closer to the bed, dragging his hand across the dust bunnies, proof of Mabel's substandard cleaning, and groping for the elusive mouse. He lifted the edge of the quilt and peeked under the bed. Bertrand sat in the middle of the floor cleaning a paw. John-Peter wiggled his fingers, hoping the mouse would find them more distracting than a bath. Bertrand began working on the other paw.

John-Peter rolled onto his back and landed on the leprechaun. A click sounded in his head, and a series of lights flashed across his eyes. He quickly rolled off the leprechaun. The lights vanished.

Dr. Rothgard's final words exploded in his brain. *You're not human.*

He quickly sat up, cupped his hand over the leprechaun, and pressed on it. He heard the click, and the lights appeared. He let go. Another click, and the lights disappeared. He did it again. A click, and the lights returned. This time, he noticed the lights were not randomly displayed. They were lined in an organized row.

Guard your mouse.

Had Dr. Rothgard meant Bertrand? Or was he implying something else?

John-Peter slid the leprechaun slightly to the right and clicked onto the first light. The fire blazed high in the hearth. The lounging, Victorian men gave their full attention to the Bible-reading, Amish man. John Simons stretched out his hand toward John-Peter and offered him the dark crimson liquid in his half-full goblet.

"For the blood," John Simons said, "is the life."

Behind him, Karla inhaled deeply. "Oh, gosh, John-Peter! What does this mean?"

"I don't know," John-Peter said, "but I'm going to find out."

CHAPTER 16: WHEN A DOOR CLOSES, OPEN WINDOWS

John-Peter skimmed the questions on his driver's education test.

Cake.

He glanced across the room at Karla, who was scribbling with astonishing speed, and tapped her shoulder.

"Later," she messaged back.

"This afternoon?"

"You bet!"

He slid the heel of his hand along his jeans and over the bump in his right pocket.

Guard your mouse.

Dr. Rothgard needn't worry. John-Peter had no intention of letting that leprechaun out of his sight, not after last night. Two seats on his right, Courtney paused over her test and frowned. Figured.

Your short fingers tell me you view reality only from your own perspective.

The correct perspective.

Was it really his perspective, or had someone hypnotized him, using the leprechaun as a mouse to trigger a suggestion and response?

Trenton threw down his pen and picked up a book. Courtney fidgeted in her chair and looked as if she might cry. Lauren was still writing, but she was on page two. Curtis was probably still working on the test, but he was behind John-Peter. The boy folded his arms, gingerly the avoiding decreasing, but still painful, lump, leaned back in his chair, and raised his eyes to the wall clock. A few more minutes to go.

A dozen years ago, a jury denounced Dr. Rothgard as insane for stealing his patients' blood samples. Was Dr. Rothgard into mind control as well as body fluids? And why did Uncle Ed "adjust" the leprechaun from time to time? Maybe Uncle Ed really believed the graven image carried good luck powers. Who knows? Maybe the Steward had once taken it home, stood under a full moon, and waved the tiny figure over his head while reciting a Druid incantation.

John-Peter looked at the clock again. Five minutes before the bell. Karla shook her head ever so slightly, trying not to smile. He picked up the pen and swiftly scrawled his answers.

"You crack me up," Karla messaged.

"It's more fun this way."

Courtney stopped him as he entered the lunchroom. "Are you working at Happy Hunting Grounds this week?"

He scanned the room for Trenton. "That's up to Mephistopheles."

"Well, I'm working every night this week except Friday. If you can get away..."

There he was in the food line. Curtis' mother was ladling something into plastic bowels. Evelyn Chandler must have gone back to Boston, where she belonged.

"That's what gets me through the day." John-Peter cut behind Trenton and left Courtney to her fantasies.

The large vat contained chicken noodle soup. John-Peter held his breath against its stench as he obediently held his bowl for Mrs. Chandler to fill. She met his innocent gaze head-on, but the look on her face shouted rage, rage, rage. Was it his fault if Karla valued friendship over a silly infatuation? Curtis would get over it. If not, he could always soothe his broken heart in Lauren's welcoming arms.

John-Peter opened the kitchen door. His mother was sitting at the table eating a sandwich and reading a book.

"I brought you some soup," he said, setting the bowl next to her.

"Thanks, John-Peter, but I already had some."

"Rejected by my own mother. Well, maybe some other famished teacher will appreciate it."

"Is this guilt trip your way of telling me you're not prepared for today's 'Tale of Two Cities' quiz?"

John-Peter grabbed his lunch from the refrigerator, refilled his water jug, and settled across from Melissa, at the chair nearest the sunny window.

"Charles Darnay and Sydney Carton look alike," he said. "Both fall in love with Lucie Manette, but Darnay gets her, after they are properly married of course. Carton nobly dies in Darnay's place. The end."

Melissa set the book on the table, pages down. "You skipped a few parts."

"Why divulge all the answers?"

He took a bite from the sandwich Mabel made from last night's lentil loaf, infinitely tastier than anything Aunt Cindy could make, and reached for the salt. Miss Elbert walked into the kitchen, poured a cup of coffee, and sat next to John-Peter.

"I wish I had gotten here sooner. The sandwiches were great, but they're all out of soup, and I really wanted to try some. I heard Madeleine Chandler made it."

Melissa pushed her bowl across the table. "Here. Take mine."

"Why, thank you, Melissa."

She picked up her book. "Ironically, John-Peter, you'll miss the quiz after all. Arthur is coming for you after fifth period."

"This is an outrage!"

"Kellen bought the land behind the funeral home for a pet cemetery, and he's been deluged with advance orders. Even with hiring extra help, he's still overwhelmed. He asked if you could skip my class just this one time."

"'It is a far, far better thing that I do, than I have ever done.'"

"I hate to deflate your happiness, but that quiz will be waiting at your dinner break."

John-Peter unwrapped the second sandwich. "Double pay?"

Melissa turned a page. "Don't get your hopes up. The new credit card bill is sitting on Kellen's dresser."

John-Peter unwrapped his third sandwich and messaged the news to Karla. She sounded equally as disappointed.

"I was really looking forward to exploring your brain," she said. "Do you have to work tomorrow, too?"

"How should I know? I'm just their puppet."

"Well, don't do anything fun with the leprechaun until I can be there."

Rows of cars poured into the parking lot of Happy Hunting Grounds, wrapped around the building, and spilled into the street, backing up traffic. John-Peter figured he sold more animal plots than the cemetery would contain, but that was Kellen's problem.

One of the new girls relieved Grace at five o'clock. Grace still stopped by John-Peter's stall before she left.

"You know why your stepfather's racking up all these sales, don't you?" She zipped up her coat.

"Please drive up to window four to pay." John-Peter closed the glass. "No, why?"

"He's pronounced all Tuesdays as 'Bury Your Dog Day.' Everyone who pre-buys a plot for their dog gets a free burial, if the funeral is on a Tuesday."

"And if Fido audaciously dies on Wednesday morning?"

Grace cupped the muffs over her ears. "Check out the basement. Kellen bought a ton of deep freezers. Don't tell me he doesn't know what he's doing."

A car horn gave a loud, long blast that made them both jump. John-Peter opened the window. "Good afternoon. Welcome to Happy Hunting Grounds. Please hold." He shut the window again.

"Are you coming back after dinner, Grace?"

"Not till the morning, thank goodness. It's a madhouse in here."

"'You have been the last dream of my soul.'"

Grace grinned and moved her hand in a friendly way as she walked out the door.

John-Peter slid back the window. "I'm sorry for the delay. May I take your order?"

"I'd like to buy an HHG Pet Plot."

"Certainly, sir. Would you like shade or sun?"

"Sun. Wait. Hold on."

John-Peter contemplated the bare trees against the graying landscape. Even the crisp leaves lining the grounds had faded to brown, but they would soon disappear under a cloak of darkness. The temperatures dropped with the sun, and the night's chill seeped through the glass. Karla was right. They would have no opportunity to investigate the vibrations until spring, and it was all her fault.

His speaker crackled. "The wife says shade if we can have a maple tree."

"We have a few maples in stock. Trees are complimentary with each HHG Pet Plot, but other landscaping is extra."

"No, we're fine with just the tree for now. What about a headstone?"

"You purchase that when you make the actual funeral arrangements."

The man guffawed so hard, John-Peter almost fell off his stool. "Well, he's just a pup so hopefully we won't need that for a while."

"Anything else, sir?"

"I think we've got everything."

"Two thousand even. Please drive up to window five."

Kellen shut down operations at eight o'clock when he knew for sure all plots had been sold. John-Peter could not remember the last time his stepfather looked so pleased with himself.

"This went better than I dreamed, John-Peter. I've already started buying up property near the other franchises."

"You're brilliant, Kellen, there's no doubt about it." A Parisian vacation should be the logical next step.

"Your literature quiz is in the fifth meeting room from my office. Ordered you a big kettle of pasta fagiole and a loaf of French bread to go with it. Might as well celebrate. You're a born salesman, John-Peter. If you ever abandon those concert pianist notions of yours..."

"Joining me for dinner, Kellen?"

"Nah. I had prime rib an hour ago. I've got these reports to finish, but I'll be ready to leave in an hour. Your mother will string me up if I bring you home late again on a school night."

John-Peter zipped down the hall to Meeting Room Five so he wouldn't laugh in front of Kellen. Couldn't his stepfather do the math? It was a two-hour ride to Munsonville.

But the reports took Kellen twice as long as he had anticipated. John-Peter took a pain pill before they left the funeral home and fell asleep in the limousine. A livid Melissa, hands on her hips, met them at the front door.

"It's after one o'clock!"

Kellen tried pushing past her and tripped on the dangling sash of her purple bathrobe. A rose petal fell and landed on his mother's purple slipper. "Here we go again."

"He's got school in the morning!"

"So? And I've got work! Which one supports this family, tell me that?"

John-Peter ducked under his mother's arm and headed for the stairs. What if a starving Bertrand had eaten a hole through his box and escaped? Fortunately, Kellen hadn't made it off the front porch.

"This is the last time, Kellen. The boy's not your personal slave."

"No, but you are, and don't you forget it. Now let me inside!"

John-Peter softly closed the bedroom door. A movement from inside his closet caught his eyes. He eased back the door and stared into the mournful eyes of the princess, the first time he had seen her since returning from Grover's Park.

He pressed his fingertips onto the glass and the princess did the same.

"They forced me to leave," John-Peter whispered to the image, "but now I have returned."

The princess simultaneously mouthed soundless words. John-Peter opened his hand and pressed his palm against the mirror, the only thing that separated their physical contact, and moved his face closer to hers.

"Hey, John-Peter!"

The princess faded away. John-Peter stared into the eyes of his own reflection. "You're still up?"

"I knew you'd be worried about Bertrand," Karla said, "so I wanted you to know I fed him a cheese sandwich."

"My mother let you into my room?"

"You're a hoot. I'm practicing teleportation."

"How do you know it worked?"

Weariness returned with such force his legs buckled. John-Peter knelt on the floor and lifted the lid of Bertrand's shoebox. The mouse was fast asleep on his back, limbs stretched out in a large "X," and snoring.

"The sandwich dematerialized, so I'm assuming it showed up in your room."

He closed the closet door, stretched across the bed, and kicked off his shoes. He was done. "Karla, you'll make him sick giving him an entire sandwich."

His eyelids weighed a ton. Any attempt at opening them made his head whirl and his stomach lurch. Safer to keep them closed. A whole sandwich? No wonder Bertrand had passed out.

"Thanks for the vote of confidence. Who kept him safe for five days; tell me that? Besides, I only sent him one bite at a time."

The bed bobbed up and down as John-Peter floated on somnolent waves. Kellen, in full pirate costume, manned the captain's wheel. "Melissa!"

The boat vanished; the water evaporated; but the bed still swayed. "What about this credit card bill?"

A fuzzy blanket lay across his cramped limbs. Eyes shrank from bright light. Joints creaked as he hoisted himself to a sitting position; his head pounded with the effort. He rubbed gritty eyes and tried focusing on the clock. Eleven! Why hadn't his mother wakened him?

Never minding the cold floor on his bare feet, John-Peter stumbled to the door and opened it. Taped to the door was a note that read: "I called you in sick. Hope you got some rest. The last lentil loaf is in the refrigerator. Love, Mother."

So much for going to Karla's after school today. She messaged during geometry class just as John-Peter took the lentil loaf from the microwave.

"I peeked at your driver's ed test. You got a hundred."

"Surprised?"

"Not really. I figured you might not be in school today. So, we wait a day."

"Easy for you to say, missy. You're not the one walking around with a microchip in your brain."

"Might not be a microchip. Maybe someone is brainwashing you and making you think you've got a microchip."

"For what purpose?"

"Who knows? World domination? I've got to dissect this angle."

She dropped a door before he could answer.

John-Peter spent the next three hours in the conservatory creating a piano arrangement for the tune he played on the tin whistle at Uncle Brian's house, and it was daunting task. No piece he ever composed stirred such elusive longings inside him, and it was hard work to replicate it. He recalled his family's tears. It was a powerful piece, to be sure.

Melissa opened the door and stuck her head inside the room. "I brought your homework."

He shut the lid. "Forgive me if I don't clasp my hands in rapture."

"It's pretty light. Bet you're done before dinner. By the way, you aced the literature quiz."

"She said as she slipped the noose around Carton's neck."

"It'll probably take you an hour, at best. You're not in any position for debate. Kellen is furious about the latest credit card bill."

Lucky for him, Kellen, swamped with pet plot orders in three states, did not come home for dinner that night. Besides, with all the money pouring in, why would Kellen waste his valuable energy on a measly few hundred dollars?

That night, after John-Peter had readied for bed, he watched bits of cheese sandwich float through the air and into Bertrand's box where the mouse stood on his hind legs, nose to the air, mouth open to the jaw, to receive the food Karla dropped into it.

One piece missed its mark and landed on Bertrand's whiskers. The mouse whacked his paw against it and dug the morsel out of the newspaper.

"Lousy aim, Karla. Good thing you're not a guy."

"One time! What's the big deal about missing one time?"

"Tell that to Mabel."

In the distance, the telephone rang.

"So no excuses for tomorrow, right, John-Peter?"

John-Peter heard a knock on the door.

"Telephone call," Melissa said. "It's Ed Calkins. You may take it in my room."

Just what he needed. A spy.

Melissa had returned to her desk and the homework she was correcting. John-Peter picked up the receiver. His mother didn't fool him. He knew she was listening.

"John-Peter, are you running with me this weekend?"

"Of course. Why wouldn't I?"

"You've skipped out twice in the last month."

"I was kidnapped and held against my will."

"There's plenty of extra work with Christmas coming. If you can't make it, I'll have to hire someone who's available for work."

"I'll be there." John-Peter decided it was worth a try. "By the way, I think the mouse needs a few adjustments."

Melissa stopped writing.

"Mouse?" Ed sounded puzzled. "What mouse?"

"The one in your office. It's sticking."

A momentary silence and then Ed said, "It worked fine this morning. But I'll take a look at it. Be ready half an hour early on Friday. It's annoying to shout at your bedroom window."

"Okay."

Uncle Ed seemed clueless about the leprechaun. He had to find a way to talk to Dr. Rothgard. How could he weasel the password from his mother?

Karla was waiting for him by the lockers when John-Peter arrived at school the next morning. "Good so far, John-Peter?"

"So far."

By the time the final bell rang, it looked as if today might really be the day. Karla ran outside with Amy and Megan, messaging John-Peter as the door slammed behind her.

"How soon before you get there?"

"Half hour or so. I hope your mom bought more soy milk."

John-Peter forced down the excitement rising into his throat and covered it with a trap door. Be casual. Let Karla feel privileged to help. No way would he let her know he daren't take this journey alone.

Karla met him at the door. "This is the most exciting thing we have done so far." She held out her hand. "Can I look at the leprechaun?"

"What for?"

"I've never seen it up close."

The second he retrieved it, Karla seized the charm. "Gosh, he's ugly, isn't he?" She handed it back to him. "Okay, John-Peter, get down on the floor."

"Why the floor?"

"Since I'm going into those windows with you, we both hold onto the leprechaun."

He complied with the first request, but balked when Karla put her hand over the leprechaun before he did. "I'm on top."

"'Fraid not, John-Peter. I'm in control this time."

"No."

"Yes, because if I think we should bail, we bail. And I don't trust you to cooperate."

"Sure, I would," John-Peter lied, but, inwardly knowing Karla was right, he conceded.

Karla took a deep breath. "Ready?"

"Now or never."

They pressed down on the leprechaun. John-Peter heard the familiar click and saw the equally familiar rows of lights.

"Which one had the parsonage?"

"The first one."

"Then go to the next one. We've seen the parsonage.

John-Peter ran toward Melissa, heart pounding and clutching a piece of paper. "Mother! I drew this for you!"

Melissa scooped him in her arms and together they studied a childish likeness surrounded by an abstract blend of earthen colors. The boy anxiously searched her eyes. "Do you like it?"

She smiled and kissed him. "I love it."

John-Peter squirmed in her arms. "There's Uncle Brian! Down, Mother!" He sped toward Brian.

The scene faded into black. John-Peter turned wondering eyes up at Karla. "Did this happen?"

"You mean, is it a real memory?"

Still looking at her, he shrugged.

"John-Peter, don't you know?"

"No."

"Then I don't either. Try the next one, John-Peter. Maybe if we see enough of them, we'll figure it out.

John-Peter proudly stood next to John Simons while the large man glared at them from the front porch.

"Name's Mark Blake. I live next door. My dog's dead, and my kid Andy saw you kill it."

Fury rushed through John-Peter. "That's a lie! My father wouldn't hurt your decrepit beast!"

That scene, too, went black.

"John-Peter, what's with all the John Simons memories?"

"How should I know?"

"Do you recognize them?"

"I don't know. Maybe?"

"Click on another one."

John-Peter, clad in pajamas, knelt on the piano bench and carefully played *Bryony* as John Simons watched over him. Although John nodded approval, his eyes shone with a sinister light.

Karla nudged his hand. "Log off, John-Peter. We're stopping."

"Why?"

"Something doesn't feel right. I know people say your dad looked like John Simons, but..."

You're not human. Your father was a vampire.

John-Peter pressed down hard, clicked out of the window, and highlighted the next one. Karla's hand squirmed under his.

"Hey, what are you doing? I said, 'Click...'"

But he tightened his grip and pressed down hard enough for Karla to cry out. His mother's screams cut through the air. John Simons flew into the room, grabbed her shoulders, and swung her around.

"Stop! You're scaring the baby!"

John-Peter exited that window and entered the next and the next and the next. Uncle Brian praised the wisdom in his eyes. With a bandana on his head, a sword in his hand, and a black patch over one eye, John-Peter forced Katie to walk the plank. Grandma Simotes whipped him with a belt for accidentally urinating in his pants.

"Stop it!" Karla struggled to break free of his grasp. "John-Peter, listen to me." She twisted her wrist, but his hand was like a vise. "You'll crash!"

He huddled in a corner at the motor home, fingers jammed inside his ears to blunt his father's shrieks as Cornell Dyer repeatedly zapped him with an electric rod.

Karla's teeth sank into his fingers, but John-Peter kept going. He huddled on a work station while Dr. Rothgard shown a flashlight into his eyes, and Uncle Ed twisted something inside the leprechaun. The light hurt, but he couldn't dodge it, because John Simons had tied his little arms behind his back.

"No more!" Karla was crying hard now. "Oh, please, stop, John-Peter!"

John-Peter clutched the edges of his car seat and fearfully watched the silent, midnight sky. An unearthly scream, an inhuman roar, and finally, that awful slushing and grunting near the front tire where his father crouched and devoured that night's prey.

"John-Peter!"

Karla's punch to his gut took away his breath, but John Simons crept closer, blood streaming from his mouth, and pushed John-Peter's mouth over the gash in his arm.

"For the blood," his father said as he clawed the squirming boy's neck with one hand and pushed him over the wound, "is the life."

"John-Peter!" Karla sobbed as she buried her head in his neck. "Oh, John-Peter, please say you're okay."

He clicked out of the window and threw the leprechaun across the room. Karla flung her arms around him as he cried and cried and cried.

CHAPTER 17: THE GIFT FROM THE GRAVE

John-Peter splashed one, last handful of cold water against his face and fumbled along the wall for the faded pink towel.

His eyes still burned, but he could not hide in the Dyer's bathroom forever. He did not want to face Karla and not only because he had cried in front of her, as if that was not bad enough.

He shrank at the mere thought of uncovering any more buried memories.

They had talked, briefly, before he sought asylum. Karla hypothesized that the visions were not memories at all, that someone had implanted them and then provided John-Peter with the mouse as a way to access them. It could have been an interesting concept if only the sudden remembrance had not been so strong. His stomach still quivered at the taste of blood.

Slowly, the boy lowered the towel and regarded his blotchy face. He looked like a total idiot, but he couldn't help that now. Reluctantly, he looped the towel back through its ring, averting his eyes from the yellow and crumbling "wallpaper:" *Ghost Hunter Locates Buried Treasure. Séance Frees Man from Family Curse. College Student Wins Lottery after Palm Reading.*

Any visitor availing himself of the Dyer's water closet came face to face with yet another story of Cornell Dyer and his famous exploits. John-Peter himself had read them all long ago. Before venturing back into reality, John-Peter double checked the leprechaun's placement in his pocket. Good thing he remembered to retrieve it. How unwise it would be to lose that mouse now.

A loud clunk back from the back of the motor home made him jump. John-Peter flung open the door, sped toward the living room, and stopped short in the doorway.

"Oh hey, John-Peter." Karla dropped the chain on Cornell's desk. At her feet lay a pair of bolt cutters.

"Your mother will kill you."

"No she won't, not if you run down to Dalton's and buy me a new chain and lock."

John-Peter started to object, but Karla held up a hand. "She'll never know the difference, trust me. Help me lug this stuff to the bedroom, okay?"

"She'll make you put them back. And I can't buy you anything because Kellen swiped my credit card."

"I thought you had memorized the number. Oh well, I'll deal with my mother later. Anyhow, I'm not that worried. She has to find them first."

John-Peter balanced a stack of binders in his arms and toddled toward the door. "How many hiding places can there be in a tiny bedroom?"

"You'd be surprised."

"Where'd you get the bolt cutters?"

"Garage. Daddy left some awesome tools out there."

Karla dropped the last stack onto her bed and surveyed the mess.

"Whew! Well, I won't get through those in one night." She rubbed her hands on her jeans. "Gosh, you wouldn't think a bunch of locked-up books would be so dusty." She looked up at him with a half-smile. "Sorry to be rude, but you've got to go. I'll only be able to read so much before Mom comes home."

He grabbed his water jug and edged towards the door, glad for a way out of the uncomfortable situation. "It's cool. Thanks, Karla."

Once outside, the boy removed his shoes and socks and sprinted home over the frigid pavement. How could he ever go back to Karla's house after the way he reacted to the scenes in his mind?

Mabel was stirring something in a pot, and Melissa was rinsing a dish when John-Peter flew through the back door. She glimpsed his bare feet as he ran past her.

"Aren't you cold?"

"Nope!"

"John-Peter, where are you going? Dinner is almost ready."

"Be right back."

He dashed up the stairs and then paused at the door of his dark bedroom, silently panting to catch his breath. After treading lightly on his toes to the closet door, John-Peter slowly and deliberately moved his hand to the knob and eased open the door. No princess.

A quick snap of the switch and the ceiling light illuminated the room. John-Peter reached into the hall for his shoes and socks and shut the door. The walk to his bed felt like a hundred miles. He sank into the pillow and shuddered, still feeling sticky, warm blood trickling into his mouth. A slight movement inside the closet caught his attention. In three steps he was at the door, but he still saw only himself. Unmoving, scarcely breathing, he waited and waited and waited until a soft knock on his bedroom door interrupted his blissful trance.

"John-Peter, are you awake? Dinner is getting cold."

He couldn't take his eyes away from the mirror. "Sorry. Must have dozed off."

"Well, come join us. I don't want you running around all night on an empty stomach."

What a typical mother thing to say. "Will do."

The mirror compelled him to stay, but he couldn't gape at his face all night. He started to close the door, and suddenly she was there, gazing at him with those beautiful, melancholy, brown eyes of hers. With unbroken concentration, they simultaneously pressed their flattened palms on the glass. His eyes watered with the strain of keeping them open, but the princess didn't blink either. He bit his lip to keep it from trembling.

"Help me," the princess mouthed.

His parents had nearly finished dinner by the time John-Peter arrived downstairs. Kellen greeted him with a "Humph! You're late," but otherwise refrained from conversation in his direction. Their voices floated around him as John-Peter picked at Mabel's tofu quiche and wondered what the princess meant.

"Melissa, did I tell you the Chandlers bought the old Cummings place? They've been there about a month, I think."

"Oh by the way, Kellen, we're not going to Grover's Park for Christmas. Brian and his family are coming here instead."

"A Florida retirement community wants an HHG satellite on their premises. I'm flying down there next week to discuss a pilot program."

Karla tapped his shoulder. "John-Peter, you're not going to believe this. Are you sitting down?"

His fork cut through the quiche. "Yes'm."

"Daddy says your father really was John Simons."

John-Peter swallowed twice before the quiche obeyed his command. "How does he know?"

"Research. Experiments. Remember the scene with the rod? Daddy wasn't torturing your father. He was testing electrical impulses. They're supposed to be faster and more intense in vampires than in humans. Your dad gave full consent."

You're not hu...your father was a vampi...

He pushed away his plate. "Mother, may I be excused?"

Melissa glanced at the nearly full plate and back at John-Peter. "Honey, are you feeling all right?"

"Tired."

"Go into my room, and take a ten out of my purse. Make Ed stop and buy you a snack tonight, okay?"

"Sure."

He dragged his leaden body to the stairs, bypassing Melissa's room, and ignoring Kellen's, "So you allow him to waste food and then reward him with..."

"John-Peter, are you still there?"

"Karla, can it wait? I have to go to bed."

"Bed? Why it's only... never mind, I forgot about the route."

But sleep and the chance to escape the avalanche of horrible knowledge eluded him. As the boy contemplated the ceiling cracks, he hoped for early trucks and quick delivery, but John-Peter abandoned that hope after Ed's shouting jolted him awake. A steady stream of snowflakes floated past his window.

Ten minutes later, the roads were already thick with the slippery mass. Ed peered between the frozen smears his old wipers left on his windshield as he guided his car toward Main Street.

"John-Peter, it's a good thing Irishmen have an abiding sense of tragedy. It sustains them through temporary periods of joy."

"I never heard that saying." The yawn escaped his lips before he could stop it. "Did you make it up?"

"No, 'tis as old as the hills of Ireland."

The boy huddled deeper within his coat and leaned his head against the frozen window. A thirty-minute nap was more welcoming than listening to Ed quote Irish proverbs. He woke with a start. Shivering, he pulled the musty old burlap that served as a blanket around his neck and peeped into the parking lot. Thick layers of heavy, still-falling snow covered the vehicles. Carriers, eyes at half mast to block the driving wetness as they left the building's shelter, struggled to push their carts through the slush.

A cart handle scraped the car, but the carrier kept going without a single apology. John-Peter opened the door, stepped out, and sank halfway to his knees. He wasn't surprised, only cold and damp. Intense snowfalls were a part of every winter he'd ever known. He shuffled and slid to the center and then blinked against the bright lights.

Ed Calkins, standing tall on a work station, cupped his hands around his mouth, and called out, "The Queen of Christmas!"

The winner was one of the new carriers, a tiny woman who barely reached John-Peter's shoulder. Her girlish giggling at being honored in this manner belied the oily, gray strands drooping onto her forehead. With mincing steps, the woman approached Ed Calkins, climbed onto the station beside him, and allowed him to place a jingle bell tiara on her head.

"All hail Gloria Nefstead, our new Queen of Christmas!"

One carrier yelled, "Hurray!" A few more clapped their hands. Most ignored the festivities as they hurriedly double-bagged their papers. Clutching the back of the work table, Ed lowered himself to a sitting position and then bounced to the ground. That's when he noticed John-Peter.

"Good. You're awake. Three new drivers need to sign my petition. Can you bag the Munsonville Weeklies while I go hunt them up?"

"Sure, Uncle Ed."

"Don't forget. Double bag."

The plows were working their way down the main roads, and the sky was hinting at a few pink streaks by the time Eircheard's Emporium came into view. Eircheard was just setting two freshly baked loaves as John-Peter and Ed slid through the door. John-Peter devoured the first loaf with half the contents in his water jug before Ed made his first deal of the day.

"Got any elf costumes?"

The little old man leaned back in his chair and relit his pipe, puffing on it a few times before he spoke. "Didn't you buy one last year?"

"Look how the boy has grown. He's not going to fit into that costume. Hey, you didn't sell that collection of Irish toasts I was reading here yesterday?"

"I've seen plenty an Irish lad grow big and strong on my bread. And, no, I didn't sell the book yet. It's around here somewhere."

John-Peter swallowed the last mouthful and cut a thick slice from the second loaf. He didn't doubt the superiority of Eircheard's bread. He tasted heaven with every bite.

Ed sifted through a table of paperbacks. "So what about that elf costume?"

Eircheard rose to his feet and spoke around his pipe. "I've got a leprechaun costume in the back that might fit him. He could wear that with your elf's hat."

"No!" John-Peter shouted before he could squelch it.

Ed dropped the paperback, and Eircheard's hand, already on the curtain, paused. Surprised at his outburst, John-Peter slid his hand down his jeans and over the bump in his right pocket. *Guard your mouse.*

"The boy is right, Eircheard. 'Twouldn't be right."

John-Peter spread a thick slab across the last piece of bread. "I can wear a green shirt with my suit coat and your hat. That's more elfish than any leprechaun costume."

Lucky for him, the Steward of Tara agreed.

Waking at noon under the warm confines of several quilts was much more pleasant than the frigid front seat of Ed Calkins' rusty, compact car. They hadn't finished filling the boxes until eight o'clock, and John-Peter barely recalled climbing into bed. He took his time stretching his limbs and especially his toes, reveling in that delicious, half-awake state between dreaming and full alertness.

Somewhere, a telephone rang.

Only one more night and then no more paper route until after the new year, which suited John-Peter just fine. He looked forward to Ed Calkins' annual Atlantic City trip as much as his uncle did. It was a good chance to catch up on reading and composing.

He heard a gentle rap on his door. "John-Peter, are you awake?"

John-Peter stretched a final time, pushed back the quilt, and padded to the door. He opened it a crack and peeped around.

"That was your grandfather. He wants to drive into Simons Woods for a Christmas tree. Your grandmother said he can go if you ride with him. He's really not supposed to be driving, but he was adamant about doing it, so she compromised."

He was instantly wide awake. John-Peter hadn't been in a car with just his grandfather since summer. "Sure!"

Melissa smiled as she swept a lock of her son's hair over his shoulder. "Good. I'll call him right back. Want anything special for breakfast?"

"A dozen peanut butter sandwiches to go?"

"Coming right up."

A loud rustling noise came from inside the closet. "And one for Bertrand?"

"And one for Bertrand. Tell you what. I'll even feed him so you can leave."

The afternoon sun sparkled on the clean Munsonville snow. John-Peter inhaled pure cold air as he munched the sandwiches while trudging down Bass Street toward his grandparents' fishing cottage, glad for the trip back into normalcy. The boy almost wished he'd never laid eyes on Grandma Marchellis' diary. If that box hadn't broken...

Steve sat inside the running car, rubbing his gloved hands together to warm them. His eyes lit up when he saw John-Peter, and he scooted over to the passenger side. At his feet was a gallon of water.

"Remember everything I taught you?" Steve asked as John-Peter shut the door and reached for the seat belt.

"I think so. Aren't you worried Grandma might see us?"

"Your grandmother took Mrs. Dalton Christmas shopping in Jenson."

John-Peter slid the seat closer to the steering window and adjusted the rear view mirror. "That was nice of her."

"So I figured this was our chance. When do you get that permit?"

"Not until after Christmas."

"Well, you should have plenty of experience by then."

John-Peter remembered his blinker even though he was only turning into the woods. "What kind of a tree are you looking for, Grandpa?"

"Something small enough to fit into my living room and large enough for the whole house to smell like pine."

"Sounds easy enough. Who's going back for it?"

"Jack Cooper. He offered to cut it next week and set it up for me. All I have to do is mark it."

"What if someone else gets it before you do?"

"Unlikely with as far into the woods as we're going."

Only a bit of bare branch here and there broke the stark white of the woods. Steve, a contented expression on his face, leaned back in his seat and enjoyed the winter wonderland from the confines of his window.

"You know, John-Peter, this is what pleases me about Munsonville. Nothing ever changes. Look at this snow. It snows like this year after year. I have no reason to expect that this winter will be any different from all the other winters I have known. Munsonville is safe, dependable, just like God."

"What was Christmas like when you were little, Grandpa?"

Steve shaded his eyes from the glare of the sun as it filtered through the trees and reflected off the snow. "Busy, although we couldn't close the diner until noon. It was tradition for people to come to us for breakfast after Sunday morning services. Of course, we didn't go to church because my family was busy serving everyone breakfast."

"Beg pardon?"

His grandfather chuckled. "My father opened Sue's Diner and named it for my mother."

That piece of news surprised John-Peter. "Not the Coopers?"

"They bought it after my parents' death. I even ran it for a while, after they became too feeble to keep it going. You're not going to believe this, but I learned how to cook before I learned to read. But once Ma and Pa died, I didn't have the heart to run the diner anymore. So I sold it to Jack's father."

The blinding sun made John-Peter's eyes water, and he reached for the visor. "So you had to work on Christmas?"

"It didn't feel like work because all our friends came to the diner. It just felt like one big Christmas party."

"And once you went home?"

"We ate leftovers and opened a present or two. We had little money, so gifts were simple, maybe a new hat or gloves. Mostly we rested. It was the only afternoon we took off all year."

John-Peter thought of the expensive gifts his mother and Kellen bought each December and said nothing. He couldn't imagine celebrating the stark Christmas his grandfather had described. Poor Steve.

"Slow down, John-Peter. This is the best place to look. Do you want to go with me or keep the car running?"

"I think I'll keep the car warm, if you don't mind. I got my fill of snow last night."

For a first attempt on a sleek surface, John-Peter didn't skid too badly as he pulled to the side of the road. Steve grabbed a coil of rope from the back seat and shut the door behind him. John-Peter watched from the frosty, passenger window as Steve walked several paces into the woods. The boy reached for the water jug and tried not to think about blood, Karla's research, or dressing up as an elf in a few hours. A quarter of an hour passed, and Steve came back grinning.

"Got it and she's a beauty. That tree's so far off the beaten path that no one will find it. It's safe until Jack comes back here with his axe."

"How will he know where to find it?"

"He'll know. Jack Cooper knows these woods like the back of his hand."

John-Peter waited until they neared the entrance of the woods before he switched places with his grandfather. The normalcy of the afternoon dimmed the horror of the previous day, but now that they had returned to the village, scintillating images flashed in his mind.

His mother's screams as he played *Bryony*. Dr. Rothgard shining a light into his eyes. The crunching of an animal's skull. The taste of his father's blood.

They were back at Steve's driveway. "Now you'll come back next week and help me decorate it, won't you?"

"Wouldn't miss it, Grandpa."

Melissa was placing the last sugar cookie into a large container when John-Peter stepped into the kitchen. She greeted him with a warm smile and said, "Mabel and I baked these for your Christmas party tonight."

"It's not a Christmas party."

She slid the container next to the others. "Maybe it would feel like a party if you treated it like a party. I'll bet those toys Ed buys will be the only ones some of the poorer kids will receive."

"I know how they feel," John-Peter said irritably. "For two years, I've asked for a cell phone."

Karla was absent from school the next morning, and, to his utter bewilderment, she rebuffed all of John-Peter's attempts to contact her. Was she angry with him for cutting her off Friday night? She hadn't seemed mad when he'd gone to bed, but with girls, you never could tell.

John-Peter was sitting in the lunchroom listening to Trenton rattle about the nervous system of beetles when he heard Amy's voice ring out, "Karla! Where've you been?"

Even from across the room, John-Peter saw the agitation in Karla's flushed face. She raised a door and messaged, "Big blow-up at the house."

"She found the binders?"

"Of course not. But I'm grounded until I produce them, and then she'll discuss my punishment."

"You didn't give them back to her?"

"I'm not that stupid."

She didn't message him again until he walked out of school once classes were done.

"Well, are you ready?"

John-Peter dropped a door and headed for home.

"Come on. One trip before my mother gets home."

"One trip where?" He was not prepared to explore his brain again.

"The parsonage. We've got to find out why you keep seeing John Simons there."

He shrank at the name. "I've got a lot of homework."

Suddenly, Karla was beside him, tugging on his suit coat.

"John-Peter, what's gotten into you?" Karla said aloud.

"Shh," John-Peter glanced cautiously around him. "Okay, I'll come over."

The Dyers' kitchen table was spread full of Cornell's vampire research books. Karla was copying something from one of them into a spiral notebook. Stalling, John-Peter studied the refrigerator shelves.

"Soy milk's in the door," Karla said. "As if you didn't know."

John-Peter slowly, slowly drained one carton and brought the second one to the table with him. Karla slid the open binder across to him and pointed to the middle of the page. Reluctantly, John-Peter read the text and then choked on the milk.

"The real reason for Professor Simotes' frequent visits," Karla said.

"How could he!"

"When his blood treatments stopped working, your dad offered himself to my dad for scientific research."

"What do you mean, 'blood treatments?'"

Karla tapped a binder. "It's all in the books, John-Peter."

John-Peter could no longer escape the truth. Cornell had logged page after page of evidence, beginning with the professor's bizarre confession that he was John Simons all the way through the night he solicited Melissa as his host, his subsequent return of human nature, and the gradual dissipation of the cure. The boy's hands shook, and his eyes burned, but, this time, he maintained control.

"If Cornell didn't have so much proof," John-Peter said, raising his head to meet Karla's sympathetic gaze. "I'd say he was as demented as Grandma Marchellis."

Karla closed her notebook. "But she wasn't demented. She told the truth as it really happened to her."

"I can sense my father's disintegration as it happened: the hyperactive reflexes, his acute senses, the increase in blood pressure and heart rate…"

He remembered standing at the counter and cooking with his father; he felt a strong arm holding him as he drank a bottle. John-Peter looked at the ceiling and forced back hot tears.

Karla nodded happily. "I know. What an amazing opportunity for Daddy. The only time he could ever study vampires was after he staked them. He lost lots of valuable information that way. John Simons is a healed vampire. He is resting in peace and therefore cannot be called up."

"Karla! You're talking about my father!"

"Yes, and he did a heroic thing. Don't you get it, John-Peter? He didn't want to go back. He gave himself up as a test subject and then hired Daddy to stake him so he wouldn't hurt anyone else. How many vampires do you think would be so unselfish? You should be proud of him!"

She stomped into the living room. John-Peter remained in his seat, glowering. She had no right to cast judgment. She wasn't living with his knowledge and twisted memories; her father wasn't a vampire. Karla sat at the end of the coffee table, impatiently drumming her feet.

They were running out of time. Katie would be home in a couple of hours. Another trip into the confines of his mind terrified him, even with Karla sheltering him, but his mouth refused to utter the cowardly words. Trembling, John-Peter stood to join Karla.

"We're only going into the parlor," she said as John-Peter dug his bare heels into the cushion. "If we see anything we don't like, we're out of there, okay?"

"Fine, whatever. But I'm on top this time."

"John-Peter..."

"We do it my way, or we don't do it at all."

John-Peter set the leprechaun on the table and cupped his hand over it. Karla heaved an exaggerated sigh of concession and placed her hand over his, curling and stretching her fingers in a feeble attempt to touch the mouse.

"Anytime you're ready." She sounded annoyed.

The boy clicked once, and the icons lit up. He grazed over the first and clicked again. He stood in the searing hot parlor where the Amish man read from the Bible and all of the men, including John Simons, listened attentively.

"Move out of the doorway," Karla messaged to him.

"And go where?"

"Closer to the preacher. I want to see the guy next to him. He looks familiar to you."

"What if they see me?"

"We'll punt."

John-Peter hugged the wall as he meandered to far end of the room. The fire blazed higher; the men sweated harder as they shifted in their chairs; and still the voice from the man in black droned on and on.

He felt Karla relax, so the boy guessed that meant no one in the room had observed them. The shortest man, the one sitting closest to the fireplace, took off his glasses and rubbed them on his shirt. Karla gasped the same time John-Peter's heart lunged.

It was Dr. Rothgard.

"Click out!" Karla hissed.

John-Peter did, and Karla removed her hand. John-Peter tried shoving the leprechaun back into his pocket, but his trembling hand missed, and the mouse slipped behind the cushion. Karla wrapped her arms around her waist and rocked back and forth as she thought.

"See? I was right. Those aren't real memories. Someone made them up and downloaded them into your mind."

"Karla, you're wrong. I remembered them the second we opened them."

"They can't be real! You and Dr. Rothgard weren't alive a hundred years ago."

"Maybe it's not my memory."

Karla stopped rocking, puzzled. "What are you talking about?"

"Someone created files of my memories, right? What if that person wanted to add a few more that didn't belong to me?"

"I can't see the sense in it."

"Karla, none of this makes sense."

She kneeled against the couch and leaned over John-Peter. Her locket grazed his cheek, and he raised his head in surprise. "What are you doing?"

"Finding the leprechaun. We're going back in."

"What for?"

"To talk to the person with the answers." She pulled her hand out from under the cushion. "Got it!"

Karla set the leprechaun back on the table, but the boy folded his hands across his belly and looked away from her and that ugly, little man in green. "I'm not doing it."

"Fine, but I've got the mouse, and I'm opening the file anyway. So if you don't put your hand on mine, you'll be stuck in there by yourself."

She mustn't think he was afraid. He couldn't bear it if she did. John-Peter counted to ten in French and then positioned his left hand over hers. A click, and the lights went up. A second click, and they were back inside the parlor just in time to see John Simons extend his goblet.

"For the blood," John Simons said, "is the life."

Karla poked John-Peter in the small of his back. He took a deep breath and said, "Father, where shall I obtain this blood?"

The beguiling expression became a leer; and a set of sharp white canine teeth appeared. John Simons' eyes glowed red and looked straight through John-Peter. The boy shrank back.

"Ask your mother," he sneered.

The scene turned black. Karla clicked the mouse, and they were back inside the motor home.

"Oh, wow!" Karla whispered. "You were programmed to ask all along."

It was true. Someone was really controlling his mind. "So...now what?"

"I don't know." Her eyes rested on the wall clock. "Oh, gosh, John-Peter, get out of here! My mother will be home any minute."

It took an effort to lift his aching, buzzing head from the couch. That should make homework fun tonight. Karla was already gathering up the binders from the table. He plodded home in the cold twilight. Just as he opened the back door, Karla messaged him.

"Daddy said Dr. Rothgard was the one overseeing the blood treatments. You need to go to Thornton and talk to him."

"I can't. My mother placed a password to his account."

"Well, slide extra hard down the tree or something. You've got to see him."

He didn't like the muffled tone of her thoughts. Karla was communicating behind a door. Karla was holding out on him. "Okay, Karla, what gives?"

The hesitation before her answer gave Karla away. "I don't know what you're talking about."

"You either tell me what you know or plan to be awake all night. Because if you don't, when you're asleep, I'll pry your little mind open and find out for myself!"

"You wouldn't!"

John-Peter opened the back door of his house and started to close the interior one to Karla.

"Okay, okay. Dr. Rothgard started host experiments a lot earlier than we thought."

Mabel beamed at him as she pulled a casserole dish from the oven. "Kellen's in Florida, so I made you this."

She lifted the steaming, glass lid and John-Peter peered inside and sniffed the mouthwatering macaroni and soy cheese, speckled with analog ham. "Is it done?"

"Five minutes."

"I'll be there with bells on. Where's Mother?"

"Watching the news. She's trying to catch Kellen's new commercial."

Melissa patted the spot next to her when she saw John-Peter, and he sank gratefully into the plushy softness, while messaging, "How much earlier, Karla?"

"Almost a century."

John-Peter turned his head slightly toward Melissa. "So, Mother, Kellen has a new commercial?"

"That's what he said, but I haven't seen it yet." The picture melted into wavy lines. "John-Peter, would you please adjust those rabbit ears."

He did, while messaging back to Karla, "You're not talking about Grandma Marchellis' blood donating, are you?" The picture returned to its former clarity. "Because that wasn't Dr. Rothgard facilitating, it was…"

"But he did. He's a vampire, too, John-Peter."

The boy started at the picture on the screen as the newscaster began.

"Forty-seven year old Marcus O'Reilly disappeared from his home last night, and police have no clues to his whereabouts. O'Reilly, a filing clerk in the Evansville law offices of Gunderson and Smith, was scheduled for a book signing this evening at the Jenson Public Library to promote his self-published poetry books, *I Have a Secret in My Attic*, and *Tulips*

250

in the Garden. O'Reilly was last seen wearing his trademark suit jacket. If anyone has any clue to his whereabouts, contact..."

The boy squirmed under his mother's incredulous stare. Even she couldn't deny it. The suit coat in that photograph of Marcus O'Reilly was identical to the one John-Peter now wore.

Mabel appeared in the doorway. "Dinner's ready," she said impatiently, hands on her hips. "Didn't anyone hear me calling?"

It was a quiet dinner. At bedtime, John-Peter tried messaging Karla, but she had shut all her doors. The princess wasn't in the closet. Even Bertrand was sound asleep. He lay awake and stared at the ceiling for a very long time.

The next day, John-Peter was dialing the combination on his locker when Karla and Megan walked past him, heads together while they chattered like magpies. He never understood how girls could be so interested in absolutely nothing. Where was her fervor last night when he tried contacting her?

"I'll call you later," Megan promised as she sailed past his locker. "Okay!" Karla said, while lightly touched John-Peter's arm. She lowered her voice. "Sorry about last night. I heard you calling, but I..."

John-Peter shut his locker. "Come with me to Jenson today."

"Jenson? Why?"

"I want to see Grandma Simotes, and I don't want to go by myself."

"Does your mother know?"

"No."

"Then how will you get there?"

John-Peter lost patience with her drilling. "So will you go or not?"

"Might as well. I'm already in trouble."

The taxi was waiting for them in front of the school. Karla entered first, and John-Peter slid beside her. "Jenson Nursing Home," he told to the driver.

The man flipped his meter and started down Main Street. John-Peter sensed Karla's questions so he looked out the window to quell any suspicions the man might raise.

"I thought you didn't have Kellen's credit card anymore."

"I don't."

"So how are you paying for this?"

"I'm charging it to Kellen's account."

"Your stepfather won't like that, John-Peter."

He dropped a door.

When the cab pulled up in front of the old one-story, yellow-brick building, John-Peter wondered why his mother had insisted on keeping Grandma Simotes in this shabby place when Kellen had offered to pay for her care at Golden Years. Sure, Jenson Nursing Home was closer to Munsonville, but how often did his mother really drive out to see Grandma? Karla didn't think a single word, but worded thoughts were unnecessary. Inside, the pale, dingy green walls sighed for fresh paint. The trapped air hinted of urine and death.

"Carol Simotes," John-Peter announced to the woman working the reception desk.

Once in the room, they just stood there, staring first at the sleeping figure of Grandma Simotes as she took shallow, uneven breaths, and then at the worn, rosebud wallpaper and white curtains yellowed with age. A periwinkle vinyl chair sat at one side of the bed; a nightstand with a beige plastic cup and pitcher stood at the other.

"How long do you think she'll sleep?" Karla murmured.

"She always sleeps, Karla."

"You don't think she'll wake up?"

"Nope."

Karla slipped her hand inside John-Peter's. "I'm sorry."

"Don't be. She's almost dead anyway."

She snatched away her hand and said in a soft, shocked tone, "How can you be so hard-hearted?"

"Me? She's the one that hit a defenseless baby."

A few minutes later they were back on the front steps of the nursing home. A van pulled up just past them: Don Cates, Exterminator. Karla strained her neck to read a sign across the street. "Is that the pawn shop?"

"Yes. Would you like to see it?"

"Oh, may I?"

No scent of Irish soda bread greeted John-Peter at the door, but he didn't expect it either, not this late in the afternoon.

At the sound of the bell, the little old man stumbled from behind the curtain and uttered his stock phrase.

"If you break it, you buy it." Then Eircheard recognized John-Peter. "This is a mite unusual, so early in the week."

"This is Karla, my friend from school."

"Hi," Karla said without enthusiasm. She pretended to browse a table stacked full of fairy rag dolls while John-Peter pretended to read a book of medieval Irish poetry.

"John-Peter, I know this place," she said into his mind. "I was here with my parents when I was a baby."

He almost dropped the book. "You were?"

"Daddy paid that guy good money for information about a portal."

"Portal? What kind of portal?"

"I don't know. We never came back. And then Daddy died."

So Katie thought Eircheard's Emporium was seedy? Yeah, maybe she had another reason for avoiding it.

"I called you last night to tell you about a local writer who disappeared from his home a couple of days ago," John-Peter messaged back. "I think I have his suit coat."

"The one you're wearing now?"

"Yes. But, Karla, he was wearing it when he disappeared. I bought it weeks ago."

"I want to go home."

They silently discussed it all the way to Munsonville. Several times the driver, disbelieving the stillness, turned around, as if intending to catch them mischief-making. But both passengers intently studied the bleak landscape outside their respective windows.

"What kind of a portal was Cornell looking for?"

"How should I know? I was just a baby."

"Then why are you certain he paid a lot of money for its knowledge?"

"Because he carried it all in a paper sack and counted out bills for a long time."

"And what did he gain?"

"Nothing but a stupid sentence."

"Come again?"

"That little troll said something about doors opening and closing. I don't remember it exactly."

Silence.

"John-Peter, what's behind that curtain?"

"I don't know. Storage, maybe."

"What if it's the way to the portal?"

"Highly unlikely."

"You bought a coat there weeks ago that some guy was wearing a couple of days ago, and now he's missing. Doesn't that seem odd to you?"

"*If* it's the same coat."

"Maybe Eircheard kidnapped him."

"Perhaps."

"There's only one way to find out. After school tomorrow?"

Despite the emotional toll from the voyages into his brain, John-Peter felt strangely excited about this trip. The only other physical location they had explored together was the parsonage, and everyone knew its ghost rumors. The emporium was common, every day, and Eircheard would be sitting there while John-Peter's incorporeal spirit entered it. Might the pawn shop be the headquarters of some great conspiracy?

Soon it was after school, and, following some snarky comments from Karla about taking it easy on the soy milk because "Mom's getting suspicious," John-Peter was lying on the couch with Karla beside him, feeling his body growing light and feathery until it wisped out of his body.

"Is there enough silver cord to make it to Jenson?"

"That's up to you, John-Peter."

The boy unraveled gossamer threads until he reached the pawn shop. He hovered over the large keyhole in its front door, pointed, and messaged, "I'm going inside this way."

"Quit being a show-off."

He spun like a whirlwind until he'd wound up tightly enough to slip through the hole, tugging his silver cord behind him. He unrolled himself as he floated to the ground. His feet touched, and the boy paused, waiting for dizziness to depart and balance to return.

"The curtain, John-Peter."

He obediently wafted past the sleeping Eircheard, softly snoring around his pipe, and moved aside the curtain.

"Well?"

"It's a basement stairway."

"Go down."

"Right-o."

He followed the dank wood steps to the underground, dirt-floored room, which, except for an assortment of damp logs and rotting tree stumps, was empty and hollow.

"Nothing here, Karla."

"Okay." He could plainly hear the disappointment in her voice. "And I was so sure."

As John-Peter flitted past the snoring Eircheard, he blew a light airy stream across the old man's left ear. Eircheard muttered in his sleep, stirred slightly, and scratched his ear. The boy was halfway across the room when he had an idea.

"Karla, how do you know this isn't my imagination?"

"John-Peter, of course, you're really there."

"Then let's prove it by taking something home with us."

"Like what?"

John-Peter scanned the merchandise tables for something suitable, something unique to Eircheard's, something they could not explain away.

"Hurry up, John-Peter. It's getting late."

"Don't rush me."

He continued browsing until, with a start, he found it. Leering up at him from amongst a cluster of pottery was a ceramic leprechaun. Its tiny black eyes sat under a pair of bushy red eyebrows, and its wild red hair poked out from a tall green hat. Across its belt were the words: "Cha d'dhuin doras nach d'fhosgail doras."

"John-Peter!"

"Karla, you won't believe this. I've found the most amazing thing."

"John-Peter, hurry up!"

"How do I get it to you?"

"Take it by the window!"

John-Peter rushed to the glass. He held it out, and it was gone. A door slammed; his heart skipped a beat; and he felt Karla scoot away from him. In surprise, John-Peter grabbed the back of the couch, sat up straight, and his heart sank.

What was Katie doing home from work so early?

CHAPTER 18: FALLEN HERO

"Well now, John-Peter," Steve said, "Are they straight?"

John-Peter edged away from the tree, picked up his water jug, and studied the results. His grandfather hadn't lost the knack for perfect lights. No crooked rows, no bare patches.

"It looks great, Grandpa," John-Peter said.

"Then see if you can find the star while I check the chili and start the cornbread. Maybe we can get all the ornaments hung before lunch."

"Ten-four."

John-Peter gave the lights another approving look. The tree scented the entire room with pine, and it was, as Steve had said, a real beauty. It stood just shy enough from the ceiling to hold a topper and its lush, bluish branches partly obscured the room's large picture window.

With less than a week left until Christmas, most people in Munsonville had their Christmas trees up and decorated, but not his grandfather. Steve wanted to maximize its freshness. He hadn't sent Jack to fetch it until yesterday.

John-Peter knelt on the floor by the smallest box and peeled back the tape. Nothing but the manger scene. He moved to another box. He was dying to go back to Eircheard's, but an opportunity to do so would be long in coming. During Katie's work hours, Karla now had to stay at her grandparents' house. He wished Karla would hurry up and perfect teleportation. Then maybe she could figure out a way to get him back inside the pawn shop from their respective residences. That would thwart Katie's control trip.

The star wasn't in this box either. The boy scooted to the next box. What kind of portal had Cornell been seeking? And why did he think Eircheard could direct him to it?

An agitated Karla had called him that first night, once the mothers had finished their respective, loud venting, demanding an answer: Why did Eircheard have a leprechaun that matched the one John-Peter carried in his pocket?

"Maybe they were mass produced back in the 1960s, and Eircheard got lucky," John-Peter had said, watching Bertrand swat at a tiny cheese cracker Karla hovered just out his reach.

"Will you get serious? Who'd want to buy such an ugly thing?" She tossed the cracker past the blocks, and Bertrand leaped over them in frantic pursuit of dinner. "I wonder what the words mean."

John-Peter leaned against the bed and clasped his hands behind his neck. "That's easy."

"You can read them?"

"Yes, ma'am."

"So are you going to tell?"

"Bertrand wants another cracker."

A shower of orange squares rattled onto the floor. Bertrand's eyes bulged with delight, and he dove into the pile. "Satisfied?"

John-Peter ignored the smirk in her voice. "Remember how you said Cornell was looking for a portal, and Eircheard said something about doors?"

"Yeah, so?"

"'Cha d'dhuin doras nach d'fhosgail doras' means 'No door ever closed, but another opened.'"

Karla was quiet for a moment. "How do you know that?" The sarcastic tone was gone.

John-Peter closed his eyes and sleepiness sailed him to the top of a large oak tree where the wind rustled the leaves, and the boughs echoed with the hollow notes of Fawn's tin whistle. He reopened his eyes, but the lids remained heavy, and he had to concentrate on forming the words.

"I'm not certain," John-Peter said slowly as he watched Bertrand enthusiastically nibbled a corner off one cracker, then another, and another. "I just know it."

Still no star. He reached for the last box. Even before he unwrapped the first package, the boy felt points poking out of the newspaper. "Got it!"

The response from the kitchen was a loud clatter.

"Grandpa!"

Silence, scary silence.

John-Peter scrambled to his feet and reached the doorway in three quick steps. A drawer lay upside down on the floor. The cornmeal bag had spilled over the scattered silverware. Steve lay motionless in a crumpled heap.

With a pounding heart, John-Peter crouched over the too-still figure and nudged Steve's shoulder.

"Grandpa?" he whispered.

He held his hand over Steve's nose. His grandfather was breathing!

John-Peter quickly turned off the chili and sped to the phone. Megan's dad picked up on the second ring. "Fire department."

"My grandfather fell."

"John-Peter?"

"Yes, sir."

"At home?"

"Yes, sir."

"Don't move him. We'll be right there."

John-Peter hung up the phone and braced himself against the counter. Steve's face was gray, and his breath came in short, irregular gasps. What was taking them so long?

The screen door banged opened, and Megan's dad, with two more firemen behind, burst into the room. In seconds they were on the floor, surrounding Steve. The youngest looked back at John-Peter, pointed to the living room, and said sternly, "Out!"

"But this is my grandfa..."

Megan's father looked up. "Git!"

John-Peter got. The soft tree lights hurt his eyes, so he stood before the window and gazed over Lake Munson's slate waters, not thinking. After what felt like a century, Megan's dad appeared in the doorway.

"We're taking him to Jenson Memorial. Where's your grandmother?"

"In Jenson shopping with my mother."

"Are you able to contact them?"

"Sure, on her cell."

"Well, do it." Megan's dad turned on his heel.

"May I ride along?"

"No."

The door slammed shut. His mind whirling with half-formed, fearful thoughts, John-Peter picked up the receiver. His mother answered on the third ring.

"Hello?" Melissa sounded out of breath.

He paused and willed his voice to remain steady. "Grandpa fell. Megan's dad is taking him to Jenson."

Melissa gasped. "We're on our way!"

John-Peter pushed the receiver button down, debated his options, and redialed.

"Merle's Taxi."

"This is John-Peter Simotes. My dad said to call you for a ride into Jenson."

The light chuckle made John-Peter's heart sink. "Sorry, kid, but after the stunt you pulled last week, Kellen left specific orders not to drive you anywhere."

Beep, beep, beep, beep, beep, beep, beep, beep.

Sue's Diner had never seemed so far away even though John-Peter's long, skinny legs quickly carried him there, so quickly that he could only pant his request to Amy's older sister.

"Sure, Jack is here," Rhonda said as she rang up a ticket. "He's in the kitchen, I think."

The smell of sizzling onions greeted John-Peter before Jack did. The steam warmed John-Peter's face, but failed to remove the icy fear trickling through him.

"Oh hey, John-Peter, what's the word?" Jack moved the onions around the large griddle.

"They took my grandfather to the hospital."

The color drained from Jack's face, and he immediately set down his spatula and turned off the burner. His apron went over his head and into the hamper at the same time Ann walked into the kitchen.

"Got three more orders for you, Jack." She laid the tickets on the counter.

"Send Trenton back here. I'm taking John-Peter to Jenson."

"Jenson? Oh God, that wasn't Steve?"

"'Fraid so." He fiddled inside his greasy pants pocket and tossed the keys to John-Peter. "Warm the car up for me. I'll be ready in a minute." Jack turned toward the back stairs and ran up them, two at a time.

Ann's eyes were full of sympathy. "I'm really sorry about your grandfather, but I'm sure he'll be fine." Her chestnut hair had almost as much gray in it as Darlene's.

"I hope so." His traitorous voice shook a little.

John-Peter walked out the service door to Jack's car. The second he inserted the key into the ignition, his mind flashed back to last Saturday when he sat in the driver's seat of Steve's car. He quickly slid into the passenger's seat.

A door slammed. Jack was trotting down the apartment stairs. The car door opened, shut, and then Jack held his gloved hands over the heater.

"Man, it's cold," Jack said with thick, white breath. "You're not running this weekend, are you?"

"No, my boss is gone until mid-January."

Jack stretched his arm across the passenger seat as he backed the car up treacherously close to the lake. "Be nice to have a break, huh?"

"I guess so."

And that was all. Once they left Main Street behind him, Jack turned the radio on low. Christmas carols crackled through the static. The sky was gray; the frozen ground was gray; and even the roads were gray from old salt. John-Peter glanced at Jack who, with a blank expression on his face, rested his arm over the steering wheel. It was clear which parent gave Trenton his brains.

The near-empty parking lot of Jenson Memorial Hospital matched John-Peter's desolation. Without a word, Jack dropped John-Peter off at the emergency room doors. The boy extended his hand and said, "Thanks for the ride, Mr. Cooper."

Jack blinked, surprised. "I'm only parking the car."

"You're coming inside?"

"I'm not leaving you alone until we find out what's going on."

"I'm not..."

John-Peter began and then stopped. He had started to say, "I'm not six," and then decided not to insult his transportation, just in case. He passed through the sliding glass doors and paced back and forth on the wet rug, wondering why parking in a deserted lot challenged Jack.

The doors moved back on their track. Jack Cooper, hands in pockets, strode between them. "What's going on?"

"I didn't ask."

Jack put his arm around John-Peter's shoulder. "Come on."

Together they approached the formidable counter of the knowledge of good and evil. John-Peter hoped its fruit was sweet. Its brown-haired angel looked up and smiled at Jack. "May I help you, sir?"

"This boy's grandfather came here by ambulance."

"Name?

"Steve Barnes."

She flipped through a stack of charts. "I'll have someone take you to the second floor. That's our cardiac unit."

Cardiac unit? For a fall? The angel was a demonic bearer of bad news after all. A chubby red-haired candy striper magically appeared from nowhere. Her freckles stood out from her face, as if ready to leap off. Obviously an unlikely candidate for Kellen's photo collection. The elevator door closed behind them and soon reopened.

His mother and grandmother were sitting by the window of the waiting room directly across from the elevator. Darlene's head rested against the back of the chair; her eyes stared up at the ceiling. Melissa was gazing at the floor. Through the window was the same bleak sky. No one else occupied the room.

John-Peter sank into the vinyl-cushioned chair across from Darlene, but, before he could speak, Jack sat next to Melissa and picked up her limp hand with his two larger ones. "How is he?"

A little, tired smile barely moved the corners of her lips as she looked up at him. "Actually, Jack, he's going to be okay. The doctor said the heart attack was mild."

"I'm glad."

Relief shook through John-Peter, and he clenched his hands to stop the trembling. His grandfather would be okay!

"A small clot caused a blockage," Melissa continued, "and they're fixing that now."

Jack Cooper smiled a wary half-smile. "Good."

"Thank you for bringing John-Peter."

"Anytime."

John-Peter looked away. Across the room, George Bailey, on bended knees, silently pleaded to Mr. Potter. Directly below the television mounted on the wall, only half of the colored, drooping strands on the tabletop Christmas tree winked.

"I have to get back." Jack removed his hands. "Do you need anything?"

Melissa shook her head. "No, I don't think so. Thank you, though, for your support. It means so much."

"Okay." Jack rose to leave and nodded at John-Peter. "Take care of the ladies."

John-Peter raised two thumbs, but he did not smile. After Jack left, Darlene, eyes now closed, asked, "Did anyone call Kellen?"

"I did," Melissa said. "Kellen's still out of town, but he wants to stay informed."

Darlene opened her eyes. "Since it's not serious, I almost wish I hadn't told Brian. He contacted a friend with a private plane, and he's probably almost here."

Melissa abruptly leaned over the arm rail for her purse.

"Here," she said, handing John-Peter a five-dollar bill. "You must be starving. Why don't you get something to eat? I saw some vending machines at the end of the hall."

"I'm not hungry." He wasn't, even though breakfast had ended eons ago.

Darlene glanced at Melissa, nodded knowingly, and then looked at John-Peter. "Well, I could use some coffee. John-Peter, will you bring me a cup?"

"And some tea for me, please?" Melissa hastily added.

"Gladly." He shoved the money on top of the leprechaun, thankful for an excuse to walk and think.

"Black, John-Peter."

"I know, Grandma."

A certain impression had nagged at John-Peter all afternoon, and he could now identify it: the automatic concern everyone had for Steve. He knew everyone liked Steve, but he now saw the depth of care, concern, and respect people had for him. It was no slight thing.

The hall curved at the end, and there, a few feet ahead, stood the vending machines. And yes, they accepted five-dollar bills, just as his mother had said. Well, she would know. She must have spent much time here when his father was sick.

His father. Something hard twisted inside him.

The slot machine gobbled his money. John-Peter made his selections. Walking back, the boy remembered a conversation with Steve earlier in the fall over the Bible verse, "Greater love hath no man than this, that a man lay down his life for his friends." Until now, John-Peter had measured greatness with artistic success, but today his arrogant confidence in that perspective had slipped a notch, and that was because of his grandfather. Steve used a different yardstick, one that valued service to others as being greater than personal fulfillment. Could it be that...

"No!"

The elevators doors opened; Uncle Brian rush through them, and his grandmother screamed again: *"No! No! No! No! No!"*

Melissa appeared in the doorway, stopping at the sight of the pleading look in her brother's face. Slowly, she turned her head from side to side. Uncle Brian's face crumpled. She held out her arms, and Uncle Brian rushed to meet them.

John-Peter stopped short, still holding a cup of coffee in his right hand and a cup of tea in his left. He had never seen his Uncle Brian cry.

CHAPTER 19: BLOOD REVENGE

John-Peter sat at the piano forcing himself to think past the fog in his head as he vainly tried perfecting *Amazing Grace*, the hymn Darlene insisted John-Peter play during the funeral service because it was Steve's favorite.

For once, his heart was not into music, and his mistakes reflected it. The wake was tomorrow; the funeral was the following day, so he berated his lack of polish and ordered the return of composure and self-control. He had no for room for missteps.

But another succession of flat chords, bad rhythms, and inappropriate syncopations destroyed the last of John-Peter's motivation. Wearily, but, reluctantly, he shut the lid. He was in no hurry to end this day and rush the advent of tomorrow.

And that had nothing to do with having to wear his gray and lavender homecoming suit.

His mother was in her room packing for their stay in Thornton. John-Peter's own suitcase waited near his bedroom, needing only to be dropped inside the trunk of his mother's car. His grandmother and Uncle Brian were at the funeral home finalizing last minute details. Aunt Cindy and the girls had arrived earlier in the day and were probably enjoying the indoor heated pool.

Although his grandfather's unexpected death stunned him, what followed it bewildered him. No matter how much people had liked Steve when he was alive, those sentiments were nothing compared to the attention Munsonville bestowed upon him in death. It seemed as if the whole town died with him.

The mayor, Bert Joyce, whose wife was the secretary at Munsonville School, declared a two-day holiday for Steve's wake and funeral. Munsonville School, already on Christmas break, delayed the restart of school by a week; stores closed for business; and even Sue's diner shut its doors. Katie relented enough to allow Karla to babysit Bertrand while John-Peter was staying in Thornton.

Perhaps John-Peter's biggest surprise was the courtesy, deference, and respect Kellen was showing to his grandmother. For although Darlene vastly preferred the dignified atmosphere of Franklin & Mores, Steve—true to his abiding family loyalties—had long ago made it clear that when the time came, Kellen would handle the funeral arrangements.

And handle it Kellen did, from the velvet-lined, mahogany casket to the gourmet, post-funeral banquet inside the HHG Hotel's grand ballroom. When John-Peter had overheard Melissa telling Darlene everything was free, the boy had nearly fallen off his piano bench. Kellen's funerals weren't cheap.

His stepfather had pleaded, yes, actually pleaded, for Darlene to let him hold Steve's body until Christmas, at least, had passed, so she would not have to bury her husband on Christmas Eve, but Darlene's "No" was loud and firm. What a miserable way to spend a holiday and an eighteenth birthday. If ever he needed the princess to come to him, it was now.

The open sheet music reproached him for neglecting the practice session, but John-Peter didn't care. It took supreme effort to simply force his heavy limbs off the bench, much less play anything spectacular. He shuffled to the door, switched off the light, and hoped, all the way down the hall.

He paused before his mother's room, knocked, and called out, "I'm taking a shower."

"Let me know when you're out," Melissa called back. "I still need one."

"Yep."

John-Peter stopped at the entranceway to his dark room, silently begging the mirror to give up its secrets for him, just for tonight. Then, without a sound, he entered and closed the door. With equal quietness, the boy opened the closet, peeped into the magic glass, and gazed at a pair of green-flecked brown eyes.

So much for paradise. He kicked the door shut and flicked on the light. It sure felt lonesome without Bertrand. As he slipped off his shoes, John-Peter noticed Mabel had pressed his suit and hung it on the back of the door, a banner of the heartache awaiting him. He would just have to get through it. There was no other way.

He kept his shower brief, on the outside chance the princess might show up after all. On the way to his mother's room, John-Peter tossed his towel in the laundry room, not caring if it fell near the hamper or not.

"I'm out!" John-Peter called as he gave one, hard thump on Melissa's door. He did not wait for her response.

For more than an hour John-Peter stood motionless in front of his mirror and willed the princess to appear, fighting against his drooping eyes and sagging frame. Before he lay down, the boy locked his bedroom door and positioned the closet door to get a full view of the mirror from the bed. Just in case.

Memories of his grandfather floated in and out of his dreams: a game of badminton in Grover's Park, emptying garbage cans at Copy 'N' Print, mulching the extensive vegetable garden, and stifling yawns during Steve's methodical readings from picture Bibles.

Just before dawn the princess came to him, looking strangely like Karla and clothed only in lavender. She slipped between the quilts and snuggled next to him, delightfully comforting the aching desolation he'd felt all day. He held his breath as she covered his face with sweet kisses, but when he could no longer suppress the urge to touch the petals in her hair, she vanished. Even after John-Peter awakened, he swore the faint essence of lavender still clung to his sheets.

Arthur and the sun arrived simultaneously, just as John-Peter popped a vitamin pill, and Melissa swallowed the last of her tea. The icy cold spell had departed, and the weather was mild and filled with bright sunshine. The wake would not officially start until two o'clock, which made John-Peter Chief Babysitter. He and his three nieces would remain inside Brian's suite until that time, so the adults could finalize the arrangements with Kellen.

"Just let them watch as much TV as they like, and I promise you they'll be perfect vegetables," Aunt Cindy said as she looped the long handle of her purse over her shoulder and glanced anxiously at her wristwatch. Uncle Brian had already left. "We monitor it at home, so this will be a real treat for them."

For the next several hours, the little girls gobbled up cartoon after cartoon while John-Peter tried blocking from his mind the crunching sound of tiny bones as his father gnawed on them. He didn't see what was so funny about the cartoons and told them so.

"Oh, John-Peter, they're not real," Deanna said with a roll of her eyes. "Mommy says you're way too sensitive where animals are concerned."

That kind of superior tone from such a little girl rankled him. "Oh she did, did she? Wait till I get you a kitten for Christmas!"

Ellie flew to his side, her face full of alarm. "Don't do it, John-Peter!"

"Oh Ellie, quit being such a baby." Deanna tossed her head. John-Peter's just being mean."

Fawn stopped chewing on her index finger long enough to wail, "I want a kitten!"

"You know what Daddy said." Ellie's voice was hushed, as if she had just disclosed a great secret.

John-Peter stretched and threw his legs on the Parnian cocktail table. "But do you know why he's against it?"

"Yes. Because everyone doesn't dote on animals like you do."

"Wrong, Deanna. It's because every pet your ever father owned died."

Fawn's finger fell out of her mouth. Ellie's eyes filled with tears, and she snuggled close to John-Peter.

"That's so sad," Ellie murmured. "Poor Daddy."

Deanna cocked her head and narrowed her eyes. "He's lying. Daddy never had any pets. He said so."

"Really? Ask him about Scooter, Snowbell, and Charcoal. Wild animal, house fire, and mail truck, in that order."

The telephone rang, and Deanna jumped up and grabbed it.

"Truth hurts, baby, doesn't it?" John-Peter called after her with a smirk.

"Hello?" Deanna said in her most grown-up voice. "Fine, thank you. Yes, I will tell him." She hung up the phone and smiled smugly at John-Peter. "Daddy said for you to bring us across the street."

With a feigned, bored yawn, John-Peter reached behind him for the remote control and clicked off the television. "I have to comb my hair."

"Daddy said, 'Now.'"

Ellie dragged her fingers through the tangled strands of red and looked worried. "Will it take long? You have an awful lot of hair."

John-Peter gently pushed her away and stood. "Best put your coats on while I'm gone."

Fawn threw back her head and howled.

"She can't do it by herself," Ellie said.

"Deanna will help her."

He sauntered past Deanna's aghast expression to the oversized bathroom, which sported such luxuries as twin marble tubs, solid gold fixtures, and a hot tub, and shut the door. It took an entire five minutes to run a comb through the knotted locks and to toss the stray strands from the suit coat onto the floor. Finally, John-Peter smoothed the lines of his jacket. No spoiling of lavender, not after last night.

A little fist thumped on the door. "John-Peter, you'd better get out here right now!"

The boy opened the door and laughed at the spectacle greeting his eyes. Fawn's arms were stuck in her sleeves, and Ellie was vainly struggling to free them. Deanna, arms crossed, plopped onto the forsaken cocktail table, glared at John-Peter, and rudely tapped her foot.

John-Peter merely tweaked Deanna's cheek. "Guess you're not as smart as you thought." He knelt in front of Fawn, slid off her coat, and pulled the cuffs of her dress into her hands.

"Hold," John-Peter said, and Fawn's fingers obediently curled around the lace. The coat glided into place, and he turned his attention to Ellie fumbling with the large, slippery buttons on her best coat.

"I'll get them for you, honey," he said to Ellie, who rewarded his efforts with a wet, smacking kiss on his nose.

"I have a muff," Deanna said, brandishing her prize before Fawn, which elicited an ear-splitting shriek.

John-Peter grabbed his water jug and ushered the girls to the door. As Deanna passed him, the boy snatched away the white fur.

"Hey!" Deanna cried with an outstretched hand and a leap into the air. "You give that back right now, John-Peter!"

John-Peter wadded the fluff up his sleeve. "When you learn respect."

Down in the lobby, John-Peter grabbed Fawn's hand with his right one, while Ellie slipped hung onto his left wrist. He led his bobbing gaggle out the hotel door and into that of HHG. Deanna plodded behind them, head down, as befitting her position, until they cleared the entrance.

"I'm gonna tell!" Deanna dashed ahead and smacked into an elegantly dressed elderly couple. John-Peter reined her back and stuffed the muff into the back of her coat. He was never having children.

Despite the foyer's crowds, a despairing stillness pervaded the air, broken only by the occasional sound of weeping. Even the little girls must have felt it because their eyes grew large, and not one uttered another word until Fawn whimpered, "I want Mommy."

"I'm looking for her now," John-Peter said, intensifying his grip on the little girls' hands and frantically searching for Cindy.

He wedged them through the mob to the front of his grandfather's viewing room, positioned himself near a window, and slid his water jug behind a row of floral displays. His aunt was standing near the casket with Uncle Brian. After a chorus of, "Mom!" his nieces bounded away to their mother. Each person in attendance wore black, and that made John-Peter in his gray and lavender suit feel more conspicuous than his green skin ever had. Yet, as the afternoon limped along, it appeared obvious no one noticed his inappropriate pastels.

His grandmother greeted visitors with easy grace and only an occasional catch in her throat. His mother continually dabbed her eyes, but that didn't affect her ability to be nice.

Uncle Brian, on the other hand, cried fresh tears each time a former client of Steve's approached him, especially if that person praised Steve's honesty, integrity, and superior manner of conducting business. With each encounter, Uncle Brian's eyes grew redder and puffier, but he did not seem to notice. He only clutched Aunt Cindy a lot tighter.

John-Peter solemnly shook each proffered hand, even the one attached to Curtis Chandler, meekly acquiesced to hug after and hug, and submitted to tear-streaked women planting raspberry lipstick on his cheeks. One by one, the entire population of Munsonville filed their way through the room, including the Daltons, the Walkers, the Harpers, and every single one of the Millers. The Rogers family came, too, except for Courtney.

"She's at work," Mrs. Rogers brushed her cheek against John-Peter's. "She'll stop in on break."

Lauren pretended to be crying because she was at a wake, but Trenton shifted his eyes away as he mumbled, "I'm sorry."

Katie allowed Karla to approach John-Peter and give him a hug. Over the top of her head, John-Peter saw Curtis monitor their every move.

Karla pulled back to look up at him with eyes full of mist. "I'm really, really, really sorry about your grandfather."

Sudden anguish filled his throat and burned his eyes. John-Peter quickly looked down and inspected the crimson carpet for signs of lint.

"Me, too," he choked out.

Courtney arrived thirty minutes later and stayed only long enough to pay her condolences to the immediate family. She did, however, linger near John-Peter.

"Is it true you're staying in Thornton all week?"

"Yes."

"I'm working overtime this weekend. Everyone's in for the holidays, ya know?"

"Have fun."

Courtney blushed as red as the rug. "What I'm trying to say, John-Peter, is that if you need to talk, stop by. Okay?"

Luckily, Mrs. Clements was behind her, and John-Peter didn't think it polite to ignore the librarian.

One hour, two hours passed, and still the line hadn't diminished, but Kellen bestowed his most solicitous attention on Darlene. Kellen literally tripped over his shiny, black shoes to bring her newly brewed cups of coffee; one lace-trimmed, HHG monogrammed handkerchief after another; plates of fresh melons and strawberries from the refreshment room; and a single red rose. Once, Kellen even linked his arm through Darlene's and drew her to a soft, burgundy easy chair, insisting she needed a break. No wonder Kellen was successful.

"Dale Carnegie classes?" John-Peter scornfully asked when he bumped into Kellen while leaving his stepfather's private bathroom. Kellen shrugged his shoulders and ignored John-Peter's breach of his rules.

"It's quite simple, kid," Kellen said. "Most people are suckers that fall for any faddish item under the sun, especially if their neighbor got one first. They deserve to have their money taken." His face softened. "And then you meet those rare good-hearted individuals, where it's a privilege to lie at their feet. Your grandmother is one of them."

John-Peter quickly assessed Kellen's pale countenance to see if he was joking, but his stepfather's face bore no guile.

"Skip the refreshment room if you're hungry because I doubt there's anything vegan in there. Just grab something from the freezer."

"Merci beaucoup."

On the way to the kitchen, John-Peter reflected upon Kellen's words and wondered if Kellen might have built his empire with qualities other than sheer gimmickry. As he neared the refreshment room, John-Peter decided to grab a plate of fruit while he heated his pizza, until he heard the all-too-familiar voices of the detestable Chandlers.

"It's too bad about Steve," Madeline said. "He just missed meeting the new pastor."

"Especially with tomorrow night's midnight service," Evelyn added. "Christmas was always Steve's favorite holiday. Well, it will be nice to open up the old church. You say this new pastor is aware of its ghost story?"

"Fairy tales don't frighten ex-missionaries," Max said, "especially those accustomed to rough areas. I understand he specifically asked for this assignment."

"How funny," Madeleine said. "And you say he's not originally from Munsonville?"

"No, he's from..."

John-Peter hurried to the kitchen. He'd lost his taste for melons and berries. The Chandlers' words rattled inside his head as he rummaged through the freezer for a few pizzas. His grandfather had said nothing about the reopening of Munsonville Congregational Church, but, then again, why should he have mentioned it? To be refused once again by his only grandson?

He slammed the microwave door and set the timer. He'd gladly have attended a million church services if only they would bring back his grandfather.

Ellie and Fawn walked into the kitchen as he swallowed the last bite from the last pizza.

"We're bored," Ellie said.

"Can't help you." John-Peter rose to leave. His nanny stint had ended.

"Yes, you can," Ellie said. "Get it, Fawn."

The little girl opened the cabinet under the sink, pulled out her tin whistle, and brought it to John-Peter.

"Play," Fawn said.

John-Peter raised an eyebrow and glanced at Ellie.

"Fawn kept blowing it yesterday. Daddy told her to put it away, or he would to throw it away. So we hid it."

The boy knew better, but his hand irresistibly closed over the sleek metal rod before he could stop it. Far away melodies enticed him; they squirmed and begged for release.

"Shut the door," John-Peter hissed.

Ellie flew to obey him. Fawn dropped to the cold tile floor and then, bright-eyed and cross-legged, leaned forward with all ten fingers dangling from her mouth. Ellie joined her sister.

"What do you want to hear?" John-Peter whispered, as he moved the whistle to his trembling lips.

"Christmas songs!" the girls shouted in unison.

Fawn wriggled excitedly, and Ellie clasped her hands close to her heart.

"Shh," the boy said.

He produced one round of *We Wish You a Merry Christmas*, accompanied by the off-key, but sweet, voices of Ellie and Fawn, yet his spirit wouldn't honor the upbeat tune. So he switched to the haunting *O Come, O Come Emmanuel*, which was better, but even that melody failed to relieve the churning.

In honor of tomorrow night's midnight service, John-Peter played a gentle *Silent Night*, as the little girls sat quietly awestruck at the beautiful notes, but that piece also did not satisfy. John-Peter lowered the whistle.

"More, John-Peter," Ellie said.

Fawn, now sucking her thumb, nodded.

The dam broke. John-Peter again raised the instrument, blew the first, halting notes of *Coventry Carol,* and the song took flight. Each tingling note grew louder, more assured, until Herod's soldiers slashed tiny children and bludgeoned interfering parents. Blood cascaded from bodies, streamed out of houses, flowed into streets, and drifted into the ditches along the robbers' highways.

The kitchen door banged open, and Melissa burst into the room. She marched straight to John-Peter, yanked the whistle from his lips, and cried out, "You have a lot of nerve! How can you be so cruel?"

With angry, flashing eyes, Melissa faced the girls, who shrank back. "Didn't your father tell you yesterday to put this away?"

Ellie swallowed hard. Fawn's eyes puddled.

"Now it's mine." Melissa pointed to the door. "Get out of the kitchen."

Both girls fled. *Cruel?* Couldn't she see *his* suffering?

"John-Peter, if you won't stand in the receiving line with the rest of us peons, please stop mocking a sad and solemn occasion."

He stiffly rose to meet her gaze.

"I need air," was all he said.

The boy strode down the hall to the rear exit and out into the winter twilight, leaving his mother to stew over his supposed insolence. Acres of field stood before him. In the spring, this would become HHG's first pet cemetery. Each step was long and deliberate, yet John-Peter hadn't a clue to his destination. The funeral home's oppression followed him. First stars appeared in the sky. Was his grandfather now a part of something bigger, or was he simply gone?

"John-Peter!"

The boy hesitated at the sound of Karla's voice, but only on the inside. He did not break pace.

"Wait, John-Peter! Stop!"

He reached the lone oak tree in the center of the field and leaned against it, panting against the cold breath burning his chest and catching his throat. The frozen ground crunched louder and louder as Karla's footsteps grew closer and closer. The frosty air pierced his bones like tiny needles, but his breathing came easier.

A few more quick crunches, and Karla had reached the tree. "Why'd you keep going? Didn't you hear me?" She took his cold hand into her gloved one.

John-Peter rested his head against the trunk, looked upward, and closed his eyes. Karla moved into him.

"I heard everything," she said in a low voice.

Night descended like a garment and wrapped his spirit within its dark cloak. Time melted into nothing and left John-Peter behind.

"And, John-Peter, I just wanted you to know..."

Karla's voice faltered, and she took a deep breath.

"If you need me, John-Peter, I'm here."

John-Peter turned his head and faced her with dull and half-interested eyes. Beneath the white hood framing the dark curls and pink cheeks, Karla gazed back steadily, expectantly. They were best friends. They shook hands over deals, held hands during séances, and high-fived over victories. They lay on the grass in the middle of woods during the pre-dawn hours and shared their dreams. He was as comfortable with Karla's body as he was with his own.

She was not the princess, true. But she was here.

Karla's palm cracked across his cheek. "John-Peter Simotes! I can't believe you'd think..."

"Hey!" Defensive pride jerked him to reality. "I wasn't thinking anythi..."

"Oh! Your grandfather would be so ashamed of you!"

She gave him a little shove and ran back to the funeral home. Bitch! He ought to look up Courtney. That'd show her.

Courtney.

He repeated the name, aloud this time. Then laughter bubbled up inside him until peals escaped his lips and dispersed into the night. Why, of course. *Courtney.* She'd been the way home all along.

Only briefly did John-Peter consider announcing his departure but quickly dismissed that thought. He wasn't going far, and he'd return before anyone, especially his mother, missed him.

It was time he got some answers.

The traffic of holiday visitors and businessmen rushing home for dinner lined the streets of downtown Thornton. Although it was now dark, distracted shoppers still filled the sidewalks, dashing in and out of stores to find a can't be beat deal on those last Christmas presents. Taylor's department store cranked carols into the night; the metallic notes of *Silver Bells* followed him into the lobby of The Golden Years Retirement & Nursing Home. Courtney kept vigil at the front desk, just as she had said.

John-Peter patiently waited while Courtney helped a young couple sign the register and call for a volunteer to navigate them through Wing D. The retirement's name certainly fit its design: gold carpet with just a hint of dark wood floors gleaming like glass below it, gold archways, gold chandeliers and soft wall lights, and groups of brushed, golden mustard armchairs arranged in scattered groupings around the colossal room.

As the couple moved away, Courtney saw John-Peter, and her face lit up like the garish Christmas lights framing the entranceway to Dalton's Dry Goods.

"I knew you'd come!" Courtney rested her arms on the counter and leaned forward.

John-Peter laid his hands on top and brought his face as close to hers as his stomach would allow.

"I need your help," he said, hoping Courtney noticed the pleading in his eyes.

Courtney moved closer, her quick breaths tickling his nose. Don't sneeze, he told himself.

"Anything, John-Peter."

"I'm *really* having a hard time with my grandfather's death." John-Peter felt a pang at this manipulation of his grandfather, but he saw no way around it.

Her head bobbed in total understanding. "I know, John-Peter, I know."

"I..."John-Peter stopped, looked down, braced himself, and slowly raised his eyes. "I don't want to be alone tonight."

The joy in her eyes unsettled his stomach.

"I'm off work in a couple of hours," Courtney said with a wide, happy smile.

John-Peter slowly shook his head. "That's a long time to wait."

"But you *will* wait?"

"Certainly. But in the meantime, I was wondering..."

"Yes, John-Peter?"

"Would you do me a favor?"

"Anything!"

John-Peter blinked hard. "I'd like to see Dr. Rothgard, but I'm so distraught, I forgot his password. I..."

"Oh, John-Peter, is that all? Of course, you may see him. It's not like you're a stranger."

"May I skip the escort? I'm not in the best shape for superficial chatter."

Courtney's delight softened into sympathy, and she squeezed his hands. "You go ahead, John-Peter. Take as long as you need."

"You're the best."

Behind him, a man loudly cleared his throat. John-Peter threw Courtney one last look of longing, and then, with head hung low, dragged his feet toward the psycho wing, all the while watching Courtney from the corner of his eye. When she turned toward the filing cabinet, the boy took an abrupt left and headed in the opposite direction.

The hall bustled with servers unloading tray after tray of covered dishes for the evening meal. Everyone was so preoccupied that no one paid attention to the boy as he stalked into the kitchen and up to the tall, young man washing dishes.

"Evening, Armand. Mind if I refill my jug?"

"Not at all." Armand stepped aside. "Been to see the old man?"

"Just leaving." John-Peter pushed a cart of dirty pans toward the counter. "These, right?"

"Nah, gotta do all the utensils first."

"Sorry. This tray on the table?"

"That's the one."

John-Peter selected his item and then set the aforementioned tray on the counter near the sink and smoothed his suit coat over his waist.

"My mother's waiting, Armand. Have a good Christmas."

"Same to you, man."

John-Peter ducked down the service hallway to the north wing and cut across to the mental institution. Those patients ate first so that area was long deserted. No light emerged from Dr. Rothgard's room, but the doorknob swung freely under his touch. The form beneath the sheets did not stir, but John-Peter noted raspy breathing as he stealthily inched closer to the bed.

With one swift motion, John-Peter removed the carving knife from under his coat, pressed it into Dr. Rothgard's throat, and whispered, "Talk to me now, you stupid, old fool, or I'll soak the pillow with your blood."

Dr. Rothgard cracked open an eye; his face twisted into a sneer.

"Do it," the elderly man shot back, glancing down at the knife. "I'll gladly take my secrets to the grave."

With the blade's tip, the boy raised the old man's face for a better look. "You're Dr. Gothart."

"I am."

"A vampire."

"No."

John-Peter jammed the knife harder. "Liar!"

Dr. Rothgard replied with a dark chuckle. The boy lowered his weapon and studied him hard. "Then...what are you?"

"A really, really, really old man."

"You're alive?"

"Very much so."

Stunned, John-Peter dropped the knife on the bed. Dr. Rothgard picked it up, set it on the nightstand, and then struggled into a sitting position, wheezing from the effort.

"Enough of this nonsense. Let's have a little tete-a-tete as you say, shall we?"

John-Peter sank onto the doctor's bed, disbelieving this twist in his plans. Dr. Rothgard swung his legs over the side and gripped the headboard as he pulled himself to his feet.

"My robe, John-Peter."

The boy felt along the sheets for the piece of terrycloth and handed it over to him. The doctor walked with surprising agility across the room to unfasten the latch on the window. John-Peter shivered against the sliver of frigid air, yet his eyes irresistibly riveted upon the ancient physician as he settled himself in the chair and picked up his pipe. The gray smoke curled away from the draft and vanished into the night. Dr. Rothgard smoked in silence for a long time before he spoke.

"I suppose you've heard of Countess Elizabeth Bathory."

"Don't insult my intelligence."

"Not at all, my boy, I'm simply giving my strange, little tale a beginning point. To look at me now, one would never know I once served Hungarian royalty."

"I don't believe you," John-Peter said, but his voice lacked the resolve he no longer felt.

Dr. Rothgard smiled and puffed contentedly before answering. "Shall I not continue?"

John-Peter looked away and said nothing.

"The trouble began after Count Ferenc Nádasdy's death. Perhaps the loss of her husband caused the unraveling of the countess' mind. As I'd been away from Csejte Castle for many months, I did not realize its horrors until my return when a panic-stricken servant ambushed me on the way to see the countess and shared them with me.

"With a firm hold on Eniko, I entered Countess Bathory's private chambers and beheld her gaily splashing about in a large vat of blood. I dropped the servant's arm, took three steps, and yanked the countess from the tub.

"'Grab a wrap!' I shouted to the girl who immediately fled for appropriate covering. Once I'd properly draped the countess, I peered into feral eyes, seeking some semblance of the woman I'd known all these years.

"'My God, Elizabeth,' I cried, 'have you no fear for your immortal soul?'

"But Elizabeth's eyes continued dancing with a strange light, as she murmured, 'Take a closer look and see for yourself if I don't wear the bloom of my youth.'

"I examined her, amazed at the vibrancy of her smooth skin, now freed from the tiny lines that belied her true age. Elizabeth acknowledged my astonishment with a happy snarl, which hinted at the atrocities hidden in the bowels of Csejte Castle, where all but one of her servants refused to take me.

"Eniko led me down a remote staircase that even the servants avoided, as multitudes of rats had claimed it, never minding the treacherous dampness on the stairs or the dripping water behind the stone walls.

"The bottom step led to a large, bolted door. Eniko paused before it and crossed herself three times before she removed the barriers. 'In there, doctor,' she said, stepping aside to allow me to pass.

"Nothing Eniko had previously said prepared me for the magnitude of Elizabeth's crimes. Hundreds upon hundreds of female bodies filled that dungeon and hung from hooks on the walls: dead bodies, live bodies, mutilated bodies, and remnants of bodies, all with unholy terror frozen on their faces. Amongst the bruises, lacerations, and teeth marks were the holes Elizabeth's crew had drilled when they harvested their blood for the countess's grisly beauty ritual. Oh, damn!"

Dr. Rothgard relit the pipe and drew on it several times to ensure it stayed lit. He continued to regard John-Peter with a calm expression.

"However monstrous this sounds, you have to remember your history, John-Peter. Although medical science understood the significance of blood, it had yet discovered how to manipulate its use to better man. Most of those early transfusions failed, but the ones that led to restored health intrigued me. Perhaps Elizabeth, in her wanton vanity, had stumbled upon the true fountain of life.

"I was about to leave when a low moan stopped me. Eniko remained on the other side of the room; her voice would not have carried these many yards. Had one of these poor souls returned from death to condemn me?

"I heard it again. Looking around me, I beheld the piteous countenance of a young girl, she couldn't have been more than seventeen, chained to the wall and looking at me with bloodshot eyes of sheer fright. Her mouth worked, but no further sound issued forth. I reversed my course.

"'What do you wish, my girl?' I asked her.

"So…thirsty…"

"Her gazed moved to the flask at my belt, so I removed it and held it up. "This?"

"She moaned again.

"I uncapped it and slowly poured its contents on the ground, then I took a blade from the wall, held my flask under her chin, and slit her throat. When I finished the first draught, I refilled the jug and drank again. Elizabeth subsequently paid for her atrocities behind the walls of her own prison, I made certain of it, but I, being smarter, lived.

"Locating new sources of blood was not difficult, not with the abundance of workhouses and asylums consistently requiring a doctor compassionate enough to enter them. The poor have many delightful ways of paying for the service, and, given the circumstances, I could indulge all manner of delights without worrying about tarnishing my sterling reputation. How fortunate, John-Peter, that the dead don't tell."

Dr. Rothgard leaned over to the ashtray sitting on the windowsill and knocked out the ashes, while John-Peter watched, thinking. The old man didn't belong at Golden Years. He needed a padded cell and constant sedation.

"When the nineteenth century brought the rise of penny dreadfuls with its oft-present themes of vampires and ghouls, I became intrigued with the possibilities of using blood to reanimate life instead of merely extending it. I shared my fledgling experiments, resurrecting animals and the turning of one creature into another through complete blood transfusions, merely in the context of drawing room entertainment. To others, they were amusing stories, nothing more. To me, each success brought me closer to controlling life and death through medical treatments employing the blood of the living."

John-Peter recalled Dr. Rothgard's presence in the parsonage's parlor and the words, "For the blood is the life." With a calm John-Peter did not feel, he locked his gaze on the doctor. "You said my father was a vampire."

"I'm coming to that. One lovely spring morning, I stepped outside for the morning newspaper and there, off in the bushes, was the sound of an infant's cries. Someone had hidden a basket there, and, yes, inside it was a tiny thing all swaddled in pink. Tucked inside the basket was a note: *It's your turn now.*"

"The baby was yours?"

Dr. Rothgard chuckled. "I could not mistake the red hair of my youth, my father's brow, and my mother's sweet mouth."

"And the infant's mother?"

The old man shrugged. "Who knows? The genetics are buried with the mother. Yet, by accepting the care of a destitute orphan, I raised my reputation in the community.

"Now Millicent, for that was her name, grew beautiful and intelligent, but she possessed a hellish streak, her downfall, as you shall see. If only she'd heeded reason. But passion ruled Millicent, not reason, and the one man of whom she was most passionate was a certain writer named Henry Matthews.

Unhappily for her, he did not return her amorous and rather embarrassingly straightforward affections.

"To me, the solution was a simple one: find her a decent man to marry. Women, for all their charms, are rather simple creatures, and I was convinced that a few flowers and declarations of love from another would erase all thoughts of Henry from Millicent's mind. For a time, my plan worked. The suitor was an intelligent sort, recently graduated from medical school, and a chap to whom I could perhaps one day leave my practice, the one I conducted on the surface. He bought Millicent a diamond; they set a date; and I congratulated my strategic move. Then Bryony died."

"You're balmy," John-Peter said,

The raised eyebrow and twisted smile on Dr. Rothgard's face showed he knew the boy didn't believe it.

"Now perhaps if John had permitted my presence at the birth from the beginning...or perhaps if he'd sent for me sooner...anyway, it was nearly two o'clock in the morning by the time I'd left Simons Mansion and retired to the fire with a cup of broth, a loaf of bread, and a toasting fork. I was happily buttering my third slice when a soft thud outside my door caused me to pause.

"'Millicent?' I called out for she had been milling about the house tending to my needs, and I thought perhaps she had come to check on me. But she did not reply, so I decided the noise was the product of an overtired brain. Two bites later, I heard it again. Alarmed now, I set down the fork.

"'Who's there?' my tremulous voice cried although I did my best to control it. Yet silence again was the response, so I rose from my chair to discern its presence. I performed a thorough search of the room and the hall but detected no one. I had just reentered my chambers when the door shut behind me. I whirled around but saw no one, which really unnerved me. Still, I managed to warble a brave, 'Show yourself!'

Slowly, a figure stepped out of the shadows. It resembled John Simons, but oh, how different he now appeared. I held up my candle for a better look. His hair was disheveled, and his face bore the ghastly color of chalk, but it was the lifeless appearance of his eyes and the stench of death that sorely frightened me.

"'Good Lord, John, what happened?'

"John motioned to my seat, which I took as quickly as my timorous limbs would carry me. I nonchalantly speared another piece of bread and invited him to dine with him.

"But John was restless and roamed about my room while I nervously ate half the loaf. He picked up an ornament here and leafed through a book there while my stomach quivered under its heavy load of bread. Finally, he spoke.

"'How is your vampire research progressing?"

"So that was it! John, insane with grief, had killed himself and was now paying for his poor judgment with eternal unrest. Too late, I regretted my previous foolish boastings because in reality, John-Peter, I had done almost no research at all.

"'Well, John,' I hedged, 'one must be patient with such matters. Quickening the dead is a difficult task."

"'How long?"

"'It's really impossible to say. I...'

"In a flash, John secured my arms held behind my back and dragged me out of that chair to the window. Down below, Henry was tying the horses to the fence post while Millicent hung by the gate chattering like a squirrel.

"'Oh, I couldn't,' I heard Millicent say, 'My father would kill me.'

"'I promise you,' Henry said as he looped the rope, 'it will remain our secret.'

"Millicent glanced around, scarcely containing her excitement. I started to shout out, and a vise clamped over my face. I couldn't believe John's strength, even as Millicent asked, 'How long do you think John and my father...'

"'Long enough,' Henry said as he opened the carriage door.

"Millicent lifted her skirts and sprang into the carriage. Henry started to follow, paused, and then turned his face up to me. His eyes shone yellow; the pupils glowed red. Between a leering parted mouth were large canine teeth, sharp and ready to feed. I struggled; John held me fast. A heart-wrenching shriek came from the inside of the carriage. John removed his hand and said, 'You now have good reason to expedite your work.' And he was gone."

"Did you save Millicent?"

"The vampire that cursed your stepfather to the same fate? No, she remained as wanton in death as she was in life. A Serbian priest staked her at the beginning of the twentieth century."

"I'm very sorry, Dr. Rothgard."

"It was a long time ago."

Dr. Rothgard revived his pipe and reflected a long time, gazing straight ahead. All John-Peter could think was, *You're not human. Your father was a vampire.*

"Soooo," the boy slowly said, "John Simons is my father." He watched Dr. Rothgard closely for his reaction.

"Not...exactly."

"Which means?"

"I decided to test a legend older than the Bathory's, one that was ancient even when I was a boy. Regular and precisely measured amounts of blood from one human source might neutralize the effects of vampirism and restore not only animation, but full, bodily function. The theory had always intrigued me, but I'd never found a vampire cooperative enough to sufficiently test it. Millicent, shall we say, was not a good candidate. Your father, however, was extremely motivated, and thus we began.

"His first host was your great-grandmother. Because she was still a child, her blood had desirable, youthful qualities. And because she was fond of both Bryony and John when they were alive, the notion of John siphoning her blood did not repulse her. But the experiment failed, so John waited for the next compatible match. He wanted similar blood composition. He wanted your mother."

John-Peter bolted upright. "Sir, your accusations go too far. My mother would never submit to such a beastly act."

"She can, and she did, twice. She now plays host to your stepfather."

"Untrue!"

Even as the words left his mouth, John-Peter recalled the numerous times his stepfather sniffed his mother's neck. He now cursed his blasted curiosity. If only he'd stayed at the funeral home. If only he hadn't crossed his personal Rubicon!

"Not only was your father's transformation an absolute success, more victories soon followed, including that of your stepfather. As vampirism disappeared from each of my subjects, I pronounced them cured and exhorted them to adopt maintenance treatments to retain life. John, as usual, ignored my heeding and this led to his eventual detriment."

Dr. Rothgard paused, and, with a sly glance at John-Peter, said, "But this isn't what you came to hear, is it?"

John-Peter stared back. The truth was coming, and he could no longer stop it, whether or not he still wished to know it. He said nothing.

"Your father never recovered from the loss of his infant son in death. The fact he could no longer conceive a child meant nothing to him. He had decided he was going to have a son, and, by golly, that's what he set out to do. Now most men might have settled for adoption or artificial insemination, but John was not like most men. Oh, I don't mean that he was a past vampire for plenty of men have that history, and they still father children. No, John had only one way of doing things, and that was his way. So he asked me to..."

John-Peter interrupted him. "Derek Granger and Debbie Polis are not my biological parents?"

"No."

"I wasn't switched at birth?"

"No. Shall I continue my story?"

Again, John-Peter had no reply.

"I laughed, a bit nervously I must confess, because John was not one to converse hypothetically. If John had a request, he had something concrete in mind. But before I could speak, John unfolded his plan. You see, John-Peter, fairy blood must be periodically strengthened with human blood to keep the fey race intact. Historically, the pixies accomplished this in one of two ways. They would kidnap a human child and leave a sickly fairy child in its place. Or, it would replace the human child with an enchanted piece of wood. This last is exactly what your father had in mind. He wanted me to create his son from an inanimate object.

"By his own hands he destroyed his most prized possession, severed one of its legs to form your frame, and soaked that leg with his blood. He arranged an adoption with a pregnant piano student, and I arranged for her demise on the operating table, smuggling her infant daughter to the leprechaun hired for the purpose of spiriting her away and replacing that baby with you. It should have been a flawless plan, but there is a lamentable consequence of raising a changeling. They never reach adulthood."

John-Peter thought of the eighteenth birthday that was only two days away and recalled the skeleton riding on a horse. *Death.*

"However, you were only a baby, so time was on our side. As I researched, tested, and experimented, your fairy nature attempted to appease its constant hunger with blood from your mother. Yet, it was that challenge that led to our first success. By supplementing your diet with your father's blood, we regulated your hunger even as we prepared your body to accept what one day must be yours."

That vision of him sitting in his car seat and sucking blood from his father's arm really happened? Impossible! John-Peter rose to leave. He had wasted his time. The old man really was insane. Dr. Rothgard watched him and smiled.

"Don't believe me, huh? Dr. Rothgard said. "What do you think is in your vitamins?"

The pizza came back up without warning, but Dr. Rothgard must have seen it coming because the bedside wastebasket was instantly under the boy's mouth and a box of tissues was thrust into his hand. John-Peter slammed them into the trash cash, wiped his mouth across his sleeve, and turned to leave. His mind refused to accept Dr. Rothgard's words, but John-Peter knew in his heart each one was true. As his hand closed around the door handle, John-Peter turned and faced Dr. Rothgard.

"I have wasted my time in coming here," John-Peter said. "It does not matter how long I shall live. My father is dead. There is none of his blood left to bring me life."

"Untrue. He hid it before his death."

"Hid it where?"

Dr. Rothgard hesitated and set down his pipe. His face bore a mixture of sympathy and regret. "Inside your mother."

Whosever blood ran inside John-Peter now ran cold. He could no longer return to ignorance. "And how do I obtain this blood?"

"You'll need a complete transfusion of her synthesized blood before your eighteenth birthday."

"That's in two days."

Dr. Rothgard lowered the pipe and gazed at John-Peter with a placid expression. John-Peter had to know.

"And if I choose to believe nothing you're telling me?"

The doctor shrugged, knocked the tobacco onto the ground, and shut the window. John-Peter stood.

"What happened to Derek?"

"Let's just say he got nosy, and I halted his curiosity."

A shake began inside the boy that quickly spread to his limbs. The man before him was no longer the eccentric doctor from his childhood that periodically removed splinters from his hands and sympathized with his antisocial nature. "You killed him?"

Dr. Rothgard's expression remained serene. "No one interferes in my work."

That did it. John-Peter sped out of the room and bumped into an orderly carrying an armful of towels, scattering the snowy white linens everywhere.

"Sorry," John-Peter mumbled as stooped to help the man pick them up.

"No problem," the orderly said, although he looked annoyed.

As the man started down the hall, John-Peter called out, "Wait."

The man stopped, irritation clearly showing now. "Look, kid, I've got a job..."

"The girl at the front desk has a crush on me and might, you know, be waiting. Is there another way out?"

The orderly sighed and motioned with a jerk of his head. John-Peter followed him down the deserted wing to the delivery entrance. The man pushed a few buttons to silence the alarm and held open the door.

"Thanks!" John-Peter said with sincere appreciation.

And with a superhuman burst of speed, he bounded away into the night.

CHAPTER 20: HEARTBREAK

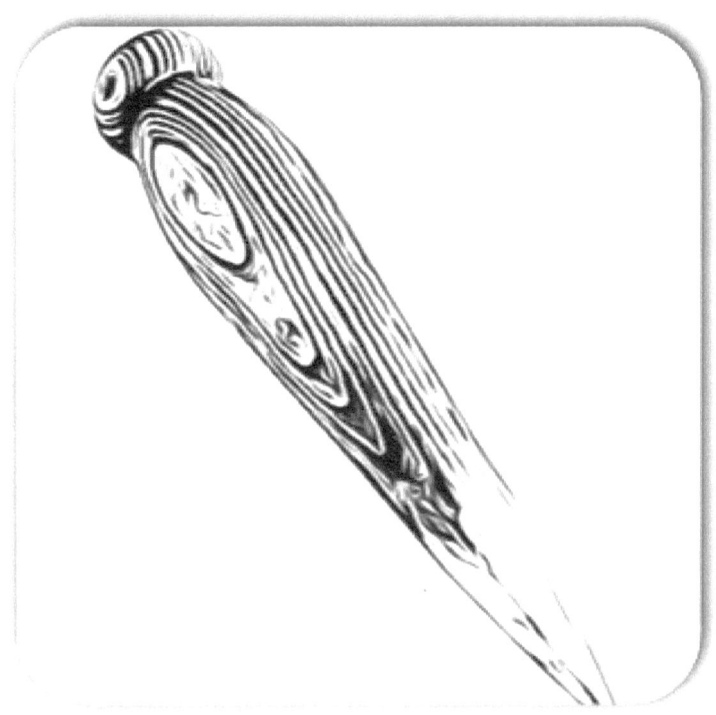

John-Peter sped through HHG's back door and bumped into Kellen for the second time that night. Although late, Kellen's black undertaker garb still appeared perfectly creased and pressed, his rose remained velvety, bright, and fragrant. John-Peter instinctively swiped his hands over his own rumpled jacket.

"Where've you been?" Kellen asked sharply. "Everyone's waiting for you."

"Getting air. Mother knew."

"You've been gone long enough to deplete all of Thornton's oxygen."

"Break room?"

"Kitchen. Go. I'm locking up."

But John-Peter didn't move. With the scrutiny of a forensic scientist, John-Peter observed Kellen as he secured the back door, set the security code, and pocketed his keys. Was his mountebank stepfather a bonafide vampire? Kellen noticed, took a step forward, and peered into John-Peter's face.

"Boy, are you ill? You look like you've seen a ghost."

John-Peter stared back at Kellen's pallid complexion. "Tired."

In silence, they walked down the dimly lit and silent hall. Kellen stopped at his office.

"You're not eating with us?" John-Peter asked.

"I'll grab a bite later. Got business to finish."

The kitchen's dazzling overhead lights accentuated John-Peter's dismal fog. His family sat around the largest table and passed trays of sandwiches and pans of salads. Beside Deanna sat a platter of falafel in pita and a fresh water jug. Cindy was cutting Fawn's sandwich into bite-sized pieces. All conversation ceased when he entered the room and slid into the empty seat beside Deanna.

"Daddy made us wait," she whispered.

Brian regarded his eldest daughter with his severest expression. "We wanted to wait."

"You worried us to death," Darlene began and then stopped, realizing what she had said. Tears rushed to her eyes, and she covered it by reaching for the mustard.

Melissa simply glared at him. "What got into you, taking off like that?"

"Leave him alone," Brian said shortly.

A look of surprise crossed Melissa's face, and she opened her mouth to retort.

"Look, everyone's hurting," Brian said. "Ellie, bring me a pop."

With full eyes and a trembling lower lip, Darlene struggled to raise a sandwich to her lips. She was about to take a bite when Brian moved her arm down.

"Brian, what in the world has gotten..."

"Shouldn't we pray first?"

"Beg pardon?" Aunt Cindy said, about to bite into her own sandwich.

"If Steve was here," Brian said, "he would want us to pray first."

Melissa set down her sandwich and looked at Darlene. "Mom, he's right."

Darlene sighed, but she obediently folded her hands and sat back in her chair

"All right," she said, her voice quavering, "Go ahead."

Brian slid his paper plate aside, leaned his elbows on the table, clasped his hands, and closed his eyes. A giggle escaped Ellie's lips, and she clapped her hands over her mouth the same instant John-Peter leaned around Deanna to tug one of Ellie's pig tails.

"God, if you exist and can hear me, I want you to know I'm not very good at this."

Brian's voice caught in his throat, and he leaned his forehead on his hands. John-Peter glanced sideways at Deanna, expecting a wisecrack, but none came. Instead, she remained still and mute, hands folded, head demurely bowed.

"And I ask you to bless this food, this family, and the great man you called home to be with you. Amen."

"A...Men!" Fawn echoed with a dramatic nod of her head. Cindy gave Brian a quick hug, but he only picked up a knife, and, with visibly shaking hands, cut Ellie's sandwich in half.

Few words were spoken during the rest of the quiet meal. Even the little girls, fatigued from the long day, ceased their senseless chatter. The falafel was mediocre. His grandfather would have used more cumin and less coriander.

It was nearly eleven o'clock when he, Melissa, and Darlene stepped off the seventh floor elevator and headed to their adjoining suites.

"I'll be right in, Mom," Melissa said, lingering outside John-Peter's door as he inserted his key card.

"All right," Darlene said weakly, as she unlocked the door. She looked exhausted.

Melissa waited until Darlene was gone from sight before opening her purse and removing the tin whistle.

"Here," she said. "Fawn wants you to keep it."

"Thanks." John-Peter accepted the instrument and stepped into the room.

"I'm sorry for overreacting this after..."

"I understand. Good night, Mother."

John-Peter shut and bolted the door, tossed the tin whistle on the black leather sectional couch, and then strutted to the other side of the spacious room. He scanned the numbers on the laminated card next to the phone and pressed five.

"Laundry services."

"I need a suit cleaned and pressed by morning."

"Certainly, sir. Room number?

"712."

"Write the instructions on the ID tag in the top drawer of your nightstand and hang it outside the door. When do you need it returned?"

"By six a.m."

"Consider it done. Have a good night, sir."

John-Peter swapped the suit for an HHG red monogrammed black robe and placed the suit outside his room. He opened his hand and looked down. The leprechaun's spiraling numbers had dropped to five digits. He tried not to dwell on that fact as he walked to the bedroom to slide the mouse underneath one of the many overstuffed pillows on his king-sized, platform bed. However, the image remained, making his shower brief and of the strictest utility, never minding the twin hot tubs. He started to fasten the towel around his waist as he opened the bathroom door, remembered he had the suite to himself, and tossed the towel under the counter. The boy headed straight for the tin whistle, reclined against the arm rest of the couch, propped his feet under the middle cushion, and sent heavenward the notes of the ballad he played at Uncle Brian's house over Thanksgiving. That tune inspired another more haunting than the first, and the lucid, pure notes elevated him to the comforting embrace of the oak tree's branches until he couldn't tell the tree's limbs from his own. The reeds bent in time to the music, and a ground fairy settled under a mushroom cloud with a wide smile across her face.

And still John-Peter played.

The wind murmured condolences through the leaves, and the stars ceased their twinkling to listen. An owl poked his head through a tree hole to tap its wing. Two gray squirrels frolicked on the ground. The delicate flower fairies reposed across the corn chamomile, flapped their translucent wings, and hummed in perfect harmony.

But as the moon's radiance waned; the evening air cooled; and the breeze from the lake no longer blew warm; John-Peter shuddered against the chill and woke up. The sky was still dark but showed several slashes of pink. With the musical refrains tumbling about his ears, John-Peter, freezing cold, set down the tin whistle and stumbled to the bedroom. The warm arms of the princess greeted him and quickly lured him to sleep under the soothing balm of fragrant lavender.

He awakened in earnest several hours later. The princess was gone, but an aura of lavender loitered in his room. Tomorrow, he would be eighteen, but other concerns crowded that concept from his mind.

Concepts like survival.

Clutching the black satin bedspread around his shivering frame, John-Peter walked out of the bedroom to the front door and cracked it open. His suit was hanging there, as ordered, and so was a large covered tray. He lifted the suit with one hand and held the door open with the other one as his nudged the tray into the room. John-Peter then hung the suit on a nearby hook and let the bedspread fall in favor of breakfast: a large bowl of scrambled tofu, a loaf of whole wheat toast, and a good pound of fresh berries. He was just buttoning his shirt over a new thatch of splinters when the telephone rang.

"Oh good, you're up," Melissa said. "Did you sleep all right?"

John-Peter looked longingly at the bed and wished for a meadow of lavender. "Sure."

"I'm going to the funeral home. You don't need to bring the girls. Aunt Cindy and Uncle Brian are feeding them breakfast, and then they're going to meet us there."

"Okay."

"Don't forget your vitamins."

Less people were present than yesterday, but still they overflowed Kellen's largest showing room and into the hall, despite the extra folding chairs he kept adding. Many of the

Grover's Park guests had already returned home for Christmas, but most of the villagers had stayed.

Curtis sat with his family and not with Karla. Good boy. Not good was Karla's refusal to acknowledge him, verbally or otherwise. Courtney, dressed in black lace with a black silk rose in her hair, was there with her parents, but she didn't look very happy. That didn't worry John-Peter. He could fix her by tonight. Julie Drake sat alone; David couldn't spare the time away from his clients, she had said. In the middle row, Ann was motioning over Jack's head, bent over a hand-held video game, for Trenton to close his book. Lauren seized that opportunity to whip out a compact from her beaded purse, black with clear glass pebbles, which suited the hag that she was, and admire her reflection.

The graying, liver-spotted minister from Jenson Bible Church approached him and inquired how quickly John-Peter could learn new songs.

"How quickly do you need them?"

"Well," the minister said as he fumbled through the sheets of paper in his hands. "I'll be weaving a few through my talk, if you don't mind."

"Like 'Amazing Grace?'"

"We'll end with that one."

"You better."

The minister raised his eyebrows in surprise, but his blue eyes behind the silver-rimmed bifocals looked severe.

"The music will be on the piano," he said and stiffly walked away.

Immediately, a familiar hand grasped John-Peter's collar.

"You rang?" John-Peter retorted.

"Today isn't about you," Brian said. "Remember that."

Before John-Peter could retaliate, Uncle Brian was hustling Fawn in the direction of the bathrooms. So John-Peter walked to the front of the room where the Regence Style Concert Grand Piano, created by French piano producer Sebastien Erard, rested opposite where his grandfather lay in Kellen's most expensive coffin: mahogany lined with scarlet velvet and embellished with fourteen carat gold handles and hinges. Kellen had offered a box in solid gold, but Darlene had adamantly refused as ostentatious never suited Steve. If his grandmother had known Kellen had paid five hundred thousand dollars wholesale for her husband's final resting place, she'd have her own stroke. But it was the piano that fascinated John-Peter. His fingers tingled merely thinking about touching those keys.

That instrument, all six hundred and sixty-six yards of it, had made its premiere appearance in 1889 at the International Universal Exposition of Industry in Paris. Kellen had paid over five hundred thousand dollars for it, too. Its unique features included gold legs and a hand-painted case featuring still life paintings, along with a signature of its artist, the famous Flemish painter Heber Lippmann. Only the minister's mimeographed hymns plopped over the keys marred its majesty. John-Peter was sifting through that sheet music and scanning their chords when he heard the minister announce, "Let us all stand for our first hymn, 'Holy God We Praise Thy Name.'"

A general rustling ensued as the crowd rose to its feet. The minister's strong tenor wafted over the tuneless warblings of the mourners, but at least the minister could sing. At the hymn's conclusion, the minister motioned his audience to sit by flapping his hands like the wings of an overgrown chicken. When he had more or less attained their cooperation, the minister smiled benignly and began.

"Good morning. For those who don't know me, I am Pastor Clyde Balshum from Jenson Bible Church. But who I am is not important. As I gaze out amongst all of you, I see people from all walks of life: babies, little girls and little boys, teenagers, parents, and even a few with one or two gray hairs, like me."

Here, the minister touched the side of his head. A light titter ran through the crowd. The minister looked pleased.

"Yet every one of us is here today to pay tribute to the life of Steve Barnes: son, husband, father, grandfather, worker, community servant, and, most importantly, a humble man of God. You see, as I'm sure all of you know, Steve loved nothing more than attending church on Sunday morning, and he showed that faithfulness by his heartfelt participation and generous financial support of our various programs. Why just last week Steve came up to me and said, 'Pastor, I'm merely a poor, sick man, but if there is something more I can do for you, don't hesitate to call.' Now I'm sure all of you who knew and loved Steve can recall a time when he helped you, too."

Deanna's hand shot up in the air. The minister nodded approvingly at her.

"Grandpa taught me to ride a two-wheeler," Deanna proudly said.

Aunt Cindy beamed and hugged Deanna.

A man in the back row put up his hand. "Several years ago, when I was in the hospital, Steve cleaned my warehouse for an entire month, free of charge."

A young woman wearing an imitation fur stole sat on the edge of her folding chair and waved her hand in the air. The minister recognized her with a smile and a nod.

"When my father died before the spring planting," the woman said, "Steve saved my mother's entire vegetable garden. Steve's kindness guaranteed her an income that summer."

It continued that way for an hour. One person after another had a tale to share about Steve. Even Uncle Brian, looking more composed than John-Peter had seen him in days, mentioned that Steve used to help him with his homework. John-Peter had never heard half of the stories, but, then again, Steve had never bragged about his accomplishments.

When the anecdotes ran dry, the minister asked everyone to stand and sing, *Take My Life and Let it Be*. This piece was not as easy to play, not because the music itself was difficult, but because of the lyrics accompanying it. Amazing Grace might have been his grandfather's favorite hymn, but this one truly illustrated his life.

> "Take my life and let it be
> "Consecrated, Lord, to thee.
> "Take my moments and my days;
> "Let them flow in ceaseless praise.
> "Take my hands and let them move
> "At the impulse of thy love.
> "Take my feet and let them be
> "Swift and beautiful for thee.
>
> "Take my voice and let me sing.

"Always, only, for my King.
"Take my lips and let them be
"Filled with message from thee,
"Take my silver and my gold
"Not a mite would I withhold.
"Take my intellect, and use
"Every power as thou shalt choose.

"Take my will, and make it thine;
"It shall no longer be mine.
"Take my heart, it is thine own;
"It shall be thy royal throne.
"Take my love, my Lord, I pour
"At thy feet its treasure-store.
"Take myself and I will be
"Ever, only, all for thee."

This time, at the hymn's conclusion, the crowd needed no coaxing from the minister; almost in unison, they reclaimed their chairs. They were catching on. The minister quickly studied his notes then held them behind his back.

"Next to his love of God, was Steve's love of family. Nothing was more important to him than..."

John-Peter tuned out the rest. Uncle Brian was already sniffling, and he'd be next if he listened to anymore.

"...but even more than the family business Steve built from the ground up with his own bare hands was the legacy of faith he left for his family, a legacy that I'm sure will grow more precious to them with the passing of each day." And he nodded at John-Peter.

With resentment approaching open hostility, John-Peter began *Faith of our Fathers*, while the crowd followed his lead with broken voices. What was this guy, some kind of sadist?

At the hymn's end, the minister invited final comments and announced the serving of a memorial lunch at the HHG hotel following the interment right on HHG's own cemetery. Then John-Peter filled the room with *Amazing Grace* and realized the simplicity of the hymn had fooled him. It was decidedly the hardest piece he had ever played.

The minister kept the graveside services mercifully brief. They consisted of *The Lord's Prayer*, a few final words, and the repeat luncheon announcement. Uncle Brian patted the coffin, said a low, "Good-bye, Steve," and then quickly grabbed his two youngest daughters hands, and walked briskly toward the hotel. Aunt Cindy trailed behind with Deanna at her heels.

Courtney caught up to John-Peter just as he reached the entrance to the grand ballroom. As she opened her mouth to deliver a spiteful lecture, John-Peter blurted out, "You left!"

She stood there, open-mouthed.

"Courtney, how could you?"

She shook her head in disgusted disbelief. "What!"

"You promised!"

Her face flushed. Confused, she fumbled for words. "John-Peter, I...I waited until eleven o'clock!"

"I feel asleep. You couldn't check on me?"

"Well...I..."

"See if I trust you again."

Cake. Courtney would now do anything to make it up to him.

Kellen had ordered an extravagant display of food. Row after row of white draped, two-tiered tables lined the perimeter of the massive room; about a fourth of the offerings were vegan. In the center, stood round tables with matching linens. In the middle of each sat a mirror topped with crystal bowls that floated lightly scented candles and fragrant rose petals. A chamber orchestra of a dozen musicians filled the air with elegant renditions of Steve's favorite hymns. Although Kellen spread similar feasts for his other funerals, John-Peter knew this flamboyance was for his grandfather. At every third item they passed, Deanna tugged John-Peter's sleeve and asked him to identify accordingly.

"What's that? It looks like rabbit poop."

"Caviar."

"Is it good?"

"If you like fish eggs."

Deanna made a face, plopped cottage cheese onto her plate, and continued down the aisle. "And this purple stuff, John-Peter?"

"Squid."

"Huh?"

"You know, like octopus."

"Yuck. Why no fish sticks?"

"Look again, dearie, two trays down."

They had reached the meats. Deanna grabbed a set of tongs, but John-Peter jerked them from her hand.

"Hey, you give them ba..."

"That's not chicken," John-Peter warned, setting the utensils back in the pan.

"It looks like chicken."

"It's pheasant. Fried chicken's on the opposite side."

After they'd heaped their plates, John-Peter deposited Deanna with Aunt Cindy and set out to find Trenton, who sat next to the desserts and dug his way through a mound of gravy-laden mashed potatoes.

"Nice service," Trenton said over the top of his book.

"Whatever." John-Peter unfolded the cloth napkin and snagged his hand on the way down to his lap. Damn splinters!

While devouring chicken-style seitan crepes, John-Peter scanned the room and estimated Kellen had set up tables and chairs for close to five hundred guests. Melissa sat two tables away talking and smiling with two women John-Peter had never met until yesterday, friends from her Grover's Park years. As Melissa passed John-Peter on her way to the desserts, Kellen approached her and said, "I hate to say it, but I'm flying out shortly."

"More break-ins?"

"I'm afraid so. These aren't common burglars. One of them threatened to stake my best manager. Mark my words, Melissa. Someone will get hurt."

Ellie's voice rose above the din. "Daddy, we want to go swimming!" followed by Aunt Cindy's reply of, "Daddy's tired, but I'll get John-Pe..." A roar of laughter from the adjacent table drowned the rest.

John-Peter braced himself for the inevitable, but, to his surprise, he heard Uncle Brian say, "I think it's high time I taught Deanna to swim."

Squeals of delight emitted from Deanna as she flew from her chair and threw her arms around Brian's neck. "Just like Grandpa taught you?"

Katie and Karla were putting on their coats. Karla still had not greeted him. Courtney was pretending to check out the cakes while gazing at him from the corner of her eye.

"John-Peter, did you hear me?"

His mother's voice returned him to the present.

"Sorry?"

"I'm going to the mall with Shelly and Laura. Your grandmother needs some alone time. Uncle Brian is taking the girls swimming. Did you want to go with them?"

"I'll pass."

"My cell phone is on, if you need me."

John-Peter waited until his mother left before pushing his chair away from the table. Trenton turned a page.

"Later, Trent."

"Yep."

Courtney was now sitting at a corner table, chortling over something with Lauren. Neither looked as if they were leaving anytime soon. Might be a good time, John-Peter decided, for a nap. He strode to the elevators and pushed "up."

Twilight was settling over downtown Thornton when John-Peter woke. The red light on the phone was flashing, signaling a voice message. It was his mother.

"We're going out to dinner," Melissa's voice droned. "You may eat with Uncle Brian or ask room service to send something up. I hope you had a nice nap."

If only he had a camera to capture the look of astonishment on Courtney's face when he walked through the front door of Golden Years. Head cast down, hands in his pockets, John-Peter meandered up to the front desk to beg pardon from Courtney.

"I'm sorry for saying mean things to you today. I don't know what came over me."

Courtney bit her lip and twice blinked fast. "It's okay, John-Peter," she said in her softest voice. "You don't have to explain yourself to me."

"May I see you tonight?"

Her eyes grew round with disbelief. "I work until eight."

"So I can return then?"

"Yes! Eight is perfect!"

John-Peter turned to leave then spun around as if he had abruptly remembered something. "Dr. Rothgard seemed really worried about me last night. He asked me to check in with him today. Do you mind, just for a couple of minutes?"

She smiled a broad, knowing smile. "You know the way."

Less than twenty-four hours had passed since John-Peter had seen Dr. Rothgard, but the old man appeared thinner, paler, and frailer than he had last night.

"Well, John-Peter, this is a surprise," the doctor said as he set down his pipe and shut the window.

John-Peter held up both hands. "Splinters," he said. "Everywhere."

Dr. Rothgard tipped the pipe's bulb over the ashtray and tapped it. "Get my bag," he said. "You must expect this. You're rotting."

For a solid hour, John-Peter submitted to the poking of his trunk while prodding Dr. Rothgard for additional details to last night's narrative, but Dr. Rothgard appeared reluctant to share. So when the splinter removal commenced on his hands, John-Peter tried another route.

"Dr. Rothgard," the boy began, "did you conduct any of your experiments in Simons Woods?"

"Thousands." Dr. Rothgard jabbed again. Strange that his poking no longer hurt. "Why?"

"Karla and I sensed vibrations there," John-Peter said, examining his left hand for stray wood slivers and then offering Dr. Rothgard his right. "She said they weren't positive."

"I should think not. I spilled much innocent blood in those woods. I'm surprised the ground doesn't rip apart with cries for vengeance."

"But it's different with my mother?"

Dr. Rothgard sighed and set down the tweezers. John-Peter grabbed the old man by the neck of his nightshirt and pulled him halfway off the bed.

"Listen you putrid corpse! Does my mother know she carries my father's blood?"

A wheeze and then gurgle escaped Dr. Rothgard's lips. Why, the old fool was laughing at him! John-Peter shook him like a rag doll. "Answer me, now, or I swear I'll...I'll..."

"Yes!" Dr. Rothgard hissed through a spreading grin.

John-Peter let the doctor go. The old man fell limply against the pillows, panting and rubbing his neck. His skin matched the bleached sheets.

"And does she know I require a transfusion? And what happens to her when I get one?"

"My head is throbbing. Bring me an aspirin, boy. Top drawer by the bed."

John-Peter complied, but only because he was afraid Dr. Rothgard might die before revealing the rest of his secrets. The doctor took a sip of water and then motioned to the bed. John-Peter sat.

"Your vitamin pills were to prepare your body to accept a complete blood transfusion with the artificial blood I once manufactured. Vampires under my care no longer kill for food. I saved many blameless lives that way."

"Used to, Dr. Rothgard? You no longer fabricate blood?"

"My assistant, Dottie Sherman, left me today and took all my formulas with her. 'Doesn't need me anymore,' she said. 'Can start her own career.' I'm a condemned man, John-Peter. I can't run a practice from these walls without her."

"So there's no blood for me?"

"There's no blood for anyone."

The magnitude of Dr. Rothgard's words hit him full force. "Not even you?"

"Not even me."

"But without blood you can't..."

"You need to leave. They'll be coming shortly with my dinner tray."

"But what about me? How do I get the blood I need?"

Dr. Rothgard gazed at the ceiling with insane calm of a condemned man at peace with his fate. Instantly, the boy had his collar and jerked him back with a shake.

"Look at me, you quack! Are you saying my mother wants me to kill her?"

"Be quiet. Your mother knows nothing about your dilemma. However, it's your life, so do as you please. Of course, you could choose the other path."

"I don't get it."

"Oh, I think you do." Dr. Rothgard's voice slurred as he glided into the warm drowsiness that precedes real sleep. He popped open hazy eyes. "You're not a victim, John-Peter. But you must make a serious decision."

"Kill or be killed. Both choices suck."

"As I've often told you, if a man cannot face himself in the mirror, he must right the wrong."

"I think Michigan should reinstate the death penalty."

"Good-bye, John-Peter."

Filled with disgust for the fiendish megalomaniac that could never play physician to him again, John-Peter spun on his heel, stalked out of the room, and proceeded to the same rear door the orderly opened for him the previous evening. Swiftly, the boy typed the code he'd memorized at the time and stepped into the frosty night. He was starving; Brummings was only a block away. He ordered three vegan pizzas to go, took his time eating them by cutting through the back ends of businesses and across the immense grounds of HHG's cemetery, and pondered Dr. Rothgard's words from the past two nights. John-Peter longed to attribute Dr. Rothgard's confession to the ravings of a delusional psychopath, but the man's previous comments, couple with the discoveries from his and Karla's psychic adventures, stood in the way.

Karla.

He wished he could take back the other night. He wished he could talk to her.

The pizza did little to assuage the ravenous hunger growing more urgent by the minute. He'd keep room service hopping tonight. To distract him, John-Peter pulled Fawn's tin whistle from his pocket and allowed his fingers to choose the music. HHG came into view, and John-Peter quickened his pace as he grew closer to the future animal plots, the very place where he and Karla had argued. As he neared the funeral home, a shadow shifted near the kitchen window. John-Peter stopped short, desperately licking tomato sauce from his frozen fingers.

Was it an illusion? A corpse of Kellen's come to life? Copycat vandals ravaging the main branch? Mere hours ago, his grandfather had lain in this very building. No one should desecrate it. John-Peter could call the police, but there would be no glory in it for him. Besides, no punk kid could intimidate John-Peter, and if the intruder was something else, well, John-Peter knew how to deal with that, too.

The boy fixed his gaze on the window as he took stealthy, but purposeful steps to the service door, the silence only momentarily breaking with the squealing of an ambulance as it fled down the street. With rapid, practiced movements, John-Peter overrode the fourteen-digit security code, undid the locks with the extra set of keys Kellen had tossed him weeks ago and forgotten to reclaim, and entered the dark passageway. The door to Kellen's bathroom stood ajar, but his private chambers remained closed and locked. The boy held his breath and strained his ears, but he heard only the galloping of his heart.

Satisfied no trespasser lurked in the present vicinity, John-Peter turned left and tiptoed past the offices where Kellen, or one of his representatives, often consulted with clients. With every third pace, John-Peter paused, muscles taut, trying to detect any muffled sound that might hint at the intruder's whereabouts. He briefly debated the wisdom of a flashlight then discarded the idea. Might as well use a megaphone to announce his arrival.

Hours seemed to pass before John-Peter reached the main foyer. The doors to each visitation room were wide open; all coffins were closed. If one of the dearly departed had risen, he practiced tidy habits.

A flutter of black swept around the corner. Scalp prickling with the thrill of the hunt, John-Peter took halting steps toward the wing that held the support group meeting rooms. He saw nothing, but heard a fleeting swish. Was something behind a door? Or was it the rush of blood inside his head?

Somewhere, a faraway door closed with a faint click, and John-Peter's mouth went dry.

He vacillated only for a moment. Then John-Peter lightly sprinted down the hall toward the cellar, feverishly typed *that* code, and gently opened the door. His fingers snapped the switch for the fluorescent lights, and the boy flew down the stairs. When his feet touched bottom, John-Peter didn't hesitate but dashed straight to the rear of the preparation area to the vault where Kellen stored his cryptic supplies.

After manipulating yet another keypad, John-Peter swung back the heavy door, groped for the light, and entered the spacious vault. Walking up and down the aisles, John-Peter quickly scanned the various weapons, every one designed to counteract against specific metaphysical threats. An oak stake was unwieldy; a mahogany club was clumsy, and the Osage bow was just plain useless for this situation. A sword offered more control. He selected a silver one and examined it. Its handle of ebony wood felt commanding, and he mimed a few ferocious poses before he returned the vault to its customary darkness and shut the door. He plunged forward and then froze, pointing the blade at an imaginary assailant. That should scare away any trespasser, alive or not.

Carefully holding the sword from his body, John-Peter marched to the staircase and trod lightly up the steps, pausing at the landing before closing the door, making certain of no presence in the area except his.

Still keeping the weapon a safe distance away, but poised to pounce, John-Peter crept back down the hall and peeped around the corner before re-entering the main foyer. He stopped and suppressed the urge for further movement and waited until his eyes adjusted to the dim security lights. He glanced around the information desk and the display cases. The room was empty.

Despite his thudding ears and the inability to take a deep breath, John-Peter advanced, little by little, toward the opposite hallway. A black streak flitted into the opaque gloom, and he heard a giggle that a low voice silenced. He switched hands, wiped a cold, wet palm across homecoming pants, and then retightened his grip on the sword.

He stopped in front of each office to peer around the door and listen. Nothing, except the conference tables with its cushioned-backed chairs patiently awaiting the next day's clients. Everything appeared to be in order. None of ghost-shaped mints inside the candy dishes were disturbed, and the reference books reposed on their shelves. Not one HHG pencil had jumped out of place. Could the streetlights have played tricks on him?

But streetlights do not laugh.

John-Peter leaned against the wall and closed his eyes, the tip of the sword resting against his leg. Perhaps the trespasser sensed his presence. If he appeared less vigilant, the coward might show himself. He imagined Kellen's gratefulness at John-Peter's brave defense of his property and entertained possible rewards. He might see that vintage convertible and a cell phone yet.

A whisper was followed by a low moan. He opened his eyes. Kellen's office door now stood ajar. John-Peter raised his sword, clenched his teeth, and soundlessly scurried toward his stepfather's sanctuary. Whoever had entered it unbidden would soon wish he had smaller gonads.

The glow from the computer's screen saver showed the room was deserted; however, the door to Kellen's den was open. Inaudible voices emanated from it, oblivious to the young swashbuckler on the other side. Inch by mincing inch, John-Peter slid noiseless feet across the plush and peeped through the crack in the door. Two shadowy forms frolicked on the couch.

He steadied his nerves and then, with a loud shout and sword brandished for attack, John-Peter leaped into the room. The tumbling ceased, and a growling figure raised its head. The beast leaped off the body with a snarl, and John-Peter plunged the sword. Sticky warmth spattered onto his face, and the figure on the couch screamed. With the ravenous desperation of a starving man, John-Peter swiftly wiped away the blood, frantically licked his hands, and dropped to his knees. As a newborn babe latches onto its mother's breast, John-Peter's mouth rooted around the crumpled frame for the life-gushing wound and then sucked and sucked and sucked its blood down his parched throat. Exhausted, but finally sated, John-Peter lifted his head and panted.

The screaming continued and brought John-Peter back to his senses. He leaped to his feet and hastily switched on a lamp. There, lying motionless on the floor, was the rapidly decomposing frame of his stepfather. The red in the rose was fading; its source of life no longer flowed into the stem that Kellen had inserted into his chest.

The girl's howling increased as she scrunched further and deeper into the corner of the couch, which did nothing to alleviate

John-Peter's mounting, shaking panic. Her shredded emerald gown revealed the corded petticoat splayed across the cushions. Her titian curls fell over face, but they did not hide the puncture marks at the left side of her throat or the dual trails of blood trickling from them.

She beat her fists against nothing and shouted, "Mon Dieu! Mon Dieu! Mon Dieu!"

He had to shut her up. He couldn't think. He waved his hands before her face and blurted a series of "Shh! Shh! Shh!" all the while glancing toward the streetlights. Could anyone outside hear the racket? It was not yet that late.

The girl...woman...shushed her shrieks to hysterical whimpers. Why wouldn't she be quiet? She had to stop.

"Parlez-vous anglais?"

His question disarmed her. Still breathing heavy, the girl made a fist, bit it, and mumbled a sorrowful, "Non," as she rocked herself back and forth. At least she was calmer.

"Comment appellez-vous?"

"Colette."

"Ou habitez-vous?"

"Mersault."

"Le roi?"

She drew blood, looked to the ceiling, and wailed.

"Le Roi!"

"Louis le Prudent!" And she buried her head into her arms and half-shrieked, half-cried.

John-Peter's mind whirled. Louis the IX? The girl was fucked. No one, especially the police, would believe a single word she'd utter, once they found an interpreter that understood twelfth century Northern Gaul dialect, but at least he was off the hook. He wouldn't spend his days in prison, not over Kellen, although if he did, he'd serve the shortest life sentence in history if he didn't quickly locate an adequate substitute for his father's blood.

The boy took the leprechaun from his pocket and contemplated it. Twenty-five thousand and counting down. He cast a final glance at the weeping girl. He hoped she wasn't too attached to home because she was never, ever going to see it again. He retrieved Collette's headpiece that had fallen on the floor, wiped the handle of the sword, mopped his face, and tossed the cloth onto her lap. Before he left Collette to bemoan her fate, John-Peter stooped to touch the remaining petals on Kellen's lapel. They crumbled at his touch.

He now realized how prophetic Dr. Rothgard's words had been. John-Peter had just taken that first step toward setting things right. He could never have faced himself in the mirror if he had allowed Kellen to live, knowing that his stepfather really and truly was a monster. What would the princess have thought of him?

Razor-sharp memory propelled him back to Dr. Rothgard's bed. He felt the sting of tweezers.

Slide down that oak tree pretty fast again?
My boy, why do you put yourself at odds with the rest of the world?
A man needs to face himself in the mirror.
You have to right the wrong.

Understanding snapped to life as effortlessly as the iconic windows of memory had once flashed. John-Peter hailed a taxi, and once he settled into its back seat, he began banging on Karla's doors. He, a number four, just might beat that death card yet.

A man needs to face himself.

But Karla tonight was behaving like a typical self-righteous girl. She ignored him.

"Come on, Karla, open up!"

She pulled up a door just far enough to be heard. "Go away, John-Peter! I'm still mad at you!"

"Be mad at me tomorrow, for I need you tonight. I'm en route to Munsonville."

"Munsonville?" Karla was so surprised she forgot to be angry. "I thought you guys were staying in Thornton until school started."

"Too complicated to explain. Just meet me in my bedroom in two hours."

The door instantly dropped, but John-Peter was expecting it. He quickly slid his foot underneath and propped it open.

"Get off it already! I've found your father's portal!"

CHAPTER 21: THE LAND BEYOND THE DREAMS

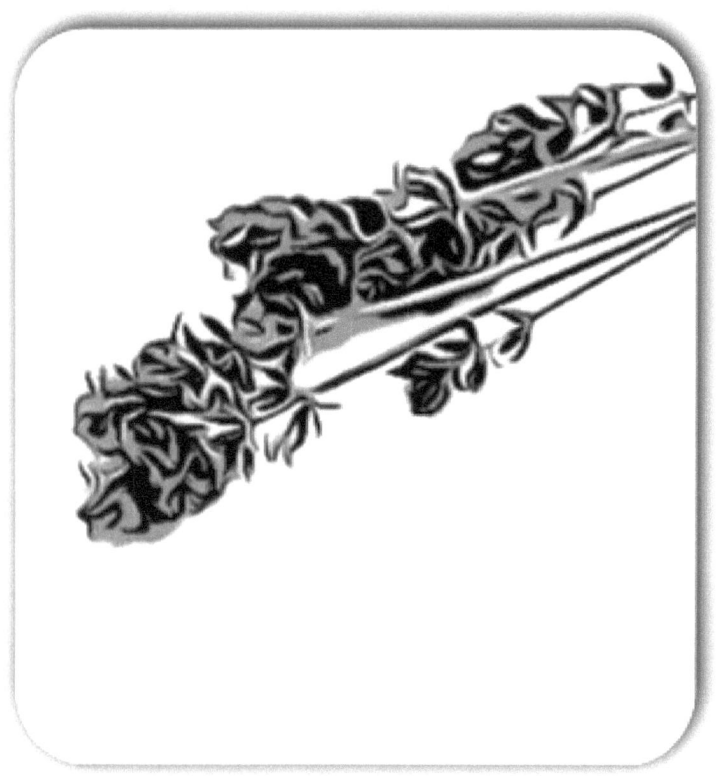

"Wait here," John-Peter said to the cab driver as he opened the car door. "I'll return promptly with the money."

His feet thudded up the familiar steps, and his hand slipped the key into the equally familiar lock. Had only several days passed since he had executed these daily motions? With all the events that had transpired, it seemed they had departed for Steve's funeral centuries ago.

The foyer felt cold as death, but John-Peter didn't stop to adjust the thermostat. No need to heat the entire house when he wasn't staying. He headed straight for the downstairs master bedroom Grandma Simotes no longer inhabited, marched up to Kellen's desk, forced open the locked roll top with a couple of hard jerks, and unrolled two hundred dollars from the left cubby. The pale green glow of the little bat-shaped clock read nine-fifteen. Nearly two hours had passed since he had called Karla. Where was that girl?

The boy dashed back to the cab and watched, with a rather grim satisfaction of the spending of Kellen's cash, the driver's mouth quickly switched from an impatient scowl to a broad grin as the man closed a beefy hand around the bills. With the tip of his cap and involuntary shake of his abundant jowls, the man sped down the hill.

The boy shoved his cold hands deep into his pockets, closed his fingers around the leprechaun, and watched the cab vanish into the clear dark night. Although it was nineteen ninety-four, Munsonville still had not installed streetlights. Even worse, no Karla yet. He tried messaging her, but she still had not unlocked and opened any of her doors. Restless and irritable, he stomped his numb feet and then climbed up to the porch to wait, alone. He watched his frosty breath drift into nothingness, the same nothingness his life would soon become. He had killed his stepfather and partaken of his father's blood from that ancient corpse as it rotted before his eyes. A maiden from a distant past would be now committed to a twentieth century insane asylum for a deed she did not commit. With sudden horror, John-Peter realized the redheads stored in Kellen's private computer were not part of his personal pornography collection but a catalogue of unfortunate victims. The grandfather clock struck ten.

You're not human. Your father was a vampire.

In John-Peter's distant mind, a skeleton and his equally gaunt steed gallop into view. *Death.*

Karla and her all-knowing, magical cards were right. Death loomed all around him. His father was dead; his grandfather was dead; Dr. Rothgard would soon be dead; and the delusional Ed Calkins ought to be dead. His stepfather had met a most deserving death, a little late, but, oh so marvelously, fitting.

The family heritage he had once claimed turned out to be dust; the legacy awaiting him had shriveled dry. And now...

A sudden north wind blasted through his bones; his cheeks burned like fire. Worse, his limbs prickled and smarted against the invasion. With a jolt of panic, John-Peter pushed up his sleeve and ran a hand across his arm. The skin remained smooth, but for how long? Today, Dr. Rothgard blamed the intrusive splinters on Professor John Simotes' decaying piano leg, but that did not explain the faint hint of green beneath the surface of that condemned skin. Looks like Dr. Rothgard forgot one important detail in his deathbed confession. Looks like John-Peter forgot to ask him to explain it. Crap.

Still, John-Peter couldn't help smiling, a morose type of grin, true, but a grin nevertheless, despite the mirage of a guillotine hanging unsteadily over his head. Because of John-Peter's valor, one less vampire roamed the earth tonight. The clock chimed eleven times.

"Damn it, Karla!" John-Peter shouted to ears that probably didn't hear it. What had happened to her?

More agitated than ever, John-Peter fidgeted with the leprechaun, running his fingers over its sculpted hat, molded hair, sneering face, and clear plastic showcasing the numbers that hurried to complete its course. He pulled it out and examined it. Eighteen thousand had come and gone. Soon he would see only a row of four. Then what? John-Peter shoved the mouse back inside his pocket and shuddered. No amount of survival instinct would compel him to kill his mother, even though she had lied to him, served as his father's host, and permitted Kellen to drink his father's blood right out of her body.

Thanks to Dr. Rothgard, he now knew his life's purpose. Thanks to Dr. Rothgard, he now had a contingency plan.

Sure it was risky. He might end up as dead as everyone else, but he had to take it, for his sake, for the sake of what remained of his family, and, most importantly, for the princess' sake and their future together.

He shivered again, less from the cold and more from his rapidly approaching mission. He was a number four and a musical genius, a combination that, if Karla had dealt those picture cards differently, and fate had provided better options, should have sunk an awestruck world to its knees.

Tonight the universe chose him to save just a small portion of the world with only giddy moments in lavender as his reward. Even more perplexing was the fact that he was perfectly fine with it, nay, ecstatic about it. The torment from years of waiting shot paroxysms of longing and desire through him with a force that alarmed him. That degree of passion should be reserved for music alone, not some girl in his mirror, even if she was a princess.

Still...

Lavender, or C Major 7? It really was not a difficult choice.

Just as staking Kellen had not been a difficult choice.

John-Peter jumped at the tap on his shoulder, and he whirled around. There stood Karla, huddled inside a thin denim jacket, her lips attempting a weak smile around her chattering teeth.

"Just me," Karla sputtered out. "Sorry I'm late."

John-Peter looked around and then back at Karla. "How'd you get here?"

"I materialized. Been practicing at home. Cool, huh?"

He merely moved her aside to open the screen door.

"So," Karla said, "where's the portal?"

The boy held open the door for her, but Karla hung back and regarded him with troubled, questioning eyes.

"I told you," John-Peter said as he nudged her through the entranceway. "It's in my bedroom." He paused only long enough to lock the door. Karla lingered on the doormat while John-Peter dashed to the top of the staircase.

"How did it get there?" she called up to him.

He refused to engage her in time-wasting conversation and refrained from eye contact so he might not unwittingly encourage it. "It's been there all along. Now come on!"

John-Peter waited at the stop of the steps and listened for the soft thumping Karla's straggling feet. When he heard her land on the last step, he walked to his bedroom and switched on the light. It wouldn't do for Karla to see the princess just yet. He opened the closet door and saw only his reflection. Cool beans.

"Ok, Karla, here's the plan," John-Peter said as he turned around.

But Karla stood frozen in the doorway, twisting her gloves into a tight knot.

"Now, what?"

"It's your bedroom, John-Peter." She unconsciously shrank back into the hall.

"It's a room."

"I know. It's just..."

"Don't get coy with me now, Karla. This is no big deal. I've been in your bedroom dozens of times." He bet she never acted like this in Curtis' bedroom.

"That's different. I can't expl..."

"And did anything bad happen?"

"No, but..."

"Karla!"

"Okay, okay."

Karla took several hesitant steps into the room, slid off her jacket, and then reached back into its side pocket. Out came the ceramic leprechaun John-Peter stole from Eircheard's Emporium, the one identical to the mouse tucked inside John-Peter's pocket. Its tiny black eyes sat under a pair of bushy red eyebrows, and its wild red hair poked out from a tall green hat. Across its belt were the words: "Cha d'dhuin doras nach d'fhosgail doras."

"I brought it," Karla said, "in case we needed it."

"Good thinking."

He took the leprechaun from her hand and set it beside his closet door. The thing leered up at him with a knowing expression in its beady little eyes as John-Peter gestured to the mirror. "This is the portal."

She bit her lip with a puzzled look and glanced from it to him. "The mirror? John-Peter, don't you think..."

"Listen, Karla. Your father didn't pay for information but for this mirror, a mirror that Eircheard had either already sold to my Uncle Ed or allowed him to buy before your father came back for it."

"But..."

"Uncle Ed gave me this mirror when we moved here. He told me to expect anything from it because it was a magic mirror."

"John-Peter, that doesn't mean..."

"So when I saw a reflection that wasn't my own, I didn't question it."

"When you saw a reflection? John-Peter, you never told me that..."

"Until tonight."

Karla leaned against the wall and intently studied John-Peter. He didn't like the queer expression on her face. What was the matter with her? She was usually ripe for adventure.

"Tonight?" Her voice trembled as she said it. "What happened tonight?"

"You know, Karla, I can't tell you how many times Dr. Rothgard had told me that if a man cannot face himself in the mirror, he must right the wrong. Don't you see? I haven't always been facing myself in the mirror because I sometimes see someone else."

Karla's face was the color of bonfire ash.

"Who do you see?" she whispered.

"So tonight I began righting that wrong, and I shall not stop until it is accomplished. I go forth to meet my destiny. Will you help me?"

"I...I don't know. There's something different about you. There's...John-Peter, you're drenched! Are you sick? Look at yourself!" John-Peter pushed his damp hair from his face and looked into the mirror. Karla was right, because how could a mirror lie? He had soaked his lavender shirt and gray suit coat with sweat; his cheeks shone blotchy and pink; and the green-flecked, brown irises around his dilated pupils glittered like glass.

But none of that was important right now, not when eternity with the princess was so close to fulfillment. He turned to Karla. "Well?"

Karla still looked worried. "If this is really a portal, I can't promise we'll stay together. A lot of unknowns are out there. Something might separate us and..."

"I know. Just do your best."

"John-Peter."

"Please, Karla!"

"Well...all right. But don't lie down this time," Karla added with alarm as John-Peter sat down on the bed to retie a shoe. "Just...stay by the mirror."

Fine by him. That's where the princess dwelled. He returned to the glass and vowed never to leave it. He opened the door wide until it touched the wall. He then leaned on it for support as he gently stroked the mirror's smooth oak frame. After all these years, he was finally rescuing his princess. He didn't have a white horse, but he didn't need one. He had Karla.

"John-Peter?"

He shifted slightly to see her. "Yes?"

Her face reddened, and she looked away. "Nothing," she muttered. "Just close your eyes and picture yourself fading into the mirror."

"No."

She blinked and glanced back at him. "No?"

"I want to see it when it happens."

"Then you might not get in there."

"I will if you envision it for me." And he took Karla's cold and shaking hand firmly in his and contemplated his reflection.

The boy had often kept a late watch on Christmas Eve, except this time he wasn't waiting for the Santa Claus he had always known did not exist. He was coming to claim the princess who had been promised to him since his boyhood.

"John-Peter, remember when you accused me of clouding my mental faculties with trivial emotion?"

He remembered, and he knew why she mentioned it. How dare she compare his magnificent mirror with some cheap crystal ball!

"For your information, missy, emotion is not trivial."

"John-Peter, you're blocking your own results with..."

Had she read him to the depths of his soul? John-Peter doubted it, because he'd shut and bolted all doors labeled, "Princess." Still, Karla was sensing something from him. Slowly, he looked away from the mirror and towards Karla. "How am I blocking my results?"

"By your stupid insistence that I conjure the illusion."

He returned to the mirror, slid a hand into his pocket, and grasped the leprechaun. For the first time in his entire life, he didn't quite trust Karla, and he didn't know why. Because of it, he wouldn't put it past Karla to spirit the mouse right out of his pants.

"Call my insistence what you will," John-Peter said in a voice that could only sound this calm when one was suppressing a storm. "This time, I'm on top."

And, with a heart so filled with the passion and devotion characteristic of a sun in Capricorn, he willed the princess to summon him. How long he stood there, John-Peter did not know, but the grandfather clock chiming twelve reluctantly returned him to reality.

"John-Peter?"

"Hmm."

"Happy birthday."

"Maybe. Too early to tell."

Just how grateful did princesses feel toward their rescuers? Really grateful, he hoped, especially when the hero might be a dying man. He saw Karla turn over *The Lovers* card. It was his birthday, and the thought of how he and the princess could celebrate it made his heart beat fast and chaotically. Then he remembered whose blood his heart pumped and the vitamin pills he swallowed with every breakfast he'd eaten since early childhood.

I spilled innocent blood in those woods, Dr. Rothgard had said a few, short hours ago. *I'm surprised the ground doesn't rip apart with cries for vengeance.*

How many people's blood had supplied John Simons? How many different types of blood ran through his veins? Enough to shake the entire woods?

"Karla?"

"Yes, John-Peter?"

"You were right. The vibrations are not good."

"I didn't think so."

He waited and waited and waited, but the princess remained hidden. The grandfather clock struck once. Karla said his moon in Leo made him charming, but was that sufficient for a princess living within an enchanted mirror? Would a mandrake have helped his cause? With all the ones he'd ordered for Karla, you'd think he'd purchase one for himself.

His ankles shook, and his knees buckled, but John-Peter locked his exhausted, traitorous limbs and dug his heels further into the floor. The clock struck twice.

Karla's fingertips grazed John-Peter's palm. "Bertrand ate a whole piece of chicken tonight. He..."

"Shh."

For a brief moment, John-Peter had thought the mirror had quivered. He strained his eyes until they watered, but the specter regarding him was his own likeness. It couldn't be long now. Salvation approached; his being sensed it. John-Peter was a knight upholding a wand of victory and steering his powerful horse. He was a hanged man no more because his life no longer dangled in suspension. The reward...

His toes painfully curled to the balls of his feet. Instantly, he flexed them to the ground, and yet the cramps fired up his legs.

"Damn it!" John-Peter cried out as he struggled to flatten his feet.

"Let's take a break," Karla suggested hopefully.

"No!"

A pinprick in the mirror's center rippled; the painful spasms disappeared. He was Connla the Fair waiting with an uncommon eagerness for the crystal boat. The sweet taste of freshly picked apples watered his mouth.

"Did you see that, Karla?" he asked excitedly.

"See what?" Karla said, and her voice was soft and hushed.

Mesmerized, John-Peter watched the hole of light stretch into diamonds. They spawned bright and scintillating daggers curving away from the shimmering nucleus and scattered lightning bolts across the mirror. As the distortion grew, the beams intersected into oscillating shapes that rotated and shifted like a giant, sparkling kaleidoscope with an ever-widening, soupy puddle for its core.

Slowly, irresistibly, John-Peter extended his right hand toward the liquid center while keeping a firm grasp on Karla with his left hand. He poked it with his index finger, and it slid past the glass as easily as if he'd thrust it inside a thick bowl of pudding. Karla clutched his hand harder and took a step back. This is the moment he craved. She would not hold him back, she would not!

Bit by bit John-Peter entered, pulling the unwilling Karla along, until he could only see his elbow, and his face almost touched the melting glass. He saw no sign of the princess. Was she on the other side waiting for him?

"John-Peter…" Karla began in a voice almost too low to hear.

The boy did not wait to hear the rest. With a swift and single jerk, he freed his hand and stepped into the mirror, a narrow, flashing prism bouncing rainbow light waves against tens of transparent sides. He gazed around the barricade surrounding and encasing him, but the dazzling display toyed with his depth perception, and he could not discern the extent of his prison. As he fought to see between the hypnotic, dancing lines, John-Peter stretched out his hands to touch the margins of the mirror, but they remained beyond his reach. He tried again, but the surfaces eluded him as if they were miles away. He took three halting steps and braced his muscles for the inevitable smack against his face. It did not happen.

His pace quickened as his confidence grew; the boundaries of his confinement adapted with him. The mirror's edges softened into a cone-shaped channel, and the sharp points of the multicolored streaks rounded until they no longer hurled and jabbed but chased their tails in an eternal, elliptical path. Farther and farther into the channel John-Peter strode, but the passage was an endless coil that drove him on and on and on and on and on.

A hole of illumination appeared at the tunnel's far end, a chasm that expanded and brightened as the darkening walls compressed and squeezed John-Peter toward the elusive exit.

"It's like being born in reverse." Karla's voice looped through John-Peter's mind and reverberated off the walls.

"I don't remember," he sent back to her.

Until that moment, John-Peter had forgotten Karla's flawless memory, but, right now, he really didn't care. The accentuating constriction squeezed his lungs, and John-Peter strained his ribcage to take even a partial breath. His head buzzed; his limbs spasmodically wriggled, twitched, and lurched. The hole widely spread open its elastic; John-Peter's head popped out, and his body followed.

He flopped down onto level ground and blissfully gulped pure, clean air. The sun warmed him from head to toe, despite the cool breeze blowing off the blue-green lake, far off on his left. The rolling green hills of the underworld lay before him, dotted with sporadic patches of darker greenery. This lent an almost checkerboard effect to the landscape under the deep blue sky.

France was nowhere in sight.

The boy sat up and glanced over his shoulder. The mirror was still there, a tiny clear hole glinting from deep within the dense, shaded forest. John-Peter stretched his toes, slowly stood, and felt his back pocket. Good. The tin whistle had survived the trip. Without any hesitation, John-Peter turned a sharp right and set off toward the fields of goldenrods. The yellow heads turned upward to greet him even as the stems bowed low with respect and then leaned backward to allow the boy to pass.

Wading through the dense, waist-high, pungent plants winding up the steep hill was annoying enough without contending with a winged, insect-like creature persistently buzzing about his head. John-Peter waved away the pest with one hand only for the drone to hum into his opposite ear and then fly back and forth across his face.

When the overgrown butterfly nipped his chin, John-Peter pinched two fingers around its waist and held it fast while his captive beat translucent, green wings and twisted its long, slender body back and forth to free itself. Sagging with exhaustion, the mite fixed black eyes at John-Peter and delivered its most reproachful stare.

"What are you doing here?" the creature said in a crisp, hoarse voice.

John-Peter threw back his head and laughed with the exhilaration and abandon of a young man whose triumphant time has arrived.

"I've come home," John-Peter said.

CHAPTER 22: LIVING ON THE EDGE

The sun set low in the orange-gold and black sky, while the evening wind commenced its wispy lullaby. The boughs and wildflowers bent and swayed, even as the shivering littlest pixies scurried to their respective abodes, where they would bundle into tufts of cotton and toast their diminutive toes before matchstick bonfires.

Initial audience departed, Glorna ceased his reel and cocked his head to listen to the first alluring notes of the evening wind, always a delightful surprise, whether they crooned a fluttering breeze or blasted an occasional fortissimo gale.

Assured he could reproduce tonight's song, Glorna coiled his toes around the old, gnarled branches; rested his head against the broad, lobed leaves; raised his pointed face to the moon; and scattered his musical strains across the heavens. Each piping perfectly complemented the whistle blowing through his oak, and he contentedly sighed and merged with the ethereal music.

While he played, the filmy, cornflower-blue fairies flitted about the evening primroses and moonflowers. They pried open the delicate blooms and released into the night air the hundreds of supernatural beings that dwelled within them. Soon, the ground sylphs emerged, their transparent, mauve wings glowing under the full moonlight. Even the gray water sprites hovering over Quixotic Pond, paused their patrol to bask in the haunting tune.

It was a perfect life, and he was grateful for the steward's generous gift of consciousness. One moment he did not exist, and the next he sat cross-legged under a toadstool, the tips of his pointed ears grazing its velvety, cone-shaped cap as he blew a treble jig. When he willed it, Glorna expanded to the height of a full-grown man, one that kept an immaculate cottage and bountiful garden. Other times, he shrank smaller than a butterfly, scaled trees with the agility of a lizard, and glided through the air with the easy speed of a dragonfly.

With his profound musical abilities and passion for song and dance, he should have happily dwelled in the mounds with the other trooping fairies, their home ever since the Milesians defeated the Tuatha de Danaan. However, his mischievous tendencies, high intelligence, and preference for toiling alone set him apart from that group and turned the poor steward's hair white with worry over how and where to classify this atypical sprite, as he didn't neatly fit any category in the steward's entire kingdom.

He certainly could have made a fine leprechaun, for his solitary nature suited it, if only his penchant was shoemaking, not music. He enjoyed mischief, but that alone was too shallow for him, so becoming a fear dearg or pooka was unthinkable. He abhorred strong drink, so joining the cluricahns was impossible. He was too full of life to enjoy an existence as a dullahan, but his marked preference for human traits prohibited roanism. However, this fairy had a fierce, protective spirit, which made the steward seriously consider deeming him a dinnshenchas, although he worried about Glorna's scornful tendencies. He finally deemed the fairy a wood sprite, and, with the first challenge settled, the steward began the search for a proper vocation.

The rebellion began with his name. The steward called him Lugh because of the enchanting effect his melodic whistling had on human and sidhe alike. It provoked euphoria during times of feasting and frolicking, released poignant emotion during moments of sadness, comforted under affliction, and eliminated insomnia by inducing a deliciously, soporific state.

It was the steward's right to name him, and no one disputed it. But the strong winds during a particularly heavy rainfall so badly whipped the branches of the oaks that its limbs scratched his windowpane, as they begged him for relief: "Glorna! Glorna!" The fairy decided that sacred trees were wiser than a nonexistent steward and adopted the name, which generated his first censure by verse:

> The wood sprite tied to his pride
> Should heed the one guarding his hide
> When he nurtured the gall
> To make his own call
> Something great inside of him died.

Perhaps the steward was right, because after the first offense, Glorna's sense of propriety became greatly reduced, and more daring infractions followed: conversing with mortals in their sleep, tripping anyone who stepped on a fairy mound, tossing acorns onto mortals' paths, and risking real exposure by leaving tracks of dancing footprints in botanical gardens. With each offense, the steward increased Glorna's verbal chastisement, which only caused Glorna to laugh with glee and scamper away to the next escapade.

Nearing despair, the steward changed tactics. He summoned Glorna to his chamber and slyly praised Glorna's superlative talents as an independent fairy. Instead of punishment, the steward offered him a reward, the position of protecting a very old oak tree in southwest France, a tree older than the steward himself. Duties included consuming the grubs and fungus threatening to destroy it and nipping any axes poised to chop it down. In the evenings, Glorna would be free to make his music. The bargain was struck, the first Glorna would make with the desperate steward.

The initial few centuries were glorious ones, for Glorna was free to live as he pleased, answering to no one, for he was far from the steward's controlling grasp. The feeling was mutual, for the steward no longer endured complaints from the other fairies about this mutinous fabrication of his mind, leaving him free to rule with the ruthlessness he so esteemed. Glorna's voracious appetite soon eliminated any pestilence lurking on the tree, and his sharp, little teeth cut deeply into the arms of all axmen who approached it, frightening them into abandoning their tools and fleeing for safety miles away from Glorna's tree. Then came the attacker that changed the direction of the story.

Looking back, Glorna wasn't certain if this particular lumberjack was not easily daunted, or if Glorna merely had tired of dining on insects and molds, because, this time, he drew blood. Glorna had eaten meat once at Clancy's house and enjoyed it, but the sting of red flesh straight from its source enflamed him, and, for a moment, he felt one with the dearg-due who rose at night to drink the blood of past lovers. Glorna hesitated no longer. With siphon-like power, the fairy drained every drop.

If only his action hadn't made the news! That particular tree, his beloved tree, was slated for destruction to make room for a highway. A national movement began to save the enchanted tree, which now attracted thousands of tourists. Reports of French vampire oak trees circulated past reality and into the deluded realm of the steward. With wringing hands, the steward sought out Glorna and demanded the reason for this audacity. Glorna defended his actions, for wasn't he sent to protect the tree? The steward worried that once a sprite tasted blood, he might frantically seek more, jeopardizing the entire sidhe race, something the steward could not allow. Glorna minimized the steward's alarm, but a growing frenzy for more blood now consumed him, and he wondered how long he could repress it. This new thirst scared him, even as it excited him, and he wondered if blood gulped by night tasted as good as blood quaffed by day. The fearsome light in the steward's eyes told him that an eternal, rhyming punishment awaited him, even if he curbed his lust, for what might the other fairies attempt if they knew what Glorna had accomplished with no penalty? Luckily for him, the all-wise, all-knowing, and all-powerful steward had a wonderful solution.

Every fairy knows that consistent breeding weakens its bloodline, consequently producing hideously malformed offspring, which can only be strengthened once again with the fairest of human blood. Yet, trying to stop a fairy from breeding, especially during nights of feasting and frolicking, is like trying to stop night from following day. Co-mingling humans with the leprechauns is the optimal solution, but enticing real people to the job is nearly impossible. Historically, fairies swapped their unwanted infants for human ones, raised them as their own, and appropriately betrothed them in due time. Occasionally, when these fairy children expired at a rate quicker than their parents could reproduce them, carefully selected pieces of wood were magically quickened and charged with the duty of imitating their human counterparts. Furious with the steward for the lack of respect for his tree and eager to explore new lands, Glorna accepted the title of "changeling." With eyes of wonder, Glorna examined the oak piano leg that would soon become a new "him."

The glow was short-lived. The steward hailed a woodsman, indicated Glorna's tree, and ordered its immediate death, as punishment for the fairy's murderous deed. An anguished Glorna vigorously protested, but the steward heartlessly laughed, wound a spool of thread around the fairy, as neatly as any seamstress might, and tucked him into his kilt for the journey back to the underworld, a journey that could be hard or easy, long or quick, depending on the steward's present mood, for he controlled all elements of the story.

These circumstances abruptly changed, for Glorna, still raging and vowing to avenge his noble tree, was suddenly inside the ramshackle cottage of Eircheard, the steward's head shoemaker and aspiring woodworker. Eircheard, while not exactly compassionate, pitied the trapped sprite, unrolled him from his threaded prison, and fed him a slice of his famed Irish soda bread.

As Glorna munched the wonderfully tangy food, as flavorful as any grub he'd ever eaten, Eircheard carefully took measurements for Glorna's human outer wrap, leaving sufficient space for the computer chip brain. The steward watched each step with eyes hungry for power and control, but Eircheard foiled them both. He, respectfully, of course, informed the steward that he worked better unsupervised. In the meantime, didn't the steward have ruthless business somewhere in time to conduct?

With a promise to return by the morrow and threats of rhyming reprimands if the task was not complete, the steward exited the cottage by way of the front door, an amazing occurrence for Glorna, since he was accustomed to seeing the steward blend into air. After pouring a large draught into a tin mug, draining it, pouring another, and then shoving stout clay pipe between his teeth, Eircheard grabbed Glorna and the rest of his home brew and then stepped outside to the clearing in front of his hut. Dark, thick woods surrounded Eircheard's property on all sides, lit only by the unprotected, crackling fire several yards from his door.

Eircheard set his mug near the fire and settled himself on the wide, old log before it. A collection of tools and the scuffed piano leg lay close by. Glorna, really curious now, speculated how the tipsy dwarf might create a new being from this odd assortment of implements and materials. With a chuckle, Eircheard stuffed Glorna into his shirt pocket, but Glorna's fingers grabbed the edge and pulled himself up to observe the process. He didn't have long to wait, for Eircheard picked up his hand drill and the piano leg. Balancing the misshapen wood between his stubby legs, Eircheard bored a hole three-quarters into the wood and then dropped Glorna into the abyss. Glorna opened his mouth to object, but wood chips sealed his prison shut. The actual carving now began. Bored, Glorna sank into sleep. When he awakened, he was lying inside a clear plastic bin in a completely new world. Its sun, a bright glass ball attached to the sky with a steel arm, hovered over a figure, completely covered with a cloth, except for her bloated, blue face. Tufts of blonde hair strayed from the figure's fitted cap, and Glorna wondered if this was a human destined for fairy breeding. He decided it must be so, for the other creatures in the room paid frenzied homage to her, while she, unmoving, passively accepted it.

He turned his attention to the other beings. They wore blue gowns and hats, hid their faces behind white masks, allowing only their eyes to peep out, and worked frantically with thin, sharp metal tools. One of the blue-gowned creatures slapped him hard on his bottom and shouted, "It's a boy!" which made him scream, while another creature smuggled a white-wrapped bundle from the room. A voice cried out, "We've lost her," which confused Glorna, since no one had left the room except the creature and the bundle, and everyone saw that happen. Glorna opened his mouth to say so, but a giant, rubbery bulb leaped inside and tried to suck the life from him. Glorna squirmed and gagged and ultimately prevailed, for the creature that had slapped him decided he must be tired and laid him on a cold, metal bed for a nap. "Eight pounds even," the creature bellowed and quickly removed him. The quick lie-down scarcely refreshed him, but perhaps these creatures required less sleep than he did. He shivered in the chilly room. The sun did a poor heating job. Before Glorna could complain, another creature spun a white cloth around him. Glorna peered up at his savior, a tall leprechaun with dark, slicked back hair. This leprechaun was different from the rest. It had an extra set of eyes, heavy black ones that fit across his face and over the bridge of his nose, and his robe was green. Nevertheless, the leprechaun handled him as well as the mighty steward once had, for he carried him out from one world and down a busy passageway to a second world. This one was filled with the wailing of other white-bundled creatures, also living in clear crates. Occasionally, a creature lifted a bundle and examined it. So, Glorna mused, this is earth.

Another creature, this one wearing a white robe, stood much taller than the leprechaun and had long, blond ribbons hanging from his head. The four-eyed creature transferred Glorna to the tall, fair-haired creature, obviously less confident than the leprechaun, for his hands were actually trembling.

The tall being said to the leprechaun, "Dr. Rothgard, I..."

Dr. Rothgard reached up, patted the other on his shoulder, and said in a gruff voice, "I'll check in later." He briskly walked through the swinging double doors and disappeared into another universe.

The large creature's arms tighten around him. Glorna held his breath, fearing the worse, but the being regarded him with such loving tenderness that Glorna relaxed and decided he liked this new treatment very much. Surely, the steward had paid him a rare favor, a second chance in this strange new world. The creature cradled him close to his chest, and Glorna felt a thumping from the inside, similar to the drums the trooping fairies produced on their marches. The creature cupped a strong hand over Glorna's head and ran it along his cheek, which increased the chest thumping's speed and force.

A slim, blue-robed creature said in a voice as musical as any midsummer night, "Would you like to sit down? We have several rocking chairs available."

Glorna gazed up. The tall creature's eyes looked moist, but the creature settled into a curved wooden chair, so different from a toadstool or Eircheard's log. There the creature sat, closed its eyes, and rocked Glorna for a long time. Glorna decided this must be the way these beings slept, and, greatly fatigued from his transformation and voyage into an unknown land, drifted away into peaceful repose. When he awoke, it was to the easy rock of the chair and the watchful, loving look of the creature's eyes.

"Now," the creature said.

With a firm, but soothing, grasp around Glorna's little body, the creature rose, carried Glorna down another passageway, and into yet a third world, where Glorna heard a voice cry out, "John!"

Then he heard the tall creature say, "John-Peter, it's time to meet your mother."

Thus, Glorna learned his new identity and sallied forth to begin his new life.

CHAPTER 23: CREATURE COMFORTS

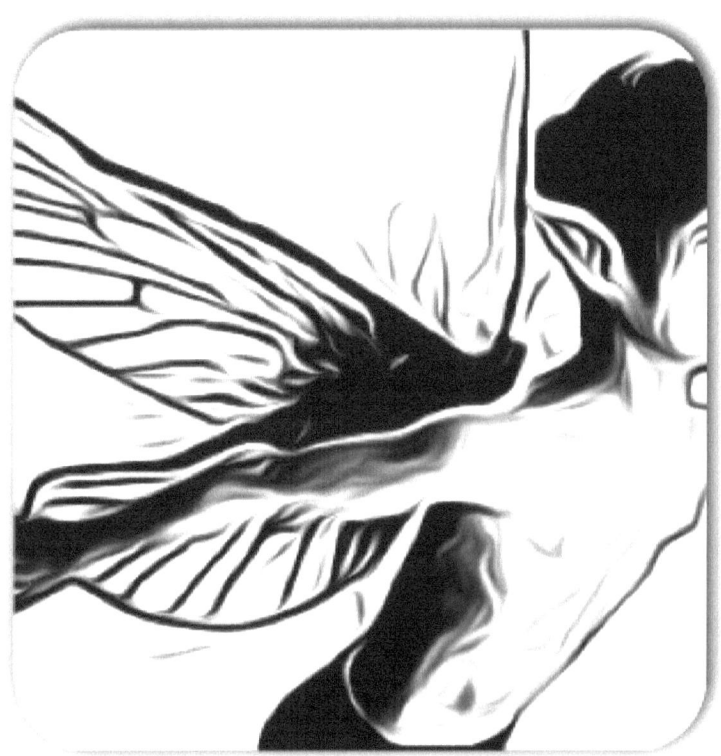

A steady wisp rose from Quixotic Pond as the warmth from the dawning sun seeped through the dark sky and gently pushed aside last night's cool air. The yellow rays had just begun overtaking the pink ones when John-Peter's eyes rolled awake, his head still resting against the trunk of the rowan tree he called "friend."

Even before his hazy sight focused and the disorientation cleared, he was groping along the damp moss for the tin whistle, the instrument of bliss, which had paid homage to Aine, the Irish goddess of summer. A faint whiff of a dying bonfire hovered in the background, the final, lingering sensation of the midsummer celebration, the last thing he remembered before electricity overtook him, and he faded away. In long, past ages, a similar morning might compel John-Peter to loiter at this area for a lunar cycle or two, piping lazy melodies to the more industrious dragonflies as they busily hunted gnats and mosquitoes for breakfast, while he grabbed an occasional meal from whatever crawled past him. However, the experiences of the last seventeen years had changed him. Mere pleasure no longer satisfied him. He had set his sights higher. He had a destiny to fulfill.

An angry clicking sounded from the pond's edge, and a cloud of monarch butterflies shot from the purple milkweed, hotly pursuing the flower sprites that preyed on their nectar. A hearty laugh broke through John-Peter's lips and fluttered away into the woods. Although reluctant to leave such serenity, he stood, hungry now for something more than dandelions and ground beetles. He chuckled to himself. Those butterflies would never catch the fairy pack, especially with Aodhan leading it. Better for them to find another source of nectar. His soaked pants surprised him, for the ground had not felt that wet. He stuffed his suit coat pockets with wild garlic and turned onto the path that led to Daragh Hill.

The wet fabric clung annoyingly to his legs and resisted his trudging efforts up the steep, familiar route, but John-Peter pushed forward anyway. As he walked, he recalled the dream from the beginning of the school year, where the princess refused to marry a certain dwarf, and that the shrunken man imprisoned her in a mirror at Eircheard's Emporium, intending to retrieve the glass at a later date. Ed Calkins discovered this enchanted mirror and hid it inside John-Peter's closet. Why hadn't he recognized the princess's captor before today, or was that another of Ed Calkins' tampering of his files? If the cluricahn hid her, would John-Peter find her in this great land, its length and breadth hampered only by the bounds of the steward's endless imagination?

He neared the top. The oak trees surrounding him moaned his name, and the cool breeze rippled their leaves, as well as the tender grasses, causing them to dance about his feet. John-Peter, the oaks' national hero, acknowledged their greeting with a detached nod. From here, the earth sloped downward, but John-

Peter saw the top of the thatched roof of the tiny mud and grass cottage he forsook centuries ago. Even before he reached his home, he spied the overgrown weeds of what used to be his garden and decided he might have to hoe and plant before he brought the princess here, just in case she didn't hunt for her food. Still, he waded through the tall greenery and stumbled upon a few cabbages and potatoes, entirely inappropriate for an ancient, abandoned, Irish garden, but this wasn't his fantasy, and, besides, he was plenty thankful for their existence. He gathered an armful of food and trotted back to the cottage. Today's breakfast, at least, was assured, thanks to the steward's benevolence. He noted the cord of wood, as he pushed through the grassy, rear doorway. What a surprise. That wood should have rotted eons ago.

John-Peter deposited the vegetables on the mud floor, grabbed the wooden bucket near the exit, and headed for the well. When the bucket was full, he dunked his head, slurped a long drink, and splashed water over his face, wiping the dripping remains with the front of his shirt. He carried the rest into his house. Everything was as he had left it, including his few knives, but unless the steward had imagined an intruder or two, there was no reason to expect otherwise. He felt a faint tapping in the back of his head, vaguely familiar, which he promptly ignored. He had important matters to settle.

Soon a fire crackled in the stone fireplace, and the water he poured into his iron kettle boiled his vegetables. His homecoming pants hung near the fireplace to dry. He poked a potato with a long-handled fork to test its doneness and made his plans. Before he cultivated a garden, he must first locate the princess and ensure her safety. He doubted Clancy would willingly give up that information, especially if he intended to harm her, but John-Peter would arm himself with bribes and consequences. He'd use whichever worked, both if necessary. He glanced at the pile of dry leaves at the cottage's far end. He must replace those before the princess shared his bed.

When the vegetable were fork tender, he ladled them into a large clay bowl, which he carried to the log table by the open-air window. The grain of the bench was worn smooth with age, but what did a few splinters matter when was rotting from the inside out? He took a large bite and raised his spoon; a sharp prick stung his cheek. Startled, John-Peter dropped his spoon and gave the translucent green creature sitting on his shoulder and peering into his lap his most threatening stare.

"Do you mind?" John-Peter said, pushing the creature's pointed chin away from him. "I'm eating."

"You have a lot of parts." The creature turned his long, thin face to meet John-Peter's gaze. "How do you fly?"

"Unless first engaging a machine, humans only take flights of fancy," John-Peter said, retrieving his spoon and wiping the dirt onto a dry spot on his shirt. "Streamlining is not strictly necessary, as it is to sprites like you."

"Dare you contrast yourself with the steward?"

John-Peter did not reply, so the creature folded his wings and admired his own sleek appearance; he then stretched full-length across John-Peter's shoulder. With intense interest, it watched each up and down movement of the spoon.

"Still, it must be rather disagreeable to be human," it said. "Such vast amounts of food are required to sustain you. A bit of sweet nectar, and I'm off to new adventures."

"A limited culinary experience," John-Peter said, "but then, you never tasted tofu kabobs from Brummings."

"Or blood from a man."

"Touché. Hang on. I'm getting up."

The creature gripped its dagger-like fingers onto John-Peter's ear, as the boy carried his empty bowl to the stew pot and refilled it.

"Iron, Glorna? No changeling can withstand it."

"I'm fearless, Aodhan."

"Or the myths are false."

"I prefer fearless."

John-Peter dipped a clay mug into the water bucket and carried both plate and mug to the table. The creature promptly let go, perched at the edge of the mug, dangled its teeny toes in the water, and said, "If we're not careful, Glorna, humans will overrun the place."

"Two is hardly a population explosion, Aodhan."

"Ha! Two! Not with the farm Clancy runs."

John-Peter slowly lowered his spoon and poked the fairy's diminutive belly with the handle, which caused the said Aodhan to anxiously grip the sides of the mug for support.

"Clancy operates a human farm?" the boy said. "Since when?"

"Since you left, Glorna. Oh, it's been bad here, real bad. Clancy's arrogance has led to unrest amongst all the leprechauns, and there's talk of mutiny. That's why we're thrilled the steward is paying a visit. He should be here tonight, if Amerigen's latest poetry report is correct. The steward'll put things to rights. Oh, I wouldn't be in Clancy's silver-buckled shoes for anything."

"The steward is unaware of the farm?"

"Do you think he'd approve it? Only he decides when to strengthen the stock. Although I must tell you, Glorna, I almost can't blame Clancy. This latest supply of fairy offspring is mighty ugly. Even their mothers don't want them, not when they can raise a human child instead."

"Describe these humans."

"Fair, all of them, just like the others. But enough about Homo sapiens. Come, and be reacquainted. Everyone wants to hear your tales of the upper world."

With a scornful look, John-Peter brushed Aodhan onto the table and lifted his mug. "Bambi and his mother greet their woodland friends?" He took a swig and slammed the mug on the table, but the sprite zipped away in time. "Be off with you. I've no time for social calls."

Aodhan spread his wings to full length. "I see time spent on earth has not improved your manners," he said, with real reproach in his voice. "Permanent separation may be best."

With a calmness that belied the excitement that stormed inside him, John-Peter said, "Bring your chums at dusk, and I shall play. Now go, for I've important business to conduct."

"So, that's why you're here! Well, I'm not one to interfere with the work of the steward. Wait until everyone discovers he allowed you back."

"Not a word to anyone, Aodhan."

The sprite prepared for liftoff, but at John-Peter's words, he fluttered onto the table. "The steward has knowledge of your presence?"

"Who else could authorize it? Let this be our surprise to everyone."

A happy nod, a whirring of wings, and Aodhan was gone. John-Peter cleared his few dishes and smiled to himself. Clancy would be surprised to see him, all right. Hopefully, he would be surprised enough to surrender the princess without a fight. He and the princess might begin the rest of their lives this very night!

He banked the fire and peered inside the kettle. Only a few spoonfuls remained, but these he rapidly consumed. He felt his clothes. The fire's warmth reduced them to mere dampness. That must suffice, for John-Peter could wait no longer. He kicked his shoes to one side, happy to finally discard them. Twice, when he dressed, John-Peter felt the strange tapping in the back of his head, but, twice again, he paid no heed. Yet, the sensation oddly reminded him of earth, and he glanced at the shoes. Suddenly, he felt like wearing them.

Aodhan flew inside the window, as John-Peter tied the last shoe. His left index finger snapped in two, and the boy cried out in pain.

"Who's Bambi?" Aodhan said, with a curious cock of his head.

The sun was high in the sky and on its downward bent when John-Peter finished splinting his finger and finally left the cottage for the realm of the cluricahns. He had no use for sots; his feet rebelled against taking him there. Only a real princess could compel him to visit it. The cluricahns built shabby little huts in close proximity to each other and spent their days drinking ale. This they obtained from pushing their children through the fairy mounds armed with stern prohibitions against returning empty-handed. Troll-like, but clad in the red suits and feather-topped green hats of their so-called fathers, these youngest cluricahns would crawl through the cellars of lavish inns and rich households to swipe everything alcoholic in sight, biting the ankles of anyone who tried to stop them.

The throbbing in his finger subsided, but the prickling of hundreds of reappearing splinters worried him. How long since Dr. Rothgard had removed the last batch? All sense of normal, linear time had evaporated in this world; there was only the eternal present. The sweat rolled off his neck and down his back, but John-Peter stubbornly refused to remove the suit coat, and he had no idea why. He rubbed his head to relieve the infernal tapping and tried to remember exactly what the mad scientist had told him.

Time was running out. He would die without his father's blood, but he must kill his mother to obtain it. The only known means of escaping his fate was to return to his native homeland, but only if the steward, who abhorred bloodshed, nullified his sentence. Safety and ultimate security lay beneath these fairy mounds. He was a fool to renounce them, and for what? His own will, a will the steward had infused into him. He should have obeyed, but, perhaps, rescuing the princess would restore his position. He hoped it wasn't too late.

Yet, he was a number four. Karla said so. That meant he could not die, for it would leave the princess bereft of a rescuer. The skeleton on the horse galloped into his memory. Maybe, it meant what his grandfather believed, a dying to himself, to his own way, his own plans, and an adherence to the role the steward once planned for him, a role that include loving the princess forever. Maybe, the steward had arranged this very day, so John-Peter would not have to kill anyone. Maybe.

John-Peter smelled the cluricahn abodes before he saw them. A stench of yesterday's greasy bacon and cabbage dinner combined with raw sewage and decaying potato and onion scraps pervaded the air and formed low, overcast clouds of stench that forever barred the sunshine from entering that division. Hordes of cluricahn tots sat in the road, patting mud into pie-shapes and licking their grimy palms. One of them, noisily sucking his fingers, looked up, and, from beady eyes sunk into a pale, puffy face, recognized John-Peter with a leer.

"My father said you best not show your face here again," the young cluricahn jeered.

"Screw your father," John-Peter said. "Is he home?"

A reply was unnecessary, for the deformed lad ran into the house bellowing, "Pa, that wicked fairy is back!"

The other cluricahns scooted away from John-Peter, as he stepped amongst them to reach Clancy's home, but Clancy, his square face encircled with a gray smoke cloud, appeared at the threshold, a crooked smile forming around the pipe stub he bit with thick lips and blackened teeth.

"My, my, Glorna, this *is* a shock to the old ticker. You're staying for dinner?"

"No meat."

Clancy raised his thick, shaggy eyebrows, but otherwise did not respond. John-Peter followed him into the dark shack where Clancy kicked a stool in John-Peter's direction and took the one near the fire for himself. Swaying and puffing heavily on his pipe, Clancy's bloodshot eyes surveyed John-Peter with a mixture of disbelief and fierce dislike. "I thought exile was forever."

"The steward makes exceptions for his favorites."

"Ah." Clancy smiled, but John-Peter knew by the way he looked at him, Clancy mistrusted his words.

A grossly obese cluricahn, this one in a red dress and green apron, jiggled into the room with two bowlfuls of food.

"No pig's feet for the wood sprite," Clancy said, snatching his meal from his wife.

She shoved the potato cakes and boiled onions at John-Peter and stomped from the room. An image of the princess gazing at him from the closet mirror prevented John-Peter from vomiting, for the oily stench steaming from Clancy's bowl was truly nauseating. Instead, he said, "Been farming much?"

Clancy's eyes momentarily narrowed, then he shoveled a huge spoonful into his mouth and grinned. "I make a living."

"Rather odd for a cluricahn to assume an honest occupation."

"Gotta set a good example for the young'uns. Can't all be thieves and misers. You lookin' at tattlin'?"

"I'm looking at buying, if you've anything worth purchasing."

"What's a fairy gonna do with a breeder?"

"Look again, Clancy. I'm no longer a mere fairy. Maybe I'll start my own race."

Clancy ran his tongue through the inside of his bowl then roared, "More!"

Instantly, his wife returned with another large bowl and whisked the empty one away to the back room. Clancy's self-designated authority privileged him to a two-room slum. Without bothering to remove his pipe, he ate several scoops of food before regarding John-Peter with disgust. "You be insulting my goods?"

"I'm seeking something particular."

"If you want it, odds are I got it."

"Show me."

"Under there." Clancy pointed to John-Peter's stool.

John-Peter stood and knocked over the stool to reveals an iron handle glinting through the dirt. Without hesitation, John-Peter lifted the latch and descended the wooden stairs, unmindful of Clancy shouting, "I thought changelings couldn't take iron!"

"Think again!" John-Peter slammed the lid, but not before he caught a glimpse of the pile of candles on the floor.

He flew down the stairs and fumbled for a candle, wondering how he would light it, when a glare made him blink. It was Clancy, clutching a lantern in one hand and gesturing to his basement with the other.

"You'll scare the cattle if you come at them like that," he said with a smirk. "I'll give you a real look-see."

This time, it was John-Peter's turn to be surprised. The light that radiated the underground prison, thick with centuries of mounting dust and debris and filled with cells of yellow-haired, young girls, failed to show its full extent, for it traveled indefinitely in both directions.

"Not what you expected, huh, Glorna?"

"Not even close."

"If you want it, I got it."

It took hours for John-Peter and Clancy to walk the entire moldy prison, because the boy insisted Clancy shine the lantern into each dank cavity, so he could properly examine the features on each despairing girl's tear-stained face. None of them could be more than sixteen, none of them appeared to weigh more than a hundred pounds, and none of them resembled the princess.

Clancy grew impatient with John-Peter's version of hide and seek. "Thought you were buyin'?"

"The cache?"

"Stuff your high-falootin' words, Glorna."

"The other merchandise you're hiding."

Clancy didn't even try to hide his annoyance. "There ain't no other merchandise, but you're through wasting my time."

"You're lying. I've seen others."

"Then, they're already sold."

"Sold? To whom?"

"Doggone brownies bought up most of the last batch for their confounded night work."

"Thanks, Clancy!"

With a burst of speed that only Aodhan could match, John-Peter raced past the caves of wailing girls and toward the stairs that might lead him to the princess. Clancy's screams of, "Where's my money, you danged time-thief?" soon turned into muffled cursing, as John-Peter reached the stairs and swiftly bounded up them. He flung open the cellar door, popped up his head, and smacked into the billowing knees of Clancy's wife.

"Sorry," John-Peter said, easing himself onto the floor, standing, and giving her a respectful half-bow. She was a type of woman, after all.

"Watch where ye goin," she snarled, the loose flesh jostling so hard it threatened her balance.

"Yes'm!"

Twilight had cleared the streets of the cluricahn boys and girls, giving John-Peter easy access to the hole-filled road and out of the town toward the meadow of the brownies. Here, they camped, between assignments, underneath trees and bushes, although the more sophisticated ones, the brownies most experienced in the ways of humans, actually pitched tents and constructed temporary shacks. It was completely dark by the time he reached their land. Aodhan and his companions were probably waiting at the cottage, anticipating a night of dancing to reels under the full moon. Well, it couldn't be helped.

He settled under a large oak tree to wait. As the night deepened, even the insects halted their evening song and went to sleep. Soon afterward, the brownies, one by one, emerged from their hiding places and trooped across the meadow to secretly help the humans. John-Peter waited until every last straggler had left the campground. A quick cursory search under every green plant revealed no breeders, so he donned his most official persona and approached the first tent.

"Sorry to bother you, miss," John-Peter said in his most authoritative tone, "but the Steward of Tara sent me to speak to you."

A rustle inside and a thin hand moved aside the tent flap. "Miss, I'm from the license to breed census bureau, and I'm here to log the number of breeders living at this residence."

Titters filled the air.

"Two?" the girl said.

John-Peter tapped his stick pencil against the long strip of bark that served as his notebook. "The truth, missy."

The giggling stopped. "Okay, five. Miranda joined us yesterday."

What could a brownie do with five breeders? John-Peter dutifully scratched the information onto his bark. The laughter resumed.

"That all?" the girl asked.

"Yes, ma'am. The Steward of Tara thanks you."

It was that way at every tent and hut he visited. Each brownie kept anywhere from one to half a dozen blonde-haired girls, but none of them came remotely close to the one who lived inside his closet. He walked all night, broke two toes in the process, and still no princess. The barest hint of day lightened the black sky to gray, although not enough to call it dawn, when the last brownie home appeared in view. If the princess was not here, he would have no choice but to give up the search, at least for today. All the brownies would return from their midnight tasks and ready themselves for bed. There would be no opportunity to question any more girls.

With a heart heavy in defeat, John-Peter knocked on the hollow door. He heard a shuffling noise and a very sleepy waif of a girl—she didn't even look twelve—slowly opened it and peered wary eyes at him. "Sir?"

"I'm very sorry to disturb your sleep, miss, but I'm from the license to breed census bureau, and the Steward of Tara sent me here tonight to log the number of breeders living at this residence. There's a discrepancy in his numbers, you see."

"It's just me, sir."

John-Peter swallowed the growing lump swelling his throat. Disappointment really did taste bitter. "You're sure? It's unwise to lie to the steward's emissary."

"I'm certain, sir."

"I've heard reports of another."

"Not here, sir."

Had he a wooden heart, too, for he felt it breaking with reality of certain loss. Dr. Rothgard did not mention this aspect of his anatomy. Nevertheless, he forced a weak smile and said, "Thank you for your time."

He turned to leave when she called out, "Oh, sir, wait!"

Hope exploded inside him, and he tightened his fingers around the twig to keep them from shaking. One of his fingers popped under the pressure, but he dismissed the pain, as thoughts of the princess consumed him. "Yes, miss?"

"There's a family of brownies who live out yonder, rather remote like," and she pointed in the direction of the woods. "I know it's unusual, sir, but they keep to themselves. They don't mix much with humans like regular brownies do. They're more into farming, but maybe, they keep a breeder."

The joy of long-contained desire surged inside John-Peter, and he restrained himself to keep from hugging the girl.

"The steward appreciates this information," he said in a carefully modulated voice.

"Glad to oblige, sir."

He casually sauntered away from the cottage, but the second the girl shut the door, John-Peter sped into the woods. Even the spasms from his broken toes couldn't hinder his resolve, for now he could not waver until he found her. How long he ran, he did not know, but he saw the wafting smoke long before he actually neared the concealed cottage. Acres of fenced, cleared ground extended from the main house far into the distance, but it was the sight of chickens running around the area, and a hard knock on the back of his head that stopped John-Peter from going any further.

"John-Peter!" a voice inside him called.

He couldn't believe it. "Karla?"

She could barely speak between sobs. "Oh, John-Peter, I thought I lost you. Don't worry. Everything's going to be fine."

He already knew it, for the back door opened, and a young girl stepped into the yard carrying a bucket of feed that she scattered on the ground for the hungry fowl crowding around her feet. Her hair was the color and texture of straw, and, as John-Peter walked closer to her, he saw her eyes were darker brown than his. The faint smattering of tan freckles across her nose and cheeks proved Clancy didn't know his own business, for it was obvious this girl worked in heat of the day. She no longer wore the regal appearance of the apparition in his closet. She was just a plain, ordinary girl, but she was still the princess he adored. The moment for which he waited all his life arrived; fate reached out to him with wide, open arms; and John-Peter rushed to embrace it.

"John-Peter, do you hear me?" Karla cried. "The paramedics are here. You've had a seizure!"

He dropped the door and bolted it.

"Excuse me, miss," he began.

The girl startled at the sound of his voice and her eyes widened, then misted. She was afraid, but she must know John-Peter was there to rescue her from her doomed fate, so he edged closer to reassure her.

"I mean you no harm," he said. "I only wish to..."

She raised her hand to ward him off. "You mustn't come any closer."

"But..." He took a step forward.

"John-Peter, don't touch me!"

She knew his name? But how?

"Princess..."

A rooster loudly crowed his morning song, and the girl jumped and dropped the bucket of feed. The gleeful chickens rushed to claim their prize, pecking each other to eliminate the competition. Great tears fell from the girl's eyes.

"John-Peter," she said. "I think I'm your sister."

CHAPTER 24: POT OF GOLD

The heat of the afternoon diminished, although the sun still remained high in the sky. John-Peter twisted and squirmed on his leafy bed, restless, and only partially awake, although he had not really slept. He pulled the leprechaun from his pocket and tipped it toward the windows to watch the descending numbers that slowed nearly to a stop: 10, 815. Maybe the battery needed changing. He'd ask Ed about it, after the first of the year, when he returned from Atlantic City, if the leprechaun lasted that long.

He watched the lengthening shadows and recalled this morning's tongue lashing from Aodhan, for the meadow sprite buzzed about the entranceway quite agitated that John-Peter stood him up and caused him to endure much taunting and jeering from his spritely pals. However, the boy only swatted Aodhan away from his ear with the same consideration he'd give a fly. Weightier issues occupied his mind. The princess claimed she was his sister. He must go back and talk to her.

Of course, he would have pressed her further right then and there had not her emaciated brownie owner stood on tiptoes and jammed a musket into the small of his back, ordering him off the property, and pledging he'd blow a hole through his liver if he ever caught him sniffing around his breeder again. With nary a backward glance, John-Peter took the hint and left, but the brownie had to go to work sometime and then…

In the meantime, John-Peter, nearly feverish from the previous night's lack of sleep and the ecliptic journey from reality to make-believe, spent the day attempting a facsimile of rest. As he wove in and out of consciousness, the pleading eyes of the princess gazing out at him from inside her mirror prison haunted him. John-Peter did not know where she received her information, but she had to be wrong. He felt it deep within him. The way she looked at him…this was not the look of a sister.

He shoved the leprechaun back inside his pocket. Hunger finally lured him away from the bed, although it was really fear he might faint en route to the princess that motivated him to the garden to collect some food. He literally grabbed breakfast on the run this morning, a handful of bilberries here and a smattering of knotgrass there. About halfway through the woods, he reached an empty area containing a single, dilapidated cottage decorated only by the stout tree stump several yards away from the front door. He slowed his pace, studying the only place in the entire woods exempt from foliage. The entire view was strangely familiar to him, although whether it was a real memory or a superimposed one, he could not tell.

After John-Peter filled the kettle with water and scallions and set it over the fire, he stooped to pick a basketful of goosefoot. Derbail provided the basket, which she wove from Irish waxed linen, an improbable material for this remote area. The work was slow, for he kept raising his eyes toward the distant woods, which beckoned him to enter, and he silently ordered his thudding heart to be patient. It would be hours before the brownies left their region for work.

The goosefoot filled the kettle to the top and then some, but John-Peter mashed the dark green leaves together until they all fit. Then, he settled on the three-legged stool before the fire, watching the flames leap and twist with the same vigor as the grove full of fairies did at the midsummer celebration, just two nights ago. There, they gleefully danced in the fields, round the trees, and over the bonfire. Then, the music he played filled his heart with the anticipation of his quest. Last night sowed doubt in his heart. What if the princess really was his sister?

The boy filled his clay bowl with the vegetables and sat down in his open doorway to eat them. Mouthful after mouthful he consumed, yet not once did John-Peter break his vigil of the darkening woods. The princess was on the other side of it. The brownies worked by night. A light breeze tickled his ear.

"Blasted wing's still sore," a raspy voice said.

With one swift motion, John-Peter jabbed his fork toward his shoulder, but Aodhan was quicker than he. He floated away and landed on John-Peter's knee, his transparent wings billowing like a parachute around him. The tip of his left wing curled toward the ground, but the sprite merely crossed his threadlike arms and huffed and harrumphed in profound indignation.

"I already told you," John-Peter said, scraping up the last of the leaves that clung to the edges of the bowl. "I was summoned to business of monumental importance."

"Tell that to a cavalcade of frisky fairies," Aodhan said. "You owe me, Glorna. All the favors I've done for you and what do I get, but this..." He shook his wings to their full glory, but the left wing stayed bent, and he cast a forlorn glance on it.

"If it's a listing of favors you're declaring, don't forget how I rescued you from the hungry bat that swooped down on you while you napped carefree on a sprig of wild thyme. Or the giant wasp when it..."

"Now don't get sore. 'Tis news they're wanting, news and a bit of fun. No one can whistle as you, not even the steward himself although the poetry reports proclaim even Lugh would swoon in rapture at his feet. What do you say? Tonight then? Got a sweet nectar mead I've been dying to..."

"No, not tonight," John-Peter said, with anxious eyes on the dimming sun. "I have a prior engagement."

The smile vanished from Aodhan's face as quickly as it came; a stern frown replaced it. "Remember that a secret is a weapon, as well as a friend." he said, preparing for take-off. "Be careful it doesn't turn against you."

John-Peter stood at the exact moment Aodhan flew into the air. The sprite wavered before the boy's face to with a sorrowful expression, then vanished in a rainbow of sparklers. John-Peter returned to the house and banked the fire. He'd wash his few dishes in the morning. Outside again, he broke into a run, the inferno in his heart urging his feet to faster and faster speeds. The brownies should be gone for the night by the time he reached the farm. If anything, last night's rounds attested to the girls' inclination against early bedtime. He was glad the princess lived in solitude, far from the chattering and squealing of the prisoners. Was that how Karla sounded during sleepovers with Megan and Amy?

He cleared the garden and ran free across the open field, straight for the dense woods ahead. No entranceway was visible amongst the trees thickly bordering the tall weeds, but John-Peter wasn't worried. Two oak trees bowed their leafy boughs at his approach and moved silently aside to admit him. With a whisper of rustling leaves, the gap closed. The fading sun sent tangerine stripes through the tree tops and scattered them among the undergrowth, but John-Peter required no light, weak, or otherwise, to spur him to his destination. The orange dimmed into pale yellow and eventually disappeared. No matter. He always saw well at night, one of the reasons Ed Calkins relied on him; instinct, memory, and bursting desire for the princess supplied the rest. Her face appeared in his mind, clear as daylight. He could not get lost.

How long he ran, he wasn't certain, but a gradual lightening of the woods insinuated he was halfway there. His feet pounded the ground with heavy thump, thump, thumps. The light increased as the packed trees thinned, and he flew past that now all-too-familiar cottage, catching a whiff of heavenly Irish soda bread as it baked, a smell that made him briefly wish for home and the Saturday mornings he threw papers with Ed Calkins. He wondered what Eircheard was doing this Christmas day and decided he didn't care.

The last half of the journey took forever; the closer he came to the vicinity of the brownie farm, the more it eluded him. As darkness blanketed the woods, an unusual shyness struck him from nowhere, and a vague uneasiness slowed his steps; the trees no longer whizzed past him; the bushes were no longer fuzzy, moving objects. He breathed hard, but not too hard, for his long, slender legs were meant for racing at high speeds. The sweat that formed on his palms had nothing to do with running, and he nervously wiped his hands down the sides of his gray pants. The princess forbade him to approach her last night, but then again, she didn't know he was there to liberate her. He approached the end of the woods. This was it.

With a deep breath and a heart full of intense hope, John-Peter stepped between the two great oaks that guarded all the secrets of the foliage and onto brownie territory. He couldn't fathom why brownies kept a farm when they must earn their keep by assisting humans every night. Certainly, the stock towered over them. The rugged, gray dormitory-appearance of the farmhouse lacked any welcoming warmth; the thick, sturdy boards of the fence surrounding the property underscored the owners' disenchantment with visitors. The two, rickety barns would not endure any wind stronger than a breeze. Not an animal was in sight and neither was the princess. He took halting steps toward the farm. He wanted to see the princess, but not just yet. The timing had to be right. She had to accept him. She…

The back door opened, a gold head peeped around it, looking this way and that, until, slowly, the thin form of the princess slipped into the yard. Even from his hiding place, John-Peter could see large knots where she had tied her ragged clothes together. She eased around the grounds with languid and carefully timed movements, and they hypnotized John-Peter into a thorough, delightful inspection of them, each one endearing him more to her than the last. He knew she was worried about something, for several times she lifted a foot, as if to take a step, and then set it down again, but there was something very charming about the way she did it, and the manner in which her fingers repeatedly combed her stringy hair from her eyes mesmerized him. Still cautious and still scanning her surroundings, the princess glided toward the south end of the farm. John-Peter ducked around the side of a barn to avoid her spotting him. From around the corner, he watched her lift the latch of the gate, close it without a sound, and dash toward the waist-high goldenrods he waded through on that first day home.

"Princess!" John-Peter heard a voice shout out, and, to his surprise, he realized it was his.

The girl jumped at the sound and froze in place, not turning to see who called her, even after John-Peter had caught up to her. With no glass separating them, his initial boldness forsook him. Inwardly cursing his timidity and ordering his quelling stomach to behave, the boy placed cold, shaking hands onto her shoulders and gently spun her to face him. Even in the darkness, she couldn't hide the look of astonishment that crept across her face despite her efforts to hide it.

"Princess?" he softly repeated.

"John-Peter, is it really you?" the girl whispered, and he noticed she was trembling, too.

She knew him! Ecstasy was short-lived, however, because she quickly added, "You must go where you belong, where it's safe."

His eyes locked onto her soft brown ones, and John-Peter hoped she saw, in addition to the green flecks, how much he truly cared for her.

"It's not safe here?" he asked, hoping to entice an explanation from her.

She bit her lip and looked at the ground. "Why do you call me 'Princess?'"

"Because you are a princess, and I don't know your real name." Feeling slightly braver at her response, he removed one hand from her shoulder and slid it under her chin, tipping it up for another intoxicating stare into those limpid eyes melting back at him, without the barrier of his bedroom mirror.

"I don't have a name. I'm just number forty-two."

"Princess, I don't understand."

"My place is to bear babies. I don't need a name for that."

She spoke with an earnestness that broke John-Peter's heart to hear. She would never be a breeder like the girls Clancy locked beneath his house; he would fight to the death to ensure it, for he could never call her by a number. Living with the fairies obviously destroyed her faith in the glorious future that was theirs to take. The temptation to steal her away with him this very night overwhelmed him, but logic spoke in a louder voice: *Make her trust you first.*

The princess however, edged away from his touch and turned toward the farm.

"Don't feel bad for me," she said in a voice so low John-Peter scarcely heard it. "I like babies."

He grabbed her hand before she could escape. "When does your master return?"

"Oh, the entire family is gone until sun up. I'm here alone."

"Not alone tonight. I'm staying with you."

"John-Peter, you mustn't!"

"I'll be gone before sunrise, my word as a gentleman."

The alarm on her face turned to panic. "Leave, now!"

"I am not your brother."

There, he said it, and the words were not as fearsome as he imagined. What's more, even the princess relaxed, a little, but it was enough to encourage him. It was only a tiny chance, but John-Peter risked it. He might not get another. She did not remove her hand.

"Where can we go?" the boy asked.

"Not inside the farmhouse." She glanced across the goldenrods, toward the lake, but, disappointingly, did not suggest going there. "We can sit near the woods. That way, we can watch for the brownies' return, and you can flee into the woods without anyone seeing you."

Not the privacy he preferred, even accounting for the remoteness of the area. Still, it was better than nothing, for he would be alone with the princess for many hours; nightfall had just begun. Maintaining a firm, but easy hold onto the girl, John-Peter led the way back to the woods. The princess shivered, but he couldn't decide whether it was from the cool evening air that descended, as the moon rose higher in the sky, or an attack of nerves from disobeying the brownies; perhaps, a mixture of both? He backed off her hand, removed his suit coat, and guided it over her shoulders. Then he took her arm, steered her to a grand old apple tree and gestured for her to sit. Its wide trunk accommodated both their heads, and they gazed upwards into the starry sky. Her hand rested limply inside his, but she did not try to take it away; he sensed the merest touch of her shoulder against his arm. He contemplated those glowing spheres of gases far off in the universe and decided former cravings for cell phones and vintage convertibles seemed trivial compared to this delectable moment with the princess. The word "sister" popped into his mind, and he glibly passed over it. It couldn't be true, but, if it was, he dwelled in a world where anything happened. This night more than proved it. He would find a way. No, change that. *They* would find a way.

For a long while they sat there, neither one speaking, and, although the princess did not appear cold, every now and again a faint tremor rippled through her body. The cooling temperatures did not affect John-Peter; warmth smoldered inside him, and he fought to contain it, but, at the same time, he hoped the heat from his hand reassured her. She was afraid, and yet, she stayed, which greatly heartened him, until, looking heavenward, she stunned him by saying, "If you are not my brother, who are you?"

The question disquieted him, but he kept his gaze fixed on the sky while he considered his answer. He could not say, "lover," for fear of sending her scuttling back to the brownie farm, although Karla's "The Lovers" card loomed in his mind, but he also would not say, "rescuer," without a plan to accomplish it.

Instead, he hedged. "What makes you think I'm your brother?"

The princess dropped her hand, pulled a solitary blade of grass from the ground, and peeled it down the middle. "Eircheard says you are."

Eircheard! John-Peter's heart took off like a rocket, and a storm of conflicting emotions, desire, loathing, and, yes, even rage, boiled inside him. Not the Eircheard of Eircheard's Emporium, the very place where Ed Calkins purchased an enchanted mirror for him? What was Eircheard doing around the princess, and what were the odds it was the very same man?

"Who is this Eircheard?" John-Peter said, deliberately enunciating each word to steady the voice that threatened to betray the turbulence he felt inside. Control, he told himself, stay in control.

"He's my betrothed," the princess said, giving another piece of grass the same treatment as its cousin. "He caught me watching you one day in the mirage by the lake and told me how wicked it was for me to gaze upon you, because I belonged to him, and, because, you were my brother."

He swallowed hard at the memory of the two of them, standing immobile and unblinking, on their respective sides of the mirror. "Gaze upon me, princess?"

She reached past her slippers for a piece of clover, and her hair fell across her cheeks, so John-Peter wasn't certain that she blushed, but her evasive actions suggested it. He brushed the silken strands over her shoulder, and her cheek felt hot under his fingers. She didn't say it, but there was no need. The princess loved him, too. He was in.

"Mama B. always came to the lake to wash the clothes, with me and all her little baby brownies traipsing behind her. Being larger than they and clumsier, I could never play as they did, leaping from tree to tree and scaling underbrush with the speed of a blue hare, so I often amused myself by picking heather and watching the frolics of the water sprites. One day, while I gathered an enormous bouquet as a surprise to Mama, I saw a clear, sparkling light shining in the forest. I forgot the flowers, and I forgot the other brownies, so captivating was that light, I just had to follow it. I don't know how I hurried over all those hills, for I don't think I was very old, so my legs must have been rather short, but somehow I made it. The light seemed to fade the closer I came, and, for a second, I thought my eyes played tricks on me, but then it was there again, and you were inside it, looking back at me. I was lost, but I didn't care. You made me feel safe."

John-Peter thought he heard a tremor in her voice, but with her head bent low away from him, he couldn't be sure. He wasn't even two years old the first time her reflection visited him, when Ed Calkins presented him with the enchanted mirror as a housewarming present. He remembered telling Ed about seeing the princess, and he could still hear the old steward's laugh and casual remark that he wasn't surprised, that anything could happen inside a mirror with supernatural powers.

The princess continued in a quiet voice. "After a long time, I grew very sleepy, for the sun was hot, and I had missed my nap that day. Under the security of your watch, I lay down amongst a clump of sorrel and wild strawberry leaves and fell asleep. I had the strangest dreams that day, dreams of you playing the most beautiful music until someone called your name, and of me rolling around in dark, warm waters, and hearing echoing women's voices as they repeated over and over again, "Angela, oh, Angela." When I woke, it was dark and Papa B. was carrying me home over an open field. I fastened my arms around his neck lest his high leaping caused me to fall, but my eyes irresistibly drew themselves to the forest I no longer saw and to the strange music I still heard. I knew I had to go back."

He edged closer to her and put his arm around her shoulder. "Princess, you were only a small child. However did you accomplish it?"

"It wasn't easy," she said, and John-Peter wished she would look at him. He yearned to see the expression in her eyes. "Until I was old enough to do the laundry or take a bath by myself, I could only go when Mama B. did, and, naturally, after Papa's upbraiding, she kept a closer eye on me. Still, I could always find an excuse to drift away from her sight and sneak into the woods to see if you were there. I cried such bitter tears the first time you were not."

Something lurched inside him, and John-Peter tightened his grip on her. He didn't want to think about the princess crying.

"As I grew older, I relieved Mama of many household burdens, which gave me more reasons to visit the lake, even if it meant taking a beating when I was late coming home. I always knew I was different from Mama's other brownie children, but I didn't really understand, until recently, what Papa meant. He always was telling me that one day I would marry Eircheard and reinforce the fairy race by having many babies. I just thought it sounded altogether lovely to have such a romantic future waiting for me."

"So, you do understand now what is required of you?"

"Oh, yes, Eircheard explained it all to me. He said that because I shall soon marry him, I'm not to fall in love with anyone, especially my brother, and, oh, John-Peter, that's made me so sad!"

The thought of the princess climbing into a pile of leaves with that wizened, smelly old leprechaun, even if he did bake good bread, turned his stomach.

"Princess, this making of babies…"

She vigorously shook her head. "I'm not worried about that, at all. It can't be too difficult, because fairy women have so many of them. Such an ugly bunch those children are, too, with coarse hair sticking up at all angles, their pudgy cheeks and screwed-up, beady eyes. I can do much better than that. Papa B. told me so. I don't even have to raise them after they can walk, which is a good thing, because fairy children are such brats. I just get to have another baby, and I like that. Babies are so sweet, even brownie babies. That's when I realized Eircheard was right. You are my brother, because soon after I heard the words, "It's a girl," people dashed in and out of the room and another voice said, "It's a boy." Mama B. always had her babies by threes and fours and the midwife always spoke those very, same words. It's not fair."

John-Peter's mouth turned to cotton, and he was instantly transported back to the days when, as a little boy, on trips into Jenson, with closed eyes and open mouth, he'd hung his head out the car window to pretend he was flying. The giddiness he felt then paled to the rushing currents inside his head. She had no idea what Eircheard would demand of her.

He swallowed hard and said, "So, then, are you in love?"

The princess sighed, but made no other reply. John-Peter tried again. "What would you say if I told you we could leave this place for another one and be together forever?"

She turned to him now, with a look that was almost defiant. "There is no escape from here. Everyone knows that, even the peist, although he tried many times."

"I am living proof of it. I came from here, lived somewhere else for a while, and returned to take you back with me."

"No," she said, with a little shake of her pretty head. "It's hopeless, especially for a breeder."

"It's not hopeless," John-Peter said, reaching out to stroke her hair. "I know someone who can help us."

The princess's eyes were wide with wonder. "Who?"

John-Peter smiled with a confidence he hadn't felt in a long time. "The Steward of Tara."

She gave a little gasp and covered her mouth in shock. "You know him?"

"I not only know him, he's a very good friend of mine, and will arrive tomorrow. I shall pay him a visit at once. The steward's a fair man, so this is good as done." The happiness that radiated in her face made all trepidation worth it, for John-Peter wasn't entirely certain the steward would be glad to see him back. "Princess, did you know this is a magic apple tree?"

"It is?" she said in a tiny, faint voice.

"Yes, for it grew the apple the fairy enchanted and sent to Connla the Fair to nourish him for a month, until she returned with a crystal boat and bewitched him away forever. Princess, you have bewitched me, except I'm the one who will take you away, and, when I do, no one will ever frighten or harm you ever again."

"It sounds wonderful, only…"

"Only what? Speak it, and I will make it so for you."

"You're lucky to have a regal-sounding name," she said. "I'd give anything to have a real name."

"Your dreams did not mislead you," John-Peter said. "You do have a name, and it's Angela, the very name I shall henceforth call you."

"Angela," she repeated thoughtfully, tasting each syllable. "That's a pretty name. I like it."

He scooted close enough to wrap his other arm around her, too.

"Fret no more about our supposed relationship," he said. "You are not my sister. I give you my solemn oath on it."

She did not answer him, but the merest hush of a wind filtered through the apple tree, releasing enough fragrance to remind John-Peter of his destiny and steel him for the next step. He slowly moved his head toward her and lowered his gaze, relying on intuition for his only guide, until his lips touched Angela's. He paused, heart pounding, and reopened his eyes; she was so near that her lashes brushed against his. She did not close her eyes or pull away, so, under the very same apple tree that brought Connla his eternal good fortune, John-Peter kissed her, hesitantly at first, then with jubilant abandonment, freeing the pent-up ardor he'd harbored inside, all those years when she had hidden trapped inside his closet.

CHAPTER 25: THE STEWARD OF TARA

Just as he promised, John-Peter departed from Angela's sight the very instant daylight began nudging away the darkness, but not without lingering beside her for a one, last kiss and a pledge to return again the following night.

He hid in the woods the entire day, napping beneath the oak trees that humbly agreed to shelter their defender, for their relatives in southern France related his exploits to them. He climbed a particularly tall oak and maintained a constant vigil on brownie territory, until the afternoon merged into night, and the winding trail of the tiny, hopping creatures disappeared over the horizon. That's when John-Peter scampered out of the branches and jumped to the ground, speeding away for another delightful night in Angela's arms. He wondered how long he could be satisfied with merely kissing her, then remembered the poke of the brownie musket and decided kissing suited him just fine, for now.

This routine continued for a week, until Angela reminded John-Peter of his promise to visit the steward to petition her freedom. With a final taste of her lips to carry him through the next few days, he set out for home, basking in the exquisite remembrance of her warm breath against his skin. The passionate bubble of glowing feelings stayed with him the whole jaunt home, significantly shortening, in his mind, the time it took to get there. Only the sight of smoke rising from his chimney jolted him to reality. Nothing should be burning inside the fireplace.

John-Peter quickened his steps, but when he reached the back exit, a tall, lean girl, her straw hair chopped into spikes over the top of her head, met him there, brandishing his butcher knife. A younger girl, no more than four, with disheveled flaxen hair reaching to her waist, clutched the older girl's skirts and looked at John-Peter with a mixture of curiosity and fright.

"Hey!" John-Peter cried, reaching out for the knife.

The girl whipped it away, and John-Peter paused to glance at the red-beaded line forming where she grazed him from his wrist to below his fingers.

"Get your ass off my property," the girl snarled.

"Your property! Vile trespasser! Leave now, and I'll let you live."

"Finders, keepers. If you wanted it, you should've stayed home. Emmie and me, we're homesteading now. Crawl back to your woods." John-Peter watched her mouth closely when she talked and nearly laughed aloud. What a loser. She was nearly as bad as Lauren Cooper and her mawkish cohorts.

The girl advanced and pointed the knife at his face. "What're you staring at, scarecrow? Haven't you seen a tongue piercing before?"

"Sure, but it's wasted on your tongue. I would've screwed your lips together."

Her mouth dropped in astonishment, and John-Peter grabbed the knife as he pushed past her into the house. She stomped inside after him, folded her arms, and glared at him. The little girl did the same.

"So make us leave," the tall girl said.

"I wouldn't dream of it, now," John-Peter said, flopping onto his leaves; they crunched beneath his weight. "I require steady doses of amusement, and I bestow that job upon you." He scooped a handful and crumbled them between his fingers. "Your standards can't be that high, or you would've added some fresh ones."

"Do you think I'd lay my head in the same place you'd lay yours? I can do better than some moldy, makeshift bed."

From beneath the slits of his drooping eyes, John-Peter studied the morning sky that filtered through a chink in the roof directly above his head. So much for drifting off to sleep under the memory of Angela's kisses.

"One man's mold is another's fertilizer," he said with a wide yawn. "I'll expect dinner when I rise. Oh, and the place could use a bit of dusting, too."

"Make your own dinner. Emmie and me, we look after ourselves."

He rolled over to face her. "I'll bet Clancy would pay out a couple of nice, gold coins for the safe return of two runaway breeders. The old leprechaun down the road has a wife named Derbail. Tell her Glorna sent you for some barley, and she'll readily oblige you. Then, you and the tot can cook that up tonight, along with potatoes and cabbage, for there's plenty growing in the garden. Fetch some water, too. If you do a good job, you can have some."

The girl pressed her lips together and narrowed her eyes almost as tightly, so John-Peter guessed a decent fury raged inside her. Good. Served the smart-alecky chit right. Who gave her the right to soil his quarters with her obnoxious presence and then bark orders at him? The girl tossed her head, and the little girl she called Emmie tossed hers, too.

"Tell Clancy anything you want," the girl said evenly, "for he'll recoup his gold and then some from Eircheard, once both of them find out you've been hitting on forty-two."

Aodhan's words came back to accuse him: "Remember that a secret is a weapon, as well as a friend. Be careful it doesn't turn against you." Maybe, he should have played a reel or two for the sprites, for how else would this girl know about him and Angela? Just wait until he saw Aodhan. He'd have more to gripe about than a bent wing. In the meantime, maybe a change of tactic would soften the girl's disposition. A few lessons in sweetness from the princess wouldn't hurt, either.

He forced his tired body to stand and then offered his right hand to the unpleasant girl.

"Let's begin anew. I'm John-Peter Simotes, and I welcome you to my humble lodgings. You?"

Arms still crossed, the girl stuck her nose in the air and turned away from him. This time, Emmie did not mimic her, but stared, open-mouthed, unspeaking, at John-Peter.

"I'm not touching that," the older girl said, jerking her head in the direction of his hand. "I don't have my shots."

"Explains the distemper." He spat on his hand, wiped it down his pants, and once again extended it. "Since we're going to be roommates, we might as well be friends. At the very least, we could observe a few principles of basic etiquette."

"Left hand."

Suppressing the urge to wet that one, too, albeit a little more creatively, John-Peter held out the requested hand, and, amazingly, the girl returned the greeting with a hearty shake.

"Dawn Abrams, eighteen, Goose Creek, Kentucky."

"You're a long way from Kentucky, missy."

"Not long enough. There isn't enough gold at the end of the rainbow to make me go back there. Turned eighteen four days ago. Now, no one can make me do anything."

He jerked his head at the Emmie. "Your sister?"

"Nope."

"Okay, twenty questions, then who?"

"Don't know. I named her Emmie the day I met her. It's a lot better than a hundred and nine."

"Why doesn't she talk?"

"Cuz she can't talk, you nitwit. Are you blind?"

"Then, how did you know her number?"

With a look of disgust, Dawn, yanked the girl around and lifted the back of her shirt. The three digits were fused into her back. John-Peter flinched at the sight of those deep scorch marks.

Did Angela have brands like these, too? He didn't feel quite comfortable asking at their expense, so he instead said, "And you?"

"All of us, even your precious girlfriend. How else do you think Clancy keeps us all straight? On the day of my capture, Emmie was huddled in a corner, scared out of her wits. She and I are a team now. Mess with her, and you mess with me."

Dawn couldn't have humbled him more if she tried. She could keep the butcher knife in its place, for she wouldn't need to use it on him, ever.

"I'm sorry. I didn't know, and, cross my heart, I won't tell Clancy. You can stay here for as long as you like. Forget the food. I'm not hungry."

All former revelries left his mind. He pictured Clancy shoving a hot iron into Angela's back, and he coughed back the nausea socking his gut. He would not vomit before this arrogant girl. Dawn, however, paid no attention, for Emmie tugged at the older girl's skirts, and Dawn forgot about John-Peter to take the little girl's hand and lead her outside. He only felt bone-tired now, and he desperately needed to sleep if he planned to make the journey to Filiocht Hill without collapsing on the way. He lay back down on the bed, clasped his hands behind his neck, and felt a break in his shoulder that sucked his breath right from him. John-Peter closed his eyes against the pain; the throbbing that ascended into his neck wasn't intense enough to compete with sleep. He started down the stairs when his body jerked him violently awake. He grunted and drifted away again, interrupted this time by a gentle tapping in the back of his head.

"Go away, Karla," he said in muffled voice.

"What?" Dawn said from her crouch on the floor, where she tended the fire.

Karla wedged herself in the doorway, lest John-Peter tried shutting her out. He smiled through sleepiness and pain. She knew him too well.

"Listen to me, John-Peter, this is serious. You're in the hospital, and you've had another seizure."

"Later."

"No, not later. The doctors don't know what's wrong with you, but your mother does. She said you need a special kind of transfusion that only Dr. Rothgard knows how to give. Do you know what she's talking about?"

Sleep washed over him with tsunami-like waves. "Nope," his voice slurred, fading into blessed nothingness. How long he slept, he did not know, but he wakened to early morning sunshine and to the aroma of freshly baked cornbread, something he hadn't smelled in a very long time. Where had Dawn found cornmeal? No corn grew in these parts, not anytime when he lived here. He closed his eyes against the fog overtaking his brain, and when he opened them again, Emmie sat on the leaves near him, a placid, inquisitive expression on her young face.

"He up?" Dawn called.

Emmie nodded and pointed to the bucket near the doorway. John-Peter focused his eyes and saw the wet floor surrounding it, where the water sloshed out.

"Good. Go wash, John-Peter. Your food's waiting. You slept an entire day."

An anvil would be easier to lift than his painful body. With much effort, John-Peter eased to a sitting position. His shoulder felt as if someone was pouring burning ice into it; the flaming chill ran down to his fingertips. He didn't feel like washing up, much less eating, but the fact that Dawn made the trek to the well on his behalf somehow cheered him. The cold water he splashed on his face returned him to alertness, and the moth-eaten, but clean, rag she left beside the bucket warmed him on the inside. Maybe, having Dawn live here wouldn't be so bad. Besides, she might as well because, hopefully, he wouldn't need the hut anymore. He counted on the steward to make a way for him to return to Munsonville with Angela, even if he had to promise lifelong servitude to him. Dr. Rothgard couldn't be telling the entire truth about his demise. The steward helped create him, too, and John-Peter felt confident Ed Calkins would know what to do.

The spread on the table truly astounded him, and, for the second time in twenty-four hours, Dawn subdued him, no easy task to achieve. In addition to the cornbread and the boiled cabbage, she had prepared a huge bowl of Irish green peas and filled another with potatoes and leeks. She stood, hands on her hips, chin thrust forward, waiting for a jeer or a sarcastic taunt.

"Call off your dogs," John-Peter said, throwing one leg over the bench. "You won't be hearing anything negative from me. I was joking about cooking food, honest. I wasn't expecting this."

He piled large mounds of everything into his dish. Emmie sidled up beside him and noted each spoonful.

"Sit down like a good girl," John-Peter said, much as he might to Ellie, "and I'll give you some, too."

Emmie didn't move.

"We ate," Dawn said, shortly. "This is yours."

He was grateful for the meal, but the crisp note in her voice made him wary. He bit into the cornbread and was again surprised, for Dawn had mixed fresh corn into the batter. Then hunger sounded its battle cry, and John-Peter responded to it with a zealous attack. Emmie's head bobbed up and down with every mouthful.

"Make her stop," John-Peter said, dumping more potatoes into his bowl. "It's unnerving."

Dawn sat down on the bench next to him. "We want something from you."

He threw down his spoon. "I knew it. The anesthetic before the kill. Whatever it is, the answer is 'no.'"

"Rescue us, too."

"No."

Her fist slammed on the table so hard all the bowls jumped inches from their places. "Yes!"

"I can't take all three of you to Munsonville."

Dawn's mouth opened wide. "You live in Munsonville? Home of world-famous pianist John Simons?"

The cold in his shoulder crept down his spine, but he tried to sound casual. "You've heard of John Simons?" He picked up the last wedge of cornbread, split it in half, and ate it in two bites.

Emmie watched, fascinated.

"Sure, anyone who takes piano lessons from a good teacher's heard of John Simons."

"You play?"

"Played. Instruments suck. Drag racing rocks. Take us back with you."

"Are you deaf?" John-Peter picked up his spoon and resumed his meal. "I just said, 'I can't take all three of you back with me.'"

"There's more than three."

He felt the oh-too-familiar knocking inside his head.

Damn, Karla! Later!

John-Peter looked from one solemn girl to the next. Emmie only leaned her elbows on the table and smiled.. More than three? How many more girls hiding on his property? Surely, she wasn't talking about liberating Clancy's entire stock, but one look at Dawn's grim face told him she meant exactly that.

He reached for the beans and scowled. "Impossible."

Dawn placed her hand on his arm, and he looked straight into the face of the grinning skull tattooed on her forearm, scary for a girl, but, at least, her touch was mild. "We know you're in love with number forty-two, but how can you leave the rest of us behind, knowing that when you do…"

Her voice trailed away; the distress on her face uttered volumes of unspoken words. He knew what would happen after he left, but what could he do about it? Emmie's ardent monitoring of each of his movements reminded him of Fawn observing him peel apples, only creepier.

"Dawn, there's no way that…"

"You're going to see the steward. Can't you tell him to set us all free?"

"It's not that easy."

"I'll help. We'll all help. Whatever you say, we'll do."

"I've got to go."

"John-Peter…"

He didn't wait for the rest. It would take him all day to reach the top of the Filiocht Hill, so he couldn't waste any more time thinking about the breeders' plight. However, as he descended Daragh Hill, John-Peter couldn't help mentally touring the cellar prison again, except each of the faces in those cells resembled Deanna, Ellie, and Fawn. He tripped over a vine and returned to reality. Stop it, he ordered himself. Those girls are numbers, just numbers.

Filling his mind with horrors he couldn't fix wouldn't help Angela, and helping Angela was the reason for his journey.

He would be wise not to forget it. Somewhere, a red grouse called out, "Go back! Go back! Go back!" That's when he remembered to return Karla's call. He thought she sounded a bit miffed for spurning her help, not that he blamed her, although her version of what happened was hard to digest.

"Karla, how can I be in the hospital when I'm here?"

"Where's 'here,' John-Peter? I'm looking right at you."

Her words were incredulous. "What do you see?"

"You're lying in a hospital bed with a bunch of tubes sticking in you. Your eyes are shut, and you're breathing kind of funny. You twitch, sometimes."

"I'm inside the mirror, Karla."

"You seized before you ever got that far."

She was either lying, or else he was in two places at the same time. The second was more plausible; Karla never lied to him. He sidestepped a partly buried tree root to avoid another stumble and said, "It's serious?"

"Very. You won't last without a complete transfusion. The nurses at the hospital said your blood doesn't match any type they've ever seen, but they're willing to try O negative because they said hardly any one reacts badly to it. Your mom refused, and your grandma is out in the hall with her, now, trying to change her mind."

"You say my mother contacted Dr. Rothgard?"

"She tried, but she couldn't reach him. Anyway, the hospital won't allow his help. John-Peter, it's not sounding good. I'm scared."

"Don't be. I won't die. At worst, I'll be stranded here forever. At best, we'll find a solution, and I'll come home."

The steward had better have the answer, for the chances of protecting Angela forever were slim if they remained here.

"Why does your mom want Dr. Rothgard?"

"You won't believe this, Karla. Pull up a chair."

A slight, quick movement and a splash caught his eyes, as he skirted around Quixotic Pond; probably a merrow, the first of the elusive creature he almost saw since returning home.

"What's a merrow?" Karla said.

Urghh! Sometimes he wished he could switch off her mind-reading abilities like he turned off the tap water at home. "It's like a mermaid."

"Are you by a sea?"

"No, a pond."

He took a sharp right and waded through the tall yellow-green grasses toward the open fields, surprising a group of brown grasshoppers, who leaped from their hiding place in a dark cloud and then dispersed from sight among the weeds.

"I thought mermaids lived in deep water."

"Karla!"

"Okay, sorry. What's up with Dr. Rothgard?"

He told her about sneaking from the hotel to Golden Years and confronting Dr. Rothgard about his past. Not once did she interrupt him, even as he related Dr. Rothgard's association with Countess Elizabeth Bathory, his subsequent discovery of her heinous fountain of youth, and how his sharing in it eventually led to the conception of his only child, Millicent.

"You still there, Karla?"

"I think so. Wow, it's a lot to absorb, isn't it?"

She remained silent during the retelling of Millicent's infatuation with Henry, who vampirized first John, and then Millicent, and John-Peter only lightly explained the parts they already knew from Grandma Marchellis' diary and Cornell Dyer's vampire research: Dr. Rothgard's ability to reanimate the dead with blood and how Grandma Marchellis and John-Peter's mother both became cooperative hosts to satisfy John's obsession for a second human life.

"John-Peter, what does all this have to do with you?"

"I'm coming to that."

Karla was so quiet during the story of his fairy roots, the commission of a changeling son by John Simons, and the roles that Dr. Rothgard, Ed Calkins, and even Eircheard, played in his creation, that John-Peter wondered if she was paying attention and paused for her affirmation.

"Go on, John-Peter, go on."

"My dislike of meat is all part of the plan. Ed programmed me to desire no blood other than my father's. The vitamin pills Dr. Rothgard fashioned from my father's blood, which is stored inside my mother, confirmed it. For many years, he kept my father alive with increasing amounts of my mother's blood, synthetically reproduced, to ensure adequate quantities at all times. The master plan was to completely transfuse me with enough of my father's blood when the rotting piano leg completely failed. No one anticipated Dr. Rothgard would be committed and unable to manufacture anymore."

"So the only way for you to get enough blood to survive…"

"Is to murder my mother."

"Oh, John-Peter, how awful!"

"I'm on my way now to see the Steward of Tara about another matter. When I'm there, I shall ask him to reprogram me to accept Type O blood. It should be a simple matter for him, and then I'm saved."

"Hurry, John-Peter. The doctor says you don't have much time."

"Dr. Morgan is overseeing my care?"

"No, the hospital's medical director took the case because it's so unusual. You'd think that would make your mother feel good, but she's gets mad every time he walks into the room."

"She's probably just used to Dr. Morgan."

"Probably. I'll keep you updated."

"Much obliged, mademoiselle, much obliged."

Before she could utter another word, John-Peter shut the door and bolted it. He wanted to think about Angela, since he wouldn't be with her tonight, but he didn't care to share those thoughts with Karla. Of course, his musings were outside the boundaries of what they really did under Connla the Fair's apple tree, but the steward had issued no law against dreaming.

Long before the sun reached the top of the sky, John-Peter felt the first rumblings of starvation, but the combination of the day's heat, his erratic sleeping patterns of the past week, and his turbulent emotions for Angela had worked a soporific spell on him. He didn't dare stop, for fear of falling asleep, and instead, plucked steady handfuls of nonexistent vegetation all the way to the steward's residence.

Filiocht Hill was the largest of the underworld hills, the ideal place to showcase the four-story, red-brick apartment building that overlooked the countryside. The road that guided one to its double-arched doors, visible from the ground, was unlike the typical fairy paths, for it was paved and sealed and gleamed like obsidian in the afternoon sun. The smell of new tar overpowered the freshly mowed grass, and John-Peter wondered where the steward found tar and a lawn mower in the underworld.

An old white cargo van, splotched with gold where someone attempted to touch up rust with sprayed-on paint, was parked alongside the building, the first vehicle John-Peter encountered since leaving Munsonville. The side door was unlocked, so John-Peter opened it and peeked inside. A single seat for the driver, ink-smudged seams gaping here and there, was the only place to sit, except for the two bean bag chairs someone had tossed on the back floor. The yellow chair featured a fake, leopard-skin design; the black stitching on the orange vinyl chair suggested a basketball. Several, large laundry baskets held stacks of manila envelopes and spiral notebooks; another held two changes of clothes: blue jeans, socks, and striped shirts; and the last was full of old newspapers. The glove box was open and filled with hand-held video games. He grabbed one of the baskets, slid it near him, and removed one of the notebooks. The scrawling penmanship was illegible, so he tossed it into the basket and tried one of the envelopes. This was typed and formatted for submission, but the flowery prose was too clumsy to stomach. Who lived here besides the steward?

He replaced the envelope and shut the door, pondering the sea of manuscripts all the way to the front doors. He debated whether or not to knock, decided not, and turned the handle. The door freely swung open, so John-Peter stepped into the dark foyer where a set of stairs led up and another set steered to the building's lower level.

"Now what?" he said aloud.

As his eyes adjusted to the dim light, he noticed a row of mail slots on the left wall. The gold plate towering over the other names read, "The Steward of Tara," which seemed to indicate that the steward occupied the entire fourth floor. He bolted up the first floor without any problem, and he climbed the second floor with relative ease. His broken toes were pounding when he reached the third floor, and he slipped twice while climbing the last flight, which led directly to the front door of the only apartment on that floor. The boy leaned against the wall, dug his hand inside his pocket, and removed the leprechaun. The numbers barely moved from the previous time he viewed it, yet his memory hadn't diminished. Did the Steward of Tara remember to bring batteries with him? He shifted his aching feet and willed their throbbing go away. This was not why he came here. He stood straight, marched to the door, and loudly locked.

The door opened, but it wasn't the servant John-Peter assumed would wait on such an eminent person as the steward. No, the heavy ruffles on the white shirt accentuated the fine, boyish features of the man who wore it. His dark hair sleeked over the top of his head and, when he turned to call out to the steward, "He's arrived," John-Peter saw the hair ended in a pigtail at the tip of his collar. He wore brown breeches, white socks and black shoes, certainly not a typical Irishman.

"He'll be right with you," the man said. He gestured to the sagging couch, and John-Peter swore he saw a loose spring. "Won't you sit down?"

"Is it safe?"

The man shrugged but otherwise seemed unconcerned whether or not John-Peter accepted the invitation. Despite the feet that clamored to sit, John-Peter tried to look indifferent as he said, "I'd rather stand."

The man bowed his head and left the room. The sill of the large picture window overlooking the fields that John-Peter had recently traveled was thick with dust and displayed several brown plants choking in fossilized dirt. The beige carpet boasted stains small and large, and the glass coffee table, underneath millions of fingerprints, held a number of tattered periodicals, all of them pertaining to Irish gardening. Next to it, on the floor, was the stack of paperback novels Ed Calkins purchased at Eircheard's Emporium. He didn't examine the records near the old phonograph at the other end of the room, but he wouldn't be surprised if some of them featured bagpipe music.

"John-Peter!"

Ed Calkins, dressed in blue jeans and a red-striped shirt, poked his smiling head into the room. "Come back here. I want to read you something."

The boy followed the man down the hall to a small bedroom that Ed obviously used for an office, for it contained a plywood desk, a rusty metal folding chair, an electric typewriter, and several computers. A second folding chair was propped by the door, which Ed left ajar once John-Peter entered the room. The branch of a large oak tree was the only view from the window.

"Yeah, okay, Atlantic City."

"Well, John-Peter, what was I supposed to say?"

"It's a sham."

"Not really. Here, listen to this." Ed walked to his desk, picked up a notebook and read:

When it comes to matters of verse
The Steward is master of terse
He goes straight for the heart
From end to the start
With insults that are quite diverse.

He lowered the notebook, raised his eyebrows, and looked at John-Peter with a proud, happy smile. Footsteps padded down the hall, and John-Peter peered through the doorway's slight opening but saw no one.

"Well, what do you think?" Ed said, still smiling.

"Hardly worthy of my vomit."

The smile faded, and Ed dropped the notebook on the table, sadly shaking his head. "It's the story of my life. I have all these great ideas, but they never sound like I imagine them. Thank God for Amerigen."

"Amerigen? The man who answered the door?"

"Yes. He's my poet and a tremendous one, at that. He's like the minstrel of the Middle Ages, very careful to elevate my status, which means legitimizing some news and rejecting others. Instead of being bloody, well, except for the most necessary of meals, I can be very effective at praise, condemnation, mockery, and, most importantly of all, at being ruthless."

John-Peter studied the gray bark and oval leaflets on the limb outside the window, while stifling a yawn. Ed Calkins told this story on the route more times than he sang, *Sweet Molly Malone.*

"You see, John-Peter, Amerigen's poetry is not the high art, high minded poetry of the De Danann's, who were superior poets. It's vulgar poetry, the precursor to the limerick, the most superior kind of poem. Why is it superior, you ask?"

"Because people can pronounce it," John-Peter said. "They can remember it, and it flows freely from the tongue. People fear it because it immortalizes how others will remember them. Victories become defeats; missteps and misfortunes transform into epic blunders."

Ed gave a short, uncertain laugh and uneasily shuffled his feet on the floor. "Well, I can see you've paid attention. I tonsure you an honorary Irishman, but you have to take seriously your obligation to create myth."

"That's why I'm here, your stewardship. I come to beg two favors."

"Which are?"

"I want you to return the human child who took my place."

The smile vanished. "I'm afraid I can't do that."

"Are you not the caretaker of your mind, as well as Tara?"

"This is not about Ed Calkins, the man, but Ed Calkins, the myth, and I can't worry about all these details. I didn't create this myth from thin air, but from your delusion, Glorna, and I, like all creators of mythology, can't stress out over what actually happened when I can control what I imagined happened."

"It's not fair to Angela!"

"Have you stopped to consider what's fair to me? Do you know what it's like to have stories bursting inside of you, only to hand-deliver, since I was a lad, newspapers full of other people's stories, and not be able to put the right words down on paper? I'm so dyslexic and scatterbrained, even spell-check doesn't recognize my words."

"I don't care," John-Peter began, but Ed continued as if he hadn't spoken.

"So, I wind up changing the word to get past spell check, but when I keep writing that way, I kill the story. I keep trying, because I can't stop writing, yet, on the other hand, I can't finish anything. My life is full of half-begun novels. I couldn't even finish one about Hannibal, my hero, foe of Rome! So, in high school, I switched to poetry, but it never sounded like any of the poetry I ever read."

"Uncle Ed, this is real life. It's my life. It's Angela's life. It's not one of your novels."

"That, John-Peter, is where you are wrong." Ed sat on top of his desk and spread his hands apart with a swoop, but he no longer smiled. "Did you see that van out there? That's the van I was driving when your father first asked me for a route. I loved that van. It was beat up, but it made me feel strong. It was stick, so not everyone could drive it. It was like a second home. I could sleep, eat, read, and play games in it. I had practical things in it, too, like my manuscripts. It wasn't seduction bait. It was practical. I drove it until it would drive no more, and then..."

"And then what?" John-Peter asked.

Ed thought hard. "Where was I?"

John-Peter slumped into the chair by the door. Maybe, if he humored Ed, he might change his mind about Angela, just like a patient hearing of his Irish jokes was usually rewarded with a visit to Eircheard's Emporium.

"My father asked you for a route," John-Peter said.

"The only one available at the time was a country route I drove from Evansville past Thornton, because no other carrier wanted it, but your father said it was just the thing for him. I gave it to him for two reasons. It took too long for me to complete it on time, and because there was something vaguely familiar about him. This is where the story gets tricky."

Ed fell silent. The gentle rain pattered on the leaves and against the glass.

"One dark and stormy night, a car forced me off the road. A man took my wallet, stabbed me in the chest, and left me for dead. Your mother appeared out of nowhere, so I managed to give her the leprechaun, instructing her to return it to you."

John-Peter instinctively rubbed his hand over the lump deep within his pocket, looked up, and saw Ed Calkins watching him with a studious expression. "You were still alive when you programmed me?"

"I told you that it gets tricky. Some time after your mother left, your father flung open the passenger door, leaped inside the van, and told me to shut my eyes, that everything would soon be fine. I did as he told me. Something painful ripped apart my throat, and I woke up at home the next night. That's when your father told me what happened. At first, I didn't believe him, but when he opened the grocery bag at his feet and tossed a slab of raw corned beef at my feet, I eagerly devoured it, which only proved his point."

"So, when did you program me?"

"Before you were born and after I became a vampire. Now, don't ask me, John-Peter, because I don't understand it, either. Somehow, when your father decided to create a son, he had enough vampirism inside him to advance a few years in time, after he turned me into one of the undead, and order this from me. I had no choice because, since he made me, I was compelled to obey. However, unless he wanted something from me, I was free to exist in whatever manner I chose. Well, of course, I chose something Irish, something visible, but not seen in public, someone who could insult without fear of counter-insults."

"The Steward of Tara?"

"Exactly. As the steward, I maintained the property by appointing collectors, groundskeepers, masons, and carpenters to keep the place in repair. Being that Tara is a sacred site, it would be a place where I could feel important, and where I could cross kings, without being under the direct control of any king."

"Except my father."

"Well, except for him. Only once, for you, did he use that authority."

The gentle raindrops were gone; a torrential downpour replaced them, which beat against the glass, rattling with the heavy winds threatening to shatter it.

John-Peter's voice rose above the din. "Why seek your assistance?"

"Anyone working for me knows my love for all things Irish. However, John also knew I had a background in psychology and computer programming, and this interested him just as much."

The boy sat straight up and leaned forward to hear more, which immediately put a pleased smile back on Ed's face.

"You thought just because I ramble about Irish myth, you knew everything about me, didn't you? The truth is, John-Peter, I majored in psychology in college to help me with my writing. My roommate, who was also my newspaper route supervisor, had an early morning computer class, but he was afraid he'd miss it, either with late trucks or by oversleeping. So, I signed up for the class, too. Since I now worked for him, getting him to school on time secured my own job. Looking back, I'm glad I did. That computer class changed my life."

John-Peter leaned back in the chair and stretched his arms over his head, while also stretching his legs. He knew where Ed was taking this story.

"So, you quickly rose to the top of the class," the boy said, "and became the mad, genius programmer no one understood. The end."

"Actually, John-Peter, I got the lowest grade in the class, but I found out I had a knack for programming. I took a few more classes, started working for Joe Reece, and created programs for his routes, since he didn't have anyone who could do that for him. So, when the conventional method for having a son didn't work for your father, he demanded I concoct a believable substitute. It was just a simple matter of assimilating Irish changeling lore with my knowledge of human psychology and computer programming, Eircheard's skill for woodworking, and Dr. Rothgard's experimental treatments with blood reanimation and pseudogenes."

"Pseudogenes?"

"DNA garbage. Dr. Rothgard harvested any leftover usable coding material from them and gave them to me to people my kingdom. He retrieved enough from your father when he was alive to fashion you. Basically, you and your father share the same genetic makeup. Anyway, that's why your father couldn't let me die. I needed regular contact with you to install periodic upgrades, as you grew and as technology changed, to continue your illusion of humanity and retain the memories your father wanted retained. That's also why Angela stays here, where she now belongs, and you must go back. You are my masterpiece. If I can't write legend, I'll be legend. Does that answer your question?"

"You left out a part."

Puzzled, Ed, clasped his hands, gazed at the ceiling and silently counted. The he looked at John-Peter, frowned, and said, "I did? What part?"

"The treated wood."

"The piano leg?"

"The extra preservative in the leg. Changelings typically die in the first, few years of life. You've artificially prolonged my existence."

"Ah, that. You see, Glorna, it wasn't enough to feed and sustain the boy, John-Peter. I also devised a way to nourish the very wood that formed him. Why do you think I always insisted you get plenty of sun and water? Judging from your appearance, and, until now, relative good health, I call the experiment a complete success."

"So, the green in my skin is…"

"Chlorophyll," Ed Calkins said.

CHAPTER 26: RUTHLESS BUSINESS

"See?" Ed said. "You're doomed if you stay here. I recreated you for another world. You have to go back."

"I can't."

"Yes, you can. Let me see the leprechaun."

Eyes still closed, John-Peter reached his hand inside his pocket and withdrew the detestable mouse. "I think it needs new batteries," he mumbled.

"It doesn't have any batteries," Ed said. "It runs on your life force. That's why you must leave. When the numbers run out..."

"I die." John-Peter leaned his head against the wall and managed a sardonic smile. "I'm doomed either way. I need a complete transfusion with my father's blood, and there isn't any to be had."

"Of course there is. Dr. Rothgard has that under control."

"No, he doesn't. Dottie left. There is no one to manufacture the blood for him. And he's dying."

"John-Peter, open your eyes and take this."

The boy squinted through the haze of pain and distress long enough to accept the leprechaun from Ed. He could have stayed at HHG and taken his lickings from the law for all the good his escape brought him. Before he reclosed his eyes, he saw Ed Calkins lean against the desk with an encouraging smile.

"Stay here for a couple of days," Ed said. "I must attend to some ruthless business this evening, but, tomorrow night, we shall get the blood you need, and then you will go home."

"Uncle Ed, I already told you there is no more blood, except inside my mother, and I'm not hurting her to get it."

"There's all kinds of blood, if you know where to look, and you won't have to hurt anybody."

John-Peter opened his eyes and raised himself to a sitting position, willing the hope welling inside him to remain at low, manageable levels. Was he saved, after all?

"Are we still talking about my father's blood?" the boy asked warily.

"We are still talking about your father's blood. Dr. Rothgard has freezers full of it, in nineteen-eighty. I'll just take you along on my nightly spree, and we'll steal enough blood from him to make you completely human. There's only one problem."

"Which is?"

"I don't exactly know where he stores it. I'm hoping your little psychic friend can consult her crystal ball and find out."

The memory of Karla suddenly appearing behind him on his front porch flared with sharp clearness in his mind. How far did her clairvoyant powers travel? As far as Thornton?

"I don't think that will be a problem, Uncle Ed."

"Good!" Ed looked pleased with himself. "Then, it's off to a hot shower with you, and then dinner and bed. Tomorrow, you can amuse yourself in my library, and, after the sun sets, you and I will take a trip sixteen years in reverse."

Ed led the way back down the hall, past the living room where John-Peter had entered, and through the kitchen to another hall that mirrored the one they just left. This one also had three bedrooms and a bathroom. Ed opened the door to the last room on the right. It had a motel cleanness to it, with its white walls, tan carpet and chenille bedspread, a plywood bed with a matching chest of drawers and desk, along with another metal folding chair.

"There's a robe in the closet," Ed said, "and a washer and drier across the hall. Throw your clothes in there while you take a shower. You don't want to give yourself away to Dr. Rothgard by your smell. You can come to dinner in the robe. Amerigen and I, we're not fussy."

"Thanks, Uncle Ed."

After Ed shut the door, John-Peter draped the detested suit coat over the back of the chair and sat on the edge of the bed to untie his shoes, cheered at the prospect of venturing into the past. Maybe, the steward did him a favor, by giving him his freedom, which enabled him to dwell beyond the hollows of Ed's mind. He stood, undid his belt, and allowed the ruined pants to fall to the floor. Soon, he would be the human he always thought he was, and he could finally shed his fictional side. He strolled to the closet for the robe. Somehow, he must persuade Ed to allow Angela to share the real world with him. Perhaps, if the steward knew of the multitude of other breeders Clancy kept, he would be more willing to allow this one to go.

The guest bathroom was just as Spartan as the bedroom, but the white label shampoo and soap served its purpose. He turned the hot water on high, and the steamy water ran down his back and over his sore shoulder. Had he ever really enjoyed a shower before now? Even his toes felt better under the sudsy, hot water that collected in the bottom of the tub; hunger now was the greater pain. Reluctantly, John-Peter shut off the spray, squeezed the water from his hair, and reached for a towel. He hoped the steward served something good for dinner.

Ed Calkins sat at the kitchen table, scribbling into a notebook, crossing out a line here and there, and adding fresh ones. Across from him sat a variety of food, all warmed up from cans, but, which, nevertheless, smelled delicious to the starving boy. There were baked beans, vegetarian chili, a bowl of peas, a dish of potatoes, and half a loaf of store-brand white bread. John-Peter devoured half of the food before he spoke.

"What are you writing, Uncle Ed?"

"My battle plan," Ed said in low tones.

"You're going to war?"

"Hush!" Ed said, glancing furtively around him. "I don't want Amerigen to hear. I've challenged him to a duel."

"Do you think that's wise?" John-Peter grabbed another slice of bread. He had only a brief glimpse of the poet when he opened the door for him, but, judging from the way he moved, the man yielded some muscle under his pansy, colonial-style garb. An army of Ed Calkins' would be no match for Amerigen.

"Amerigen hates that too many of his poems are associated more with me, the ruthless dictator, and not with him, so I've challenged him to a duel to determine who the real poet it," Ed said. "After I defeat him, I shall install another poet. I'm going to procure him this very night."

"Sword or pistol?"

"Neither. Our weapons are the power of the spoken word." Ed bent his head over his notebook and wrote.

John-Peter scraped the last of the beans onto his plate, wondering how Ed could possibly win. He'd heard many of Ed's limericks.

"There!" A smiling Ed closed the notebook, and, with a victorious gleam in his eye, looked straight at John-Peter. "This should do it. Throw everything in the dishwasher when you're done. I'm going out for a bite and to find me a poet." He rose from his seat and added, "Get plenty of rest this evening and tomorrow. You have a long night ahead of you."

Ed tucked his notebook under his arm and skipped out of the room. A few seconds later, John-Peter heard the front door shut. He rinsed his dishes and put them in the dishwasher. The apartment was silent, except for the faint sounds of voices emitting from the television set, behind a closed door, at the end of the hall, opposite of John-Peter's bedroom. Now seemed to be a good time.

"Hey Karla," John-Peter called. "How am I doing?"

"Weak," she said. "Your mother's having no luck convincing the hospital to call Dr. Rothgard, either."

"They haven't given me the Type O blood?"

"Your mother's refused it, but your doctor is looking for a loophole that will allow him to do it, anyway, and, you know what, John-Peter? I sort of hope he finds it. I'm so afraid something bad is going to happen to you if you don't get the blood you need."

Through the kitchen window, John-Peter saw the orange-black sky of sunset. Before long, the brownies would vacate camp for work. "How far does your teleportation work?"

"Not sure. Haven't practiced long distances. Why?"

"Well, first, can you spirit some clothes from my bedroom?"

"That's easy!"

Instantly, a pair of jeans, green T-shirt, clean socks, and Marcus O'Reilly's suit coat dropped onto the floor. John-Peter quickly scooped up the clothes and headed back to his room to change.

"Next, I want you to pay a visit to Dr. Rothgard."

"Isn't he out of blood?"

The boy said nothing. He wondered if he could make it to the brownie camp and back again before Uncle Ed returned at sun-up. A warm current ran through his veins at the remembrance of Angela's soft lips, and he realized, with a start, that his sprained shoulder, as well as his broken fingers and toes, were pleasantly numb. He sensed Karla's impatience, and it brought him, grudgingly, back to reality.

"John-Peter, what are you up to?"

"Uncle Ed revealed he is a vampire, thanks to you-know-who. Tomorrow night, he's conveying me to nineteen-eighty Shelby to swindle some of my father's blood from Dr. Rothgard. Determine where he conceals it and the correct amount I require."

Karla sounded uncertain. "What makes you think he'll cooperate?"

"Tell him we'll share."

He checked the security of all doors labeled, "Princess," retrieved each piece of the suit, and lightly sprinted toward the front door.

"Leaving now," Karla said. "Wish me luck."

"May the luck of the Irish enfold you."

"Good enough." She dropped a door.

John-Peter dashed down the stairs. A large sign on the third floor read, "The Library of Ed Calkins, Steward of Tara." As he passed the second floor landing, he wondered who, or what, the other tenants were. He stepped outside, made sure the doors remained unlocked, and threw away the homecoming suit in the steward's dumpster. He ran down Filiocht Hill with a speed that astonished him, considering his rotten limbs, turned left, and sprinted toward brownie terrain. Before he reached the woods, he spotted the lavender, its leaves silvery-gray under the moonlight. The heady scent returned him to his bedroom and to his hotel suite, where twice, Angela, when he knew her as the mysterious princess, clad only in those fragrant flowers, had visited him at night. True, he was dreaming, but, thanks to that heavenly illusion, he now associated the plant with her. He stopped long enough to pick her a large bouquet, congratulating himself for his suave move. If he caught her off guard, who knows how touched she might be…or how she might show it?

As he stepped from the woods into the clearing, John-Peter saw Angela, hands clasped behind her back, near the apple tree waiting for him. He forced himself to pause, to assimilate her beauty and to humbly contemplate how thankful he was to have it, lest, in his eagerness, he foolishly pounce on her. Her pale, almost colorless hair, shimmered golden under the moon's rays, and, every so often, she turned her head from side to side, scanning the horizon for a glimpse of him. He advanced slightly for a better look, and a twig snapped under his feet. Angela spun around in alarm, saw him, and then smiled in relief. Lavender held high behind his back, he ran to meet her. His plans for greeting her with a tender kiss and a dramatic flourish of the bouquet dissolved when she began violently sneezing. She covered her face with a hand and cried out, "Oh, John-Peter, that's not lavender, is it?"

"Lavender?" His good spirits took a rapid flight, leaving him holding the forlorn posies that now drooped, too. "Where?"

"Behind your back. Oh, please say it isn't. I'm awfully allergic to lavender."

Curses! He hurled the traitorous flowers in the direction of the woods and once more approached Angela, but she took a step backward. "You have to wash your hands, to get the smell off."

Irritation was chasing away ardor at an alarmingly quick pace. This was not the way he had envisioned it. "Where?"

Still holding her nose, Angela pointed toward the brownie farm. "There's a stream that runs just beyond the barns."

He headed in the direction she indicated, but John-Peter no longer felt like running. Allergic! Why did he have to dream her wearing lavender, of all things? Now, whenever he conjured up that delightful vision, his remembrance of Angela's reaction tonight would eclipse it. Pleasant reveries forever ruined, and all because of pollen.

John-Peter found the stream, just as Angela said, and swished his hands around it. He started to wipe them on his jeans, thought better of it, then stopped to dry them on the grass, remembered the lavender, wondered if grass bothered her as well, and so thought better of that, too. Instead, he shook the dampness into the cooling night air and debated whether or not to turn back to the steward's apartment. Remembering how Angela's lips tasted between his own still pulled him; wasn't it unreasonable to expect smooth plans all the time? Unconsciously, he picked up speed. By the time he reached the apple tree, his plodding had become an easy jog. He noted, with joy, that she was still waiting for him. When he reached her, he stretched out his arms, as if to embrace her, then held up his hands before her face.

"Do I pass?" he said, unsmiling, but with a docile earnestness that surprised him.

She nodded, her eyes bright with anticipation, a wide joyful smile lighting up her face. John-Peter lowered his hands to her cheeks and pulled her face close to his. The moment his lips touched hers, a fire broke out inside him, but, when he really started kissing her, she pulled away. Now what?

"What's wrong?" he said.

"My nose is too stuffy," she said. "I can't breathe when you, you know, do that."

He paused, willing patience, and reminding himself this wasn't her fault. The way the night was transpiring, it was senseless to stay, but he couldn't bear the thought of leaving, not yet, so he removed his suit coat and set it on the ground.

"Here," he said, "no use aggravating congestion with grass pollen."

John-Peter took her hand and guided her, spreading the edge of the coat around her, making sure no part of her body touched the grass. With joyful eyes, coupled with the panting that often accompanies mouth-breathing, she watched him adjust the coat and guide her shoulders back toward the tree trunk. When her head touched the tree, she closed her eyes, and he started to kiss her again, leaving her enough space to breathe. Yet, her quick breaths against his cheek were annoying, so he decided to avoid her mouth altogether and console himself with tiny pecks around her lips.

"This is nice," she said, and he believed her, for the rapture on her face couldn't lie. Then, she spoiled it by adding, "What happened last night? I waited and waited for you."

"I had an errand," he murmured, daring for a nip close to her ear, but, just when he reached it, she sat up, narrowed her eyes, and wrinkled her nose in disapproval. "What kind of errand?"

"Who cares?" He tightened his hold around her waist and tried again for that soft spot just under her left ear lobe.

Angela scooted out of his reach, off the suit coat and onto the grass, and she didn't even sneeze. "What kind of an answer is that? I care! I missed you last night."

John-Peter sighed and leaned against the tree she vacated. He gazed into the distance, past the brownie camps, and toward the cluricahns' slums, so he wouldn't notice her pout.

"If you must know, I called on the Steward of Tara to secure your release, as I promised I would do."

Her eyes and mouth opened in disbelief. "Oh, John-Peter, did he agree?"

"Not yet, but he soon shall." The lilt in her voice was intoxicating, and he relented. "Come sit close to me and give me something pleasant to recall on the way back."

A crestfallen demeanor replaced that hopeful one. "You're not leaving?"

"Yes, soon. I must return before the steward misses me."

He held his arms open, and she accepted them, laying her head on his chest and breathing with tiny gasps. For a long time, John-Peter stroked her hair, wishing for the mythical crystal boat to appear and take them both away to a place where the need for antihistamines and blood transfusions didn't exist. How long they sat there, he knew not, for when John-Peter perceived reality once more, he was under the rowan tree near Daragh Hill. This time, his jeans were dry and the ground was soaked with evening dew.

"I feel like Gideon," John-Peter said aloud.

Thinking of Gideon made John-Peter remember his grandfather and the burial that occurred only yesterday. Sudden grief stabbed him hard, and he feared he might cry, so he leaped to his feet, hoping that action might thwart that menacing cloudburst. Dawn had not yet broken, but the dark sky was turning to gray. It was time to return to Ed Calkins' apartment. A knock sounded on his bedroom door, causing John-Peter to jump and sit straight up in bed.

"Who is it?" he cried out in alarm.

"Amerigen," said the voice on the other side. "Just seeing if you'd like some breakfast."

"Be right there."

He lay still, pondering the events of the night. He remembered, now. In a haze, he walked Angela back to the brownie farm, where she finally let him nuzzle her neck, and, in an equal haze, he navigated the woods, forgetting that he wasn't returning to his cottage for the night, but to the steward's apartment. Exhaustion overtook him at the bottom of Daragh Hill, so he sought rest under the shelter of his favorite rowan tree. Whether he slept, John-Peter did not know, but the trip back to Ed Calkins' place was a dreamlike, chimerical fog, broken only by the mournful wail of the banshee, foretelling someone's approaching death. He tumbled into bed just as the rooster crowed, and the boy knew nothing until Amerigen awakened him. He sat up and instinctively felt for the leprechaun. The numbers, 7,500, barely moved at all, but they were definitely decreasing.

The kitchen was empty; Amerigen was nowhere to be seen. Three cereal boxes sat on the table, along with two gallons of soy milk. All the doors down that hall were closed, although John-Peter heard the low rumble of snoring. He assumed that was Ed Calkins, home from the hunt. He wondered if he'd found a poet to replace Amerigen.

Twenty minutes later, John-Peter had eaten all the food, placed his dishes in the dishwasher, and thrown the garbage away. He had a lot of hours until nightfall, and wondered how to fill them, until the ringing inside his head reminded him he had little sleep last night and would have less tonight. A nap seemed like a good way to pass the time, so he returned to the bedroom, hid the leprechaun underneath his pillow as he used to do, and drew the covers up to his chin.

"Hey, John-Peter," Karla called.

The boy struggled back to consciousness and mumbled, "What happened with Dr. Rothgard?"

"Um, we have a problem."

Now he was wide awake. "What problem?"

"He's gone."

It didn't take long for Dr. Rothgard's life source to fizzle out. "As in dead?"

"As in gone. Three orderlies were found stabbed to death in his room, and..."

Stunned, John-Peter bolted up. "And what?"

"Their bodies had been completely drained of blood."

"So he escaped?"

"It appears that way, but the police are puzzled. Dr. Rothgard had been under constant maximum security. What stupid idiot slipped up and allowed him to get a knife?"

John-Peter saw himself remove the carving knife from under his coat and press it into Dr. Rothgard's throat.

Talk to me now, you stupid, old fool, or I'll soak the pillow with your blood.

He recalled fleeing after Dr. Rothgard's insane tale of vampires, changelings, and blood transfusions. He did not recall taking the carving knife with him. *Shit.*

"I can't imagine," John-Peter mumbled and dropped the door containing that memory.

"So now what?"

John-Peter sank back onto the pillow and thought hard. Karla needed to get to Dr. Rothgard, but how? To what extent had Karla mastered materialization?

"I'm just in the beginning stages," Karla said, "but I'm getting better every day. Why?"

"Are you limited to the present tense?"

"You mean real time?"

"Yes."

Karla squealed loudly, and John-Peter raised a weary hand to rub his ear. Now was not the time for Karla to act all girlie.

"So you want me to visit Dr. Rothgard yesterday?"

John-Peter yawned loudly before he could stop it. "Is it possible?"

"I'm sure it is, if I concentrate really hard."

"Well, do it," he slurred, drowsiness engulfing him into a merciful black hole of nothingness. Just before John-Peter lost all awareness, a thought pierced his fading mind: Why did lying on the mouse no longer activate it? The clicks he often heard inside his head were conspicuously absent. Were those also under the control of his waning life force?

The boy woke to sunshine and stifling heat; he bolted upright, kicked off the blankets, and looked at the shamrock alarm clock beside his bed: three o'clock. He didn't know what time Ed Calkins rose, but guessed it might be awhile. He decided to check out the library.

The apartment remained silent and stagnant; the snoring still emitted from the room next door to Ed Calkins' office; he saw nothing of Amerigen. Outside the steward's quarters, the rest of the apartment was equally quiet. Did anyone else occupy this building except Ed, Amerigen, and him?

Like the fourth floor residence, the library encompassed the entire third floor. Although not as large as the small Munsonville Library back home, Ed's collection of books was, nevertheless, an impressive one. Row after row of bookcases filled the room; it was impossible that Ed had read them all, or that each one could possibly pertain to Ireland. Curious to what Ed enjoyed, John-Peter pulled a random book of the shelf and laughed out loud. It said, *Limericks,* by Ed Calkins.

He replaced the book and then selected the one next to it: *More Limericks*, by Ed Calkins. He put that back, then moved to another aisle, and reached for a book, *The Best of Irish Limericks*, by Ed Calkins. Another section contained epic poetry, all about Ed Calkins. For the next half hour, John-Peter skimmed book title, after book title, but all pertained to Ed and boasted Ed as its author: *Ed Calkins' Original Limericks, More Ed Calkins' Original Limericks, Limericks of the Underworld, The Royal Order of the Limerick, Limerick, Fact or Fiction, How to Be a Limerick Master in 30 Days,* and *Limericks for All Occasions.* John-Peter opened one of the books, flipped through its pages and read:

> *The battle was done; the victory was won*
> *So Ed Calkins, grubby and unbloody,*
> *Took his rest*
> *At the foot of the best*
> *Well, under the noonday sun*
>
> *Then out from the wood, one by one*
> *Came five DeDannan maidens ruddy*
> *Whose beauty cast*
> *On Ed who, happy, at last,*
> *The time had come for some fun*
>
> *They carried buckets; they sought a drink,*
> *So to Ed Calkins' well they came*
> *And petitioned of him*
> *To fill to the brim*
> *Their containers, they said with a wink.*

Ed readily agreed, but with a catch
For the maidens were lovely and fair
He wanted a kiss
But only Colpa did this
And to him became quickly attached.

A tap on the back of his head, thankfully, interrupted the rest. "Hey, John-Peter, are you in there?"

"Unfortunately, yes," John-Peter said, shutting the book and returning it to the empty space between, *The Ed Calkins Book of Epic Battles by Verse* and *The Lyrical Adventures of Ed Calkins*. He wandered to the next row of books and studied their titles. "Did you talk to Dr. Rothgard?"

Karla giggled, an annoying tickle on the undamaged eardrum. "I wish you saw his face, John-Peter, when I materialized inside his room. I thought he'd have a heart attack!"

"Was he helpful?"

"Oh, very. He said to take about a dozen quarts. It's more than what you need, but it doesn't hurt to have extra, just in case, especially once I told him you were sharing it with him. He doesn't need it now, of course, but he didn't know it then."

"How do I ensure freshness?"

"Well, he keeps it in a freezer, but, because it's synthetic, he said it can go a little while without refrigeration. How long before you come back with it?"

"Not too long, I hope. How am I doing?"

"Still hanging in there. Your breathing just sounds so weird."

"Any more seizures?"

"One, last night, but it was a little one. You're not feeling anything strange?"

John-Peter considered his hazy recollections of the previous night. Was that when he convulsed?

"No," he lied, feeling a strong desire to change the subject. "Where does he keep the blood?"

"At his house. Can you write down his address?"

"Scanning for writing utensils. Please hold. A stealthy representative will be with you shortly."

His eyes passed over the room, trying to determine where Ed might keep pen and paper. He saw only the rows of books and the three reading tables in the middle of the room. He walked among those tables, peering under them for a stray pen. Finally, he spied one, sticking out from underneath the last chair on the left. He saw no paper, so he took a book off the shelf, removed its frontispiece, and called out to Karla, "Ready!"

"Dr. Rothgard lives at 931 Elm Street. He said Ed Calkins will know where it is, because he services a newspaper box at the convenience store a couple blocks away. His basement has all kinds of freezers, but he labeled them all. He said you'll just have to look for the one that says, 'John Simotes.'"

"How do I gain entrance?"

"He always leaves his second floor bedroom window open. The latch on the screen is broken, so you can easily remove it, okay?"

"Young Mr. Simotes, may I have a word with you?"

It was Amerigen.

"Karla, I've got to go. Wish me luck."

She blew him a kiss. "Good luck, John-Peter. Call if you need something."

John-Peter folded the paper and stuffed it into his left pocket. He turned to face Amerigen, who had shut the library door behind him and was now walking toward the back of the room. "I have a proposition for you."

Amerigen propped one foot on a chair; his face wore calm assurance. "If you help me, I will gladly assist you in Angela's rescue, and so will the others."

"What do you wish of me?"

"Take me back with you."

"You're not from my time."

Amerigen gave a short laugh. "That's rather obvious, don't you think? I'm unconcerned what time period I enter. Any era is preferable to remaining here, especially once I defeat the steward at the duel."

"You're not from Ed Calkins' mind?"

"No, and neither are the others. Ed spirited me away from my father's print shop, circa seventeen sixty-five. My father and I had an argument, you see, for I spent more time writing poetry, than minding my orders. I stayed late to sift through the backlog, when a gray-haired and gray-bearded, bespectacled, pot-bellied man of average height dressed in a plaid kilt, matching cap, and gold and bronze wristlets appeared and offered me a fulltime job writing poetry. The offer was so heady, I failed to stop and envision the consequences. I've slaved for him ever since, while he takes the credit for my work."

"Who are "these others" you mention?"

"The other writers confined here. I thought you knew. This is no ordinary apartment building, Mr. Simotes. It's an author mill."

"A *what*?"

Amerigen's face remained tranquil. "An author mill. Who do you suppose composed these tomes of great literature?" He gestured to the books with a graceful, lazy wave of his hand.

"How many authors has he kidnapped?"

"Eight of us currently reside here. Being the head poet, I have a special office in the steward's private quarters and the largest second floor apartment. The others rarely leave their domains, as they are tethered to their computers. You've heard of ball and chain, I suppose? Well, their fetters are similar, except they drag a weight on each foot, one large dictionary and one equally large thesaurus. The steward and I have the only keys, and, even then, recess is reserved for library trips."

John-Peter reflected upon Dawn's similar request, freedom for her and the other breeders. How would he squeeze eight grown writers and more than two hundred girls into the portal? It might collapse under their combined weight, killing them all. Would it be so wrong of him to leave them there?

Amerigen leaned on his leg and fixed keen eyes on the boy, so John-Peter carefully chose his words, saying, "I don't think the portal could safely carry everyone."

"There is a second portal."

"*What?*"

"Of course," Amerigen calmly replied. "However do you think we appeared?"

"Ed Calkins is a vampire. Didn't he just teleport you in here?"

"Yes, Mr. Simotes, by way of a portal."

John-Peter couldn't believe his ears. "Do you know where it is?"

"We believe it is underground, below Clancy's house. Would you like an introduction to the others?"

John-Peter's glance shifted to the windows, but the sun still brightly shone. "Is there time?"

"I don't begin preparations for the steward's dinner for another hour. We have time."

The boy's fractured knees felt weaker at the knowledge that more humans lived in this shadow of a world, but, just the same, John-Peter was curious to meet them.

"Well then, Mr. Amerigen, perhaps we should address our options."

Amerigen walked back to the library door, opened it, and called out," You may come in now!"

And come in they did: a tiny wrinkled woman with wiry gray hair pulled into a bun, an acne-faced teenager who bumped into a table despite his thick and taped glasses, and a bleached blonde housewife in designer jeans and cashmere sweater. Before John-Peter assessed the remaining writers, a voice from the back rang out, "My jacket!"

A chunky man in tinted glasses, and a head full of thick, wavy hair that could only be manufactured in a beauty salon, rushed toward him and pointed at the suit coat. "My jacket! How did you get it?"

Marcus O'Reilly!

"I bought it," John-Peter stammered under the man's indignant stare, "at a pawn shop."

"Eircheard's Emporium?"

John-Peter's legs buckled; instantly, a smiling Amerigen slid a chair underneath him.

"It seems we have much to discuss," Amerigen said. "Shall we begin our meeting?"

Marcus folded his arms and glared at John-Peter. "I want my jacket back."

"Reimburse me, first."

"I'll do no such thing!"

Marcus lunged at John-Peter, but an elderly man tripped him with his cane. Marcus stumbled and caught the back of the chair, but he did not fall.

"Watch where ye goin' young feller," the old man said. "You nearly stepped on my heirloom cane. Solid oak, it is, too."

"Gentlemen, please," Amerigen said. "In the interest of mutual concern, let us set aside all differences. We all desire escape, and, today you have a young man in our midst who just may hold the final key to our puzzle."

"Here, here," a male hippie in flowered shirt said. His long waves of brown unkempt hair matched his equally long and equally unkempt beard.

"Let the boy speak," a sweet, high-pitched feminine voice agreed.

John-Peter turned at its sound. The young woman who uttered it was so large she occupied three of the seats. He wondered if she resided in the largest first floor apartment, and decided the steward was most unfair, if she did not.

The boy looked straight at Marcus. "How do you know Eircheard's Emporium?"

"I was there scheduling a book signing, when a gray-haired and gray-bearded, bespectacled, pot-bellied man of average height dressed in a plaid kilt, matching cap, and gold and bronze wristlets appeared, drugged me, and dragged me into the back room and down the stairs. The next thing I knew, I was inside Clancy's farm, where he and several other cluricahns hauled me up the stairs and over to this joint. I'm convinced the way out lies through Clancy's walls, but no one believes me."

"Man, we've examined that wall a thousand times," the hippie said. "It's miles of solid rock. There's no way to get into it."

Cha d'dhuin doras nach d'fhosgail doras.

Those were the words across the belt on the leprechaun that sat inside his Munsonville bedroom. Cornell Dyer paid Eircheard good money to learn words about doors opening and closing. Marcus had to be onto something. Even Karla was convinced her father understood the portal to be located below the pawn shop.

"I think Marcus is right," John-Peter said. "I believe there is a portal beneath Eircheard's Emporium that leads to Clancy's house. I don't know how to access it, but I know two someones who can help find out."

He hoped Dawn wouldn't protest too much when he returned Emmie and her to the farm. They found a way out; hopefully, they could pinpoint the location of the secret exit. On impulse, he unbuttoned the suit coat, slid it off, and handed it to Marcus.

"It's too hot for me," he said, "and it really belongs to you."

Marcus sniffed, but he accepted the coat. "

"Thank you for taking good care of it," he said stiffly. "Hate to be unreasonable, but it's my lucky coat. I can't write well without it."

Recalling the titles of Marcus' two books, *I Have a Secret in My Attic*, and *Tulips in the Garden.?*, John-Peter doubted the filing clerk wrote too well with it.

"John-Peter, how soon can you consult your sources?" Amerigen said.

"Not until tomorrow. I have an out-of-town meeting with the steward tonight."

Amerigen nodded and then swept his eyes over the other writers. "Another meeting in twenty-four hours, same time, same place? Necessity requires haste. The duel is in two days."

A chorus of acceptance murmured around the table. They rose, almost in unison, and walked back to the door. Amerigen extended his hand toward John-Peter. "We are much obliged to you, sir. You may be the salvation of us all."

Amerigen turned to catch up with the others, who waited, single file, for him to lead them back into their strongholds.

The door to Ed Calkins' bedroom was opened, but the one to the office was closed when John-Peter returned to the steward's apartment. Had Ed noticed his absence? He knocked on the door and heard Ed's cheerful voice call, "Come in!"

John-Peter did, and, to his relief, Ed sat, preoccupied, at the computer.

"Change of plans tonight, John-Peter," Ed said. "I have to pick up my poet tonight, so we can't go to nineteen-eighty."

"But, Uncle Ed…"

"Now hold on," Ed said, swerving his chair to face the boy. "We still have some time. Tomorrow night, do, or die, we go to Shelby. After that, you may stay one more day to see my glorious triumph over Amerigen, and then it's back to Munsonville you go."

"Do I have to stay here again tonight?"

"That's entirely up to you. Is there a reason you want to leave?"

"Homesick. I want to spend one last night in my cottage."

Ed beamed with delight. "I did imagine some nice quarters for you, at that. Okay, John-Peter, stay for dinner and then be off. No use having to cook, when you get home. Where shall I meet you tomorrow night?"

"I'll come back here?"

"Sunset, then. Don't be late."

"I won't."

John-Peter shut the door behind him and bumped smack into Amerigen.

"You're leaving us, young Mr. Simotes?"

John-Peter put a finger to his lips and said in a low voice, "I'm leaving to speak with my contacts, but I'll return for our meeting tomorrow. Uncle Ed's made other plans until then."

"Splendid, Mr. Simotes. You'll find dinner waiting for you in the kitchen."

"The name's John-Peter."

With an amiable smile, Amerigen lowered his head in assent and then retreated into his office. The poet had prepared a large pot of pre-packaged soy macaroni and vegan cheese and a large pan of plain iceberg salad, unimaginative, but filling. When John-Peter finally was able to leave the apartment, he slowly descended the stairs, contemplating the people that lived behind each door he passed. All differed from each other, yet bonded in their love of writing. How had Ed persuaded each of them to leave their world for his, or had he kidnapped them all, as he had Marcus?

John-Peter scarcely cleared Filiocht Hill when Aodhan alighted on his shoulder.

"Still hiding out at the steward's?" he asked, flicking John-Peter's sore ear with the bent wing.

John-Peter did not smile, but neither did he brush the fairy away. "How many sprites, like us, do you supposed the steward created?"

"Haven't a clue," Aodhan said. "I never stopped to count them, and, besides, that all depends on how many the steward imagines. That number could change from day to day."

"Well summon your favorite ones, for tonight I play."

Aodhan glowed like a firefly. "You mean it, for sure, this time?"

"I'm on my way there, now. Tell Dawn we're celebrating. I've decided to honor her request."

The sprite stretched his body to full elongation to bring his eyes face to face with John-Peter's. "What request be that?"

"Never you mind. She knows. Now, hurry."

"She won't be happy. I'll be coming to collect from her, anyway."

Aodhan crouched for take-off, but John-Peter caught the sprite around his middle just as he sprang into the air. "Collect, what?"

"A jar of sap," Aodhan struggled against John-Peter's grasp. "We bet you weren't coming back, and she lost."

John-Peter grinned and released his friend, imagining Dawn's heated reaction at his homecoming. He stuffed his hands inside his pockets and happily whistled all the way to Daragh Hill, the first time he'd made music since Midsummer's Eve. Dawn again met him at the door, this time minus the butcher knife and her sullen attitude.

"You had a successful meeting with the steward?" she asked, more pleasantly than he anticipated.

"More or less," John-Peter said, peering into the pot hanging over the fire.

Emmie sat by the hearth, head flung back and working her mouth up and down in a most unsettling way.

"Aodhan sent word you were coming, so I made extra. How about some details? When are we leaving?"

"I'd prefer not to spoil the evening with rescue plans. Tonight we carouse. Tomorrow we scheme."

"Fair enough." Dawn walked over to the fire, picked up a large spoon, and stirred the pot's contents. "I don't like it, but fair enough."

Emmie now shook her head, as she puckered her lips, grimaced, opened her mouth wide, and strained until the veins bulged in her neck.

"Make her stop those dreadful contortions."

"Why should she? She's singing."

Singing?

John-Peter started to retort and then decided not to spoil a promising evening by arguing with Dawn. He removed his tin whistle from the shelf, slipped off his shoes, and curled his toes around the fire iron, as he played a jangle of discordant notes. Emmie shielded her ears from the noise and ran from the cottage. John-Peter smiled around the mouthpiece as he continued piping. Good. It worked.

That evening, the ground and air alike buzzed with the patter of tiny feet and the whirring of miniscule wings, as sprites from all four elements rejoiced in the music John-Peter piped. Dawn merely leaned against the cottage and observed the fun, but, at least she didn't hibernate inside the cottage. John-Peter noted that, from time to time, one of Dawn's feet irresistibly tapped to the beat. However, it was Emmie who enjoyed herself best, and it was in this way that John-Peter hoped to remember her.

With outstretched arms and little face turned upward to the moon, the little girl swayed and spun in perfect time to each melodic sound. Sometimes, she whirled ever so lightly and, at others, the music propelled her into a near frenzy. The air elementals caught her spirit, for they wafted around her, creating colorful, flashing specks resembling magical crystals. Far into the wee hours of the night they danced, until the little girl dropped to the ground, exhausted, but with a playful smile lingering on her lips. Eventually, even the fairies grew sluggish until most of them flew away, and John-Peter announced the party was done. Dawn walked over to the little heap on the ground and picked up her precious bundle. Emmie immediately nestled her face into her guardian's neck, as Dawn carried her into the cottage.

Aodhan flew right in front of John-Peter just before the boy stepped through the rear entranceway.

"A thrilling night to remember," Aodhan said. "We are all beholden to you."

Then, in a rainbow spray of pastels, Aodhan was gone.

John-Peter returned his pipe to its place, and, exhausted beyond all strength, dropped onto his leaves. This night was the perfect introduction to an afternoon even more perfect, for Angela's rescue was at hand. He loved the princess, for Angela would always be a princess to him, and, although waiting to be with her sorely tried his restraint, he also felt a certain relief, as if a large burden tumbled off his back. He was confident their plans would succeed, for they represented goodness and might. Yet, despite being relaxed and tired to the bark, slumber eluded him, and the boy remained wide awake. The more John-Peter tossed and twisted, the more his efforts failed him; he could not get comfortable. He instinctively reached between his legs, then remembered Dawn and Emmie sleeping on the other side of the room, and changed his mind. Restless, he stared at the stars through the still unpatched hole in his roof and pondered this night's most blazing question.

Angela loved him, and he loved her; knowing they would soon be together forever in Munsonville filled him with unspeakable joy. So why did he get hard every time he thought of Karla?

CHAPTER 27: A ROYAL PAIN IN THE NECK

"Did you get the blood?"

Karla's voice floated in springy waves through his foggy mind. John-Peter bobbed to the surface and then submerged once again into blissful slumber.

"John-Peter!"

Her shrill voice pierced his mind, startling him into alertness. "Huh?"

"The blood, John-Peter. Where's the blood?"

"No blood yet," he muttered, rolling onto his side and burying his face in the leaves, as drowsiness melted all powers of thinking. "Not until tonight."

"What!"

That did it. With an exasperated groan, John-Peter hurled himself onto his back and looked out the ceiling at the still dark sky. "Karla..."

"Your mother's letting them give you Type O in the morning."

He brushed the leaves away from his face, and felt a needle sharp scratch across his cheek. He brought his hand down and scrunched his eyes to focus on it. Hordes of the tiniest splinters covered it, like moss on rock, only sharper. He held up the other hand, and it, too, was covered in wood. Horrified, he sat up and slowly moved his arm before his face. It looked the same as his hands.

"Why did my mother change her mind?"

Karla didn't answer, and it was her hesitation that brought John-Peter to complete consciousness. "Karla, why did my mother change her mind?"

"She was getting frantic, so I told her our plans."

John-Peter swiftly dropped a door at her blatant breech of confidence, but before it collided with the floor, Karla ducked underneath it.

"Come on, John-Peter. I had to tell her."

He turned indignantly away from her. "You're out of line."

Karla grabbed him by the shoulders and tried to make him face her, but the boy locked his knees and dug his toes into the dirt. So she circled around him and stuck her face next to his in the most maddening fashion, leaving him the choices of closing his eyes or intimidating her with his most hateful glare. He selected the latter.

"Karla, seeing that you can't take a hint..."

"Your mother had them type her blood, and it was a match. She was on her way to beg for a direct blood transfusion, when I remembered what you told me about the amount of her blood you needed to survive, and I got scared of what she might do."

Her voice broke off in a choked sob and, this time, it was Karla who looked away. He didn't want Karla to see how badly her words affected him. So, cross-legged, he examined the splinters in his arms while contemplating Karla's speech. He was, as she hinted, in a rather, nasty predicament.

"So, why am I receiving Type O blood?"

Karla snuffled, and John-Peter saw her swipe at her face, but she kept her back toward him while she did it.

"She thought it might buy you some time," she said in a low voice. "Not much time, but enough until the blood arrives. I just thought you'd get it here by now."

He lifted his shirt. Splinters covered entire trunk. It would've taken Dr. Rothgard a month to remove them.

"It can't be helped, Karla. The steward had other obligations."

"Well, you're just lucky that your doctor at Jenson Memorial specializes in mysterious cases." A strange note entered Karla's voice, and she added, "Hey, John-Peter, your suit coat is gone. It was right here on the chair."

"I returned it to Marcus O'Reilly."

"The missing writer?"

"The very same."

"Come on, John-Peter, details!"

"Suffice to say I have much information to share upon my return, enough to start your own binder, oh ye gifted progeny of the renowned Cornell Dyer."

Karla spun on her heel, grinning now, and dropped onto the floor across from John-Peter with a little giggle. "Wait until my mom reads it. That should make her forgive and forget."

"Questionable. Forgive, perhaps. Forget, not a chance. The image of us rising from the couch will stick with her for a long time."

Karla was so close that John-Peter almost forgot she was only a mental apparition, but, after last night's meditations, viewing her from a safe, physical distance might be a blessing. Karla just shrugged her shoulders at John-Peter's concerns regarding Katie.

"Not when she realizes we were conducting scientific research," she said. "Mom can be stubborn, but she's not unreasonable."

How could a girl with sixth sense tolerate blinders? He recalled Katie's reaction years ago when she found them studying anatomy. She wasn't crazy about their experimentation then, either. The direction of the conversation annoyed him, although he did not know why, so he changed its course.

"How's Bertrand?"

"Oh, he's fine. I've been feeding him dematerialized peanut butter crackers from the vending machine all night." She cocked her head to one side and listened. "Someone just came into your room. Time to be nosy. Gotta go."

"Much obliged for mademoiselle's assistance."

Enough light now pervaded the room that John-Peter could see Emmie stir and then flop an arm across Dawn's neck, even as she burrowed her face deeper into her sleeping bag. Between his absorption with Angela and the lack of pain in the broken areas of his body, John-Peter had stopped paying attention to the splinters that overtook his body, that is, until now. He sat up again and dug into his pocket for the leprechaun. If the numbers moved any slower they would stop: 7,209. Just how much time did that leave him in the real world? The unexpected volume of splinters momentarily scared him, but he felt composure return. Of course, he was worrying; who would not? Yet, he was not worried to the extent of anxiety. With his own hands, the steward had fashioned him; no one better knew his capabilities and his weaknesses. John-Peter's demise would weaken the steward's artificially inflated concept of himself. Surely, if Ed Calkins really thought the situation perilous, he would never have delayed their blood quest.

Dawn's eyes popped open. They noticed John-Peter staring at her, and she immediately narrowed them. "What're you looking at, gremlin?"

He said nothing but merely rose and brushed the leaves off his legs, smiling to himself that his control had returned. Plenty of time to answer that question.

Annoyed that he ignored her, Dawn threw her arms above her head, stretched luxuriously, and tried again. "What was that awful racket last night?"

John-Peter removed the poker from its stand and jabbed at the fire's dying embers. "A crazy damsel's hallucination, perhaps?"

"Ha, ha. I'm talking about that creepy wailing. It kept Emmie and me up half the night."

He replaced the poker, then tossed a few sticks onto the fire.

"Oh," he said in an offhand manner. "You must mean the banshee."

Dawn gingerly unwound Emmie's arm from her neck and slowly sat up. Emmie mumbled wordlessly in her sleep, then slid a hand under her cheek and breathed easily. Dawn unzipped her sleeping bag, stood, and fluffed out her hair.

"What's a banshee?"

"A female messenger of death."

She stomped across the room, bumped into John-Peter on purpose, and started heading for the water bucket when the boy grabbed her arm, covering the leering skull so that only its eyes peeped over his fingers.

"Smother pretension now, or lose my gracious help."

Keeping a firm hold on her arm, he rose to meet her angry eyes.

"Look, John-Peter, stop messing with my head."

He let go, picked up a log, and squatted to set it on the fire. "You dwell among imaginary beings. Adjust to our reality." The flames looped hungry tongues around the wood. John-Peter rested on his haunches and watched the fire grow. "Death catches us not unawares, as it does you humans. We herald its coming."

"With a terrible noise?"

He turned to see Dawn's eyes open wide in dismay.

"Whose death is she foretelling?"

John-Peter smiled and paused, drawing the anticipated reaction to his reply. "Ah, well, that's the rub. She never says. Could be yours, even."

"You're impossible!"

Dawn snatched the bucket from the floor and trounced out the back exit. He watched the fire until she returned carrying two buckets. She set one down by the back door and then filled the iron kettle with water. Wondering, John-Peter walked to the back door and inspected the contents in the other bucket. It was half full of milk.

"From Derbail," Dawn said, sifting barley through her fingers and stirring down the grains with a large spoon. "She's brought some everyday for Emmie and me."

He glanced at the little girl, who was now awake and cradling a large rock in a cabbage leaf. She rocked it back and forth, silently moving her mouth up and down. John-Peter shoved his hands into his pockets, pushed down the leprechaun, and leaned against the wall, watching her.

"Don't tell me," he said. "She's singing a lullaby."

Dawn did not look up. "You're smarter than you look."

"How did you escape?"

"What's it to you?"

"Because I'm sending you back the way you came."

She turned pale, but continued stirring. "You can't do that."

"You must. We can't rescue the other girls if you don't."

Dawn set the spoon on the shelf and faced him. Her hands were on her hips and she jutted her jaw, but her eyes wore the look of a scared rabbit. "So, tell me about your great escape plans."

"Ed Calkins oversees an author mill. He plans to fight his poet tomorrow night. The steward thinks he will win. Amerigen, his poet, is planning otherwise. The writers and I are meeting today to formulate a plan. Everyone wants out, and you, who have escaped, can show the way."

"Hate to disappoint you, elf, but we sneaked out after Clancy and his fat, ugly family went to sleep."

Was she telling the truth? John-Peter felt his hopes for Marcus' portal theory, Cornell's too, waning. Then he remembered, "Cha d'dhuin doras nach d'fhosgail doras." Was it only by coincidence that Eircheard had a matching leprechaun at his shop with those words, or was he flaunting his secret, while laughing at them on the inside? He probed her eyes with his, and she quickly picked up the spoon and stirred the bubbling mass inside the pot. Dawn wasn't telling everything. He was certain of it.

"There's more," he said, gently.

Dawn colored, took a deep breath, and shook her head to show she didn't care what John-Peter thought.

"We're not stupid, like the other girls. They're resigned to their fate. Not us."

"So, you just snapped the chains and fled."

"Pretty much."

"With your bare hands?"

"With Emmie's voice."

"Beg pardon?"

Dawn removed the iron pot from the fire. This time, John-Peter took it by the handle and carried it to the table.

"Keep talking," he said.

"There isn't much to tell," she said, following him with the bowels and spoons. "Emmie really is singing. I found that out my first night there. Clancy came round to check on us, and he kept covering his ears and yelling at her to be quiet."

"Your point?"

"It's like opera singers who shatter glass with their high notes," Dawn said, motioning for Emmie. The little girl tucked the sleeping bag around the cabbage leaf and trotted to the table. "I figured Emmie's notes were so high, they might destroy steel."

John-Peter scooped barley into Emmie's bowl. The little girl leaned her elbow on the table and pillowed her cheek into her hand, watching him with intense interest. Dawn returned with two mugs of milk. John-Peter handed Emmie a spoon and grinned at her, and she grinned right back at him. As Dawn sat down, she noted the exchange with a pleased expression.

"Tell Emmie to use her voice sparingly for the next day," John-Peter said, reaching for Dawn's bowl and filling it full of barley. "She has many girls to release."

Daylight had fully broken when John-Peter left the cottage and headed down Daragh Hill for the steward's apartment. He awakened with a start, sitting under the rowan tree and smiling to himself. The meeting had gone well, despite the old man's continual bellowing of, "Hate to part with an heirloom. Solid oak it was, too." Their strategy was laid, although their time together was prematurely halted with Ed Calkins' summons for Amerigen to begin his dinner preparations. Amerigen had smiled at John-Peter's perplexed look.

"I'm not cooking anything," Amerigen said. "I write the limericks he tells his victims, before he consumes them."

Surprise details about the other writers had abounded that afternoon. The hippie had won an archery badge in scouting; only the rich housewife could drive stick shift; and Marcus owned rechargeable batteries. Only the old man grudgingly conceded to their plans.

"I supposed it's better than gasping my final breath in this remote place," the old man admitted, "although I hated to part with an heirloom. Solid oak it was, too."

John-Peter did not run straight to the rowan tree. He detoured through the woods, past Eircheard's cottage, and straight to the brownie farm to inform Angela of the rescue mission and her need to be ready when her transport arrived. Aodhan accompanied him most of the way, alternatively pestering him with the meeting's details and humming a hornpipe in his ear, but the boy scarcely noticed him, so bent was he on reaching Angela. It had been two days since he had kissed her. The deprivation was killing him.

Aodhan landed on his shoulder, crossed his legs, leaned a diminutive hand against John-Peter's cheek, and gazed up at him with excitement flashing in his crystalline eyes.

"Tell me again what the steward said."

John-Peter scratched his cheek where Aodhan touched it, causing the sprite to lose his balance, so he spread his wings and quickly grabbed the boy's ear.

"He didn't say much," John-Peter said, wondering how he could attract Angela's attention without announcing his presence to her brownie owners. "Just that he created thousands." He recalled the dreamy, far-away look in the steward's eyes when he stated it and brushed the memory away. Much more interesting was the mix of apprehension and longing he saw in Angela's eyes before he kissed her for the very first time.

Aodhan sighed with immense satisfaction. "I'm the commander of a legion, a vast army of epic proportions, a towering fortress of heroism, a…"

John-Peter tuned out the rest. Was Angela allergic only to lavender, or could he bring her some other flower? Aodhan leaped off John-Peter's shoulder and landed on his friend's hip, patting the clip now attached to his belt. "What's that?"

"A communication system for clumsy humans." John-Peter glanced down at Aodhan who inspected the screen, ran a finger up the antenna, and jumped up and down on the bulge in John-Peter's left pocket. "And this?"

"You're awfully nosy today."

Aodhan grunted, removed his hand, and looked away, but he still tapped his feet around the straining pocket with a puzzled air.

"I still say flying is more useful and versatile, with far less unnecessary components."

"Being human has its rewards."

"Oh? Like what?"

The woods lightened. *Soon.* John-Peter extended an index finger to Aodhan, who accepted the lift that carried him just inches from John-Peter's dancing eyes.

"Observe," John-Peter said, "and learn."

He reached the clearing. Aodhan flew up to the branch of an oak tree, then straddled a slender branch and leaned against the trunk, prepared for the lesson. John-Peter hoped it was a good one. It would be the fitting reward for his patience and the perfect way to prove to Aodhan that humanity was indeed an improvement over fantasy. Smoke wafted into the sky from the farmhouse's chimney. Just what time did brownies rise for the day?

With a backward leer at Aodhan, John-Peter crept closer to the farmyard, but not so close as to startle the chickens, lest their squawking alert the master of the home to his presence. When he reached the barn, he pressed his back against it and craned his face around the corner, scanning the property for signs of fey or human life. The chickens pecking at the ground was not a good sign; had he missed Angela, after all? A large collie stretched out by the kitchen door, but the pricking of his ears and the darting of his eyes told John-Peter the dog sensed an intruder. A light sweep against his arm made him jump, but he faced this new threat with a menacing glare. It was Angela, carrying a bucket of water.

"What are you doing here?" she whispered in alarm, with a glance at the farmhouse. "It's too early. They'll catch you."

He removed the handle from her skinny hands, and, with a start, took his first, real look at her in the sunlight, without the mellowing effect of mirrors or moonlight. She clumsily brushed aside the wispy hair that clung to her face from the uphill jaunt from the well, revealing the dark brown lashes framing her doe-like eyes, but he saw a dullness behind them that disturbed him. Karla's blue eyes were bright and quick, and they flashed with intelligence that often surpassed his own. Yet, she had a lissome coordination to her movements that awed him, whether she was copying notes in her sweeping, ornamental penmanship, carving a mandrake, mounting her bike to race John-Peter to Simons Woods, or taking his hand to trace the lines on his palm. Angela, even with her full, curved lips that begged to be kissed and kissed often, lacked a natural gracefulness that even Dawn inherently possessed.

Sweeping aside these negative impressions in favor of deeper pleasures, John-Peter set the bucket on the grass, gently cupped his hands on Angela's bony shoulders, taking care his splinters didn't snag her dress, and pulled her close to him.

"I had to see you," he said in a strained voice.

She closed her eyes, waiting for the kiss that he more than happily bestowed, but halfway into it, his passion waned, for although the little moan in her throat was thrilling, her passive acceptance of him was deflating. Not once in all the times he was with her did Angela kiss him back, and he didn't know why that bothered him. Certainly, her inexperience matched his, and he could teach her and have plenty of fun doing it, but, for some reason, he felt no motivation to do so. He finished with an indifferent nip on her bottom lip and pulled away to look at her. She didn't smile or say a single word, but she met his eyes with the same trusting expression that Fawn wore Thanksgiving weekend when she handed him the penny whistle to play, and that childlike look redeemed her. New fire rose up inside him at her perfect faith in him, and he kissed her again, with more fervor than the last time, and, this time, he meant every bit of it. Angela wanted him and needed him, and that, in turn, overwhelmed and enthralled him. He couldn't wait to get her back to Munsonville. Without warning, she tensed, which, disappointingly, returned him to reality. While he calmed his mind, she broke away and reached down for the bucket.

"I have to get back," Angela said, "before they miss me."

"Tomorrow's the day."

Her hand shook, and she missed the handle. Angela straightened and said in a hushed voice, "Tomorrow?"

"Yes."

"So…so soon?"

"Yes." Her uncertainty annoyed him. He expected a violent rush of happy emotion, perhaps a flinging of her arms around his neck in profound thankfulness, accompanied by some passionate fondling that she initiated. Wasn't she as eager as he to leave Ed Calkins' vivid hallucination? "Do you have a problem with that?"

He hadn't meant to sound brusque, but the crispness in his voice spoke his heart more effectively than words, for Angela's face softened and a shy smile formed around the lips that screamed for another kiss.

"No, no," she stammered. "It's just that, well, I didn't know. How did you make it happen so fast?"

"Tomorrow afternoon, the steward will…"

The dog barked; a door slammed; and Angela grabbed the bucket.

"Just be ready," John-Peter whispered.

She blew him a kiss and trotted away, the bucket banging on her shins. He heard unintelligible brownie grumbling but waited for another slam of the door to slink away. Aodhan was still in the tree, his thorax quivering with laughter, and his wings curled around the limb to keep from falling.

"Too funny!" He wiped his eyes with a cleft hand. "Oh, what a show! Glorna, has midnight piping annihilated your finer sensibilities, or did your heavy baggage make you forget the heady rush air travel produces?"

"What do I care for your disdain?" John-Peter said with a lofty toss of his head. "In real time, a fly swatter would permanently cease your heckling. Are you in or out?"

The words "fly swatter" calmed all but the occasional sputter from Aodhan's mouth, as he righted himself and assumed a serious demeanor.

"In, of course," he said, an indignant note creeping into a voice that longed to break free with laughter. "Who wouldn't be up for such an adventure?"

"Remove the smirk, and pay heed."

Aodhan lighted near John-Peter's elbow and braced his hands on the boy's forearm, then turned his most pensive gaze upward. Not one time did he interrupt or jeer, but absorbed every word with the attention befitting a sergeant receiving his orders. Only the sound from Eircheard's cottage disturbed his concentration.

"Glorna, what is that sickening noise?"

"Humming."

The floral sprite tilted his head and listened. "It sounds like an out of tune foghorn."

"It's 'The Wedding March.' Eircheard's betrothed to Angela."

"Who?"

"Number forty-two," John-Peter said, with a grim look at the open window as they passed it. "He bought her from the brownies."

Aodhan shook his head with a disappointed air.

"What a sorry fate for such a pretty creature. Have no fear, Glorna. We won't let you down."

"Much obliged, Aodhan, much obliged."

A salute of the wing, and Aodhan was gone. John-Peter's arm twitched the moment Aodhan left it, and he stood inside the cottage's front doorway watching Dawn ladle stew into Emmie's bowl.

"No meat, only lots of peas and potatoes," she said, without looking up.

"I'm famished," was all an astonished John-Peter managed to say. How had he gotten home?

"Then get your ass over here and eat."

Too tired to argue, too hungry to care, John-Peter complied, and, without another word, ate plate after plate of stew.

"Slow down," Dawn barked once. "You'll get sick."

When John-Peter did not reply, she thunked him hard on his arm. The resulting crack was loud enough to make Emmie jump and drop her spoon, but Dawn turned so white, she didn't notice.

"What the hell just happened?" Dawn reached out and gingerly touched the rapidly growing swelling on John-Peter's upper arm. "John-Peter?"

He had doubled over against the pain, but was now regaining control. He dragged the pot of stew closer to him and began heaping spoonfuls into his dish. No way would Dawn get the satisfaction of hurting him.

"I am, as they say, rotten to the core," he said in a strained, but mocking, tone. "Emmie, more stew?"

Tears sprang to the little girl's eyes, and she shrank against the wall, eyeing first the open window and then John-Peter's wound, but she stayed put. Something wet cooled the inferno under his skin. Dawn was wrapping a wet rag around him. John-Peter relented on the inside and let her. Dawn's face was staid, but her fingers trembled.

"I wish this godforsaken place had ice," she said, tying a knot to hold the bandage in place. Her harsh voice couldn't hide the anxiety mapped all over her face. When John-Peter didn't answer, she peered closer at him. "What do you mean by 'rotten to the core?'"

He patted her cheek in mock affection.

"Florence Nightingale needn't trouble her spiky little head over trifles. Tend, rather to the masses who need you, for tomorrow morning you and Emmie return to Clancy's."

Her face contorted with rage, crowding out her concern for the arm. "I'll die first!"

"You'll die if you don't."

John-Peter carefully recounted the afternoon's meeting, paying special attention to the rapid, intense vocal training the girls would need if they wanted to survive Ed Calkins' verbal combat with Amerigen. With each detail John-Peter provided, Dawn grew more sober. Finally, there was nothing more to say. Emmie rested her head against the windowsill and stared at John-Peter with a mixture of pure hatred and the calm expression of one accepting her fate at the guillotine.

410

Dawn took John-Peter's scratchy hand into hers. He quickly looked at her, but all of her brashness had fled, despite the splinters that must be digging into her hand.

"John-Peter, if I don't see you again, I want you to know…"

Did Dawn, of all people, have to get sentimental on him? He yanked his hand away and snarled, "Just be ready," when his body jerked violently, an arm jackknifed, and John-Peter smacked his head on the dashboard. Ed Calkins reached out an arm and eased John-Peter back into passenger seat. "Pay attention. You're missing too many throws."

John-Peter looked out the side mirror to see downtown Jenson disappearing from view. "You're going the wrong way, Uncle Ed."

Ed Calkins threw back his head and laughed. His sharp teeth seemed especially white in the glowing light from the full moon, and an evil gleam had replaced his smiling, Irish eyes, but Ed only said, "We're subbing for the Shelby driver tonight, but I'm stopping for food before we begin. If you're hungry, say so now."

Dawn's hearty stew was only a memory. How long since he had eaten? Hours? Days?

"So, now," John-Peter said.

"Good," Ed Calkins said. "There's a little sandwich place right before we get to Shelby. We'll eat there."

"Don't trouble yourself. I can wait until Shelby."

"I can't. Besides, remote is safer."

The cornfields were already blanketed under the cover of night, but, even if they had been driving with the noonday sun to guide them, John-Peter's only thoughts consisted of Angela. He wasn't sure if he should fault time, distance, or both, for the remembrances of her that he conjured were fuzzy and lacked the allure that ordinarily made him squirm with feverish anticipation of the next visit. Instead, he brought Angela into what used to be his present time and kissed her through the closet mirror that melted at his command. Her lips felt unusually limp and unresponsive, and another pair replaced them in his mind, lips that spouted, "Emotion, for your information, is not trivial,"

"Hey, John-Peter, do you need a wake-up call?" and, "If you need me, John-Peter, I'm here."

Ed Calkins peered into the night over the steering wheel. "It should be just up the road a bit more to the left...Ah, here, we are, John-Peter. This is the place."

John-Peter looked through Ed Calkins' window to see, a completely squared, grayish-white building, with a sign that boasted, "Sammy's Sandwiches." As Ed turned into the parking lot, John-Peter saw that the paint peeled in numerous places, one, loose, gray shingle hung at a perilous angle, and that two shingles were missing altogether.

"Sue's Diner in twenty years, maybe?" Ed chuckled when he said this, until he saw John-Peter's unsmiling face. Uncle Ed had a lot of nerve comparing this dung heap to his grandfather's former establishment. "Come on, John-Peter. Betcha the food's good."

John-Peter hoped so, for the inside was as dismal as the outside. The dim lighting failed to obscure the yellowed wax on the black and white tile, yet, as Ed said, the food inside the display case, at least, looked appealing. Four round tables and chairs occupied the opposite end of the shop, but the room, save for the petite, deeply-tanned, dark-haired girl slicing tomatoes, was empty.

"Can I help you?" she asked in a flat tone. She dumped the freshly cut tomatoes into the bin next to the shredded lettuce.

John-Peter waited for Ed to order, but he merely stood near the cash register and gave the girl his most menacing, Count Dracula stare. John-Peter read the nametag on the girl's large apron, Rosa, and said, "As many vegetables as you can fit between a loaf of bread."

Rosa raised an eyebrow at this unusual request, but she grabbed a French roll and sliced it open. "Which vegetables?"

"All of them."

John-Peter looked back at Ed Calkins, who was steadily observing each of Rosa's movements, beginning with her piling on lettuce to sprinkling the last of the purple onions with oregano and replacing the bread's top. She reached for a sheet of waxed paper and wrapped the sandwich with automatic, practiced folds.

"Anything to drink?" Rosa slid the sandwich to the cash register.

"Soy milk?"

"This ain't no health club, kid."

"Water. Extra-large."

Ed Calkins sighed, leaned forward, and intensified his threatening gaze.

"You gotta pay for the cup."

"My uncle will."

Rosa grabbed a giant cup, opened the ice bin, and dragged the cup through it. The room was so quiet that the water flowing from the dispenser sounded like someone was filling a bathtub, and the plastic lip she snapped on top echoed off the walls like a gun shot. She grabbed a paper-wrapped straw on her way back to the cash register and looked dispassionately at Ed Calkins.

"And for you, sir?"

Ed tossed a five-dollar bill at her, cleared his throat, and then leaned further across the counter to meet her gaze. He dropped his voice to its most threatening tone, then said,

Your sandwiches are useless to me
For my needs are simple, but fussy
I merely guzzle some blood
Without starting a flood
But you are too thin to be tasty.

He paused, nudged John-Peter, and sauntered out the door. Rosa, expression unchanged, processed the order and tore off the receipt. John-Peter accepted and pocketed it, but continued to hold out his hand. Rosa looked down at it, then up at him.

"Whaddya want, kid?"

"Free will offering. He used to be in vaudeville. Oh, I know the nursing home cares for most of his needs, but this buys him an occasional newspaper or a stick of gum."

Rosa slid her hand under the apron and into her jeans pocket. She withdrew two coins and dropped them into John-Peter's hand.

"It's not much, kid, but it's all I have."

John-Peter bowed with a flourish of his hand and said, "Ma'am, you have tickled an old man's heart." Then he picked up his sandwich and scampered out the door. Even before he opened the car door, he heard Ed Calkins' hysterical laughter.

"Oh, John-Peter, did you see the frightened look on her face? I've never seen anyone so scared. You saw how she dressed. She thinks she's a voluptuous beauty. She hated that I called her skinny and degraded her body fluids." He slapped his knee and then started the ignition. "Well, onto the next victim."

John-Peter unwrapped the sandwich and inspected it for minute signs of stray lunchmeat. "What about the route?" He found nothing offensive, except that Rosa could have added more onions, and took a large bite. Bread didn't crunch; vegetables were fresh. Life was good.

"It can wait. I'll die if I don't eat soon."

"Literally or figuratively?"

"Shh. I'm trying to remember where I saw that motel." Ed Calkins studied the few landmarks that preceded Shelby: a small, private airport, a billboard advertising menthol cigarettes with a bikini-clad woman smoking one, and a boarded-up gas station. "I'm looking for a street named Fulmer...up on the left...here we go, that's it."

A long, winding driveway led up to a row of doors attached to a trailer-shaped structure. Ed slowed his speed, concentrating on the units before him. He selected the one with a large, gold "5" on the door and parked in front of it. He turned off the engine, unbuckled his seat belt, and opened car door, glancing back just in time to see John-Peter brushing crumbs off his lap onto the carpet. "Aren't you coming inside with me?"

"I'll guard the car."

Ed's face fell with disappointment. John-Peter knew the steward wanted an audience for his performance.

"Suit yourself." Ed Calkins said with a sniff.

While John-Peter wadded up the wax paper, Ed slid under the door. The boy tossed the paper ball into the back seat and then cradled his swollen arm against his chest, gazing out into the night, missing Angela. What did she do when they were not together? Was she washing a last batch of dishes, sleeping, or, better yet, sitting outside under the apple tree, longing for John-Peter?

For some unknown reason, that last thought irritated him, so John-Peter restarted the car and turned on the radio, but his choices were static, a talk show about the dangers of processed meats in school lunches, and bagpipe music. He switched off the radio with more irritation than he felt when he turned it on. Ed opened the door, smacking his lips with glee, not even upset that John-Peter was wasting his gasoline.

"I gather you found something acceptable on the menu."

"You should have seen the look on her face when I told her why I'd broken into her room. Well, she shouldn't have laughed."

"So, you killed her?"

"Never! I only took enough for a meal, but I thoroughly insulted her, and let her live to feel its full effects. By the way, get that garbage off my floorboard."

John-Peter fumbled under his seat for the lever, released it, and eased his seat all the way down to retrieve the wrapper. The back was completely empty.

"Hey, Uncle Ed, where are the newspapers?"

Ed turned back onto the main road. "What made you think I had newspapers?"

"You said we're subbing the Shelby route."

"For a courier, not a carrier. I do a bit of moonlighting on the side. I've got to make a blood drop at Jenson Memorial Hospital."

"Where do you pick up the blood?"

"931 Elm. It's near a convenience store where my guy makes a box drop."

They had entered Shelby. A series of tree-lined streets jutted off Main Street, each featuring mostly old Queen Anne and neo-classical houses. Ed turned down Elm Street, pointed out Dr. Rothgard's house, a large, two story, box-shaped structure five houses down, and then proceeded to drive past it to the far end of the street, where he parked his car under a towering, oak tree.

"The house is back there," John-Peter said, craning around for a better look.

"I know. We're walking back. I can't risk raising anyone's suspicions."

Ed might as well have parked in front and blown a trumpet to signal his arrival, for he took exaggerated mincing steps, pausing every few paces to take furtive glances to the left and to the right. John-Peter was amazed that someone didn't notice and call the police, especially considering Ed was also carrying a large garbage bag. When they entered Dr. Rothgard's yard, John-Peter caught a glimpse of his former pediatrician sitting on the couch in front of a television set. He was naked except for a pair of orange and white striped boxers, and his slick, combed-back black hair was still wet from his shower. A giant apparatus of test tubing and little bottles sat on the coffee table before him; a large stand forced opened a plastic bag at its mouth. Dr. Rothgard poured red liquid from a bottle into the bag, but his eyes were fixed on the television program.

"I'll take, 'Famous Cities of the World,' for a hundred dollars, Tom."

The audience erupted into a thundering cheer. John-Peter didn't hear the question, but couldn't mistake Dr. Rothgard's yell of, "You fool! It's Berlin!"

They walked in silence, until Ed said, "You haven't asked what limerick frightened the woman in the motel. Right here, John-Peter. Back window?"

"That's what Karla said."

"Good thing the hedges are tall. No one can see us from the street. Okay, since you asked, here is the limerick:

Oh, maiden who's taking a bath
You shall soon feel the brunt of my wrath
I will now fill the tub
With a bit of your blood
Since you're too cheap to offer me one snack.

The branches scratched John-Peter's face, but he was so covered in splinters that he scarcely noticed. Of more consternation to him was the second floor window, for although Karla's reports of it being open were correct, there was no way to reach it from the ground.

"I don't suppose you brought a ladder."

"We don't need a ladder," Ed said, bending over and cupping his hands. "My shoulders are big and strong. Put a foot in here and climb up."

John-Peter's laughter rang out into the night before he could stop it. "You can't be serious!"

"Shh! Do you want to get caught? Of course I'm serious, as serious as the time we stacked the baskets on old Mrs. Dobbs' front porch to get the paper I threw into her rain gutter." He set the garbage bag on the ground and said, "Come on, I don't have all night."

Ignoring Ed Calkins' loud, "Ouch," John-Peter clamped his prickly fingers into the steward's shoulders, then pushed one foot into Ed's clasped hands, dug the second into his waist, and hoisted himself onto the old man's shoulders. The windowsill remained just out of reach.

"Can't you stand on tiptoes?" Ed Calkins cried out in a whisper.

"Can't you?" John-Peter fired back.

"We both will, on the count of three. Ready? One, two..."

John-Peter raised himself on his toes and grabbed the sill, prying onto it with one hand, while he punched in the screen with the other. Then, he hoisted himself high enough to place both legs on the side of the house and catapult into the room. He ignored Ed Calkins' faint shout of "Good job!" and "Hurry up!" Instead, the boy adjusted his eyes to the dark room, trying to discern the location of an electric outlet near the dresser. He walked across the room, unplugged the lamp, and then reached into his pocket for the charger Marcus gave him at this afternoon's meeting. He unsnapped the walkie-talkie from his belt and plugged the contraption into the wall. He had no time for a long charge, but, hopefully, tomorrow's mission wouldn't require much. Karla said Dr. Rothgard kept the blood in the basement. Getting there should be fun.

He opened the door, holding his breath against its creak, but loud applause emitting from the television set downstairs drowned out the sound. The air in this part of the house was icy cold, and, when John-Peter opened the door to the first bedroom, he discovered why: rows of giant, deep freezers lined the room.

Maybe, Dr. Rothgard kept some of his father's blood upstairs, and he wouldn't have to brave the basement. The subtle glow from the street lamplights softly illumination the room, but it was enough to read the labels: *Corinne Applebaum, Herbert Cartwright, Dottie Sherman,* and *Elise Pesavento.* None said *John Simotes.*

On tiptoes, John-Peter crept out of that room and past the bathroom, then into the bedroom across from it. This one, too, was full of freezers, but, again, none of them belonged to his father. He tried the last door, but it only contained a flight of stairs that led to an even colder attic. There were no more bedrooms on the second floor. He couldn't get around it. He'd have to sneak into the basement.

With easy, light steps, John-Peter darted to the edge of the staircase and peeped down below. By leaning his head far to the right, over the banister, he could see into the room where Dr. Rothgard sat watching television and playing with his portable laboratory. Getting to the basement would be quite a trick, especially without the guarantee that his prize would be there, yet he must accept the gamble, for his very life, and the lives of others, was at stake. He slid sweaty fingers into his pocket and closed them around the leprechaun for good luck, but, this time, he left the talisman in place. A glimpse at the few, remaining numbers might unnerve him, a risk he could ill-afford. He rubbed his hand across his shirt to dry it, steeled his will, then edged toward the top step. A blast of frigid air stopped him, foot hovering in mid-air. A warm summer night should not be so chilly. Why was it so cold near the roof of the doctor's house?

He spun around, sprinted on the tips of his toes to the attic door, softly closing it behind him, and dashed up the stairs, three at a time, and ran straight into a freezer. The attic was a spacious one, spanning one end of the house to the other, but it was not the immensity of the room that struck him; it was the contents. The attic was crammed full of freezers, with enough space between them to open and shut the lids, and John-Peter briefly wondered who wired the house to accommodate them all, and why the floor didn't sag under their weight. He bounced on the boards, but they were solid and unmoving. Dr. Rothgard would not be able to hear him in the uppermost part of his house, but, at the same time,

John-Peter could no longer hear the television set. Just how long before Dr. Rothgard decided to come upstairs and freeze the bags he had filled? He took a deep breath. There was no time for speculation. He must act now, quickly.

John-Peter trotted to the far end of the room and swiftly wove among the freezers, skimming their labels: *Bob Ellenburg, Carlton Randich,* and *Marianne Farling.* Did he hear a stair squeak, or was it just his imagination? He held his breath, but detected nothing. A chill ran through him, and he shuddered; instinctively, the boy wiped the sweat from his brow and began anew. His breath came in forced, white gasps, yet he increased his speed with each aisle: *Edna Johnston, Paulette DeFabre,* and *Dwayne Zabora.* Two more rows to go. His legs shook so hard, they barely carried him, but John-Peter slapped them into obedience and continued: *Samantha Cree, Opal Minter, George Barber,* and *John Simotes.* He stood shock still at the freezer before him, mentally preparing himself to steal what was inside, the very blood that flowed through the veins of the father he no longer remembered. He yanked the handle and lifted it, but nothing budged, except his left shoulder as it wrenched from its socket. He strangled the cry of pain that convulsed his throat, but another agonizing paroxysm followed it, and ripped that howl from his teeth, and he didn't care whether or not Dr. Rothgard heard it. Dr. Rothgard had toyed with Karla, knowing he'd catch John-Peter on the way to the basement, where John Simotes' blood was not, the final, sick joke of a dying monster. A terrible rage roared through him, smothering his earlier fears, and he braced his frame against the freezer, jerked up the lid, hard, over and over again, until his stomach churned, his sides ached, and the hinges tore, sending the lid flying onto the freezer behind it. He stacked bag after bag onto his left arm that now was numb and rested just as many against his chest. He barely noticed the cold. He ignored the pain. The puppet would beat them at their game. He'd beat them all.

Clutching the frozen bags to his chest, John-Peter ran down the stairs and into the bedroom he first entered, calling for Ed Calkins before he even approached the window. He looked through the opening to see Ed blinking the sleep from his eyes and holding open the garbage bag. John-Peter flung the bags one at a time into the sack and prepared to leap from the window when his head buzzed, and the room spun. Something slammed him to the floor and banged his head against the frame of the bed, but, even in dazed, semi-awareness, John-Peter knew he did it to himself. He rubbed the echo in his head, and he no longer sat on Dr. Rothgard's bedroom floor, but at the head table of a lavishly spread banquet, honoring Ed Calkins' defeat of the hapless Amerigen. At one end of the table sat Clancy, licking clean his wine goblet, and at the other end was Eircheard, with Angela beside him, wearing full bridal garments. John-Peter cupped his hand to hear Ed's speech and the announcement of the new poet, but the grunts of Karla on his left drowned out his voice.

"Shut up," John-Peter hissed, giving her a little shove.

Karla glared at him, she but kept jamming apple after apple into her goblet, splattering seeds over her lavender homecoming dress. Angela began to cry because Eircheard tried kissing her, and John-Peter turned to comfort her when Karla whispered in his ear, "Know *me*, John-Peter!"

He turned again to see Karla, clad only in the purest of lavender blossoms and drinking from the goblet of cider she had just pressed. All signs of the banquet evaporated; there was only Karla, solemnly holding the clear, amber liquid toward him in her outstretched hand and beseeching him with her eyes to drink it. In the distance, a banshee sent up her plaintive wail.

For some unknown reason, her request intimidated him, and he hesitated, but Karla pressed the glass to his mouth, so he cast all trepidation aside and obediently opened wide to accept it. She locked their eyes together while he drained the glass, but the moment he lowered it, Karla's lips bore down on his, and she kissed him with an intensity that astounded him and caused his head to reel in a most alarming way. He let the glass fall, and something awakened inside him; the crystal boat appeared on the horizon; and he sailed away on that beloved vessel that, at long last, finally arrived to claim him. He knew Karla by instinct, so why hadn't he realized that Karla, the mistress of teleportation, had played the fairy enchantress all along? It was she who, dressed in lavender the night of homecoming, recognized his buried desire for her and hid under the cover of real lavender, in his bedroom and inside the hotel suite, to masquerade as the princess of his dreams. Somehow, she had found a way to join him here, in this mysterious land, the product of an aging man's delusion. He doubted not his senses; Karla was no hallucination, for did phantasms taste of cider? She kissed him faster and harder; the waters grew choppy, and he sank below the waves that washed around him. Twice he clawed his way to the stop sputtering, "Karla, we can't," but Karla was insistent, and John-Peter freely drowned under her will, until, in the far-off distance, the brownies' rooster crowed its morning song, and Karla began to fade.

"No!" John-Peter cried, clutching her neck in panic. "Karla, don't go!"

Something caught between his fingers and snapped; she was gone. His hands, realizing they now grasped only air, dropped to his side. Loneliness, disappointment, and profound sadness at her disappearance rose up inside him faster than the new sun overtook the night sky. Yet, he did not need to open his hand to know Karla's locket was inside it, still hanging from the chain he had broken while struggling to keep her. The full weight of his feelings for Karla dawned on him with the day. He had loved Karla all along.

John-Peter sat there under the steadily increasing morning sunshine, reflecting on this new development. He and Karla had always been best friends. They shook hands over deals, held hands during séances, and high-fived over victories. They lay on the grass together in the middle of woods during the pre-dawn hours and shared their dreams. He was as comfortable with her body as he was with his own. They belonged together, and, somehow, she had sensed the truth they both knew long before he'd ever admitted it to himself. He was still attracted to Angela, but he didn't love her, and he could never find the lasting happiness with her that he already owned with Karla. He wondered how he could have been so blind to this significant aspect of himself, then considered his implanted memories and forgave his lapse of sound judgment.

Raising his bottom off the ground to tuck the locket underneath the leprechaun, John-Peter vowed to make everything right with Karla. He would tell her how he felt, and he would tell her soon. However, he must first complete the task fate lay before him and fulfill his destiny; he must right the wrong; he must rescue Angela and return to Munsonville, where he really belonged.

John-Peter stood before the smudged, full-length mirror in the underground rest room below the steward's amphitheater. Slowly, he buttoned the long white jacket, glad to hide the beloved green T-shirt, grimy, now, even to his own eyes. He caught the diamond-shaped cap as it tumbled from his head and readjusted its folds. He again pressed it firmly around his ears, but the provoking garment insisted on traveling up his scalp.

"White looks better on you than lavender," Karla said, giggling.

With trembling fingers, John-Peter pinched each side of the hat and pulled it hard, but, in his mind, they brushed against a million fragrant petals. He wished Karla was here.

"Nurse, medical update. How am I faring?"

"The same, but, at least you're not any worse. You and Ed got the blood, right?"

"I…think so."

John-Peter's memories of the last few days were nebulous, disjointed scenes. Had they successfully completed their mission?

"Well, someone came into your room, announced that some loopy courier in a kilt had a package, and your doctor went flying out. I figured it was your blood. It shouldn't be long before you're home."

John-Peter absorbed Karla's words. *It shouldn't be long now*, for him…and for Angela. He hoped Melissa welcomed her; he wondered what Trenton might think of her. A grin spread across his face at the thought of introducing Angela to Trenton. Poor Angela. He straightened his shoulders. The hat stayed put, but the jacket crept past his belt. John-Peter tugged the coat back into place, and the knuckles on his right hand nicked the bump in his pocket. John-Peter hesitated. Did he really want to read the dwindling row of numbers? Instead, the boy entwined his fingers around the chain of Karla's locket.

Screw the mouse. Karla's locket was the only good luck charm he needed.

"Home sounds good." John-Peter walked to the door and reached for the handle.

"John-Peter?"

"Hmm?" He opened the door and scanned the hallway for fairy folk.

"When you're fully human, will you remember things?"

The wistful sadness in Karla's voice, so unlike her, made him pause. "What things?"

"Just things."

John-Peter stepped into the deserted hallway. He had not considered the fate of Ed's program. Would John-Peter's saved files be deleted? Or would they be stored somewhere in a new, soul-infused brain and become part of his permanent collection of memories? Fear at what he might lose clamped onto his heart with vise-like strength. Would he still be John-Peter without his cache of records from the past? Would he know Karla? Would his essence allow him to forget her?

"How should I know? I've never been real."

"Okay. I just wondered."

The walkie-talkie beeped.

"Hey, John-Peter!" Marcus called.

"Karla, I've got to go."

"Wait, John-Peter, I…"

John-Peter dropped a door and turned left toward the stairs. "Speak, Marcus."

"We're at the cottage. Is Dawn always this difficult?"

The boy flew up the stairs three at a time. "Only when she's awake."

"Any sign of the brownies or the cluricahns?"

John-Peter reached the top. Swarms of sidhe milled about the spacious venue. Little by little, they filled the vast seating, but John-Peter saw no representatives from either group. He shaded his eyes and studied the top rows.

"Negative, your honor."

"Should we still…"

An elderly hoarse voice in the background broke off Marcus' question: "I hate parting with an heirloom. Solid oak it was, too."

A crackle, then silence. John-Peter squinted into the distance. The concession stand was on the opposite side of the main entrance. He was halfway there before the walkie-talkie beeped once more.

"John-Peter?"

Raucous laughter made the boy look up. A fear dearg, his tiny hands shoved into the pockets of his red trousers, and a short, gnarled pooka, all in orange, sauntered toward him. If they heard Marcus, they gave no sign. The boy waited until they passed before he answered Marcus.

"That fossil still grousing about his cane?"

"He won't shut up about that blasted thing. Should we wait at your hut?"

John-Peter turned around. A new group of creatures ascended the stairs. He caught a glimpse of the peaked sepia hats of the tiny brownies. The cluricahns were not among them.

"No, it's safe to get Angela. Call when you get there."

"Roger, roger, over and out."

The boy had reached the refreshment area. Being the only human vendor, John-Peter stood nearly two feet higher than his fellow peddlers. The uniforms of these aged fear gurthas flapped around their emaciated frames like sails in a gale. Knowing their habits, he bet they ate more than they sold.

"Next!" the leprechaun behind the stand barked. He shoved the box toward John-Peter.

The boy looped the rope around his neck and looked down. The box was full of serving-sized foam containers: skirts and kidneys, crubeens and cabbage, and drisheen. Wax-paper wrapped boxties were stacked as high as the box. A large money envelope was wedged between the food and the row of Irish coffees.

"Hey, changeling!"

John-Peter turned at the sound. A leprechaun seven rows up snapped his fingers and frantically waved his hand. When John-Peter reached him, the little man's black eyes were shooting angry sparks under his shaggy red eyebrows.

"Watcha got there, sonny?"

"Slop, with and without animal flesh."

"Gimme the skirts and kidneys."

"That'll be five oak leaves."

The leprechaun dug inside his pocket and removed a fistful. "Can you take three and an apple?"

It had been a long time since John-Peter had savored an apple. "Done!"

"Oisin," the leprechaun said, turning to the second leprechaun sitting beside him, "give the boy an apple."

The said Oisin grinned through broken teeth, removed his buckled hat, and produced a ripe and shiny red apple. He balanced it on his scaly, yellow palm, then, with a raspy chuckle, stretched his hand toward John-Peter. "I'll take a boxty."

John-Peter slid the squashed leaves into the envelope and snatched the apple from Oisin's hand before the leprechaun reconsidered his offer. He then handed the largest container to the leprechaun that first addressed him. That little man ripped off the cover and stuck his snout into the pork stew.

"That'll be three more oak leaves," John-Peter said to Oisin, raising his voice over the leprechaun's slurping.

Oisin scowled, stood, and grunted as he felt around his many pockets. John-Peter hummed a waltz. The leprechaun removed his empty hands.

"I'm fresh out of oak leaves."

"Oh, well."

John-Peter turned to leave, but Oisin leaped from the bleacher and grabbed his coattail.

"I said, 'I'll *take* a boxty."

He clawed one of the potato pancake packages and scampered away with his prize before John-Peter could stop him. Unruffled, John-Peter polished the apple on his coat and then blissfully sank his teeth into crisp skin. Aodhan lighted on his shoulder. The walkie-talkie beeped.

"Any sign of the cluricahns?" Marcus' voice boomed.

"Shh." John-Peter dropped his voice. "None noted."

A loud sigh, then Marcus lowered his voice, too. "We're starting choir practice."

John-Peter nibbled the last few bites and tossed the remains under a bleacher. Why couldn't he remember the name of that waltz? Was Ed's program failing?

Aodhan tapped John-Peter's cheek with one of his antennae. "The gladiators are coming out."

John-Peter recognized these members of the sidhe from Ed Calkins' stories. They, tall, muscular, and comely, were direct descendants of the Tuatha de Danaan, insofar as Ed envisioned them, and masters of the vulgar verse Ed so enthusiastically espoused. Proudly and confidently, the three-man teams approached their respective microphones. Ed's team wore red and white striped shirts stamped with the word, "steward." Those representing Amerigen boasted heavy, blue coats circa Revolutionary War. Pinned to their breastplates was a metal plate, "poet." The steward's first agent grabbed his microphone and bellowed a battle cry, which the crowd returned with a wild shout. Over the din, the man yelled:

A leprechaun sat mending his shoe
While enjoying a cheap, hearty brew
His lack of control
Cost him saving his sole
Now he sits all day in a stew.

Cheering rose from the stands. Down below, a row of brownies squatted on the ground and held up a row of cards. Each bore the number ten. Gradually, the applause faded. With a clear of his throat and a deep breath, Amerigen's man began:

A pooka who shunned all manner of fun
Preferred lounging all day in the sun
When tired of the jeers
That brought him to tears
He took them all out with his gun.

A hiss rippled through the stands. Again, the brownies held up their cards. All read zero.

Aodhan shook his head in disgust. "This is terrible writing. I shouldn't wonder that the steward wishes to replace him."

John-Peter remained quiet. He had read worse in the steward's library. Another round came and went, resulting in similar scores. Amerigen's team called a time-out and huddled for a conference. He could hear loud cursing in the distance, a sure sign the cluricahns had arrived. He beeped Marcus and said, "It's time."

"Golly, I hope we can pull this off."

John-Peter glanced at Aodhan's grave face and then said to Marcus, "Be brave, for we stand for truth. Be strong, for we are mighty. We shall prevail. We shall...

"Damn!" a woman's voice rang out through John-Peter's receiver.

The boy hastily covered the walkie-talkie and moved as quickly as he dared to an exit.

"What happened?" John-Peter whispered. "Marcus?"

"I broke a nail!" the woman with the cashmere sweater yelled. "I can't believe no one else can drive stick!"

The walkie-talkie beeped again. This time, it was Marcus saying, "Thanks, John-Peter. We'll keep in touch."

A chorus of shouts startled Aodhan, causing him to flutter nervously about John-Peter's head. The steward's second contestant lifted his hands to silence the crowds. When the roar dulled to an aroused murmur, the man smiled and recited:

> *A banshee complacent about wails*
> *Was judged unworthy of good fairy tales*
> *It was agreed six to naught*
> *She was too dull to be taught*
> *And was banished to scare away snails.*

This gladiator caused the same explosive reaction as the ones before him. He received a perfect score, and the clapping grew harder. Amerigen's second gladiator watched, stunned and open-mouthed. One of his teammates nudged him to the microphone. With unsure steps, the poet's delegate assumed position and lowered his head. A titter ran through the crowd, and John-Peter wondered if he'd simply throw the contest. Then the man faced the audience and belted:

> *A changeling so far from his home*
> *Misjudged how long he should roam*
> *When he leaped back in place*
> *To his own homey space*
> *His wife had run off with a gnome.*

John-Peter winced at those words. He remembered the close call with Curtis. The noon sun blazed. John-Peter shivered.

"They're taking an intermission," Aodhan said. "I must depart. I only came to inform you the troops are in formation and ready to fight."

"Thank you kindly, Aodhan," John-Peter said, with a smile and a nod at the sprite, who gazed unseeingly into the sky. John-Peter noticed, and his smile faded. "I shall miss you."

Aodhan returned to his senses and stared straight at John-Peter. "I'd say the same, but..." Here, the sprite hung his head. "I doubt enough of me will remain to miss anything."

"My grandfather believed in heaven. Maybe we will meet up there one day."

The sprite looked up and frowned. "Heaven is for humans, Glorna. You and I are only the products of a silly fool's imagination."

John-Peter stroked Aodhan's wing in what he hoped was an encouraging fashion.

"Even Ed Calkins didn't exist until a higher power envisioned him," the boy said. "Cheer up, old friend. If there is a God, we are only twice removed from him."

"Got any crubeens?"

A shriveled leprechaun swayed before him, the drool on his matted beard glistening in the heat.

"Pigs feet!" the leprechaun slurred. "I want pig's feet!"

John-Peter glanced up, but Aodhan had vanished.

Thunk!

The leprechaun had fallen flat onto the ground.

"Two Irish coffees!"

John-Peter stepped over the rumpled heap and hurried to bring the coffees to Clancy, who stood at the bottom of the stairs tapping his foot with an annoying click of his boot heel.

Clancy eyed the cups suspiciously. "That cream good and thick?"

"Should be. Regardless, they're on the house."

Clancy gulped them one after the other and then stomped on the cups.

"In that case," he said, leering and reaching inside the box, "I'll take two more."

"The gladiators are vacating the field," John-Peter said.

Clancy grabbed the last two coffees. "Takin' 'em back to share with the young 'uns."

"Brought the whole family?"

"Even the wife. Chance of a lifetime to see a verbal sparring between steward and poet."

The crowd yelled, "Steward! Steward! Steward!" and Clancy, coffee spilling over each hand, dashed off. John-Peter ducked into the building and beeped Marcus.

"Coast is clear, Marcus. The entire breeding ranch is vacated."

"We're on it!"

John-Peter sweated and shivered under the sweltering heat as he ran up and down the stairs fulfilling orders. Twice, John-Peter reloaded his box. A fear gurtha reloaded next to him.

"Skip the drisheen," the creature said. "Gives the runs."

"You don't say?"

The fear gurtha shook his head. "Terrible bad."

So John-Peter stacked container after container of the black pudding into his box. Disarming the crowd could make the rescue mission easier. The steward's voice rang out across the field: "We are gathered here today on this historic occasion..."

The walkie-talkie beeped. John-Peter ducked around the corner. "Go, Marcus."

"We're here. Every chain is cut, and the girls are pouring out. Gosh, that little girl has a powerful voice! Good thing I can't hear it."

"The main event is beginning."

"How much time, Simotes?"

"Not sure. Steward's up. Gotta go."

A hum of approval flowed through the arena. Everyone hushed in unison as Ed Calkins bent near his microphone:

When it comes to matters of verse
The Steward is master of terse
He goes straight for the heart
From end to the start
With insults that are quite diverse.

The audience perched at the edge of their seats. The brownies held up the cards. Ten! Howls of delight shook the stadium. John-Peter lurched and braced against a solid wall. Had he imagined its movement?

With a calm, easy half-smile, Amerigen patiently waited for silence. Then, in rich, fluid tones, Amerigen called out:

No amateur when penning a rhyme
Amerigen is worth every dime
Words of peril and strife
Spice up his life
And he accomplishes it every thyme.

Loud boos from the stands. The brownies cards went up. Zero! A storm of paper cups sailed onto the field. Ed Calkins stood by his microphone, grinning from side to side. The atmosphere quieted but rippled with suppressed anticipation.

The poet who thought he was best
Soon found himself put to the test
Although correct to the letter
The steward sounded much better
Now he languishes in house arrest.

The fairies screamed. They slapped each other's backs. Tiny feet drummed the floorboards. One cluricahn woman turned white and slumped; her husband knocked her to the ground. The brownies held cards high above their heads. Ten!

Amerigen's voice cut through the screams:

A computer geek who slaved for the news
Soon found himself singing the blues
When his programs all crashed
His hopes, they did dash
Turning his prideful roars into mews.

The brownies jumped up and down, angrily waving their cards. Zero!

Foam containers pelted Amerigen, coating him in black pudding. John-Peter beeped Marcus. "Are you close?"

"Lining 'em up now...oh, wait!"

"What?"

"Number sixty-three has to go to the bathroom."

"*What!*"

"Emmie's run off, too."

"You let her?"

Marcus sounded exasperated. "What'd ya want me to do?"

"It's a dirt floor!"

"John-Peter, be reasona…"

The boy let the button go. The fey audience stood and leaned forward, straining to catch the steward's final chant. Ed, exhilarating in the moment, cupped an ear to better hear the perfectly choreographed panting of a crowd in eager expectancy.

The Steward has beaten the game
Of one who thought he deserved fame
I'm sure you had guessed
I'd outdo all the rest
But it's a joy to gloat just the same.

With fierce shrieks the mob stampeded onto the playing field, pushing one another aside and stomping over the ones who didn't charge fast enough. The walkie-talkie beeped.

"The girls are back," Marcus puffed.

John-Peter fixed his eyes on the riotous scene. Everyone had forgotten that Amerigen had one last turn. With slow, calculated movements, Amerigen, for the last time, approached his microphone.

The boy put his lips near the walkie-talkie.

"Get ready," he hissed.

The sky darkened, but the foolish fey paid no heed.

Marcus beeped back. "Simotes, we're gonna blow such a hole through this place, the explosion will knock the residents of Jenson right out of their beds!"

The cloud had condensed into an opaque "V." No one on the ground noticed the oak weapon born by thousands of Ed Calkins' air elementals, the weapon that had once been the old man's treasured heirloom cane.

"You with me, Marcus?"

"All the way, Simotes!"

"One…"

The steward, who thought he'd attack
His poet, whose lines he had hacked

"Two…"

Ed began to have fun
For he thought he had won

"Three!" John-Peter shouted.

Nothing happened. The walkie-talkie had died. Disgusted, he hurled it onto the ground, shattering it into pieces. The spritely cloud loomed over Amerigen. He raised his hands for the bow, the one the hippie had skillfully crafted. The sprites, led by Aodhan, neatly dropped it into his grasp. For what seemed an eternity, Amerigen stood immobile, holding it.

Then he shouted: *"Until an arrow shot straight in his back!"*

Ed was too busy accepting his many congratulations to notice the view behind him. While the throngs worshipped from near and afar, Amerigen took aim and sunk the oaken arrow deep into Ed's heart.

CHAPTER 29: A MATTER OF LIFE AND DEATH

Ed Calkins sank to his knees. The brassy sky peeled away. John-Peter stood motionless and dazed, as this curtain descended on the last act of Ed Calkins' bizarre play. Already, many of the smaller fey lay dead. Amerigen was gone. Ed lay bleeding and gasping for breath. How long before his fantastical world disintegrated?

The stairs trembled under his feat. In the distance came a creaking, a groaning, and a roar as the entire west end of the amphitheater collapsed. Terrified shrieks filled the air as wee folk tumbled beneath the avalanching stone. John-Peter flew down crumbling stairs and landed hard, dislocating all ten toes. He dashed away on feet of fire. The quaking field broke open and swallowed the screaming gladiators as they raced for escape.

John-Peter ran on splintering feet towards the goldenrod fields. Shadows lengthened. The brilliant yellow sun that had blazed with a relentless ferocity during the games now produced as much heat and illumination as a nightlight. His narrow opportunity for flight was disappearing. He felt no loyalty to Amerigen. If the eighteenth century poet had not reached the van once John-Peter found it, the boy would leave without him. He soared full speed into the goldenrods and trampled their stalks into the dirt. The plants muttered protests. On and on he ran. A shout, a hammering of footsteps, and Amerigen was by his side, huffing and striving to keep up. The van came into view.

Amerigen clapped John-Peter's shoulder. "Well done, young Mr. Simotes," he said. "We may see victory, yet."

John-Peter hunched over and grabbed his fractured knees, panting with aching gasps. "We're...not...there...yet." His breath came easier now. John-Peter dashed away and called back, "How much time does the steward have?"

"Hard to say," Amerigen shouted. "What's that noise?"

John-Peter flung open the side door, and there was Angela, crouched into a ball and moaning. She sprang up at the sight of him and clambered over laundry baskets and sleeves of plastic bags.

"Oh, John-Peter," she cried, throwing herself against him. "I was so afraid you'd leave me!"

He strained to see past the front seat. The keys were in the ignition. He had only driven stick shift once, last year on a dirt road outside Grover's Park, when his grandfather was teaching him to drive in his pick-up truck, before the widow maker heart attack changed everything. That terrain was rough. This should be no different. A door opened, and Amerigen leaped into the front passenger seat.

"Don't look at me," Amerigen said. "I've only driven horses and buggies."

The sun flickered and died. The boy pushed Angela onto the floor and slammed the door shut. Rapidly he reviewed his grandfather's instructions: clutch in and gas off; clutch off and gas up. He popped the clutch, and the van produced an earsplitting screech vans should not make. Angela squealed like a pig, and Amerigen instinctively grabbed the dashboard.

"Hang on!" John-Peter called, ignoring Amerigen's vicious glare in his direction.

A jolting lurch, and they sped forward, flattening the last of the goldenrod and then the potato and cabbage fields. The van hiccupped and bounced over the ebbing countryside. Up ahead was the lake, and beyond that were the woods that hid the shimmering outlet to John-Peter's bedroom mirror.

"What if you never write poetry again?" John-Peter shouted over the din of the escalating destruction.

"Who cares?" Amerigen shouted back, still holding the dashboard. "I've written so much bad material, it will take years of deprogramming to cure it."

Deprogramming? Wasn't Amerigen colonial?

A glint, and John-Peter braked hard, forgot the clutch, and downshifted into first gear. They hit the glass.

Crack!

John-Peter shook away stars. Amerigen jumped out and disappeared amongst the trees. The sky vanished.

The boy hurled open the door and fell to the ground. Snap! He cried out in pain, struggled to stand on what remained of his feet, then reached for the side door and swung it hard. Angela tumbled out of the van.

"Oh, John-Peter, you're hurt!"

He grabbed her hand. "Hurry!"

Angela screamed. Ed Calkins' van had evaporated. Clutching Angela, John-Peter sped away, pain shooting up his legs and through his hips like flames. Up ahead was Amerigen, heading directly for the oscillating sparkles. With outstretched arms, the poet raced in and dissolved from sight. John-Peter forced a final burst of energy and tore into the aura. Light beams from all angles zapped him. Angela's hand ripped from his, and he heard her shout, "Ow!"

John-Peter skidded to a halt. Angela was kneeling on the other side of the portal and rubbing her forehead.

The boy dashed back to the entrance and pushed his hand through the opening. Angela clung to him, and he pulled her forward. Once again, she banged into an invisible barrier. Puzzled, John-Peter stepped through the gap.

He searched for obstacles but found none.

"Step in," John-Peter said.

Angela began to cry. "Not without you."

He shoved her hard, and Angela stumbled into the portal. He followed, smacked into an invisible barrier, and their hands broke free. Stunned, he now understood. Together, he and Angela represented a single soul in the real world. The cosmos hadn't sufficient space for them both.

Karla's cards needn't prompt him. Never had truth and destiny spoke so clearly.

Angela had returned. Her eyes widened. Half the lake had sunk into nothingness.

"John-Peter!" Karla called inside his head.

The boy thought quickly. "Got pen and paper?"

"Time's running out!"

"Karla, quickly! Pen, paper!"

A pen and notepad materialized in his hands. John-Peter scrawled a few words and ripped off a sheet. Dropping the rest, he stuffed the paper between the knotted folds of Angela's garments.

Angela clutched his shirt. "John-Peter, what's wrong?"

"Come, ON!" Karla yelled.

"It won't work," John-Peter said, forcing his voice to its calmest, most reassuring levels, "unless you go first."

Angela shook like a tree in a gale. "I can't. Oh, John-Peter, I can't!"

"Yes, you can," John-Peter said. "I'm right behind you. Run!"

She opened her mouth to object, but he thrust her backward into the tunnel and stepped away. The chasm melted into the trees, and those trees plummeted into the molten earth. John-Peter seized the leprechaun and cast it into the abyss. An oak tree fell, narrowly missing his head. John-Peter snatched its last branch before the tree melted and hobbled to the pool that was once the lake. He hoped Karla would have a good life with Curtis. He hoped she would not hate him too much.

Fists pummeled his brain. "John-Peter! You promised! Where are you? Come back! Come back! Come back!"

He wrapped his fingers around the locket chain and mustered up the hardest words he ever had to say. "I'm not coming back, Karla!"

The words echoed in the steward's vanishing imagination. For the last time, John-Peter reached up to slam a door, but his waist snapped in two, and he hit the ground. Pain faded. Karla's lips met his. Emmie mouthed a song. A newspaper sailed out the window. He bit a tofu burger.

Good afternoon, and welcome to Happy Hunting Grounds funeral home. May I take your order?

Candle-gazing with Karla. A skeleton on horseback. Midnight bicycling through Simons Woods. Irish soda bread. A toddler princess in a magic mirror. Fairy tales. Grinning leprechaun. Piano music.

For the blood is the life.

A rabbit's scream. Starvation. Black nightmare brutally shaking his cradle.
Mother!
A soft hand reached out in the dark and gently cupped his head. "I'm here, John-Peter," a soothing voice said.

Her hand, light and cool, slid to his cheek, and he instinctively buried his face in that all-familiar embrace. He opened his eyes to look at her but gazed into blackness. Had he dreamed it? The wail of the banshee rang in his ears, but his mother's comforting touch remained, so what did he care? Gratefully, he reclosed his eyes and let the nothingness enfold him under her loving hand. The banshee's wail grew louder, but John-Peter did not care, for he drifted into a delightful sensation that had been denied him all the days of his existence.

Perfect peace.

Dr. Lofield switched off the life support machine, silencing its shrill whine.

"Mrs. Wechsler," he began.

"Do you think he heard me?" Melissa gasped between sobs, her ears still ringing with that agonizing death gong.

Karla sniffed and rubbed her face across her sleeve. "He heard you," she said in a low voice, but the tears came anyway. "I'm almost sure he heard you."

She wrenched her hand away from Melissa's grasp, the grasp that allowed John-Peter's mother to communicate with him the way Karla always had. Instinctively, Melissa tightened her fingers, but Karla's lifeline to John-Peter's consciousness was severed. For a moment, Melissa's hand wavered in the air, then it dropped, empty, onto her lap. In the background, thunder rumbled.

So, this was the end. Fresh tears spilled down Melissa's face as she stroked her son's forehead. How quickly his warmth was leaving. Did it always happen this fast? John had been cold several days before he died. She absently combed her fingers through her son's damp hair, hair that soaked the pillow, hair that would never again need cutting. She could have been spared the awful truth about John-Peter for all the good it did either of them. For eighteen years, she had faithfully carried out Dr. Rothgard's orders. For over a decade, she had kept Kellen's bargain. She needn't have bothered. The dreaded finale came anyway.

"Mrs. Wechsler," Dr. Lofield said again. "Our hospital chaplain wishes to speak with you."

She leaned forward and kissed John-Peter's cold cheek. She clutched her arms around his neck and buried her face in his shoulder. The chain of Karla's locket still dangled from his fingers. She could not let him go. Not now. Not yet. Not ever.

"I hate you! Go away!"

"He's been waiting all night." Dr. Lofield pressed the call button.

"Tell him to save someone else! It's too late over here!"

"Mrs. Wechsler," Dr. Lofield said. "This isn't about your son. It's about your husband."

BOOM shook the floor and rattled the windows; the telephone near John-Peter's bed fell. Melissa snapped to attention and cried out, "What about Jo...?"

Melissa caught herself and glanced up at Dr. Lofield. Was he smirking? Thank goodness she had stopped herself from saying more. Of course, he did not mean John. She glanced back at John-Peter. His lips were blue. His body felt tight. He was really gone. She refused to crumble in front of Dr. Lofield. She had to be strong, if only for herself, in this moment, the type of dignity John wanted, and that she had denied him. She could fall apart later, at home, with no one watching her, where it would not matter. Bit by anguished bit, Melissa slid her arms away from the shell that once held John-Peter. Reluctantly, she sat erect and looked calmly into the traitorous eyes of Dr. Lofield.

"Kellen?" Melissa asked, in an uncertain voice.

"Yes, of course," Dr. Lofield said.

A nurse entered, walked to Karla, patted her hand, and reached for a tissue. She dabbed Karla's eyes with it, and, amazingly, Karla let her.

"You should step out in the hall, too." The nurse tucked the tissue between Karla's stiff fingers. "A very worried young man has been asking about you all night."

Bewildered, Karla slowly, hesitatingly, stood, but her gaze fell on the still figure in the hospital bed, and she wavered between loyalty and trusting obedience to the nurse. Noticing Karla's dilemma, Melissa, too, forced her wobbling legs to stand. Dr. Lofield wasn't smirking, but the benevolent sympathy in his eyes irritated her. No, it maddened her. John's death was horrible, thanks to him. Why did this doctor get to live, to thrive, to celebrate another Christmas, while she had nothing?

"You stay with your son as long as you like," Dr. Lofield said. "Please just meet our chaplain first."

The door opened, and another nurse appeared. "Dr. Lofield, phone call." Dr. Lofield did not respond, so the nurse tried again. "Dr. Lofield, there's a call on line…"

"Take a message. I'll call back."

The nurse glanced at Melissa, hesitated, then said, "Doctor, it's from Golden Years. You really need to answer this one."

Dr. Lofield looked squarely at Melissa. "At least think about it. We're only trying to help." He followed the nurse from the room.

Melissa looked at Karla's drooping face and black smudges beneath her eyes. Karla had walked with John-Peter every step of the long night. She must be far past exhaustion. Yet, Melissa felt profoundly thankful for Karla's intervention, and the wordless communication that she and John-Peter had mastered. Their unique interaction had given John-Peter a chance at survival. Somehow, Karla had beaten the ambulance to the house. When the paramedics arrived, it was Karla who led them.

"I guess," Melissa said, but she spoke the words listlessly and only for Karla's benefit. "A quick introduction won't hurt."

Cold sudden fear gripped her heart. Was something wrong with Kellen? Once, she would have prayed for his demise, but not now, not when Kellen was the last surviving link to John. For the first time since she had laid eyes on Kellen's despicable face, she needed him, if only for reassurance that John's blood still flowed through her. Tonight, she had to see it. She had to smell it. She had to see the rapture on Kellen's face as he drank it.

"Let's go, Karla," Melissa said.

Karla nodded, but she did not move, so Melissa nudged her toward the door, away from the oppression of John-Peter's lifeless room and into a widening void of despair. In silence, they walked down the hall to the lounge. Curtis Chandler sat hunched over the edge of his chair. His face was hard; his eyes were distant; he squeezed and released his fingers. On the wall behind him, the television flashed bright colors and murmured unintelligible tones. Katie, jacket pulled up to her chin, dozed in a chair near the back wall.

"Curtis?" Karla said in soft disbelief.

His head darted up. His eyes looked anxious, but his face relaxed. The nurse brushed Melissa's shoulder.

"I'll find the chaplain," she said.

Curtis sprang from his chair and rushed up to Karla with open arms. The joyful eagerness took a dive when he saw Melissa. He stepped backward; his arms dropped to his sides.

"Karla," he began. "I..."

Karla looked away. Curtis held out his hand, glanced at Melissa and then stopped. He wanted her permission to reach out to Karla. He needed to know she would not be angry with him, especially since he would again face her in class after the holidays. John-Peter and Karla had been inordinately close. How close, only Karla now knew. Being selfish would not bring back her son. It certainly would not ease the separation for Karla. Curtis seemed nice enough. Everyone liked him, except, of course, John-Peter, but John-Peter liked few people. Karla trusted Curtis, and Karla was intuitive. She would need someone to get her through the dark days. Ignoring the pang of jealousy at Karla's good fortune, Melissa met Curtis' eyes and nodded.

Curtis' face lit up with pure ecstasy. Tenderly, but confidently, he unwound the tissue from Karla's hands and dabbed her wet face.

"It's quieter on the other end," Curtis said. "I'll buy you a pop."

Curtis took Karla's hand and led her from the room. Melissa watched them go and felt the anguish of this second death. Melissa sank limply into a chair. The nurse had not returned. Maybe, hopefully, the chaplain was busy rattling spiritual platitudes to some other suffering soul. Her eyes met the wall. Almost four o'clock. The chaplain had exactly five minutes to make an appearance. Otherwise, Melissa was going back to John-Peter's room.

In a commercial for designer jeans, two pajama-clad youngsters tip-toed downstairs carrying a large package, so like the Christmases of her youth when she and Brian sneaked out of bed Christmas Eve night to hide presents under the tree. In this very hospital, Melissa had kept watch with John and welcomed their son on Christmas Day. John-Peter's death forever snuffed out the magic from future Christmases. She bet Steve's did the same for Brian, although her brother was luckier than she. He had Cindy and the girls. He still had a reason to live.

Two large, gray-haired women in stretch pants lumbered into the lounge. One hurriedly wobbled up to the television set and turned up the volume.

"I swear," she said, "the entire world has gone crazy tonight."

"Is there a full moon?" her companion asked.

Five minutes were up. Melissa jumped to her feet and headed to the door. Behind her, a television newscaster said, "We are here at the scene of Eircheard's Emporium after an explosion of unknown origin completely destroyed the pawn shop."

Eircheards? Where John-Peter had made charges to Kellen's card? She recalled the thunder that shook John-Peter's room. *Thunder in December?* Melissa spun around and edged her way to the television set.

"Hundreds of people are wandering around the site. One appears to be Marcus O'Reilly, the Evansville law clerk who disappeared several weeks ago."

The camera zoomed onto Marcus's face. Melissa cried out, and her hand flew to her mouth. That...suit coat...

"Most of the victims are girls, blonde, under the age of 18, and unable to speak."

One of the stretch panted women poked the second in her ribs. "Where'd all those girls come from?"

"I don't know. Eircheard's wasn't that big, was it?"

"Well, Melissa," a pleasant voice rang out. "It's been a long time."

Melissa's heart stood still. She knew that voice, although decades had passed since she last heard it. What was it doing here, in Jenson? She took a deep breath. She could pretend she was engrossed in the newscast. If she didn't turn around, he might decide it was a mistake. He might leave. That's when Melissa knew she really did want to see him. She braced herself, then whirled to face him. A few gray hairs decorated the blue-black hair, and the clerical collar was new, but the boyish face and friendly blue eyes hadn't changed one bit.

"Jason Frye!" she exclaimed in wonder. Her knees buckled, and she sank into the nearest chair. She gripped its arms to calm her thudding heart while she studied the face of the man who slid into the chair beside her. "You're the hospital chaplain?"

He grinned, obviously pleased that she recognized him. "I grew too old for the primitive life."

"Primitive life?"

"I've served as a missionary for nearly twenty years."

"Oh!" Melissa said, too dumbfounded to add more.

Her eyes traveled over the length of the suit and rested on his left hand. No ring. Was he a priest? Not Jason!

Jason caught the glance at his hand, chucked her under the chin like old times, and then immediately sobered.

"No, I'm not a priest. Listen, Melissa, I only have a few minutes." He pointed over her head to the scene on the television set. "They're going to need me in the ER. A lot of confused people are coming in."

"Look, if this is about John-Peter, I don't require..."

"It's not about your son. Someone broke into your husband's funeral home in Thornton and murdered him. Police found the body last night."

Kellen? Dead?

"This is obviously a mistake," Melissa said in a voice that felt stiff and unnatural. "Kellen left town last night, to handle another disturbance at a different location. The police are wrong."

Had someone mistaken one of Kellen's unbalanced support group attendees for its equally unbalanced leader? This suspicion Melissa would not share with Jason. He belonged to a more innocent part of her life. He didn't need to know the particulars of her feelings regarding Kellen.

"Melissa, Kellen never left town. Police have already arrested a woman they believe is responsible for killing him."

"Are they certain it's Kellen's body? He deals with many...unusual clients. Perhaps someone impersonated him?"

"They're certain."

Jason looked down at his shoes. Melissa didn't like the evasive tone in Jason's voice. There was more to the story; she was certain of it.

"Okay, what aren't you telling me?"

"It appears someone from his support group did the killing, or, should I say, 'staking."

"Staking?"

Jason sighed, but he still did not look at her.

"One of his silver swords was plunged through this heart."

"I don't believe it. Kellen was too smart for a surprise attack. The police have the wrong victim."

More likely, she reasoned, the staking was part of the break-ins to which Kellen referred at Steve's dinner. Hadn't

Kellen said someone would get hurt? She wondered who the woman really staked. An employee working late? An intruder? One of Kellen's customers, pretending to rise from the dead to walk the night?

Melissa decided to placate Jason a moment, so she could quickly return to John-Peter's side. "Who is the woman?"

"Don't know. She's dressed in goofy, old-time peasant clothing and babbling in some French dialect. People saw her inside Happy Hunting Grounds beating on the window, so they called the police. Melissa, I know this must be awful for you, and that's why I'm here to..."

He turned red and stopped. Jason still couldn't be in love with her, could he? After all these years?

"To do what, Jason?"

"To comfort you in your time of need. That's my job." He smiled and reached into his back pocket.

Her son had just died, and he had the gall to flirt with her! Dressing like a minister didn't change Jason. It was still all about him.

"Jason, given our past together, do you really think it's appropriate..."

"Here," Jason said.

"What's this?" Melissa said, accepting the packet.

The first pamphlet read, *God's Eternal Life after Death.* She flipped through the stack: *Give God Your Sorrow, He Understands Your Pain*, and *The Light at the End of Your Tunnel.* She sighed in exasperation and tossed them into his lap.

"Thanks, Jason, but I don't need these."

Jason nonchalantly set them on the magazine table next to him. "Lots of people say that, at first. Later, they change their minds."

Before Melissa could answer, she heard a voice from the television say, "Dr. Abner Rothgard, who was convicted seven years ago..."

"Go ahead, Melissa, take them. There's no donation or anything like that."

"Shut up!" She spun around in her seat to catch the rest.

"...has escaped Golden Years..."

They both jumped at the pounding of footsteps. A flurry of hospital attendants and security officers raced toward John-Peter's room. Melissa flew out of her chair, but Jason grabbed her arm and set her back down.

"Stay here," he said. "I'll find out what's..."

"No!" Melissa twisted her arm free. "I'm going, too!"

She bolted across the room and beat Jason to John-Peter's doorway just in time to hear one of the attendants say, "Has anyone paged Dr. Lofield?"

"Yes!" shouted a nurse. "And Dr. Rothgard!"

Someone else screamed, "Call the police!"

"They're on their way," one of the attendants yelled back.

Another nurse clapped her forehead. "Oh God, more publicity!"

Melissa pushed past the thick row of hospital employees to the bed. A security guard led her back to the door. "Ma'am you need to leave the room now."

"I want my son!"

The security guard snapped back as if she'd punched him. "Your son? That's *your* son?"

The first nurse's eyes widened in alarm and fright. "Get her out ! Now!"

A giggle peeled through the air. All commotion ceased. Melissa bristled at this rudeness. Not funny! The giggle turned into a snicker, then chuckle, and finally a loud bellow. Melissa could not stop laughing. One spasm of mirth followed another. Her stomach cramped, and she clutched her middle, exclaiming in pain and gasping between guffaws. She tasted salt and realized she was crying.

"Ma'am," the security guard said softly.

Were those tears in his eyes too? No, wait, wasn't it Melissa who was crying? He gently pushed her toward the door. An unseen hand pulled her from the room. The door swung behind them, and Melissa looked deeply into the eyes of a troubled Jason Frye.

"Do you have someone to drive you home?" Jason said in a most unsteady voice.

She flung back her head in gleeful, maniacal laughter. She could just picture the look on Dr. Lofield's face. Oh, he had plenty of explaining to do. Oh, how the justice system would shred his credibility. By the time the courts got through with Jenson's finest medical director, Dr. Lofield would be lucky to get a job delivering newspapers for Ed Calkins.

"Melissa, whom may I call? You really shouldn't be alone tonight."

The tears flowed hard now. Without knowing how it happened, Melissa's face became buried in Jason's shoulder. A pair of clumsy arms went around her, and the years melted. Jason might convert any number of pygmies, but he was still the same boy who shyly fumbled under her shirt in her parents' driveway.

Yet, as he held her, a poisonous green rage simmered inside Melissa. She scarcely noticed the awkward pats on her back. She wished, oh God how she wished, for another chance to hold the body of her son. Why had she left the room?

Damn Dr. Lofield for suggesting it!

Damn Jason for taking up her time, and damn Melissa for listening to them both.

She needed John-Peter, not the rotten chunk of wood in a hospital gown. Never in a million years did Melissa guess she'd once again lay eyes on John's missing piano leg.

CHAPTER 30: LOST AND FOUND

It was a silent ride to Munsonville.

Each step away from John-Peter's room meant another step toward a life without him. The years without John had been unbearably hard, but raising John's son had made them easier. She would not survive without him. Melissa even welcomed the visit from the police, for it delayed the inevitable, although their perfunctory questions floated around her head, and her answers were hazy.

She could not absorb it. Facts jumped in her brain like popping corn.

Kellen was dead. A client had murdered him. Dr. Lofield had another medical mystery, as well as a scandal of a stolen body, on his hands. Kellen's body was badly decomposed. Only John's piano leg remained of John-Peter.

After the police departed, Jason insisted she leave, and Melissa did not have the energy to fight him. By default, he became the ride. Melissa's family was still in Thornton, and Karla needed Katie. At any rate, that was Jason's argument for doing the deed himself.

It took an hour, a sedative, and two cups of strong tea to calm Melissa enough for Jason to leave her alone and place a few phone calls. While he was gone, Melissa contemplated each sip of that amber liquid. Tea was Bryony's beverage choice, and one Melissa adopted after "playing" Bryony. Oh, the awful irony.

"I called your brother," Jason had said when he returned.

Melissa half-rose from her chair. "I told you not..."

"Your family needs to know. John-Peter belonged to them, too."

Melissa sighed and sank back down.

"He offered to come get you."

"Brian's in no shape to drive all the way out here!"

Jason shook his head soberly. "That's what I told him."

So, that's how Jason had become Melissa's transportation. Yet, what other choice did she have? It would be stupid to use Kellen's credit to pay for a cab ride, and many hours had passed since she had sent Arthur home.

Actually, Jason had wanted to drive her all the way into Thornton where she could rely on the support of loved ones, but Melissa insisted otherwise. The only loved ones Melissa wanted no longer existed. The only place Melissa wanted to live was in ashes. She belonged where John belonged. She belonged where John-Peter belonged, which was...where? Jason might have been talking to the rotten piano leg, for all the good his logic did him.

"I'm going to Munsonville if I have to walk every step of the way," Melissa said.

"Fine," Jason said.

She tightened her hand around the cup and crushed it. She would not look at him. He was not John.

So here they were, in those final moments before dawn, in the outskirts of Munsonville, a place that always failed its promises of joy and bliss and consistently delivered pain and despair. To think the board once envisioned the village as a tourist attraction! What a perfect setting for Melissa to live out the rest her days, however few she chose them to be.

The question was no longer "when." It was *how*.

Jason turned off the highway and onto the familiar two-lane road that led to the village Melissa had called "home" for most of her life. Melissa supposed she ought to make some form of conversation with Jason. She wiped the steam from her window and pretended to squint at the bleak December landscape. Merry Christmas. Ha!

"Thank you for bringing me home."

Jason checked his mirrors. "Against my better judgment."

"And yet..."

"I can turn around, you know. Thornton's only a..."

"No."

Eighteen years ago, at almost the same time...

John-Peter had solidified John's commitment to her. John-Peter had made them a real family. Happy eighteenth birthday, John-Peter.

Jason turned up the defroster. The sky's slight turning from dark to gray was the only indication that night was rapidly departing. In the dim light, Melissa clearly saw Jason's drawn face and half-mast eyes, although he had cheerfully tried to hide his fatigue with occasional, banal remarks.

They passed, "Munsonville. Population: 386. Everyone Welcome Here." Melissa remembered the first time she had read that sign and hoped it was a good omen. Then she recalled passing it with Julie, when they were in college and had come to Munsonville for Ann and Jack's engagement party. Melissa's world had been so full of hopeful expectation. Now, nothing remained, except desolation and death.

"I appreciate you going out of the way for me," Melissa said, glancing at the newspaper box outside Sue's Diner and then remembering Ed Calkins was still in Atlantic City, that he would not return home until after the new year.

"It's not out of the way."

"What do you mean?"

Jason turned left up Bass Street. "I moved here last week."

What?"

"You mean, you didn't know? Your stepfather certainly did. He'd been helping me get settled."

Melissa looked blank.

"I'm the new pastor at Munsonville Congregational Church. Last house at the top, right? I think that's what Steve said."

"You're the...why didn't my mother call you when Steve died?"

"Beats me."

He pulled into Melissa's driveway, in full view of the oak tree where John-Peter spent many happy hours with a book and a sack full of apples.

"Now that I think about it, I'm not too sure your mom knew either," Jason added. "I got the impression religion's not too important with your family. No offense."

"None taken." Melissa pulled on the door handle. "Thanks for the ride, Jason. Merry Christmas."

She opened the door and set a foot on the ground when a movement in the tree stopped her short. Hope beat wildly in her chest. Only the piano leg remained in Jenson, but as for her son's body...John-Peter? Melissa' strained for a better glimpse, but detected nothing.

"Melissa?" Jason said. He lightly touched her shoulder. "Are you okay?"

"Shh." She roughly shoved his hand away.

A branch bounced. A shadow flitted across the ground. Melissa heard a soft thud and saw a figure in a heavy blue coat run into the woods. She opened her mouth to scream, then covered her mouth. Someone had leapt out of her tree! John-Peter!

Jason turned off the car.

"That's it," he said. "You're in no shape to stay by yourself."

"Didn't you see that?"

"See what?"

"That...thing...jumped out of the tree."

"Melissa, there's nothing there."

He was lying. Melissa felt it deep within her. *Someone had been inside that tree!* She peered at the thick darkness that was Simons Woods, but she saw nothing. Who was hiding in the woods? She hoped it was someone she loved. She hoped he came back for her. She glanced over her shoulder at Jason. She didn't like the odd way he watched her. She would never get rid of him, if she didn't act normally.

"You're right," she said with a sigh and a smile. "It's just nerves. I'm all right now. Thanks for the ride, Jason." She swung the other leg on the ground and started to stand. Jason opened his door. Melissa sat back down. "What are you doing?"

"Coming inside until I can get someone else to stay with you."

Her last vestige of patience fled. The last thing she needed was her former boyfriend's nosy presence. Melissa slammed the door and dashed to the front porch, with Jason right behind her. She dug inside her purse for her keys and said, "When did you get all holy and concerned?"

Jason grinned. "I'll tell you after you let me in."

For a fleeting moment, Melissa considered calling the police. What would she tell them? It was a small town. Everyone knew her lingering obsession with John. Everyone knew of Steve's death. Soon, they would also know of John-Peter's and Kellen's, if they didn't already. Captain Will Miller would probably lecture Melissa's ungratefulness, high-five Jason, and go home.

Melissa resignedly shook her head and sighed in weariness and disgust. "Fine, come inside. Just for the record, I don't make bargains anymore."

"I hope you make coffee. I sure could use some."

She unlocked the door and stepped inside. The cold cut to her bones, but Melissa was glad of it. It helped dull the knifing pain in her heart.

Jason blew on his hands. "Where's your thermostat?"

"I've got it." Melissa moved the switch and a low hum emitted from the ancient furnace in the basement.

She and Kellen had argued about replacing that, too. Melissa wanted everything inside the house to stay as they had bought it. He knew why she was averse to break with the past, yet Kellen never understood. Kellen hated the past. He always looked forward. She led the way into the kitchen and turned on the light. Its brightness seemed eerie and unnatural in the empty house, the house that would never be full again.

"Make yourself at home," Melissa said. "The coffee will be ready in a few minutes. Wouldn't it be smarter to go home and get some sleep?"

"Uh, uh. I've got a long day ahead of me."

"Do you have another service?"

"I told you," Jason said, pulling a chair away from the table and sinking into it. "Once I leave here, I'm going back to the hospital."

"Jason, you can't! You've been up all night."

"Someone has to be there for the victims of that explosion."

Melissa had forgotten about all those people at Eircheard's Emporium, the ones who got to live. "Can't someone else go?"

"Someone else did go. I got a sub from Shelby to cover me so I could take you home. It's my job to be there. I can't let all those people down."

How strange those words sounded coming from Jason. There was a time he didn't think past the next televised football game. "Black okay?"

"Cream and sugar, if you don't mind."

She made tea for herself and then carried two mugs to the kitchen table. The wall clock read six o'clock. She hoped Jason drank fast.

"So, why are you being so nice to me? Is this the way you treat all your parishioners?"

Jason actually blushed and hastily took a sip to cover it. "No, of course not," he mumbled behind the mug.

"Then why..."

"This is different. You know that."

Jason's words squirmed inside Melissa. His wet first kiss flared in her mind, and she cringed at its memory. Jason was not John. She had to change the subject, now.

"So, what brings you to Munsonville? The church hasn't kept a pastor in years."

"That's what I heard, and that's why I asked for the assignment."

"You're kidding! Because of the ghost story, I'm assuming?"

"God is bigger than a ghost."

"Oh, don't start!" She noted with relief that Jason's mug was empty. "Jason if you don't mind, I'm really tired and..."

"Hey, Melissa can I have a refill?"

THUMP!

His hand froze in mid-air.

THUMP!

Jason was out of his seat and halfway through the door muttering, "What the hell," when Melissa heard a scrabbling noise, similar to the one last fall, when they had a mouse in the attic.

"See, Jason? I told you I saw someone!"

She pushed past him, but he grabbed her sleeve. "Where are you going?"

"Upstairs."

"Not without me, you're not."

Together, they crept up the stairs, stopping every few paces to listen. Each time, they heard nothing. Deep in her heart, Melissa begged, *Please be John-Peter. Please.*

Jason paused on the top step. The second floor was silent.

"Wait here," he said. "I'll check the rooms."

"The last door down the hall leads to the attic."

Melissa waited until Jason disappeared in that direction, then quickly tiptoed past her bedroom to John-Peter's room. The oak tree led straight to his window. Maybe the figure in the woods had returned. She hoped the noise came from her son, but she would settle for a murderous intruder, too. That would make her job easier. The door was ajar. Melissa peered around it. Spindly shadows cast ghostly silhouettes across John-Peter's bed and floor, but the room was empty. The bed quilt was not crumpled. The dresser drawers were closed. Not even a stray sock married the room's perfect neatness. Blasts of frigid air swirled white. A window was open. Its screen lay on the floor.

THUNK!

"There's something inside the closet," Jason breathed behind her.

Holding Melissa at bay with one arm, Jason took three large steps toward the closet door and flung it open. There, huddled on the floor in a back corner of the closet was a frail waif of an adolescent girl. Her fair hair clung about her face like wisps of straw; her brown eyes shone wild with fright. A spray of freckles across her nose and cheeks stood out like relief against the deathly pallor of her skin.

Jason crouched on the floor and reached out to her, but she gave a little bleat and scuttled away. Her ragged skirt hiked up with her. Angry red scratches crossed her legs. Was she the figure in the tree?

"Hey," he said in a soft voice. "It's okay. We won't hurt you."

The girl hugged her knees to her chest and a folded piece of paper dropped to the floor. Melissa lunged for paper, but Jason beat her to it. She was too upset to be angry.

"Hurry, Jason, what does it say?"

Keeping one eye on the girl, Jason unfolded the sheet and read aloud:

"Mother, this is Angela. Love her in my place."

Your son,
John-Peter Simotes

Angela? Debbie Polis' baby? Oh it couldn't be! It just couldn't be, not after all these years.

Jason handed the note to Melissa and said, "Well, you just have one mystery after another following you, don't you?"

"What are you talking about?"

He stood up. "I'm calling the police. She's one of the pawn shop victims. I'm certain of it."

"Here? In Munsonville?"

456

Jason threw up his hands and then reached for his phone.

"I want her."

He stopped and spun around. "What?"

"I want to keep her. She obviously knew my son. He entrusted her to my care. That makes her mine."

"Melissa, there's more to laying legal claim to a minor than having one show up in your closet, even if she comes attached with a note."

"I know, I know, but I'm keeping her."

"That's up for the police to decide." Jason flipped open his phone and pressed zero.

She quickly hit "end," and then said in her best wheedling tone, "Do we have to call this second? She could at least use a hot bath and a meal. It's Christmas, after all."

"Do what you have to do, Melissa. I'm still calling the police."

For once, luck was on Melissa's side. She didn't hear what transpired during the phone call, for Jason placed it outside John-Peter's bedroom, with the door shut. While Jason was gone, Melissa sat on the floor next to this strange girl. She warily eyed Melissa, but she didn't move. Melissa brushed a strand from the girl's cheek. The girl flinched, but she stayed put. Melissa studied her features. It had to be Angela. She had Derek's slender frame, limpid eyes, and high cheekbones. The fair hair was definitely Debbie's. Where had John-Peter found Angela? And where was her son now? Could he really be dead when he was never truly alive?

Jason had a grim look on his face when he returned.

"You've got your way, for today," he said. "Those girls have overwhelmed the tiny committee that serves as Jenson's social services, and the entire matter is being transferred to Thornton. Will said the best he can do is pick her up and drop her off at the ER, *after* Christmas dinner." He sighed in frustration. "I guess she might as well stay here until then."

For the first time since Melissa had received that awful phone call from John-Peter that Steve had fallen, she felt the first ripple of something that might be called cautious joy.

Jason, however, was not smiling. "The thing is, can I trust you with her?"

Melissa, spark of happiness snuffed, cried out, "The idea! I'm not going to hurt her."

"I'm more worried you might hurt yourself."

Jason's voice sounded so strange that Melissa forgot to be angry. So he had caught onto her! Well, she hadn't ruled out anything, yet. However, Melissa also knew that if she did not somehow reassure Jason of her sanity, he might take Angela with him back to the hospital.

"I promise not to do anything foolish or harmful. I mean it. Someone has to look after Angela."

He still looked dubious, but, nevertheless, relented at her words. Did he believe her, or did he just want to believer her? Either way, Jason had to leave. Even if Melissa had wanted him to stay, the hospital needed him.

"I'll check on you later," Jason said. "In the meantime, if you need something..."

Melissa politely accepted his phone number and shoved it into her pocket. She'd throw it away at the first opportunity. Fortunately, Jason did not require an escort to the door. Melissa waited until she heard it close, then turned to Angela with an encouraging smile.

"How about a nice hot bath and breakfast? You must be starving."

Angela contemplated Melissa through narrowed eyes, then nodded. Melissa offered a hand to Angela, and Angela reached up a shaky hand in return and stepped into the bedroom. Her eyes swept across John-Peter's possessions, but they registered curiosity, not infatuation. How did Angela know John-Peter?

"I think I can find you something to wear, although my clothes might be a little big on you," Melissa said, trying to sound cheerful. "What size do you wear?"

"Size?" Angela said dully.

"Never mind. I'll run that bath."

Melissa took the girl's hand and led her down the hall. Angela gazed in wonder at the walls and shrank from the stairs. She stood, horrified, outside the bathroom and refused to enter it. Melissa hoped the steam rising from the tap might diminish the girl's fear and entice her into the tub, but Angela's terrified eyes only grew larger. When the tub was three-quarters full, Melissa turned off the water and laid out a towel. When Angela did not move, Melissa ran her hand through the water.

"It's not too hot," Melissa said. "See?"

Large tears splashed down Angela's face. One set of fingers clutched the door handle. The other gripped the wall trim.

"Do you want me to help you get in?"

Angela's eyes darted across the room and then landed on Melissa's face, wondering. This girl acted as if she'd never seen a bathroom. So Melissa untied the knots that held the Angela's clothes together and guided the girl to the tub. Angela lifted a foot and dipped her biggest toe in the water.

"Hot!" Angela yelled.

"What in the world?" Melissa shouted with a gasp.

Gouged into Angela's back were the numbers, "Forty-two."

She covered Angela with a towel, set her on the toilet stool, and fled to her room to call Jason. He answered on the third ring. "Pastor Frye."

"Jason, it's Melissa," she panted. "Angela has numbers burned into her back."

"I know," Jason said in a weary voice. "They all have them."

"What does it mean?"

"I wish I knew. I have to go."

The line went dead. Melissa covered her face with her hands, but she still saw the brands: "Forty-two."

Somehow, Melissa managed to get Angela into the bathtub. Finding clothes was another matter. Jeans were out of the questions because zippers frightened Angela, and, anyway, she could not manipulate them, despite a few lessons from Melissa. Sweats did not work either. No matter how tightly Melissa tied the string, the pants slid down Angela's slight frame. Finally, Melissa settled for a nightgown, robe, and slippers. Angela's face brightened at the gown's shimmery purple. While Melissa knotted the sash, Angela slipped her fingers inside the robe to stroke the fabric.

"Come on," Melissa said. "Let's find you something to eat."

That proved the greater challenge. Angela balked at cereal, eggs and toast, and even peanut butter. In desperation, Melissa scanned the refrigerator for something that might appeal to Angela. Behind her, Melissa heard Angela's thin voice say, "That."

"Potatoes?"

"Yes!"

Angela gobbled the potatoes as rapidly as Melissa microwaved them, although she ignored the tub of margarine Melissa had set on the table. Melissa nursed another mug of tea, but her stomach growled as she watched Angela. She had only picked at the food at Steve's memorial banquet. Maybe she could eat a piece of toast. After she brought Angela a seventh potato, Melissa put two slices in the toaster and sighed, wishing Brian was here to make toast. How simple life was when they were children. She set a plate on the counter, then turned to face Angela. "How do you know my son?"

"Do you have a son?" Angela said. She bit the potato in two.

Melissa swallowed hard and forced the bitter words from her throat. "I used to have a son."

Angela choked, coughed, and shoved the remainder of the potato into her mouth. "What happened to him?"

The toast popped up, and Melissa put them on her plate, glad for an excuse to avoid Angela's open mouth. Didn't her adoptive family teach her any manners? "He…died."

"Oh, that's too bad. What was his name?"

"Another potato?"

Angela nodded her head vigorously. The phone rang, and Melissa answered it on the way to the microwave.

"Hello?" she said, setting the timer for ten minutes. Even the microwave was old.

"Melissa, it's Jason. Sorry about earlier. I've only got a minute."

She glanced at Angela who dangled her paper napkin in the air and poked a finger at it.

"Go on," Melissa said.

"Everyone's going nuts here trying to find out what happened. All of the girls have brands like the one you described on Angela, and everyone, including the adults, have amnesia. No one remembers what happened."

"Even Eircheard?"

"I don't know. No one can find him. If you want temporary custody of Angela, you can probably have it. There'll be a formal hearing and all, but for now, no one's questioning it. They're too overwhelmed. Look, I've got to run."

The next two weeks passed in a blur. Melissa obtained official guardianship of Angela, and she hosted two hasty memorial services. Despite Kellen's prominence, few people showed up to pay their respects at the very last wake and funeral at his empiric Happy Hunting Grounds. She took Kellen's death soberly, for he had been the last surviving link to John. Each times his fangs pricked her neck, and each time he lustily lapped John's blood, Melissa had closed her eyes and imagined what the experience was like for John. It was the only way she could feel close to him. Now, she wouldn't even have that.

However, Kellen's bloody fountain of life was not his only well that had run dry. Although it would take months before Kellen's affairs were fully settled, the news from the head accountant had not sounded promising. Kellen had run a carefully balanced business, but had little spendable cash.

"By the time we've satisfied his debts, there won't be enough money left to bury him," the accountant had said.

So Melissa cremated what was left of her second husband.

She held John-Peter's service at Franklin & Mores in Jenson, despite Darlene's pleadings that Melissa conduct it in the same location as Steve's and against Melissa's wishes that the affair be a private one.

"John-Peter would have wanted it at Kellen's place," Darlene had tearfully said. "You know how close he and his grandfather were."

"If Steve was right about heaven, I'd say they're pretty close now," Melissa had snapped back. Her wound from Steve's death was also raw. "This isn't personal. Drop it, Mom."

Darlene dropped it, fully. She assumed her best cordial behavior, even to the gawkers, and there were plenty, for the orderlies Dr. Rothgard had reputedly stabbed were waked, closed casket fashion, in the same building. The police still had no leads on Dr. Rothgard's whereabouts, which made no sense to Melissa. Just how far could one elderly man in a nightgown get on foot?

Despite the tremendous amount of support, John-Peter's funeral ended on a flat note. Because there was no body to bury or cremate, there were also no graveside services. The police also had no leads on the disappearance of John-Peter's corpse, nor did Melissa think they'd ever have one. They certainly would not release the piano leg to Melissa. For both occasions, Jason hinted at the need for sacred representation, which Melissa promptly disregarded. She didn't need Jason weaseling into her life under religious pretexts, and she certainly didn't need his conversion services. Twice, Deanna read flowery poems that she had written for the events. Twice, Brian spouted a short eulogy. Jason attended both services anyway, but he stayed in the back of the room, where, as far as Melissa was concerned, he belonged.

For Melissa, who scarcely paid attention to anyone's words and offered none of her own, no further pious sentiments were necessary. There wasn't a prayer in the world that would resurrect John-Peter. Luckily, they wouldn't bring back Kellen, either. The few times Jason attempted civility, Melissa shunned him as if he was the bubonic plague. Ed Calkins was not present, for he did not answer his cell phone, and Melissa did not know his Atlantic City contact information.

Leaving the funeral had its own shock. Crowds swarmed the new *Book Nook* across the street. A sign in front read, *Now appearing: Marcus O'Reilly*. The pawn shop explosion had its benefits for the Evansville law clerk.

Two days later, Darlene made an announcement. She was leaving Munsonville, for absolute good this time. She had buried two husbands, and all she wanted was to return to Grover's Park, to be near her friends and Brian and his family. Brian, Cindy and the girls had left town immediately following John-Peter's memorial service, for Deanna's school Christmas vacation had ended. So, Brian returned in mid-January, and, with Melissa, spent an entire weekend packing Steve and Darlene's belongings.

They spent a quiet Saturday morning stacking possessions into boxes and taping them. The last time Melissa had helped Darlene pack was after Grandma Marchellis' sudden death. Melissa had hated every step of the task. It was so final. She remembered the first time she met Steve. She had returned from Simons Woods with Brian, and there Steve was, standing amongst her moving boxes, measuring her walls for bookshelves. This time, it was Steve's things that went into boxes. Every item reminded Melissa of another job she had been avoiding: cleaning out John-Peter's room. Getting rid of Kellen's things had been a snap. She had Angela moved into Kellen's old bedroom in a day. Melissa could not dodge the inevitable forever, for Melissa had promised her son's room to Angela.

"I can't explain it," Angela said the day Melissa caught her contemplating her reflection inside Ed Calkins' magic mirror. "I just feel comfortable here, like it's home, somehow."

"Then you must have this room," Melissa had said, but she procrastinated making it so. The slightest thought of removing any of John-Peter's belongings overwhelmed her with unbearable grief. She bit the inside of her cheek and taped another box for Darlene.

When Darlene left the room to order lunch from Sue's Diner, Brian pulled Melissa off to the side.

"I'm worried about you, Liss," Brian said. "Why don't you come home, too? There are people back there that care about you. How about a fresh start, for you, and for Angela, too?"

Melissa had yanked her arm away, but she still felt the smart of Brian's fingers through her sweater.

"Mind your own business," she hissed, looking past him to see if Darlene was still on the phone. "This is home, and I'm not leaving it."

"Liss," Brian began.

"No one, not even you, can make me."

She silently congratulated Kellen's one forethought. He had paid cash for the Smythe's old house. Her tiny school salary could never have covered its payments.

On Sunday afternoon, Darlene left with Brian. Melissa alone remained in Munsonville.

Having Angela in the large house eased the agony of the painfully lonely days. Despite her initial trepidation toward her new home, Angela adjusted with surprising ease to the suite that once belonged to Carol Simotes and stopped asking for John-Peter's bedroom. Her social and school progress was rapid, thanks to Amy and Megan's friendships and Trenton's nightly tutorial sessions. Even Courtney hung around the house, invoking Lauren's wrath.

"Are you sure you want to do this?" Melissa had said, standing in the bathroom doorway and watching Courtney apply make-up to Angela's sallow complexion. "Lauren will drop you from her group."

"It's a small group anyway," Courtney had answered. She dabbed Angela's lips with tissue and then looked up at Melissa. "I can't explain it Mrs. Wechsler. It's just something I have to do. I feel I owe it to John-Peter, somehow."

Only Karla distanced herself from Melissa and Angela. She no longer raised her hand in class, and she shunned Melissa in the hallways and the lunchroom, especially when Curtis was with her. Melissa longed to talk to her about John-Peter and the experience they shared at his death, but Karla had dropped a veil between them that Melissa felt powerless to lift. Melissa even considered inquiring about Bertrand's health just to make conversation, but she shrank from Karla's cool exterior. It was nice of Katie to let Karla keep the mouse.

Meanwhile, Jason was busy winding himself into the lives of the villagers in ways Melissa considered very sneaky. After what had transpired on Christmas Day, Melissa was afraid he'd loiter about her house like a homeless puppy. It was a wasted worry. Jason had plenty to keep him occupied, and he quickly endeared himself to the villagers.

While Melissa was busy with memorial services, Ann's mother had organized a team of women to spend an entire week inside the old parsonage, removing dusty sheets and cleaning every inch of the place until it sparkled. Ann later told Melissa that Jason and her father had spent the following weekend walking the house from floor and attic, noting areas that needed repair. The amount of work required to fix up the parsonage must have daunted Jason because Melissa heard no updates from her friends. Jason seemed content to live at Munsonville Inn by day and inside the villagers' living rooms at night. Television reception for sporting events was clearer on the hill than in town. Jason may have swapped a football helmet for a collar and car magazines for the Bible, but deep down, he was still the same shallow Jason.

Nevertheless, it hurt Melissa's pride that Jason could so easily accept her rebuffs. He had acted so concerned on Christmas morning and maintained a close orbit during the memorial services. Why wasn't he monitoring her well-being with an occasional phone call? She shared her feelings about the new pastor's Christian hypocrisy with Katie over dinner one Saturday night. It was just the two of them devouring Katie's stroganoff. Angela was spending the weekend at Amy's house. Karla and Curtis had gone to the movies in Jenson.

"That new pastor is a hoot," Katie said, twirling a noodle around her fork. "I don't think Mom ever went to any church that wasn't Catholic, but she's stayed in town the last three Sundays. Boy, you should see the amount of people that attend the old church."

Melissa scowled as she drizzled Katie's dressing over her salad. "How do you know the place is packed?"

"Silly, how do you think she gets there? Dad's too sick to go, and besides, he'd only get lost. Mom's so unsteady on her feet that she needs help. I don't mind."

"Well, I think Jason's a phony," Melissa said. She did not tell Katie she used to go steady with Jason. "He hasn't stopped by the house one time to check on Angela and me. I think it's because we don't have cable."

"I don't have cable, either," Katie said, "but Pastor Jason's been shoveling snow for us all winter."

A tomato slid down the wrong pipe. Melissa, spluttered, coughed hard, and reached for her napkin. "Jason's been here?"

"Pastor Jason's been everywhere. He's the most helpful person I've met." She slid Melissa's water glass towards her. "Are you okay, Melissa? You look a little green."

When Melissa arrived home that night, she walked straight to the thermostat and turned off the heat. She spent the night shivering under a stack of quilts, counting the minutes until morning, and never quite getting to sleep. In the hour before dawn, she called Jason.

"I hate to bother you," she said, "but we have no heat here. Can you take a look really fast?"

"Gee, I'd love to help you, Melissa, but I'm just walking out the door."

"Official business?" she teased. "When my house is freezing?"

"Well, kind of. I'm going ice fishing with Jack Cooper."

His answer chilled her hopes. He didn't even sound worried! Why should she be polite now?

"Nice try. You won't trick Jack into attending worship services."

"I don't want him in the church. I want him on the church. I need help fixing the roof."

"In this weather? Aren't you worried about ice?"

"I mean, when it warms up."

"Jason, he won't even paint the hand rail to his apartment!"

"Hey, Melissa, I've got to run. Jack's waiting. Why don't you give Eric Miller a call? He's pretty handy."

Click. Jason had hung up! With gritted teeth, Melissa marched to the thermostat and moved back the switch.

That night, Ann called Melissa to see if Angela could help at the diner on Saturdays.

"I'm going to be shorthanded," she said. "Jack will be helping Pastor Jason at the parsonage."

"Jack?" Melissa said. "You're Jack? I don't believe it."

"I wouldn't have believed it either, not until Pastor out-fished Jack."

The crushing blow came Sunday afternoon. Angela had attended church with Amy and loved it. Now, with the new-found exuberance that came from being accepted into this society, she wanted to join Jason's youth group.

"Angela, there's barely enough kids in the village to make a group," Melissa said.

"That's why I have to join! Everybody's going to be in it. Pastor Jason's taking us into Jenson every Friday night to do stuff. Those who participate get to work at a camp all summer."

"Angela…"

"Please!"

Melissa grudgingly relented. "I guess a youth group is harmless enough," she said. "But the Pied Piper of Munsonville Congregational Church will never convince parents to let their children go for an entire summer, not when family businesses need their help."

She was talking to air. Angela was already dialing Amy's number to share the good news.

As winter melted into spring, Angela gradually weaned herself from the Wechsler residence to a larger world that did not interest Melissa. The more independent Angela grew, the more introspective Melissa became, until their worlds rarely collided. Angela studied every afternoon at the library with Trenton and waitressed every evening at the diner for Ann and Jack, which conveniently allowed Angela more time with Trenton. On Friday nights, Angela accompanied the youth group into Jenson for bowling or skating. On Saturdays, she either helped at the diner or with projects at the parsonage. Sundays, of course, Angela attended church. Having to take Angela to court appearances, psychiatric testing, and counseling sessions caused major arguments, for Angela resented intrusions into her schedule. Melissa coped by huddling further into her shell. With difficulty, she prepared and administered the final exam for *A Tale of Two Cities*. Outside news poignantly reminded her of devastating losses. She canceled all newspapers and unplugged the television and radio. John-Peter's body was missing. Eircheard was missing. No one claimed the girls, known now as "the emporium orphans." Ed Calkins did not call.

Just before Easter, Melissa experienced another death, for Carol Simotes passed away quietly one night in a demented fog and was waked and buried without incident. Carol's death did not affect Melissa much at first, but when her meager affairs were settled, Melissa found she missed the sham of a mother-in-law. Although Carol had no real connection to John as Kellen had, she and Melissa had shared a common bond: John's contrived memories.

Relying on volunteer labor translated in slow renovation, but as long as Jason was welcomed into almost any home in Munsonville for dinner and sports shows, he did not mind living at the inn. After Easter break, the youth took no more trips into Jenson. Instead, they spent Friday nights sitting around Sue's Diner planning their summer. Curtis Chandler led the meetings, overseen by Jason. Several times, Jason opened the meetings for parents, too, but Melissa declined with the excuse of last-minute papers to correct and finals to prepare. She never learned the details of Jason's unusual summer camp until Memorial weekend, when Angela brought home the permission slip.

"There's a summer camp in Thornton?" Melissa said, as she accepted Jason's information sheets. "Is it new?"

"No, one of the churches there started a children's home. That's where we'll be living and working."

"A children's home? That's a rather unusual place to camp."

"It's for, you know, for the emporium orphans. They're staying there until they're adopted."

"That could take years."

"That's why they need a place to live. I can go, can't I?"

What could she say? A part of Angela was already moving away from her. Holding her back would cheat them both.

"Of course," Melissa said. "You're one of them. You have to help. Find me a pen, and I'll sign your forms."

Melissa scanned the information and then gasped loudly and covered her mouth. The children's home had two resident psychologists: Julie and David Drake.

"What's wrong?" Angela asked, her voice edged with anxiety. "I can go, can't I?"

"Of course you may go," Melissa said as she added a shaky signature, the initial shock passing. "You'll be in good hands."

The following week, Angela was gone. With no one living in the house and no school to teach, the rickety framework of Melissa's life collapsed. The past irresistibly dragged her into its clutches. Melissa drew her curtains, unplugged her phone, and let the mail pile up on the kitchen table. Shadows haunted her and blocked any real sleep. She rarely drifted into slumber before dawn and rose, hung over, in the silhouette of late afternoon. Nighttime restlessness overpowered Melissa. She paced the house and muttered. Persuading Kellen to buy the old Smythe place symbolized Melissa's first act of power, one of many that proved her equality with John's vampire manager. Her and Kellen's initial verbal sparring was in this house, at the Smythes' travesty of a dinner party, yet another event that emphasized

John's separation from her. She hated Kellen, even then, but after he murdered Cornell, she had agreed to his terms, for John-Peter's safety. Now, she hated Kellen's killer, languishing away forever in some state facility. Tucked between her mattress and box spring was an HHG silver dagger she had planned to use on Kellen, after John-Peter had become human. In the end, neither victory had been hers.

She shuffled down the basement stairs and followed Kimberly down the basement stairs at Simons Mansion, stairs that led to a secret room, where Henry painted his fantasies and ended his life and John's. She gripped the staircase to the Smythe's second floor and descended the stairs at Simons Mansions with Bryga, while marveling in wood so polished it reflected her likeness. She flashed ahead to the night of the fire. Melissa now ascended the stairs, fingers grimy with the handrail's thick coating of dust, eagerly anticipating John's arrival. Tonight, wherever she roamed, John's blood flowed through her. He entrusted her with it to save John-Peter's life, but she had to share it with Kellen to honor that trust. John-Peter was dead. She had failed.

Melissa laughed aloud. Oh, the look of surprise and terror on Dr. Rothgard's face when Melissa barged into his office, demanding the answers that made her one with John's dark world of horror. She had never seen him close a door so fast! He had hustled her into a corner, one hand around her neck, the other covering her mouth, imploring her silence. The words that followed made Melissa wished she had stayed home. John-Peter wasn't Debbie and Derek's baby. He was a figment of Ed Calkins' vivid imagination, bewitched into existence through John's piano leg, to be one day quickened into life through John's stored blood. John hadn't forced her mouth to his chest for some gruesome notion of closeness. She was a holding tank for his legacy. If she wanted her son to know human life, she must continue the daily capsule supplements of John's blood, which Dr. Rothgard periodically siphoned from her body. Gradual corpuscle build-ups were crucial; any hastening of the process might alert Kellen's senses to another delectable source of John's blood. If Kellen stole the tiny, tantalizing amount that festered inside the boy's wooden frame, the loss could destroy John-Peter.

Over time, the piano leg would rot away. At the moment of its destruction, Dr. Rothgard would perform a massive blood transfusion. Melissa would become the real mother of John's only son. The choice was simple. Melissa loved John. John wanted this. She had to do it.

In another time, in another place, Kellen might have made a good husband. Certainly, he was a practical one. Providing for his family was an ingrained concept, and he had a keen business sense to match it. If Kellen had lived longer, he would have reaped tangible rewards from his chain of funeral homes. Yet, below the surface of Kellen's success lurked the full truth behind it. He gained favors by terrorizing people with his full potential. Grateful that Kellen had spared their lives, they willingly bared their necks, opened their fat wallets, and placed significant phone calls. Melissa detested the easy life Kellen freely supplied her. It came packaged with a giddy demonic shade that ravenously plundered her veins at night.

She had reached the attic, where John-Peter had lain in wait to capture a little field mouse destined for destruction. A purple rose dropped onto the floor of her mind and a distant carriage thundered inside her brain. Henry appeared, dressed in midnight blue, and she felt his chilled gloved hands on her cheeks as he brushed his cold lips against hers.

When the walls contracted around her, Melissa left the house to roam the woods. At first, she stayed near the house, a short distance from John-Peter's oak tree. When even that vast space confined her, she tottered down Bass Street to Main Street, where dark blocks of buildings formed the perfect backdrop to black and gloomy remembrances. Gazing into the midnight waters of Lake Munson, Melissa could picture clearly, as if it were yesterday, her last-minute housewarming party invitation to Ed Calkins. How he insisted on lugging the large mirror up to John-Peter's room. With eyes large as wonder, John-Peter trailed the old steward up the stairs. In rapt fascination, John-Peter watched Ed install the mirror inside John-Peter's closet door. With each hammer of the nail, Ed explained to the toddler the marvels of magical mirrors. While John-Peter examined its features, Ed murmured in Melissa's ear his necessity for regular access to her son, to guarantee optimal hard drive function and for periodic upgrades and downloads. Ed was inordinately proud of John-Peter, his finest program. The bond between them appeared indissoluble. So, why hadn't Ed called?

She wandered into Simons Woods and demanded the once dreaded mist to appear. Opaque clouds dotted a cobalt blue sky. The mist had left with John. She yearned to see it, to be spun into its cocoon, and drown within its vapors. The ground gurgled with angry impressions of those individuals victimized by Dr. Rothgard's macabre search for immortality. Again, Melissa heard Grandma Marchellis' insistent cries of, "Blood! Blood! Blood! Blood! Blood!" Melissa wished the ground would break open and swallow her up. She plunged deeper into the woods, farther than John had taken her the afternoon he attacked her in the cove and the night he first made love to her. Both times, the earth bestowed paradise. Lying six feet beneath it offered relief. If only she didn't have Angela. She and John could be so close.

On the return trip, Melissa impulsively veered right onto the hilly, winding drive that used to lead to Simons Mansion and now ended at a park, a road she'd traversed many times by bike or on foot as a teen and had since avoided, with two exceptions. The first was when Melissa student taught at Munsonville School, when John was living, as well as caring for John-Peter, in Jenson. The servant's cottage where Melissa, Brian and Darlene had resided and where John had visited her in nocturnal illusions had become a storage building for the maintenance crew. The second trip was last fall, during Munsonville's first and only homecoming, when she and John-Peter had biked to the picnic grove, the former site of the old, gray stone, four-story Simons Mansion, with its bay windows and a wrap-around porch that had once dominated the view, before a fire destroyed Munsonville's dreams of tourists and Melissa paradisiacal abode. Green vines, grayish green leaves, and pink flowers had covered large portions of that mansion and woven itself through the estate's foliage. It was bryony, of course, specially bred by John Simons for his bride, Bryony Marseilles, a villager and daughter of Munsonville's Congregationalist minister. Steve had called the plant "a nuisance" that first day they had met him and had warned her and Brian that the grounds were full of the poisonous weed and to keep away from it. How fitting that a vampire plant should outlast its master. And now, even Steve was gone.

Melissa had reached the top. The landscape was deserted; the swings hung forsaken in the heat of the June afternoon. The air stood still. No wind bent the branches or whispered through the tall grasses. No birds chirped in the background or hopped along the ground in search of lunch. Even Melissa's footsteps made little sound as she slowly headed toward the slope that led to the servant's cottage. The box-shaped house was still too flat, too old, too gray, too small, but not too ugly, for Melissa no longer compared it to the Grover's Park ranch of her childhood: grey-blue siding, black shutters, and a manicured yard with a few perennials and tomato plants. The chain link fence that the village added after Melissa's family moved out was now rusty, but its entrance still bore a padlock. Melissa did not care. She climbed over the fence and up to the cottage. She peeked into the windows, but someone had covered them with newspaper. With a defeated sigh, Melissa wandered to the back yard that had once merged with Simons Woods only to discover Simons Woods had since overtaken the yard and swallowed up the bike path. Melissa closed her eyes, and she was standing in the dark with Scooter, under a glowing yellow moon and millions of stars, heart beating fast with a yearning she did not understand. Melissa re-opened her eyes. She now understood the longing, but that knowledge had come with an unbearable lonesomeness for John.

As she turned away, Melissa heard the rustle. She paused and listened, and then she heard it again, indistinct and faint. A swish in the woods, a parting of branches, and a young man stepped out, looking only mildly surprised at Melissa's presence, almost as if he had expected her. He was scarcely taller than Melissa, with disheveled red hair, neatly trimmed auburn beard and mustache, and a slight stoop to his medium frame. Melissa stepped back. She was trespassing, after all.

"I...uh...

Melissa did not know what to say. "I'm sorry. I used to live here and..."

Her voice trailed away when she saw the object in the young man's right hand. It was a pipe, but not any ordinary pipe. This one had polished dark wood and a large bowl with a gold lid, gold trim, and gold mouth piece. Melissa had known just one person that had owned a pipe like that. The man noticed Melissa staring at him and moved the pipe to his left hand.

"Arnold Hartgerd," the man said, with an extension of his right hand, a broad smile, and unusual intelligence gleaming in eyes of impossibly deep green. "It's fine by me if you look around. I'm the new maintenance manager."

"Maintenance...manager..." Melissa stammered, wondering if she really hadn't come unglued, unable to take her eyes off him.

Arnold took a puff from the pipe and gazed at her with the ease one displays for good acquaintances. "It's only until I finish school. Medicine's my real passion."

Melissa felt weak from head to toe. She had always known coming back was a mistake. What insanity had compelled her to do so today?

"Medicine?"

He puffed again, and Melissa followed his hand as he moved the pipe away from his lips. "Hematology, to be precise. Contacts."

"I'm...I'm sorry?"

"Contacts. That's why my eyes are this green."

"I have to go," Melissa murmured, edging away. "I have to go."

"I'll unlock the gate."

Melissa followed Arnold to the front of the cottage, but once the door opened, her legs found their strength, and she ran as fast as they would carry her.

"Nice chatting with you!" Arnold called as she fled.

After that incident, Melissa did her brooding at home. Yet as summer slowly limped away, the ache in Melissa's heart increased until it became a raw bleeding mess that even time would never heal.

One early morning before dawn, Melissa slipped out of the house and headed straight for Main Street. The muggy air of late July already hung in damp sheets around her, although the brassy sun had not quite risen. Maybe she should have let Kellen install air conditioning when they could afford it.

A man, not Ed Calkins, filled the box outside Sue's Diner. His dark pony tail grazed the end of his white T-shirt. Dirt and grease streaked his dark blue jeans. He shut the door with a bang, reset the changer for Sunday prices, and shoved his box-cutter down his back pocket. He bent to retrieve a stray blue strap and caught Melissa staring at him.

"Oh, hello," the man said, a friendly, open smile lighting up his youthful face. He stood and twisted the strap between his fingers. "I didn't see you standing there. Did you need a paper?"

Melissa looked around for Ed's car. It was unlike Ed to take more than one vacation a year. So, where was he? "I'm looking for someone."

"Oh, all right," the man said, turning to leave. "Have a good morning."

She couldn't let him go, not without knowing.

"Wait," Melissa said.

The man stopped and learned an elbow against the box. "Something I can do for you, ma'am?"

His polite, almost courtly mannerisms, clashed with the coarseness of the job. What compelled such a fine young man to run newspapers by night? He certainly didn't act as if he belonged inside a dirty warehouse.

"Where's Ed?"

The man looked baffled. "Who?"

"Ed Calkins, the man who usually delivers this route. Are you subbing for him?"

The man peered closely at her, but his glassy eyes were faraway. Had she said something wrong? "You say you know Ed?"

"Yes. We're good friends."

Surprised flickered across his face, but he calmly said, "You don't seem that old." He reached into his back pocket and removed his wallet. "Ed hasn't done this route in nearly fifteen years."

"That's ridiculous!" Melissa exclaimed. Her heart pounded hard and fast. "My son went with him every weekend until..."

A sob racked her throat, and Melissa quickly choked it back. She threw her hands on her hips and looked up into the hazy sky, willing composure to return.

"Ma'am, I don't know your son, but maybe you'd better read this." He opened his wallet, removed a ragged newspaper clipping, and unfolded it. With a little gasp, Melissa read the headline: "Newspaper Carrier Found Dead on Route."

"Responding to an early morning call for help, police stumbled upon the body of Ed Calkins, 56, of Meadowood. Calkins, a route driver for the R News 4 U agency, was found dead in his car from an apparent stab wound. No suspects have been arrested."

Melissa closed her eyes, and she was in the middle of a stormy night. John had missed his turn and pulled off the road to check the route book. Her voice cried out, "John, isn't that Ed's car?" She slipped on the mud. The rain drenched her jacket and rattled the metal of Ed's car. She opened the door and beheld Ed, sound asleep. No, not asleep. He opened his mouth and blood cascaded from it, down to the large, dark wound in his chest that stained his shirt red. He clawed her jacket and said, "For the boy," and she had snatched the grotesque leprechaun from his hand and skidded back to John and her baby. She knew what John did to Ed, but she refused to admit at the time. She followed when John drove Ed's car home. She witnessed John help Ed into the house. Bitter tears stung her eyes. John was dead. John-Peter was dead. And Ed? Where was Ed? Ed had shepherded her son after John's death. He had made John-Peter's time clock ran smoothly. He was the keeper of the boy's memories. Together, they ran a route every weekend. *This man was lying.* Old newspapers however, do not lie. Soberly and without a word, Melissa returned the clipping.

"Thanks anyway," she said.

Lack of sleep finally claimed its payment. Her exhausted legs melted into rubber. How would they carry her back up Bass Street?

"Ma'am?" the man said, stuffing the clipping inside his wallet and removing another folded sheet of paper. "Since you knew Ed, would you mind doing me a favor?"

"Sure," Melissa said. Her voice sounded as flat as she felt.

"Would you sign my petition?"

At once, she sat across from Ed Calkins at the Smythe's dinner party, while Ed fished inside his kilt.

Of course, the highlight of the year is the Calkins Day parade on February 13th my birthday, he had said. *In fact, I have a petition circulating to make February 12th through the 14th a three-day national holiday. Would you care to sign it?*

Melissa, of course, had not signed the petition that day, nor on any day for the next two decades that Ed had offered it. The elusive petition was always someplace else; Ed always promised to bring it "next time." She accepted the paper from the man's hands. It held only two signatures, Ed's and another one that read, "Bill Amerigen."

She glanced up at him, perplexed. "Are you Bill?"

The man nodded, said, "I was Ed's supervisor," and offered her a pen. She quickly wrote, "Melissa," then started to write, "Wechsler," and paused. She scratched out the, "W," and instead wrote, "Simons." A large weight fell from her shoulders. Melissa even managed a tiny smile, as she placed the pen into Bill's outstretched hand.

"Have a good weekend," she said lightly.

"You, too, ma'am."

Melissa plodded back up the hill. The houses and Main Street teetered and lurched. How long had decent rest eluded her? She drifted into the house and was half asleep by the time she reached the sofa in the television room. A loud pounding rudely returned her senses. Painfully, Melissa opened her eyes. The drums still beat inside her head; no, someone was banging on the front door. She closed her eyes against the noise. The painful knocking continued. Holding her head between both hands, Melissa stumbled to the front door and opened it a crack. It was Jason.

"God, you look like shit," he said, pushing the door back and catching Melissa before she fell. "Come on. I'm taking you to breakfast."

"Don't you have a sermon to preach?"

"Services are over. It's past noon. Let's go."

"I don't feel like eating," Melissa said dully.

"I can tell. You've lost weight. We're going to Sue's Diner if I have to carry you over my shoulder every step of the way."

The way Jason said it struck Melissa as so funny, she actually managed a weak smile. "I wouldn't try it. I might throw up."

"It's a joke. I brought my car."

How bizarre driving to Sue's Diner when the restaurant was only a long block away. Two girls with blonde pony tails were cleaning up the remains of the lunch crowd. Another blonde-haired girl rang up a customer.

"Oh, hi, Pastor Jason." She carefully counted change into the man's hand. "Just sit anyplace. I'll be right there with your menus."

Jason led Melissa to the back of the nearly empty diner.

"I need to talk to you about something," he said, "and I don't want anyone else to hear it."

Melissa was more curious about the workers. "Jason, those girls, are they…?"

"Emporium orphans?"

The girl brought two menus and poured Jason a cup of coffee. She raised the pot over Melissa's cup, but Melissa hastily said, "Oh, tea for me, thanks."

After she left, Melissa continued, "Well, yes, for a lack of a better term. They all have blonde hair."

"Curtis Chandler and I created a unique exchange program for the summer. The kids in Munsonville get a break from the home routine and a chance to minister to other youth. In turn, we've rotated the older girls into the jobs here to learn some real work skills."

The girl returned with a pot of hot water and a dish of tea bags. "Are you ready to order?"

"Janie, have you met Melissa? She's Angela's mother."

Melissa thought it strange that Jason did not introduce her as Mrs. Wechsler, but then decided the Munsonville she had known now dwelled in another era. Jason lived in the modern world.

"Hi, Melissa," Janie said, clicking her pen and turning a page in her order book. "What can I get you?"

Melissa's stomach churned at the mention of food. "Just toast. I'm not too hungry," she said, handing the menu back to Janie.

Jason said, "We'll both have the omelet supreme, bacon, and orange juice to go with that toast."

Janie scribbled the order over Melissa's objections. "Okay, Pastor Jason. It shouldn't take long."

He waited until Janie left the area then said, "Oh, stop glaring. You're going to pass out if you don't eat. Don't you want to hear details about the summer program, especially since you've ignored my meetings and Julie's phone calls?"

"I'd rather find out what you wanted to say, so I can go home."

Jason dumped a package of sugar into his coffee, then stirred in a couple of creamers.

"The worker exchange is just one portion of it," Jason said. "I've been back and forth with the village board about the old Simons estate."

Melissa's ears perked up, and she tried not to sound overly eager as she asked, "What about the estate?"

"The playground and picnic areas are nice, but there's so much wasted space. I did some research at the library, including reading a copy of your centennial report, which was very helpful, and learned John Simons had done some impressive planting when he was alive."

"So?"

"So Arnie and I want to work with the emporium orphans to recreate those gardens and orchards, except in this case, they will become a large community garden."

The hot day suddenly became very cold.

"Arnie?" Melissa whispered.

"The current groundskeeper. He's convinced a garden will thrive up there, especially with the right fertilizer combinations. But that's what you get when you combine a fourth year med student with an amateur botanist. Anyway, that's not why I asked you to breakfast."

Janie returned with the coffee pot and refilled Jason's cup. He again added cream and sugar and then said, "The renovations on the parsonage are nearly complete."

Fresh annoyance surged into Melissa's throbbing head. "That's why you brought me here?"

He took a sip of his coffee, but did not look at her. "I want you to marry me and move in, too."

"What!"

Jason waved his hand up and down. "Shh, keep it down, will you? I don't want to announce it all over the village, not yet, anyway."

Melissa lowered her voice. "Aren't you being a little sudden?"

"Sudden for you, maybe, but not sudden for me. I came here because of you."

"Because of me? I was married when you moved here, remember?"

Jason nodded and sipped his coffee. His hand shook, a little.

"I know. I just wanted to be near you, and that's the honest truth. I didn't have anything up my sleeve. Kellen's death was an unexpected bonus."

His words shocked her. "I can't believe I'm hearing this kind of talk from a preacher."

He looked straight at her. "Oh, come off it, Melissa. You weren't in love with Kellen, and you're happy he's gone. I also think it's high time you lost your obsession with Professor John Simotes. There's a whole world out here. You belong in it."

"And I think you have…"

Janie returned with the food and refilled Jason's coffee. "Anything else?"

"No, thank you, Janie," Jason said. He reached for the sugar. Melissa grabbed the creamer and moved it out of reach. Jason frowned and said, "You're being very childish."

"I think your remarks are out of line."

"They're not, and you know it. I've been following you ever since we broke up."

He reached for the creamer, but Melissa covered it with her hand. "I never knew you were the stalker type."

"Ha, ha, very funny. No one has to go very far to follow you, Melissa. Your antics, or should I say the antics of your husbands, have been all over the news. I used to think you'd gone off the deep end, until I went away and got smart."

Jason again reached for the creamer, but Melissa picked up the creamer and held it on her lap. "Jason, I have no idea what you're talking about."

"Melissa, it's like this." Jason stopped, as if uncertain if he wanted to speak or not, then took a deep breath and plunged into it. "I always thought you were cute, but you and your friends acted like little kids, until you came back from Munsonville. You seemed different, older, and I was intrigued by that."

"I always thought you liked Kimberly."

"Sure, I did, but everybody wanted Kimberly. I didn't have the nerve to date her. Shelly was just plain bland. Laura was so obviously in love with me that I did ask her out, once, just to see what that would be like, but her parents wouldn't let her go."

Melissa remembered Laura sharing that juicy bit of information, the night of Munsonville's centennial, the night Kimberly disappeared.

"I never wanted to break up with you, but you always acted so distant, like you didn't care if we were together or not. I never expected you to be fine with it. Other girls would have thrown a fuss and tried to get me back."

The eggs were growing cold, but Melissa kept the creamer on her lap.

"I guess that kind of bruised my ego. Laura was older now, so I worked it off on her all summer. I learned the hard way when not to call out the wrong girl's name."

Laura and Jason...right after she and Jason broke up? Melissa recalled the weekend Laura spent in Jenson preparing beautiful artwork for John-Peter's bedroom. Not once had Laura ever alluded to a past relationship with Jason. Then she remembered how Laura and John both knew Laura's art teacher, although John wouldn't explain that situation, either.

"In the fall, I went away to school and found more opportunities for getting into trouble. Long story short, I partied my way into flunking out. My parents weren't too happy and sent me to live out of state with my uncle. That was the best thing they ever did for me."

Melissa was silent.

"Next door to my uncle was this African missionary who was staying with his sister for a few weeks. He came over to the house one night with albums full of photographs and some fascinating stories to tell. He didn't mind the dangers, the poverty, the lack of familiar food and clean water, or the fact that he caught malaria the way the rest of us catch the common cold. I guess I got caught up in his excitement, because the next thing I knew, he was inviting me to spend a few months with him. I had no prospects for the future, so I went. I thought I was running away from myself and all my troubles. Instead, I found a God who wanted me and delivered me from my sins."

She'd didn't care for the direction this conversation was going. "Jason, I told you before, I could care less about…"

"Wait, I'm getting to the good part. The more of a real man I became, the more I wanted to return to you and win you back. Then I heard from Shelly that you'd up and gotten married. A couple years later, the professor's mysterious illness and death, followed by his staking, made all the headlines. The whole thing was so weird, I couldn't wait to contact you. I figured you must be going out of your mind."

"Jason, I…"

"Then, before I even had a chance to pack my bags, you had married Kellen, and everyone knows about his vampire persona. I decided you really were nuts and became determined to forget about us, once and for all. Then, something happened that changed my opinion of you."

He picked up his coffee, sipped it, made a wry face, and reached for the creamer. Melissa slid it close to her waist. He could not suspend the story. She had to know the rest.

"So, what happened?" she said.

Jason's face grew thoughtful. "The Africans speak in frightened tones of the adze, a vampire-like creature that turns into a firefly and drinks the blood of the living while they sleep. When captured, the adze assumes a human appearance. I always tuned out those native tales of witchcraft and voodoo. As a missionary, I was there to lead them away from their superstitious nonsense."

He raised his cup to his lips, remembered it contained no cream, then set it down again. "That is, until I encountered an adze."

Melissa's blood ran cold, and her mouth turned dry. Her fingers trembled, and she squeezed them around the creamer.

"I awoke one night and there it was, fastened to my neck and going to town. It took all my strength to rip it loose, for the darned thing had me in some kind of trance, and I found it hard to move. Finally, I threw it on the ground, but before I could smash it, it changed to a full-grown man and crawled out of my tent. I lay awake all night, shaking like a leaf and re-thinking my previous prejudices. After that, I spent a lot of time listening to what the natives had to say, instead of being the smart-ass who was going to set them straight. Once I understood what they were battling, I became more effective in bringing God to them. Then a pastor friend of mine turned down the assignment to come here. That's how I learned about the ghost stories associated with this congregational church and figured there might be something to them. I didn't think it was fair for the villagers not to have their own church, just because no one was brave enough to lead it. So, I asked to come here."

He waited for her reaction with the same, pleading look she had come to expect from him. She contemplated his offer. Life with Jason would not contain the exhilarating excitement as life with John had, but neither would it be a roller coaster ride of turbulent emotions. Jason would be a tiny flickering flame compared to John's blazing passion. On the other hand, John desired only Bryony, but Jason would love her with a steady love, like the pilot light on the stove, like Steve had loved her mother.

"I can't see a church pastor marrying someone who's had two husbands," was all Melissa said.

"I don't care what the world thinks. I care what God thinks. Stop fooling yourself. You have never been married."

"Jason, you're talking in riddles."

"Melissa," Jason said very quietly, "I don't pretend to know everything about doctrine and theology, but I do know the church has one very solid requirement for marriage."

"Which is?"

"Both spouses must be alive."

Ignoring the astonishment on Melissa's face, Jason rose halfway from his seat, reached over her plate, and took the creamer from her hands.

EPILOGUE

Melissa married Jason Frye at the Munsonville Congregational Church the Saturday morning of Labor Day weekend. The minister from Jenson Bible Church performed the ceremony, but, if he remembered Melissa from Steve's funeral, he gave no sign. She spurned the traditional white gown and veil for a light blue suit and hat; fortunately, Jason had no objections. The service was a mixture of happiness and sorrow, for images of John and Bryony's wedding invaded Melissa's thoughts and would not leave. She really had wanted to marry John here.

She forced herself to concentrate on the pious words John would not say to her and spoke them slowly, making certain she said, "Jason," and not, "John." Jason, dressed in his clerical garb, not lavender, received each word with a beaming joy that saddened Melissa. Ardor that sincere should be reciprocated. Any woman would have enjoyed receiving it. Surely, Jason could have done better than her. She could not return his feelings. She blinked, hard. Had the light played tricks on her eyes? For a moment, it seemed that Henry, dressed in gray and lavender to match John, stood in the sidelines, smiling and nodding his approval. Angela, her only attendant, excitedly fidgeted throughout the entire ceremony, for two reasons. One, Angela was thrilled to be part of the wedding. Two, Jason, with a wink at Melissa, had asked Trenton Cooper to be his best man.

Brian elected not to attend because it would interrupt the girls' school schedule again. Melissa secretly thought Brian did not take her third marriage seriously, which did not surprise her. However, Darlene did not deliver the "marrying on the rebound lecture," as she had before Melissa had married Kellen, which also surprised Melissa, although Darlene, too, stayed home.

"I can't do it," her mother had said. She sounded tired, so unlike the old Darlene. "There are just too many sad memories in Munsonville."

Julie and David were too busy to leave the children's home, but Julie sent Melissa a sweet note with her regrets. "I wish you all the joy in the world this time," Julie wrote. "You deserve it."

However, Shelly and Laura were both present. Their husbands had planned a holiday camping trip, so Shelly and Laura decided a girl's weekend was in order, and that no finer place existed for it than Munsonville. A gray-haired woman wearing a pink-striped suit and heavy make-up accompanied them. Laura introduced her at the post-wedding lunch reception at Sue's Diner.

"Melissa, this is my good friend and former teacher Colpa Ivanovich," Laura said, with a sidelong glance at Jason, who was talking earnestly to Curtis and Karla. "She specializes in Celtic art and mythology."

Colpa? Suddenly, Melissa was at the Harrington ball, sitting opposite Ed Calkins, who leaned his head on his hand and dreamily watched her eat a sandwich. Only one woman, Colpa, wanted so badly to drink from the well that she agreed to Ed Calkins' demands.

After she kissed me, I revealed my true, handsome identity and made her a wife. She had only one request: to be my only lover. Because I loved her so much, I respected her desire. In fact, her love for me may be why I became so ruthless…You see, I behaved as if I was a frog that eats flies. Colpa recognized the poet in me, so she enchanted me, empowered me, and taught me to be a prince.

Could this frumpy woman really be Ed Calkins' mythical goddess? Colpa peered through the spectacles balanced at the end of her nose and extended her hand.

"I'm happy to finally meet you, Melissa," Colpa said. "I've heard fine things about you."

In wonderment, Melissa returned the greeting. "I believe we may have had a mutual friend, Ed Calkins. Did you know him?"

The woman turned pale underneath her thick layer of blush, but she only said, "Yes, I remember Ed. We were friends, years ago, in college."

Ann interrupted the conversation by throwing her arms around Melissa and whispering, "You're lucky, Melissa, to have found someone so nice."

"I know," Melissa said.

In the far corner of the dining room, Angela and Trenton sat close, while Trenton read from a medical terminology book. Melissa envied their shared closeness and wished she felt that way about Jason.

Katie, who served punch, agreed with Ann. "He's a real keeper, isn't he?" Then she winked. "He sure changed your mind about Christian hypocrisy."

"Not at all," Melissa said lightly. "I like his eyes."

Jason reserved a room for the weekend at Munsonville Inn, where the ghost would not bother them, he had said with a grin and a playful poke in her ribs. Melissa did not mind staying in town. She had no desire for a romantic escape with anyone but John, which, of course, would never occur. After spending one night with Jason, Melissa knew she made the right decision about staying home. His love was intense, but his abilities were, at best, mediocre. She didn't have the heart to guide him, for he tried so hard to please her. Instead, Melissa mentally planned her syllabus for the next month, yawned, and set the alarm. Jason had services in the morning.

In fact, Jason had been so fervent that he dumbfounded Melissa the next day, when he returned from church, donned an old T-shirt and shorts, and lay back on the bed to watch the races. Melissa watched him, openmouthed. "You're kidding, right?"

Jason patted the pillow next to him. "You're joining me, right?"

"Jason, it's our honeymoon!"

He set the remote on the nightstand. "So, if you wanted to be near me so much, why weren't you in church?"

"We've been over that."

"Look, I didn't begrudge you the right to stay up here. So, don't begrudge me the right to watch this. Besides, there's someone I've been following."

Melissa compromised. She fluffed the pillows next to Jason and settled next to him with her a mystery novel. Melissa became lost between its pages until she heard the word, "changeling." She rested the book on her chest and said, "Jason, what are you watching?"

"Shh," he said.

"It's a play on words," the young woman said. Her cropped hair spiked at random angles. Her muscular arms bore several tattoos, including one of a grinning skull. She wore a bright green T-shirt with even brighter orange letters that said, "Changeling Ministries."

"How so?" the newscaster said.

"Well, a changeling is someone who has been switched at birth. I was switched later, after I made some foolish decisions."

"How much of the experience do you remember?"

The woman looked thoughtful. "Not much. Impressions come and go, nothing solid. I remember running away from home and getting inside a pick-up truck with this little dwarf of a man smoking a clay pipe. From there, it gets confusing. I'm not sure what's real and what's a dream."

"So why do you tour the race circuit?"

Melissa poked Jason. "Who is that?"

"Dawn Abrams. She's one of the emporium orphans."

"Really? Did you know her?"

Jason only grunted, so Melissa tried again. "Did they ever find Eircheard?"

"Come on, Melissa, be quiet."

"...so other kids won't make the same mistakes I did."

"Well, I just marvel at your maturity. Few people your age would assume fulltime guardianship of a special needs child."

"It's my pleasure. Emmie and I, we're a team."

With a yawn, Jason switched off the television and threw Melissa's book onto the nightstand. It slid off the remote and fell onto the floor.

"Hey, that's a library book," Melissa said.

Jason responded by rolling onto his side and nibbling her ear. She cringed but didn't let him see it. She wished now she had not bothered him. She would rather read.

"I thought you were watching the races," she said.

"I saw what I wanted to see. It's our honeymoon, remember?"

Her new husband's casual ghost references left Melissa unprepared for her first impression of the parsonage when she walked through its front door. The entire layout was exactly how she dreamed it. The stairs were before her; the parlor was to her right. She didn't have to walk down the hall to know it led to the church office. The mirror where she paused to smooth her hair before meeting John was conspicuously absent. Melissa sighed, and Jason looked at her. How long before she stopped seeing Bryony at every turn?

"What's wrong, Melissa? You're not upset I didn't carry you over the threshold, are you?"

Jason looked so serious, that Melissa laughed aloud. "Not at all, I was just..."

A shadow flitted up the stairs. Melissa gasped and grabbed Jason's sleeve. "Did you see that?"

"Sure, I saw it. That's my ghost. You're not scared, are you?"

"No! Well, yes! Can't you get rid of it?"

"I've said my best prayers and sprinkled my best holy water, but the thing remains. It appears harmless enough, so I'm leaving it alone, for now, anyway."

"Oh." Melissa wasn't certain how she felt about sharing her new home with a ghost.

Jason's blue eyes were teasing. "Come on, Melissa, you're not scared of a ghost, are you? You've lived with two vampires."

"I knew them," she said, suddenly feeling defensive about her past. "This thing's a stranger." Jason still stood there, grinning, so Melissa added, "Let's forget about it for now, okay? I'm starving. What's for dinner?"

"I don't know," Jason said. "I'll eat whatever you make. Don't you want to see the rest of the house?"

"Wait a minute," Melissa said. "You can't cook?"

"No, why?"

"I can't, either."

Now it was Jason's turn to be surprised. "Really? I thought all women cooked."

"Not true. We could rehire Mabel."

"Not on my small salary."

"There's my teaching salary. The old Smythe place will eventually sell, too."

Jason was almost to the kitchen. "It hasn't sold yet," he called back. "In the meantime, I know there's a frozen pizza or two in here."

Frozen pizza? John would die first. Had Steve ever made a frozen pizza? She trailed Jason into the kitchen. Jason shut the freezer door and held up two pizzas.

"I was right," he said, setting them on the counter. "Heat these up, Melissa. I'm going to check messages. When's Angela coming home?"

"After the dinner rush. Ann's feeding her." Melissa ruefully shook her head, as she ripped away the plastic. "I'll accommodate you tonight, but you have to understand something. We own an equal opportunity kitchen."

"I'm too busy winning souls for Christ." Jason tweaked her nose and sauntered down to the office. Melissa, for the second time that day, laughed out loud.

They ate the pizza at a kitchen table that only slightly wobbled and discussed their upcoming week. By day, Jason had a full schedule of hospital visits and ecumenical meetings. By evening, he rotated his sports schedule between the Daltons, the Coopers, and the Millers.

"This will keep me out of your hair while you grade papers," Jason said. He poured himself a tall glass of milk and took another slice.

Melissa wasn't certain if she liked Jason's agenda or not, but she was beginning to enjoy their relaxed, easy-going relationship. Still, having Jason gone in the evenings gave her the perfect alibi for an early bedtime.

Jason drained the glass and poured another. "Hey, what's the deal with Karla Dyer?"

"What do you mean?"

"I have the feeling she wants to get more involved with things, but Katie keeps her tethered to a short rope. What gives?"

Melissa told him about the great mystic medicine man, Cornell Dyer; Katie's obsessive infatuation with the deceased opportunist; Karla's inherent psychic abilities; and Katie's insistence Karla develop them to their fullest.

"Katie feels it's Karla's destiny to further Cornell's legacy to the world," Melissa said, raising her tea cup in a toast.

Jason looked grave. "I don't like what I'm hearing. Katie needs to loosen up."

She grinned and beat Jason to the last piece of pizza. "I thought the church encouraged people to use their gifts and talents."

"There's a difference between using them and beating them to a pulp. I'm going to have a talk tonight with Katie Dyer."

Melissa had no idea what Jason said to Katie, but it must have been good, for Katie called her a week later to ask Melissa if she was done unpacking.

"Almost," Melissa said. She ignored the shadow that edged across the wall and into the parlor. "Why?"

"Can I have some boxes? We're moving into my parents' house."

"You are? Why?"

"Mom and Dad really need someone right there caring for them, and the motor home is starting to go. I'm keeping it for Karla's studio, of course, but I'm ready for a change."

Melissa and Jason brought a carload of boxes to Katie's house after dinner that night. Jason started to help Melissa unload them, when Katie asked him to plunge the kitchen sink.

"I've tried and tried," she said. With the back of her hand, Katie brushed away a limp lock of hair.

"I'll help bring in the boxes, Mrs. Frye," Karla said.

It was the first time she had spoken to Melissa since John-Peter's death.

Silently, they moved the boxes from the car into the house. On the last trip, Melissa asked Karla, "Is everything all right?"

Karla averted her eyes. "It will never be all right." Her voice trembled when she said it. "But life, you know, goes on."

The girl's bravery despite her sadness touched Melissa's heart, and she couldn't help crying out, "Oh, Karla!" Melissa held out her arms. Karla turned tear-filled eyes to Melissa, but ignored the offer of a comforting embrace.

"We're the only ones who know the truth," Karla said. "Do you understand?"

Karla turned and walked into the motor home with her stack of boxes.

Pastor and Mrs. Frye received an unexpected windfall when Max and Madeleine Chandler bought the old Smythe house at the top of Bass Street, which Kellen had acquired for Melissa as part of their bargain shortly after their marriage.

"I can't tell you how thrilled I felt at your decision to sell it," Max had said as he signed the closing papers. "I've had my eye on the old place for a long time."

"You're actually doing me a favor," Melissa said. "The house holds too many memories for me." It did, too, her memories and Bryony's memories.

Indian summer came and went. The fall colors tore through the woods and then silently dropped from the trees.

Melissa and Jason settled into a routine that, although not highly charged, was genial and pleasant. As the days passed, Melissa grew accustomed to the ghost. She still did not see much of Angela, but Jason did, because of Angela's involvement with church activities. Melissa did not participate, but was pleased that Debbie's daughter had carved a life for herself in the village. Melissa spent most nights alone, reading and grading papers, while the shadow passed in and out of the parlor. It was not an exciting way to pass her evening, but the activity agreed with her, so Melissa never complained. Only occasionally did Melissa indulge the playing of Bryony's music box, hidden in her dresser below the jeans, for its music transported Melissa to magical ballrooms in John's arms. This made her feel disloyal to Jason, so she did not often play it. Besides, its chiming notes played tricks on her. After the music box wound down, Melissa swore the tinkling continued in the distant background.

Thanksgiving was a week away. Melissa was still not passionately in love with Jason, but she did like him very much, and was feeling especially thankful that he asked her to marry him. Each day, she remembered more and more why she had crushed on him years ago. Besides retaining his handsome, youthful appearance, Jason was just so plain *nice*. He even suggested they drive to Grover's Park for Thanksgiving, but Melissa declined.

"I'll miss your sermon, if we go," Melissa said.

She took a bite of instant mashed potatoes and resolved to check out a few cookbooks during the next library trip. Frozen dinners had gotten old, although Jason didn't seem to mind them. Now that they had the money, rehiring Mabel was not an option. When the Chandlers' housekeeper had retired, Madeline had called Mabel the very next day.

"So what? You've missed all my sermons so far."

"I'm considering attending on Thursday," Melissa said.

"You want to see why my church is the place to be Sunday mornings?"

"No, I want to hear you publically announce how thankful you are for the gift of me."

"I'd rather show you."

He did, too, even forgoing Monday night football in Jack Cooper's living room, which Melissa deemed unnecessary. Jason had insisted otherwise, so she mentally prepared a shopping list of what she needed for her first Thanksgiving dinner, told Jason she loved him, and set the alarm. As an afterthought, she kissed Jason's cheek. Then, she turned out the light.

How long Melissa slept, she did not know, but she woke to the sight of Jason leaning propped on one elbow and gazing down at her. Just enough moonlight filtered between the blinds to reveal the tears in his eyes.

"I love you, Melissa," he said. "I want to do this right. Show me how."

Melissa hesitated but not because she doubted Jason's sincerity. John's lessons had been rigid and tinged with his sense of entitlement and superiority. Had she somehow communicated those same attitudes to Jason? She need not have worried. Jason was so wildly and openly in love with her that he accepted all suggestions with wholehearted zeal. She had to give Jason credit. He was a fast learner, much faster than she, for Melissa burned her first Thanksgiving dinner beyond recognition. She fussed so long and hard, she even missed Jason's first Thanksgiving sermon. Thanks to Jason, they found refuge at the Daltons' dinner table.

Actually, that entire day had been a happy one, for Clay had custody of his two boys that weekend, and they had Angela, which eased the stinging memories of other Thanksgivings.

Julie and David joined them in time for dessert, and they enthusiastically shared stories of their work with the emporium orphans. Hearing the happiness in Julie's voice took Melissa back in time to another Julie, one that couldn't wait to leave Munsonville and its provincialism far behind her. After graduating from Jenson College, Julie and David had attended graduate school at the University of Washington; after their marriage, they opened a joint practice in Seattle. Return visits were sparse: an occasional Christmas, the weddings of David's two sisters, and the deaths of Julie's parents.

At dusk, Melissa and Julie slipped out for a walk.

"Remember Ann and Jack's engagement party, when Mrs. Miller kept sending us back to Harper's Grocery for one item after another?" Julie said with a short chuckle at the memory.

A smile spread across Melissa's face before she could stop it. The recollection stung her heart, but it didn't lacerate it, even though another image swiftly followed it, that of John making passionate love to her for the first time, on a damp bed of moss, under the stars.

"How about Katie's dad walking around with the toilet plunger?" Melissa said, and both women laughed as they turned up Bass Street.

"Hey, did I tell you?" Julie said as her parents' house came into view. "I finally sold the old homestead."

"Really? To whom?"

"Some medical student. Maybe you know him. He oversees park maintenance and said he's planning a community garden with your husband."

A shadow passed over Melissa's good spirits, but she said nothing. They continued their walk in silence.

Joviality returned at bedtime, for Melissa laughed harder than Jason when his foot cramped in the middle of the grand passion, and he fell onto the floor. She was still giggling to herself when sleep overtook her. Fuzzy feelings morphed into bitter cold, because Melissa dreamt the furnace quit working in the middle of an icy blizzard. Jason refused to come home and fix it because he was ice fishing with Jack Cooper. The air inside the parsonage was so cold that it blew in wisps across her face. Melissa startled, awakened, and felt a chill brush her cheek. A swaying, gauze-like figure hovered near her bed. It clutched a swaddled bundle against its transparent chest and gazed at Melissa with hollow, forlorn eyes. Minutes ticked away while they silently regarded one another. Melissa knew what she should do, but she wavered in her resolve. Once she spoke, she buried for eternity any lingering hopes in her heart. It was the only right thing to do, but it broke Melissa's heart to think it.

She opened her mouth, then panicked, for her fantasies of John would disappear with her words. She couldn't bear to completely lose him, yet had she ever owned him? She wondered if John would even accept Bryony into his underworld with

Henry's baby in her arms, until Melissa realized it was not her problem anymore.

"John's not here," Melissa said. "He's long gone. Everyone's gone. You can go to him, now."

Bryony continued to stare at Melissa, even as, bit by bit, she faded into translucency. Jason stirred in his sleep and instinctively reached for Melissa. She snuggled into his arms and looked back. The figure had vanished. Jason stroked her hair in such a soothing fashion that Melissa's anguish over missing John melted under his loving touch. He bent down and kissed the top of her head.

"Everything okay?" Jason mumbled.

His arms relaxed in sleep, jerked, and redoubled their hold on her. A contented feeling like Darlene's hot chocolate flowed through her.

"Yes," Melissa said, moving deeper into her husband's arms, reveling in the new-found realization that she belonged there and nowhere else. "Everything's fine."

It really was.

Denise M. Baran-Unland is a features writer, creative writing teacher, and founding member of the writer's group, WriteOn Joliet. She has six homeschooled children, three stepchildren, six godchildren, 11 grandchildren, and several cats that behave like children. Visit her at www.bryonyseries.com and www.denisembaranunland.com.

Christopher Gleason is a sales professional that also utilizes his keen communication skills in both drawing and writing. Although Gleason did illustrate his high school's arts magazine, Gleason's visual art is reserved mostly for family and a few close friends. Gleason has written about parenting, politics, faith, healthy lifestyle choices, and the importance of working to attain personal goals. Gleason also enjoys writing stories that involve heroes as main characters. He is currently writing his first novel and hopes to one day write song lyrics, too.

"IF YOU ENJOYED STAKED, CHECK OUT THE FIRST TWO BOOKS IN THE BRYONYSERIES."

"What shall I do first?" Melissa whispered.

John reached out his hands. "Touch me," he said in a low, smooth voice.

She hesitated. Even in the dim light, Melissa saw how thin and pale they were. Her insides recoiled at the thought of touching a corpse. Then Melissa remembered how much she wanted to be Bryony. This was nothing new; John had already siphoned blood from her. Could it harm her to continue for a little longer?

"I'm not afraid," she told herself, but she did not believe it. "I am not afraid. I am not afraid."

After her father's sudden death, seventeen-year-old Melissa Marchellis moves onto the former estate of nineteenth century composer and pianist John Simons, where a mysterious mist stalks her, ghostly piano music invades her bedroom, and lovely visions of John Simons' young wife Bryony, who died in childbirth, fill her dreams.

So, when John proposes a trade, a trip to the past as Bryony in exchange for her blood, Melissa happily agrees. She soon seesaws between a life of school, slumber parties, and cute boys to dancing at balls, attending formal dinner parties, and hosting garden fetes.

But fantasy and reality blur when her eccentric, middle-aged English teacher penetrates her dreams as Melissa's dashing vampire chaperone; her brother Brian adopts a peculiar stray cat after a friend disappears in a midnight exploration of the dilapidated mansion; and another girl with a similar vampire pact is gruesomely murdered.

Caught between the danger of her agreement and her escalating infatuation with John Simons, Melissa contends with other vampires and their agendas, while struggling with her feelings for an undead musician.

www.bryonyseries.com
www.bryonyseries.blogspot.com
www.facebook.com/BryonySeries

Cover Design by
CAL Graphics, Inc.
www.calgraphicsinc.com

Visage

Denise M. Baran-Unland
Illustrated by Matt Coundiff

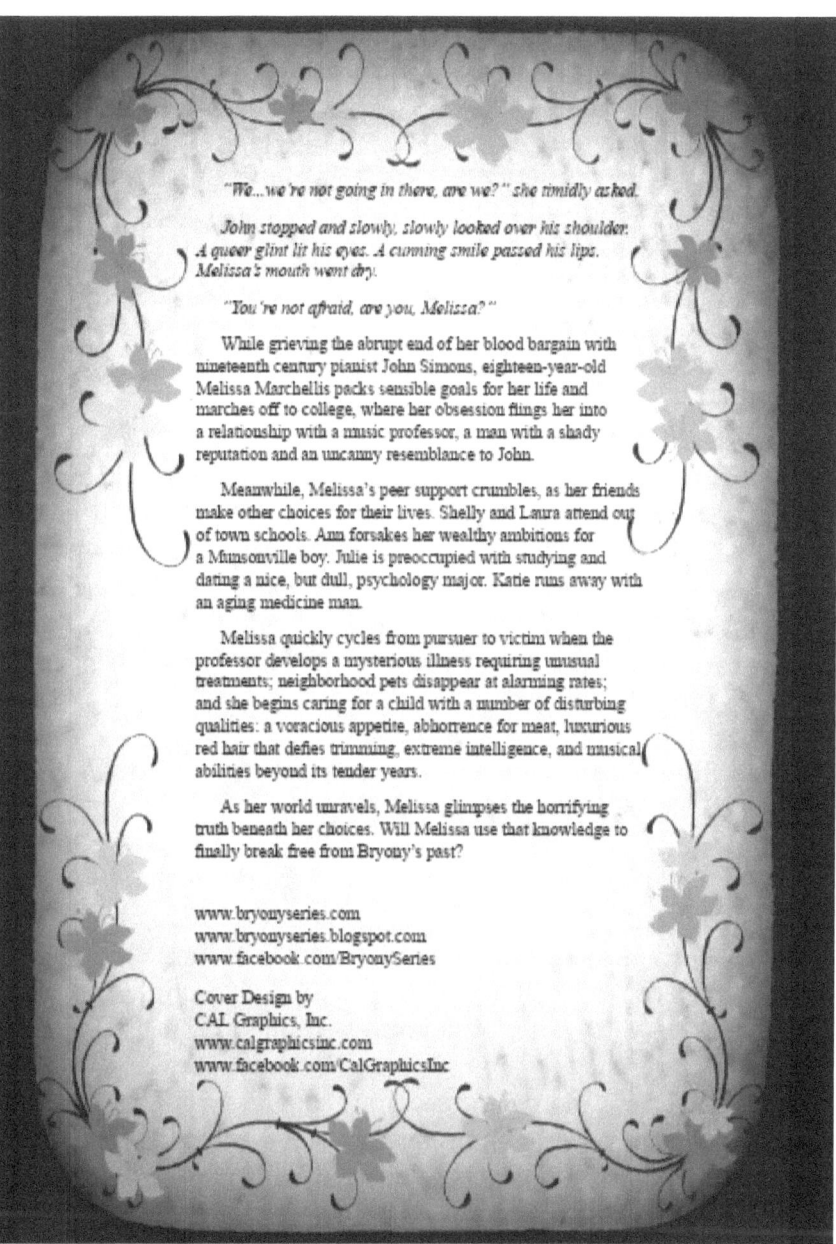

"We...we're not going in there, are we?" she timidly asked.

John stopped and slowly, slowly looked over his shoulder. A queer glint lit his eyes. A cunning smile passed his lips. Melissa's mouth went dry.

"You're not afraid, are you, Melissa?"

While grieving the abrupt end of her blood bargain with nineteenth century pianist John Simons, eighteen-year-old Melissa Marchellis packs sensible goals for her life and marches off to college, where her obsession flings her into a relationship with a music professor, a man with a shady reputation and an uncanny resemblance to John.

Meanwhile, Melissa's peer support crumbles, as her friends make other choices for their lives. Shelly and Laura attend out of town schools. Ann forsakes her wealthy ambitions for a Munsonville boy. Julie is preoccupied with studying and dating a nice, but dull, psychology major. Katie runs away with an aging medicine man.

Melissa quickly cycles from pursuer to victim when the professor develops a mysterious illness requiring unusual treatments; neighborhood pets disappear at alarming rates; and she begins caring for a child with a number of disturbing qualities: a voracious appetite, abhorrence for meat, luxurious red hair that defies trimming, extreme intelligence, and musical abilities beyond its tender years.

As her world unravels, Melissa glimpses the horrifying truth beneath her choices. Will Melissa use that knowledge to finally break free from Bryony's past?

www.bryonyseries.com
www.bryonyseries.blogspot.com
www.facebook.com/BryonySeries

Cover Design by
CAL Graphics, Inc.
www.calgraphicsinc.com
www.facebook.com/CalGraphicsInc

"This is BY FAR AND AWAY the BEST VAMPIRE book I have read since Interview with a Vampire. Unland has captured the unforgiving beastly charm and aristocratic rogue in John Simons and company. I literally read this book over three days and was clamoring 'MORE!' when it ended. I am delighted there are three more installments coming! A vampire-lover must and no sex, disturbing violence, or vulgarity. A piece of classic literature from the twenty-first century."

~Tommy Connolly, Chicago actor

"I enjoyed 'Bryony' immensely. The mixture of the past and present was fascinating. Another of my favorite things about this novel was its sheer originality. Many vampire stories have the same tired feel to them, but John was a completely unique character with an entirely individual method of 'enchanting' both Melissa and Bryony. John was wonderful, and I immediately fell in love with him. The only thing that would have been better was if I could hear him play!"

~Casey Rae Garcia, former Paperchase Supervisor, Borders Books Music & Cafe, Oak Brook, Illinois

"I really enjoyed Bryony because it wasn't like any other vampire book I'd ever read. "I can't wait to introduce this novel to my "Teaching English as a Foreign Language" students. This book is awesome because it provides a true, stark look into the world of vampires while providing lush imagery of the romantic, Victorian era then coming back around to real life in nineteen seventies America. There is so much teaching material I could use in this book, from the radical glimpses into history to the inspiring lines of poetry. I know my students will enjoy this novel as much as I did!"

~Andrea Hinz, English as a foreign language teacher, Germany.

"Unland performs brilliantly in "Bryony", successfully combining multiple views of modern perceptions of vampires.

She retains the monstrous horror of the creatures of the night not needing to display scenes of intense violence and gore, as well as presenting their seductive and sensual side without illustrating acts of unnecessary sexuality. At the same time, she weaves a tale of a girl on he cusp of womanhood attempting to decipher what her true perceptions and emotions are complicated by what may or may not be illusions granted to her by a vampire who shows a unique interest in her. It is definitely a fascinating read that I was unable to put down, and has me eagerly waiting for what will be revealed in the upcoming additions to the Bryony series."

~Dragon Alexander, Producer and Director for Blackwood X Productions LLC and 16 year member of the International Vampire LARP, One World By Night.

TO BOOK DENISE FOR AN EVENT OR SPEAKING:

Denise M. Baran-Unland is available to speak to people of all ages about her writings, (including the BryonySeries), the creative writing process and her self-publishing experiences.

Contact her through www.bryonyseries.com

I definitely recommend the author Denise Baran-Unland to visit classrooms. As the author of the new series that begins with the Bryony novel, Mrs. Baran-Unland visited my English classes and discussed the writing process (including all the editing and revising), how dreams can come true for anyone, and how her life experiences have shaped the successful person she has become. I was extremely delighted to see her interact with my Freshmen English students and keep their attention while discussing writing as well as her new series of books. I look forward to inviting her into my classroom in the near future for more conversations with the students.

~Maggie Maslowski
English
Freshmen Academy
Joliet West High School

Kudos to Denise Baran-Unland for sharing her writing and publishing journey. The members of our writers' group found her presentation both informative and inspiring. For all writers, the great dilemma is "It's done. Now what?" Denise takes you to the "now what" with practical advice based on her experience and research. Our members heard a seasoned traveler tell them that it is possible to get off the paper and to navigate the world of publishing.

~Mary Ellen Michna, co-founder with Colette Wisneski, of Word Weavers writer's group